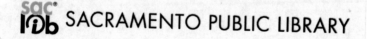

THE
MISSING
WITNESS

THE
MISSING
WITNESS

ALLISON
BRENNAN

ISBN-13: 978-0-7783-6965-3

Recycling programs
for this product may
not exist in your area.

The Missing Witness

For questions and comments about the quality of this book, please contact us at
CustomerService@Harlequin.com.

TM is a trademark of Harlequin Enterprises ULC.

Mira
22 Adelaide St. West, 41st Floor
Toronto, Ontario M5H 4E3, Canada
BookClubbish.com

Printed in U.S.A.

To Kevin Dahlgren

With admiration for your great work and sincere thanks
for your help in making this story as authentic as possible.

FEBRUARY

Eight Months Ago

1

My parking garage off Fifth was nearly a mile from where I worked at city hall. I could have paid twice as much to park two blocks from my building and avoid the rows of homeless people: the worn tents, the used needles, the stinking garbage, the aura of hopelessness and distrust that filled a corner park and bled down the streets.

I was listening to my favorite podcast, *LA with A&I*. Amy and Ian started the podcast two years ago to talk about computer gaming, technology, entertainment and Los Angeles. It had blossomed into a quasi news show and they live streamed every morning at seven. They'd riff on tech and local news as if sitting down with friends over coffee. Like me, they were nerds, born and bred in the City of Angels. I'd never met Amy or Ian in real life, but felt like I'd known them forever.

We'd chatted over Discord, teamed up to play *League of Legends*, and I often sent them interesting clips about gaming or tech that they talked about on their podcast, crediting my gaming handle. Twice, we'd tried to set up coffee dates, but I always chickened out. I didn't know why. Maybe because I thought they wouldn't like me if they met me. Maybe because I was socially awkward. Maybe because I didn't like people knowing too much about my life.

Today while I drove to work, they'd discussed the disaster that was city hall: all the digital files had been wiped out. The news story lasted for about five minutes, but it would be my life for the next month or more as my division rebuilt the data from backups and archives. It was a mess. They laughed over it; I tried to, but I was beginning to suspect the error was on purpose, not by mistake.

Now they were talking about a sweatshop that had been shut down last week.

"We don't know much," Amy said. "You'd think after eight days there'd be some big press conference, or at least a front-page story. The only thing we found was two news clips—less than ninety seconds each—and an article on *LA Crime Beat*."

"David Chen," Ian said, "a Chinese American who allegedly trafficked hundreds of women and children to run his factory in Chinatown, was arraigned on Monday, but according to *Crime Beat*, the FBI is also investigating the crime. And—get this— the guy is already out on bail."

"It's fucked," Amy said. "Look, I'm all for bail reform. I don't think some guy with weed in his pocket should have to pay thousands of bucks to stay out of jail while the justice system churns. But human trafficking is a serious crime—literally not two miles from city hall, over three hundred people were forced to work at a sweatshop for no money. They had no freedom, lived in a hovel next door to the warehouse. *Crime Beat* reported that the workers used an underground tunnel to avoid being seen—something I haven't read in the news except for one brief mention. And Chen allegedly killed one of the women as he fled from police. How did this guy get away with it? He kills someone and spends no more than a weekend behind bars?"

"According to *Crime Beat*, LAPD investigated the business for months before they raided the place," Ian said. "But Chen has been operating for *years*. How could something like this happen and no one said a word?"

I knew how. People didn't see things they didn't want to.

Case in point: the homeless encampment I now walked by.

I paused the podcast and popped my earbuds back into their charging case.

"Hello, Johnny," I said to the heroin addict with stringy hair that might be blond, if washed. I knew he was thirty-three, though he looked much older. His hair had fallen out in clumps, his teeth were rotted, and his face scarred from sores that came and went. He sat on a crusty sleeping bag, leaned against the stone wall of a DWP substation, his hollow eyes staring at nothing. As usual, he didn't acknowledge me. I knew his name because I had asked when he wasn't too far gone. Johnny, born in Minnesota. He hadn't talked to his family in years. Thought his father was dead, but didn't remember. He once talked about a sister and beamed with pride. *She's really smart. She's a teacher in*…then his face dropped because he couldn't remember where his sister lived.

Four years ago, I left a job working for a tech start-up company to work in IT for city hall. It was barely a step up from entry-level and I couldn't afford nearby parking garages. If I took a combination of buses and the metro, it would take me over ninety minutes to get to work from Burbank, so factoring the combination of time and money, driving was my best bet and I picked the cheapest garage less than a mile from work.

I used to cringe when I walked by the park. Four years ago, only a dozen homeless tents dotted the corner; the numbers had more than quadrupled. Now that I could afford a more expensive garage, I didn't want it. I knew most of the people here by name.

"Hey, Toby," I greeted the old black man wearing three coats, his long, dirty gray beard falling to his stomach. He had tied a rope around his waist and attached it to his shopping cart to avoid anyone stealing his worldly possessions when he slept off his alcohol.

"Mizvi," he said, running my name together in a slur. He called me "Miss Violet" when he was sober. He must have still been coming down off whatever he'd drank last night.

I smiled. Four years ago I never smiled at these people, fearing something undefinable. Now I did, even when I wanted to cry. I reached into my purse and pulled out a bite-size Hershey Bar. Toby loved chocolate. I handed it to him. He took it with a wide grin, revealing stained teeth.

One of the biggest myths about the homeless is that they're hungry. They have more food than they can eat. That doesn't mean many aren't malnourished. Drug and alcohol abuse can do that to a person.

A couple weeks ago a church group had thought they would bring in sandwiches and water as part of community service. It was a nice gesture, sure, but they could have asked what was needed instead of assuming that these people were starving. Most of the food went uneaten, left outside tents to become rat food. The plastic water bottles were collected to return for the deposit, which was used to buy drugs and alcohol.

But no one gave Toby chocolate, he once told me when he was half-sober. Now, whenever I saw him—once, twice a week—I gave him a Hershey Bar. He would die sooner than he should, so why couldn't I give him a small pleasure that I could afford? Toby was one of the chronics, a man who'd been on the street for years. He had no desire to be anywhere else, trusted no one, though I thought he trusted me a little. I wished I knew his story, how he came to be here, how I could reach him to show him a different path. His liver had to be slush with the amount of alcohol he consumed. Alcohol he bought because people, thinking they were helping—or just to make themselves feel better—handed him money.

As I passed the entrance to the small park, the stench of un-washed humans assaulted me. The city had put four porta-potties on the edge of the park but they emptied them once a month, if that. They were used more for getting high and prostitution than as bathrooms. The city had also put up fencing, but didn't always come around to lock the gate. Wouldn't matter; some-one would cut it open and no one would stop them. Trespass-ing was the least of the crimes in the area.

I dared to look inside the park, though I didn't expect to see her. I hadn't seen her for over a week. I found myself clutching my messenger bag that was strapped across my chest. Not be-cause I thought someone would steal it, but because I needed to hold something, as if my bag was a security blanket.

I didn't see her among the tents or the people sitting on the ground, on the dirt and cushions, broken couches and sleeping bags, among the needles and small, tin foils used to smoke fen-tanyl. I kicked aside a vial that had once held Narcan, the drug to counteract opioid overdoses. The clear and plastic vials lit-tered the ground, remnants of addiction.

There was nothing humane about allowing people to get so wasted they were on the verge of death, reviving them, then leaving them to do it over and over again. But that was the sys-tem.

The system was fucked.

Blue and red lights whirled as I approached the corner. I usu-ally crossed Fifth Street here, but today I stopped, stared at the silent police car.

The police only came when someone was dying...or dead.

Mom.

I found my feet moving toward the cops even though I wanted to run away. My heart raced, my vision blurred as tears flashed, then disappeared.

Mom.

I knew several of the local cops because I had been volunteering for the last two years with First Contact, a nonprofit that connected the homeless with available resources. I didn't recognize the first officer that got out, then I saw Officer Juan Perez. He frowned when I approached.

"Violet, you should wait here."

He wasn't surprised to see me. He knew that I walked by the park five days a week on my way to work. He understood why.

I shook my head. "I can help."

I was grateful he didn't try to dissuade me. I followed him through the broken metal gate. Juan said to his fellow officer, "Steve, this is Violet Halliday. She works with First Contact."

Steve's badge read *S Colangelo*. All LAPD officers had training with the homeless population. There were social workers who could be called upon to assist, but they were few and far between and their response time was pathetic. First Contact was made up of mostly volunteers, like me, and often arrived to a situation before the paid social workers—if they showed up at all.

The wary eyes of the homeless watched as we walked toward the far corner of the park. The cops wore sturdy boots; I had sneakers so was more cautious where I stepped.

A row of five tents were lined against the brick wall of a shelter that housed one hundred people a night. It was just as dangerous for the men and women inside the shelter as it was outside because the shelter didn't ban drugs or alcohol, had minimal security and handed out pretty little bags with clean needles and straws under the so-called "harm reduction" model. As if dying of a drug overdose was better than dying of hepatitis.

I glanced left and spotted the blue tent with a tear on the roof sealed with zebra-patterned duct tape. Flaps closed. It was the last place I'd seen my mother ten days ago when she once again told me to go to hell.

Please don't be dead. Please don't be dead.

My mom was slowly killing herself, so I knew that one day

I would pass by this park and she would be dead. But it wasn't today.

Steve spoke to a couple, a man and woman named Fletch and Gina. First Contact had been working with them since they turned up here two months ago. They hadn't shared their last names, but every time we came out, they seemed to be more receptive and friendly.

The first step to getting off the street was to obtain ID. Finding family who might pitch in or help navigate the tremendous bureaucracy of the drug or mental health programs was always beneficial. But nothing happened without official identification.

Gina sat on a foam cushion outside a faded canvas tent, Fletch with his head in her lap, eyes closed. Passed out or sleeping or ignoring the commotion. Gina paid no attention to the cops, but turned to me with sad blue eyes and said, "Bobby."

I knew Bobby's story. I'd talked to him several times because I thought he was someone I could help.

My mom made it clear that she didn't want my help, that she resented me even trying to help her, but others were more receptive. Cautious—because they had been lied to and let down in the past—but with enough time and patience, I could reach them.

Bobby was twenty-nine, like me. He got hooked on heroin when he was seventeen. In and out of rehab. Got a job here and there, but couldn't hold anything down longer than a couple months because he would go "chasing the dragon" and not show up for days. Lived with his mom, who told him no drugs but didn't enforce the rule. Because she loved him, worried about him, feared for him—all of the above. Then one night when she was working late, Bobby got wasted. He was speedballing, combined meth with heroin and was so wired that he smoked pot to calm himself down, didn't realize the pot was laced with fentanyl and "went bonkers." His words. Trashed the house, then crashed. When his mom came home, she had him arrested.

He went to jail for three days, court-ordered rehab for thirty. But under California law, any facility that took public money couldn't be dry. So he popped whatever pills were around and, when the thirty days were up, went back home high as a kite and his mother refused to let him in.

She was crying, but she didn't budge. I felt like shit, but what can I do? I tried the rehab thing, it didn't take.

Of course it didn't take, I thought. Counseling only went so far: *Don't do drugs, they're bad for you. Here, have a clean needle so you're safe.*

Bobby had been on the streets for three years. The last six months he'd been here, in this tent, never wandering far. He'd deteriorated rapidly over the last few months, as if he'd given up on living before he died.

Both Juan and Steve wore gloves. Steve pulled the latex over his watch—an expensive-looking watch with a yellow face. Gina eyed it with narrowed eyes. I knew she had a shoplifting problem, but I didn't think she'd rip off a cop.

Juan opened the flap. He didn't touch the body; the smell announced death. Bobby had died sometime in the last twenty-four hours, probably last night. Steve called it in. They would wait here until the coroner arrived.

The stiff body, the glassy eyes, the stacks of burned foil he used to smoke fentanyl. I had seen death coming. Hope had drained from Bobby's eyes with each passing week until there was nothing left.

"His name is Bobby Thomas," I told Juan. "I don't remember his mom's name, but Will knows. I'll call him."

Will Lattimer ran First Contact. He'd been my lifeline after I learned my mom was living on the streets. My sounding board. My venting partner. My punching bag.

I glanced again toward the closed blue tent with the zebra duct tape. There was movement inside. The flaps opened and a man came out. His pants were around his knees but he didn't care, made no move to pull them up. He went over to the porta-potty, tried all the doors until he was able to wrench open the last one.

Juan approached and quietly asked, "Do you want me to check on her?"

I shook my head, forcing calm, control.

I will not break down.

I cleared my throat and finally managed to speak. "She probably needed drugs and the only way she can get them is with sex."

I wasn't telling Juan anything he didn't know.

"I have to go to work," I said, my voice raw. I didn't have tears left in me, but the anger was always there. "I'll call Will."

I walked away before I changed my mind and confronted my mother. I didn't know if I could handle the emotional roller coaster today.

My family life had never been perfect, but it was okay. My parents bickered, drank too much, but they each had a job and managed to make ends meet. I'd dealt with my mom's mood swings my entire life—now I suspected she was bipolar, but she'd never been diagnosed, let alone treated. Then my dad killed himself while driving drunk and my mom had to deal with the aftermath. She started smoking pot to help with the stress, she claimed. Then she was in an accident and got a prescription for oxy.

It went downhill from there.

She lost her job, lost her house, and destroyed friendships when someone gave her a place to stay for a few weeks to get on her feet and she ended up stealing from them.

At the time, I'd been living in a studio near Pierce, a community college in Woodland Hills, attending school while working for a tech start-up. I let her move in with me, not realizing how bad she was. When she couldn't get more pain pills—legally or illegally—she would drink so heavily that she'd pass out. I offered to pay for rehab. I didn't have the money, but I had one credit card I'd never touched and I would use that. She refused. I told her she had to stop using or leave.

She left.

The guilt ate at me for years. My tech start-up did exceptionally well and when they sold it, I received a bonus—enough to put a large down payment on a small house in a quiet Burbank neighborhood. Two bedrooms, two baths—I hoped to find my mom and she could live with me. I had a fantasy—that she was clean and sober and we could be a family again.

The first time I found her, she was strung out, living in a condemned building with other strung-out junkies. I did everything to save her. I got her a new identification card. Enrolled her in rehab. Found her an apartment I paid for so she wasn't living on the streets. I enrolled her in Medi-Cal. I helped her apply for public assistance—then learned that there were plenty of places where you could use EBS cards to buy drugs. Dozens of convenience stores that were dealing in the back room would ring you up for snack food but really sell you meth, heroin, fentanyl. Her benefits ran out and she applied for disability. They awarded her money. Again, she used it for drugs. Not food, not housing, just more drugs.

Six months later, she was evicted for starting a fire. She begged me to let her move in with me. On one condition, I said: she went to rehab. She spat in my face and called me a selfish, ungrateful bitch, then walked away.

I didn't see her again for years, until I found her living on the streets.

I couldn't afford a private facility, the kind that doesn't take government money and requires patients to commit to getting clean. Will helped me find one that would have taken my mom in for ninety days and let me pay for it over a one-year period. She refused to sign the paperwork because she wouldn't be allowed to leave.

You can't force someone to get clean. You can't love someone enough to change them. If my tears were pennies, I could have paid for every man and woman in this park to get help.

I walked across Fifth Street, put my earbuds back in and called Will.

I was blunt. "Bobby's dead."

"Shit."

"Juan Perez responded."

"I'll reach out. You okay?"

"I'm done."

"You've put in a lot of time lately, you need a break."

"Not that. I'm done with these people. I'm going to expose the homeless industrial complex. People have got to realize what's going on!"

I couldn't believe that I was near tears. Tears of rage. I had to do something. I felt helpless.

"Violet, it's all there and no one cares. While I know you don't like to hear it, none of these setups are overtly illegal. I talk about this all the time to anyone who will listen, but they don't want to see the truth."

"I'll make them pay attention."

"How?"

"I don't know."

Dammit. I sounded like a whiny brat.

He was silent, and I wondered if I'd overstepped. We'd been friends for a while now, though it was a bit weird. We didn't have much in common. Will was an extrovert, talkative, a decade older than me, a veteran, and had been a social worker specializing in the homeless for the last fifteen years, ever since he got out of the military and started working with homeless veterans. I was an introverted computer geek who felt more comfortable talking to people online than I did in person.

He'd always been honest with me, which I appreciated, but mostly, he listened. I needed that after I found my mom living on the streets. Maybe I was being a Pollyanna. I should've been content—happy, even—that First Contact was productive and successful, even if I couldn't save my mom.

Then Will said, "I have a friend I can reach out to. Someone I trust, who knows the system, who might have some ideas on what we can do."

"I'll do anything, Will. This can't continue."

"I know you're upset about Bobby. But what is the first thing I told you when you started volunteering?"

I sighed. I didn't want a pep talk. "They have to want help," I mumbled.

"That has not changed. This is not going to be solved overnight. It takes weeks for some people, years for others. The important thing is that we keep going back, make contact, be available when they say, 'I'm ready.'"

"You have, what, a dozen regular volunteers? And the city has how much money?"

He sighed; I wasn't telling him anything he didn't know.

"Be patient. We're making progress."

"How many people are going to die while the city builds million-dollar units for a handful of the people living on the streets?"

"Meet me tonight at The Pulse, okay? My treat."

I didn't want to go. I pouted, angry, frustrated. Lost.

"Should be my treat," I said. "I make more money than you."

He laughed, and I almost smiled. "Five thirty good?"

"Yeah."

"Chin up. I'll let you know what I learn."

"Can you reach out to Bobby's mom? The police will tell her, but I know how she's going to feel."

That she failed her son. That she shouldn't have kicked him out. That she should have done more. That she should have forced him somehow, someway, into a program that worked. Done something different, said something else, did more, did less, fixed it. That it was all her fault.

It's what I felt every day. That I failed my mom because I couldn't help her. If I'd only been stronger. Better. Wiser.

"I'll talk to her," Will said.

I looked around, making sure no one was paying attention to my conversation; no one was even looking at me. I was a tall, skinny geek who wore no makeup and dressed as casual as I could get away with in city hall. No jeans allowed, but I didn't have to dress up. Working in the basement had its advantages.

"I'll do anything," I told him again. "The information is there. We both know it. I think—the computer virus I'm working on? I think it was planted. What could be in those files that someone would want to destroy? Maybe there's something in city hall that will help us."

"Hold that thought. We'll talk tonight."

I could dig in. Will had been hesitant because nothing these nonprofits did was illegal. They received billions of dollars to help the homeless, but so few homeless people were being helped. Not when building temporary housing was astronomically expensive—it should never cost a million dollars a unit. Not when drug treatment centers couldn't actually stop addicts from using. Not when the mental health facilities were so broken, and few social workers seemed to be trained to convince people that they *didn't* want to live on the street.

The money was there. Where there was easy money, there was corruption.

I watched the people around me. Walking quickly, on their way to work. Men in suits and ties, women in tennis shoes and skirts, their pumps in bags over their shoulders. Not a mile away, a twenty-nine-year-old drug addict died because of a system that was set up to fail. Not a mile away, a mother turned her addiction to painkillers into an addiction to fentanyl to the point where she exchanged sex for a few blue pills.

It was time to shine a light in the dark and expose those responsible for prolonging this humanitarian crisis.

"Whatever we find," I said to Will, "we can take it to the press."

"I've tried. They're not interested."

"Maybe Amy and Ian will run it."

"I don't know that a podcast is going to make a big difference."

"We have to start somewhere."

When Will didn't say anything, I said, "Talk to your friend. Whatever happens, whatever you need, I'm all in."

I ended the call and hit Play on my podcast. I wanted to know what else Amy and Ian had learned about the sweatshop in Chinatown.

I hoped the asshole who ran it went to prison for the rest of his miserable life.

MONDAY, OCTOBER 7

2

Kara Quinn relaxed once Michael dropped Matt off at FBI headquarters on their way from LAX to LAPD headquarters downtown.

Matt Costa, their team leader, would be at the courthouse to listen to her testimony, but his concern for her safety had made her tense. She understood all the reasons why, but his stress gave her one more thing to think about when she already had far too much on her plate.

"He knows this is risky," Michael said. "Cut him some slack."

She glanced at her partner. "What is that supposed to mean?"

"He doesn't think you're taking the threat seriously."

"I *am*. I just don't want to talk about it 24/7. You have my back and I trust you. Matt has talked to court security a gazillion times and we have a dozen contingencies. I'm wearing this stupid vest all day." She hit her chest. The Kevlar was wholly uncomfortable. She'd never gotten used to it when she'd been in uniform, and it didn't feel any better now.

The unspoken truth: she was in a relationship with Matt.

That was why Michael was coming with her to the courthouse. It was one thing to work together—she and Matt had proven they could be professional on the job. It was another to have the woman you cared about testifying against the criminal who had put a bounty on her head.

She changed the subject. "I wish I was a fly on the wall during Matt's meeting."

Michael grinned. "I'd join you."

Matt was meeting with Assistant Special Agent in Charge Bryce Thornton, the asshole who had nearly destroyed Kara's case against David Chen. Also in the meeting was an assistant US attorney working on federal charges against Chen. Because the state case was stronger—and because Thornton had fucked everything up seven months ago—the state was prosecuting Chen first.

Depending on what happened today at the courthouse, Kara would have to answer questions about Chen's operation tomorrow at FBI headquarters. She wasn't looking forward to it. Matt was there today to have Thornton removed from the case, something that should have happened months ago when he almost let Chen walk free and clear.

"I've never been here," Michael said.

"You've never been to Los Angeles? Are you kidding?"

"I didn't travel when I was a kid—I don't remember ever leaving Chicago until I enlisted in the Navy, and boot camp wasn't far from where I grew up. I went to SEALs training in Coronado, but never drove up here."

"I wish I could show you around. Take you to Santa Monica—that's where my condo is. One of my favorite Mexican restaurants is walking distance. Oh, and there is this amazing fish place on the pier. Best salmon I've ever had. There's so much to do here, and no one pays you any attention. Usually, I hang out at the beach on my days off."

"*You*, Ms. Workaholic, actually took days off?"

"Once or twice a month," she said jokingly, even though that was the truth.

"Don't know that we'll have the time, or if it'll be safe."

"Don't remind me," she muttered. "Lex, my boss, has someone watching the place, and there's been no sign that Chen's known associates have been checking it out. I'd really like to go by before we leave town."

The hearing was bullshit, Kara thought. Chen's attorney had moved to dismiss the entire case by having Kara's testimony and statement tossed for some legal reason she didn't quite understand. Craig Dyson, the DDA who was prosecuting Chen, and who Kara had worked with while she was undercover to prevent just these types of legal maneuvers, needed her to answer questions the judge may have. He'd told her that if she didn't show, there was a fifty-fifty chance the judge would dismiss the case. If she showed, he was confident that no evidence would be tossed and Chen would go to trial as scheduled.

"Traffic is worse than in DC," Michael complained.

Michael was following his GPS, though Kara could have navigated him to LAPD headquarters. Because the Harbor Freeway was backed up, GPS told him to continue on the 10 to the first exit, then drive through side streets.

Kara would have told him to just take the Harbor because it was a more direct route, and you never knew what you'd face on downtown streets, but in the months they'd worked together, she knew Michael didn't like backseat drivers, so she remained silent.

She looked around at her old stomping grounds. She had worked here, played here, but in the seven months she'd been gone it had changed, and not for the better. So many more homeless, the tents lining the streets leading from the freeway into the downtown area. Graffiti had plagued the city for years; it hadn't gotten better. New tags over old. Crime was always a problem, but now the smash-and-grab in broad daylight was so commonplace, most people didn't report the theft. The homeless were both victims of crime—rape, beatings, murder, theft—and the perpetrators. People preyed on people, and drug addiction made it worse.

It was sad to see, but she didn't have the answers.

The year before he was killed in the line of duty, Colton, her former sometime partner, had gone undercover in Venice Beach to find a killer targeting the homeless. The killer started here, in downtown Los Angeles, and moved west. Colton followed. Took him nearly two months, but Colton caught him. Justice served.

But the plight of these people hadn't gotten better. Colton had become invested in the communities, so angry with the politicians who talked a good game but didn't solve any problems. He'd always been tightly wound, but he'd been a damn good cop and didn't deserve to die. She still missed him. They'd had something between them—mutual respect, trust, an attraction they scratched from time to time. Colton had been the closest thing to a relationship she'd ever had, but because of who they were it had never progressed to something permanent.

Well, the closest thing to a relationship until Matt, she realized suddenly.

As they neared the government center, the rows of tents disappeared, as if law enforcement moved the homeless along until they were out of sight from the people who might be able to do something about it.

Michael turned the corner and LAPD headquarters came into view. Her heart swelled.

Home.

"That is the ugliest building I've seen yet," Michael said, "and there have been plenty of monstrosities between here and the airport."

"Jeez, what's this, rag on the West Coast week?" She tilted her head to gaze at the contemporary structure built fifteen years ago. "I guess I don't really notice it anymore. It opened before

I was a cop. But yeah, it's certainly not as nice as FBI headquarters," she said sarcastically.

"Point taken."

Michael drove to the parking garage, showed his credentials and was directed where to park. They took the elevator up to Special Operations.

Special Operations oversaw LAPD detectives, the counterterrorism squad and certain specialty units. Kara's squad, led by Sergeant Lex Popovich, was one of the few dedicated undercover units.

Kara had been one of his first hires, right out of the academy because she fit a need. Lex obtained an exemption for her to work undercover at a high school to ferret out a drug ring, à la *21 Jump Street*, and then she had to do a year in uniform when that assignment was over, before returning to the unit full-time. She loved it. She'd found a home, a place where she belonged, people who respected her, and justice.

Then it was ripped away from her. Painfully, ruthlessly, unfairly.

She missed everything. Lex, her team, the cases, even this building.

Michael let her lead the way. Lex's squad was at the north end of the fourth floor. She stopped outside double doors labeled "Special Operations Division III, Sergeant Alexander Popovich."

"I'll give you some space," Michael said, "but don't leave the building without me."

She smiled at him. "Thanks."

She appreciated Michael understanding her need to reconnect with her old squad. Trust and respect were not qualities she gave out lightly, and Michael had earned both, despite their occasional disagreements.

Kara walked in, nostalgia wrapping around her like a bittersweet blanket. The energy of the room beckoned her: ringing phones, keyboards clacking, the chatter of her fellow officers filling the space. She breathed in the familiar scents of sweat and cleanser mixed with the metallic tang of guns and the burnt aroma of old coffee.

The seven months could have been seven days or seven years. It was the same…but everything had changed. She didn't recognize half her colleagues. Her desk, the farthest on the right, was now occupied by a young, lean, black detective. He looked sharp in his blazer, jeans and skinny tie, with his badge and gun prominently displayed on his belt. His long legs were stretched out, crossed at the ankles, as he chatted on the phone.

At her desk.

Not your desk anymore.

What's that old phrase? Time stops for no one?

"Quinn? I'll be damned."

She'd recognize Detective Charlie Dean's voice anywhere. She turned and grinned at him, so happy to see a friendly, familiar face.

"I heard you were coming to town," he said, "but couldn't get any info from Lex."

Charlie rose from his desk and gave her a tight hug. In his fifties with a slight beer belly, Charlie was the kind of cop who would stay until he was forced into retirement. He didn't work undercover anymore, but now ran his own small squad within Lex's unit, focusing on fraud against senior citizens. The last case they worked together—five years ago—he'd posed as a substitute teacher at a high school and Kara had been a student. They'd uncovered an identity theft ring.

"Damn, it's great to see you," she said, feeling surprisingly emotional.

"It's not the same here without you, Q."

"Hey, hey, hey!" another familiar voice said from across the room. She turned as Pete Diaz approached and took over the hug from Charlie. Pete was a wiry Puerto Rican only an inch taller than her (just under) five foot four, with a bright smile and sharp instincts. He'd been a uniformed officer for six years before transferring over to the gang unit, then moving to Special Operations a couple years ago. She'd tapped his brain often because of his deep knowledge about gangs. He squeezed her tight, then let go. "You owe us big-time," Pete said. "No calls, not even a postcard."

"Beer's on me." As she said it she knew she couldn't go out in public. Not when David Chen had put the word out that he was paying for her head. "When all this bullshit is over," she added. "Unless you want to hang out with me and a couple of feds in a stuffy hotel room."

"We're holding you to it," Charlie said.

"So many people at their desks, you'd think there was no crime out there," she said.

Charlie rolled his eyes. "Getting new undercover gigs approved is a clusterfuck. The layers of bureaucracy have grown even since you left."

"Place isn't the same without you," Pete said.

"Well, hopefully once this is all done, it'll be like old times," she said.

Of course, nothing would be the same. Colton, her sometime partner and sometime lover, was dead. She glanced over to the far corner. His desk was empty. He wasn't coming back, but no one had filled his space. No one could. He had been one of a kind and the world was worse off with him gone.

She sensed someone watching her and when she turned, saw Lex Popovich standing in his doorway. He frowned at her. "I still can't make him happy," she said to her former colleagues, and crossed the bullpen. She smiled broadly. "Hey, boss."

He motioned her into his office, then shut his door. "What the fuck are you doing here, Quinn?"

"Good to see you, too." She plopped down in the vinyl-covered visitor's chair. It was more lopsided than she remembered.

Lex stared at her, his lips a thin line. He'd aged faster than she expected. More wrinkles, less hair, and seemed to have lost twenty pounds. Maybe he had a few to lose, but he didn't look like her boss.

"By the time you leave this building," he said, his voice low with restrained anger, "every dirtbag will be waiting to kill you. What about 'contract for your head' don't you understand?"

"I understand the threat, Lex. I have two feds watching my back every minute of every day."

He waved his hands in the air, made a point to look around his office. "Where are they? Right now, they're not watching your back."

His reaction seemed over-the-top. Kara didn't remind him she was in the heart of LAPD surrounded by hundreds of cops. "I wanted to see a friendly face and that certainly wasn't going to be in the federal building."

Lex walked behind his desk and plopped down into his worn chair with a sigh. "Nothing has changed. If anything, things are more volatile."

"I'm here because David Chen's lawyer is moving to dismiss the *entire* case. Dyson needs me. The federal case is moving as slow as molasses, but we can nail him on murder—I'm not letting him walk on it. We win this, it's a *good* thing. Murder keeps him behind bars and brings me one step closer to home."

He stared at her. "It *is* good to see you, kid."

"I knew you missed me."

"I don't miss your bullshit."

She pinched her thumb and forefinger an inch apart. "Not even a little?"

Now he laughed and every muscle in her body relaxed. "The feds treating you well?"

She shrugged. "More or less. They *are* feds."

"True." He sipped from a coffee mug on his cluttered desk, grimaced and put it down. "Greer sends me reports on your investigations. You've done some good work." Tony Greer was the FBI assistant director who oversaw the Mobile Response Team.

"Great work," I emphasized.

"They don't seem to have complaints about you."

"Don't sound so surprised."

"You look good. Happy."

"Working for the feds is much better than sitting in a safe house for a year twiddling my thumbs and binge-watching Netflix. But now that we have a trial date, this is almost over."

"The trial is still three months away. It's too dangerous for you to be on the streets of Los Angeles."

"My condo hasn't been compromised."

"Not to my knowledge, but it's risky to stay there."

"The feds got a hotel somewhere around here." She waved her hand to indicate the downtown area. "But I want to go by, check things out myself. I miss my place." It wasn't much—a tiny one-bedroom condo in Santa Monica. But it was on the beach, and it had been her eight-hundred-square-foot sanctuary for years.

"Not alone."

"Not alone," she repeated, exasperated. "Damn, Lex, I don't have a death wish. You of all people should know that."

"I don't like that Dyson couldn't get this motion quashed without you having to come back."

"Yesterday I was on a video call with Dyson going over my previous statement, the evidence, everything a thousand different ways. We're meeting before the hearing to cover all our bases."

"Court—I should have figured that's why you're all dolled up."

She grimaced. "Dolled up?"

"Slacks, blazer, blouse, *makeup*." He grinned. "Court attire."

"Yeah, well, anything to help our case. The case is tight, we have evidence to back up my testimony. These…" she waved her hand in the air "...*theatrics* are Chen's attorney blowing smoke. I'd put my money on Dyson any day of the week."

Kara took down an illegal sweatshop eight months ago, rescuing hundreds of Chinese nationals who were forced to work in horrific conditions for long hours. She'd been undercover as a clothing buyer for a big-box chain and was proud of her work until Chen killed her informant. Sunny's death still haunted her, and Kara would never forgive herself for not pulling the young woman earlier.

You tried. She wanted justice for her family and friends.

Chen, the owner of the sweatshop, filed charges of civil rights abuses against Kara after she killed his bodyguard in self-defense. Though it was a justified shooting, Kara was investigated by the LA FBI, instigated by Bryce Thornton, who she'd butted heads with the first time they met.

Thornton had his hand slapped by the FBI's Office of Professional Responsibility for opening the investigation into her actions and jeopardizing the case against Chen, but a reprimand only made assholes like Thornton more dangerous.

Chen was out of jail on a too-modest bail and had even put a hit out on Kara. Though it couldn't be proven, Lex and other authorities knew it was him. To avoid being stuck at a desk or in protective custody, Kara had joined the FBI's Mobile Response Team.

"Who's the new guy, and do I get my old desk back after the trial?"

"Rob Becker."

"He looks twelve."

"You're one to talk."

"He's the new Kara Quinn?"

"No one can replace you, Kara."

"Damn straight."

"He's taken some of the cases you would have taken," Lex acknowledged. "He went undercover with Pete at UCLA at the beginning of the school year, took down a group manufacturing date rape drugs in a campus chem lab. Just came off that case last week, lots of paperwork. And *he* doesn't complain about it."

"Me? Complain about paperwork?" She smiled. "As long as he knows that's my desk."

"When do I get to meet your partners?"

"Come listen to me be on my best behavior in court."

"I'll pass."

"Dinner? Breakfast?"

She missed Lex; she needed to reconnect with her boss so they could go back to their old comfortable camaraderie when she returned to the squad.

"Text me. I'll see if I can get out." He paused, assessed her. "You like your team, right? Costa, the others?"

"Yeah, sure." She wasn't going to mention that she and Matt were in what Matt called a *relationship*. The term made her squeamish, and she was actually looking forward to a more long-distance *relationship*. She liked Matt—a lot—and she liked sex with Matt—a lot—but it was getting…well…she didn't know how to explain it to herself, let alone someone else. She wanted to be with Matt, but she also wanted her own space, and it was increasingly difficult to balance those two needs.

"They're good cops," she continued. "They have my back, that's what's important. Why do you care?"

"Because I care about you. I want you to be happy."

"Well, happy is a tall order."

"You look good."

She shrugged. "I've been challenged, that's always good. I like the travel, which I didn't think I would. Even went to the San Juan Islands for a case, got to spend Fourth of July weekend on R & R after we solved it."

"Now *I'm* jealous."

"But there's no place like home."

"Promise me you'll be careful."

"Always."

"Let me introduce you to the new guys. Rob, of course—you'll like him—and we have a lateral move from San Francisco who has experience in sex crimes, training under Charlie because he's retiring at the end of the year."

"Retiring? *Charlie?*"

"He has twenty-plus years. He had a heart scare over the summer."

She frowned. Talking about the health of her friends and colleagues made her squeamish. She worried enough about her grandmother that she didn't want to worry about anyone else.

"I've been thinking about retiring, too," Lex said after a moment.

That surprised her. "You said a thousand times you never wanted to retire."

"Well. Yeah. The last couple years have been pretty damn crappy. I'm thinking, haven't made a decision. I have a couple cases I want to see through. But sometimes the idea of buying a couple acres in the Middle of Nowhere, Wyoming, sounds awfully good to me."

"Wyoming. With cows and horses and not much else."

"Peace, Kara. There's a lot of peace up there."

He sounded wistful. Almost…sad.

"I have to get to work," he said.

"I thought you were going to introduce me around."

"Next time. A meeting reminder just popped up on my computer. I'll walk you out, meet these feds of yours."

She rolled her eyes. "Kicking me out so soon."

Then he stared at her, eyes hard.

"It is not safe for you to be here, Kara."

"What's going on?"

"Dammit, Kara, you're not this dense."

She bristled. "This is a cop shop. I'm safest here."

"Not anymore."

She didn't want to ask, but she did. "Why?"

He was wrestling with something, and she couldn't believe he didn't want to tell her.

"What are you keeping from me?"

"I can't talk here. Shit. I told Dyson not to let you come back."

Now she knew something was going on. "What the fuck, Lex? Is this about Chen?"

In a low voice, he said, "You are not an idiot. This hearing is a smoke screen. As soon as you walked into this building, Chen knew where you were."

"So what? He knows I'll be in court this afternoon."

But then it clicked.

"Here. There's a cop *here* in headquarters who is working for Chen?" The realization made her sick to her stomach. "You know who it is?"

Lex shook his head. "It's not just your case that was compromised. I have someone I trust deep cover and that's all I'm going to say about that."

Kara stared at him. "And you didn't tell me?"

"You don't work for me anymore, Quinn."

She felt like she'd been slapped. "Not now, but—"

"Not ever. You can't come back, not until I know that every fucking prick that works for Chen is gone. And even if he goes to prison—and that's a big fucking *if*—he still has people. It's not just Chen. And if you would get your head out of your ass long enough to think, you'd realize Chen's operation couldn't have worked for so long unless he had someone high, high up protecting him."

She slowly rose from her seat. She felt gut punched.

You can't come back…

"You have work," she mumbled and turned to leave.

"Stop."

She did, but she didn't look at him. She was shaking. Anger that there was a bad cop in this building. Frustration that she wasn't here to root him out. Sorrow that Lex didn't want her back.

She felt…lost.

"Kara, I didn't mean to take this all out on you. It isn't your fault."

"I get it. Goodbye."

She walked out and Lex didn't stop her. She heard something break behind his door, but it gave her no joy.

When Michael met her in the hall he said, "What happened?"

She shook her head. She didn't want to talk about it now. "Let's go."

Lieutenant Elena Gomez picked up the call from her sergeant, Lex Popovich. "Gomez," she answered as she reviewed reports. She liked being in command; she didn't like the explosion of paperwork. It never stopped coming.

"Quinn is here."

"I know. She's testifying this afternoon. Dyson assured me that it's one hearing, and she'll be gone by tomorrow."

"We need to tell her."

She put her pen down. "Lex, *no.*"

"At the time, it was the right call to cut her out of the investigation, but she's here, she needs to know what's going on."

"She came to see you, didn't she? Now you're feeling guilty."

"You would be, too, if you had lied to her face!"

Which was precisely why Elena had avoided Kara. She had been Kara's training officer, her friend. It was better not to talk with her than to be forced to lie.

"Try to avoid her, Lex. Twenty-four hours and she'll be back on a plane to DC and we'll finish this investigation."

"She wants to come back. She thinks she can."

"Maybe—"

"Right," Lex said, barking out an angry laugh. "She'll come back and work for us when she learns we've been lying to her for months. Fuck it. She'll never forgive us. I don't know if I can forgive myself."

Even if Kara could return to LAPD, it wouldn't be in the capacity she'd want.

"Stay the course, Lex." She hung up.

Guilt washed over her, then it disappeared. It would return, but she had a job to do, and she would damn well do it.

3

Conrad James didn't need to follow Costa or Quinn from the airport to know where they were going. That they arrived on time was good enough for him.

He had a tight schedule, and didn't like to be rushed, even when he had a deadline.

The people who needed to die would all die in good time.

He listened to classical music not because he was well educated—though he was—and not because he particularly liked it—though he had an affection for Tchaikovsky—but because the music relaxed him and put him in the right mindset.

He was halfway downtown when his cell phone rang. He paused the music and answered the call.

"Yes."

"Well? What's going on?"

"Why are you calling?" He'd been working for the group for months and they still hadn't learned that he did not appreciate micromanagement.

"Because you sent me a cryptic text message while I'm in

the middle of a meeting that the game is on? What's that supposed to mean?"

"Should I have said, in writing, that Mathias Costa and his team are here, that Detective Quinn has an appointment at the courthouse at eleven thirty with Mr. Dyson? Should I have said, in writing, that the assassination is on schedule?"

"Don't be such an asshole."

Conrad bristled. He did not like this man. He didn't particularly like anyone in the group, but he was the most vulgar and, honestly, the most stupid.

"Do you have a change order?"

"No."

"Let me do the job for which I was hired." He ended the call without a goodbye.

He did not trust these people. He didn't trust anyone he worked for, which was why he had survived for as long as he had as a fixer. But these people were particularly capricious and slippery.

Yet he prided himself on doing his job well, and his plan was set. Structured, but fluid enough to adapt if necessary.

Two people would die today.

Game on.

He changed the music from Tchaikovsky to Mozart. Not his favorite, but the balanced rhythm of the sonata had a wonderful centering effect on his mind.

He had a job to do, and he would do it. After all, they paid him a lot of money to clean up their messes.

4

At its core, the FBI was a huge bureaucracy.

The Los Angeles FBI office took up the majority of the seventeen-story cement atrocity called the Federal Building, across from the Los Angeles National Cemetery. Special agent in charge of the Mobile Response Team, Mathias Costa, didn't like the architecture of the DC building that he worked out of now, but compared to LA headquarters, the Hoover Building was a work of art.

After Michael dropped him off, Matt checked in, then was led upstairs for his scheduled meeting with ASAC Rebecca Chavez, George Chandler—the assistant US attorney overseeing the federal aspect of the David Chen investigation—and ASAC Bryce Thornton.

He had been peeved when Thornton hadn't been demoted after the OPR investigation. The only consolation was that he was given a one-year probation and working directly under Chavez.

Los Angeles was the second-largest FBI office in the country and had their own assistant director in charge. Still, they answered to national headquarters, and while technically Matt was an operational "equal" to SAC Brian Granderson, Granderson deferred to him and made it clear to his staff to cooperate with Matt.

After the Chen hearing was set, Matt had talked to both Rebecca and AUSA Chandler frequently. Matt generally worked well with his colleagues, but because he had made it his mission to ensure that Thornton was under strict supervision, he hadn't made many friends in LA.

Matt had testified against Thornton at the OPR hearing. When Matt was vetting Kara's credentials for an investigation he led several months ago, Thornton had lied to him regarding an LA-FBI investigation involving Kara. The OPR investigation was broader than Matt's accusation—Thornton was accused of leaking to the press the identity of two undercover operatives, resulting in the murder of Kara's partner. He had been cleared of those charges, but received two weeks' unpaid leave for his handling of the federal investigation into David Chen, his personal motivation into recommending no prosecution, and his unsanctioned investigation into LAPD Detective Kara Quinn.

That he was still an agent irked Matt. Thornton had formally apologized, but told OPR that Matt had misunderstood him, and that he should have been clearer.

Matt did *not* misunderstand Thornton, but the panel took him at his word. Thornton admitted he had a personal beef with Kara and that his frustration with her had led to his unprofessional behavior.

Kara didn't talk about it much, but she had a lot to say about the first run-in she had with Bryce Thornton eleven years ago. While Matt waited for the meeting to begin, he thought about what Kara had told him.

Four months ago, Matt and Kara were at his house in Tucson, celebrating the successful closure of a difficult case. Matt had some loose ends to tie up—and a lot of paperwork—and Kara decided to stay. They'd needed some quality time together, away from work and any distractions.

That evening, they'd gone out with Matt's best friend, Tim Armstrong, and his wife, Sarah. They'd had a fantastic time, but when they returned to his house, Kara seemed quiet. The recent monsoon had ushered in fresh air to cool the hot night. Despite the late hour, Matt decided to turn on his hot tub and suggested they have a nightcap.

"I don't have a bathing suit," she said.

"That didn't stop you last night in the pool," he said with a half smile.

"We had sex in the pool. Is that what you want? You could have just asked."

Her tone more than her words had Matt wary. "I just want to relax." He grabbed a couple beers from the refrigerator and walked outside. "We don't have to get in the hot tub. It's a nice evening."

She followed him outside, took one look at the frothy bubbles and stripped. Taking a beer from his hand, she eased her naked body into the water.

He did the same, sat on the opposite side. Sipped his beer. Watched Kara, wished he could read her mind. Her head was back, eyes closed; she relaxed before his eyes. He breathed easier.

"Did I do or say anything tonight that upset you?"

"No. Why?"

"We were all having a good time, then you got quiet. Like you were a million miles away."

She didn't say anything at first. "You never told me that Thornton went up in front of OPR. Which I guess is the FBI's version of Internal Affairs?"

"Similar. I thought you knew."

"How would I know? I wasn't asked to tell the panel what an asshole he is."

"It's a bureaucratic process, but it usually works."

"He's still a fed."

"He was suspended without pay for two weeks."

"That's what you told Tim."

"So I did do something that upset you."

She shook her head. "It doesn't really have anything to do with me."

"Yes, it does. He violated regulations, including opening an investigation into your actions when there was no federal interest to do so. He misled the AUSA regarding your investigation of Chen. In addition to his suspension, he was placed on a one-year probation. It was serious and he was reprimanded. Getting him fired would have been a lot harder, and there wasn't enough evidence against him." He paused, added, "I didn't have any support from the local office, though they agreed that his personal animosity toward you was problematic."

She shrugged and didn't look at him. What was she really thinking? Hadn't they been through enough that she was comfortable sharing her thoughts and feelings?

"Kara, what is really bothering you?" Matt asked quietly.

Finally, she said, "I was thinking about Colton."

"Your partner."

"I know Thornton outed both of us. I'm alive, Colton is dead."

"I looked hard at that, but there was no evidence that he leaked information to the media. I swear to God, Kara, if I found even a hint that he'd talked to the press, I would have had his head."

"I believe you. And I get it—no one could prove it, so he gets away with it."

"It could have been someone else."

"There's no one who hates me that much."

"Chen's people."

"Maybe," she said, but she obviously didn't believe it.

"You miss him?"

She shrugged. "Don't be jealous. My relationship with Colton was not traditional."

He wasn't jealous; he'd known that she'd been involved, on and off, with her partner. She called it "friends with benefits"—which was what she was trying to make their relationship, but Matt was more traditional than Kara. And he knew there was something more between them than she was willing to recognize—for now.

"I'm not jealous. But answer me honestly. If he hadn't been killed, would you be with me?"

"And I hadn't been forced to leave LA? I don't know."

At least she was being honest. She was always honest.

Then she continued and said something that surprised him. "Before everything blew up in LA, I was thinking you and I would probably get together down the road. Like I told you when I left Washington, if we both had vacations at the same time, it might be fun to go away and have hot monkey sex for a few days on the beach."

He grinned. "We're not on the beach, but the sex has been amazing."

She nodded, almost absently, and he wondered what she was thinking about again.

"I'm not going to tell you that I would have sought you out or that I was going to be celibate until we got together, because I don't know. I can't tell you what I might have done in a situation I didn't face. Colton and I were just…different. Not only from other people, but each other. He was raised in a perfect middle-class home with two parents who loved him and then he enlisted in the Marines and shit happened. He didn't talk about it much, but he had his own demons and those I understood. I never had to explain anything to him, he just accepted me for who I was. Now, we didn't have this great love affair, so get that sour look off your face."

Matt wanted to say, *I accept you for who you are*, but instead he said, "I don't have a sour expression."

"Colton and I fought, and not in the good way."

"There's a good way?"

Now her eyes sparkled. "Yeah, there is. The other day, when you were mad because I let Molina kiss me as part of my cover. That was a good fight, and the makeup sex was amazing. Anyway, you think I take risks? Colton was explosive. You think I walk a fine line? Colton crossed them. Sometimes I did, too, but only if I had to. And honestly, I didn't have the strength or courage to know how to help Colton in his dark times. I'll always miss him because he was a big part of my life for so long, and I'm not talking about sex. He was my best friend."

"I respect that."

"We're not going to do this whole past relationships bullshit, are we?"

"No."

"Because I don't care who you've slept with."

"Ditto."

"You sure?"

"Yes. I only care if you sleep with anyone other than me while we're together."

"We're together?"

"I know you like this 'friends with benefits' thing, and I'm okay with that as long as it's monogamous. If you want to walk away, just tell me."

"Okay."

He believed her. Kara wasn't perfect, but she wasn't dishonest. Somehow, he felt better about what they had, even if she didn't want to think it was more than casual.

"So, why did you break Bryce Thornton's nose?" he asked.

She laughed. It sounded so good after their far-too-serious conversation.

He added, "Assaulting a federal agent could have gotten you fired."

"Hand slapped, then my squad took me out for pizza and beer and gave me a friggin' tiara." She looked pointedly at Matt. "He deserved it."

Matt waited, knowing Kara would tell him in her own time.

She drained her beer and put the bottle down. "I hate working drug cases, but back then I had less than two years on the job, and I'd do anything and everything my boss wanted. Long Beach PD needed an undercover agent—young, female, nonthreatening." She smiled, pointed at herself. "They had uncovered a drug smuggling operation at the port. The last bust failed to nab everyone. They had the boat, but smugglers can always get more boats. They had one of the dockworkers who had been paid off, but they suspected there was another. The consensus was they'd jumped the gun. They needed the distributor, had no idea who he was. So on the one hand, they got a million bucks worth of oxy off the streets—this was back before fentanyl was big—and put a handful of pricks behind bars, but they didn't shut down the network and no one was talking. Enter *moi*."

Kara got out of the hot tub and walked, naked, into the house; he watched through the window as she retrieved two more beers from the refrigerator and brought them out. His desire for her had grown each day since they met, and he wanted to take her to bed right now. But he also wanted to hear her story, especially while she was so comfortable and relaxed.

"So," Kara said, slipping back into the water and handing him one of the beers, top already off. "I joined the team that was putting together another operation. I was still new, but had already logged a half dozen undercover ops. After listening to what had gone right and wrong the last time, I made some suggestions. Bold, I know—they could have shut me down, I was practically still a rookie. It was a good team—they listened, agreed. After reading his file and watching him for a few days, I knew Jamal, the driver, wanted out. So we made him a deal. He gets me in, we get him out, wipe his record, clean slate. I went under as his girlfriend. Lived in his house. Played the part."

"Slept with him?"

"Would you care?"

He didn't know how to answer that. He didn't think that undercover cops, local or federal, should be intimately involved with suspects or informants. Yet...was that a personal or professional opinion?

"I see," she said.

"It's not because we're involved," he said. "I just want you to be honest with me."

She smiled slyly, drank, said, "We made out for show, but that's as far as we took it. Jamal was a good guy, under his bravado and bullshit. One of his friends got him hooked up with the gig after he lost his job as a bartender, then things spiraled from there. He knew it was dangerous—he was working for some serious bad guys with ties to a Mexican cartel. He also knew if he didn't get out, he'd be dead or in jail.

"Long story short, the night the shipment came in, I was there with Jamal. I'd already gone on a few jobs with him, to show I could be trusted, but this was the big one. Everything had to go right—the Coast Guard had to nab the boat as it left, LBPD had to nab the dockworker who'd been paid off, and I had to stick with Jamal through to the delivery at the distributor. Unfortunately, he wasn't alone. The thugs that brokered the deal insisted on coming with us, so we couldn't risk having LBPD follow. Even Jamal didn't know where he was going until we picked up the junk. But I had a tracker in my bra—couldn't risk a phone or any visible electronics—and LBPD would be at the house within minutes. My job, once there, was to get Jamal to safety and let LBPD get the bust.

"It didn't get that far."

Matt could almost see it before she said it.

"There was a federal investigation," she continued. "And the fucking feds didn't clue in the local police department until minutes before the raid—and they called the desk sergeant, not the chief, who knew exactly what we were doing. By the time the chief was told, it was too late to shut anything down. We were in the truck, we had the drugs in the back, I'd activated the tracker, and FBI SWAT moved in under the direction of guess who?"

He didn't have to guess, so he said nothing.

"I'm damn lucky the two assholes in the back didn't jump out guns blazing, because Jamal and I would be dead. After a few tense minutes, they got out and we all complied with the orders. I was livid. We had a good plan, and the fucking FBI blew it. They separated all of us and lucky me, I got the car with Bryce Thornton. Newly promoted to SSA, this was his first big operation. He was in charge. I immediately told him who I was, out of earshot from the goons. In the back of my mind I was hoping there was some way to salvage the op. He looked me up and down—remember, I dressed the part. Torn jeans, skimpy tank top, dyed my hair black and wore more makeup than I do in a month. He said, 'I already told you, you have the right to remain silent, so shut the fuck up.'

"At this point, I was worried about Jamal—I didn't want him to do or say anything around the thugs he planned to betray. I had promised him after tonight he would be free. Thornton got on his radio, barking orders, and I turned to the SWAT guy who was guarding me as we stood next to the SUV. I identified myself, gave my badge number, the name of my supervisor, and told him to take the cuffs off. To his credit, he looked at Thornton and said, 'Maybe we should confirm.' Thornton shut him down. I'll never forget what he said. 'She's been fucking Jamal Warner for the last three weeks. She's been with him on his last two jobs. No way she's a cop.' Then he looked at me and said, 'If you are a cop, you won't be after tonight.'"

Kara drank heavily, said, "I may have said some things that riled him up at that point."

"We're trained not to react to verbal attacks," Matt said.

"You've never been verbally attacked by me," she said, not smiling. "He was angry, and by the time my boss arrived, Thornton wanted to arrest me for assaulting a federal officer. I may have made a comment that it's not a crime to describe his tiny dick in microscopic detail. They'd already taken Jamal and the others away, and I needed to get Jamal out of this. I had *promised*."

Matt knew that Kara internalized all her cases, and her word meant everything to her.

"My boss convinced SWAT to remove the cuffs and ordered me to walk away. I had enough sense to do just that but I didn't get far. Thornton wasn't going to honor our deal with Jamal— he was getting charged with a whole series of crimes that we had told him would go away for his cooperation. We had the DA's office behind us. Thornton said he didn't have to honor it, and would also be filing a report against me, against Long Beach Police Department, yada, yada. My boss, who was cool as a cucumber until then, told him to go to hell, completely reamed him. I enjoyed watching the tongue-lashing. Probably was smirking. Thornton stormed off and passed me. He said, 'I will have your badge, and your fuck buddy Jamal Warner will not see the outside of a cage for the next twenty years.' And then I hit him."

Matt didn't say anything for a minute.

Kara finally said, "You think I was wrong."

"No. I mean, you probably should have restrained yourself, but he clearly had it coming. What happened to Jamal?"

"I almost lost him. Thornton did not back down. I was suspended for three days, told to stay far away from the case or lose my badge. I was young and stupid and thought I couldn't trust anyone. Long Beach proved me wrong. The chief of police went to bat for Jamal, went all the way to the top, shared intel with the FBI about their operation and recordings Jamal had made, and in the end, if Jamal agreed to testify, they'd put him in WITSEC and he'd have a new life. It wasn't exactly what we had promised—he had wanted to go home, where he was raised in Houston. But he was alive, and he was free, and ultimately, we put the bad guys in prison. Well, the feds got credit. As a condition of letting Jamal off the hook, the feds took our case. The only consolation was that Bryce Thornton was pulled."

"And he's held a grudge ever since."

"He's tried to bring me up on charges multiple times over the years. Lex always handled it. It seemed every time I turned around, he had a complaint about me. But I'm serious, Matt. If he had anything to do with outing Colton, I want him for murder."

"So do I," Matt said.

She looked surprised when he said it, then she smiled. Put her beer down and crossed over to where he sat on the opposite side of the hot tub. Standing, her breasts were inches from his face. She leaned over, kissed him as she straddled him. He clutched her.

"We should go inside," he said.

"In a minute or two…" she murmured against his ear. She reached down, felt how hard he was and bit his earlobe. He grabbed her waist and brought her down on him.

Then he was lost inside her.

5

Matt sat in the conference room on one side of the table. Rebecca Chavez was at the head, a small stack of files in front of her. Chandler, Thornton and Agent Tom Schroder were across from him. Opposite from Chavez was Special Agent Sloane Wagner, designated secretary for the meeting.

The setup was needlessly adversarial, but if that was the way they wanted to play it, so be it.

ASAC Rebecca Chavez had insisted on the meeting, claimed she wanted to "mend fences" with the national office over what she called "a misunderstanding." Matt had asked that Brian Granderson be present, but Chavez said it wasn't necessary to bring in her boss, that she was confident they could resolve any problems themselves.

Chavez was in her forties and appeared the consummate professional. Short, neatly styled dark hair, intelligent eyes, impeccable suit, classy jewelry. She'd been with the Bureau for as long as Matt—nearly sixteen years. Her first career had been as an accountant for a major Wall Street firm. Her specialty was white-collar crimes, and she had a solid but unremarkable career. She was known to be meticulous and didn't make waves.

George Chandler was young for an assistant US attorney, hired two years ago right out of law school. He hadn't prosecuted any high-profile cases and had been handed the Chen investigation likely because his bosses didn't see it going anywhere.

And of course Bryce Thornton. Like Matt, he'd joined the Bureau young. Worked himself up to ASAC five years ago after closing a major human-trafficking case. Matt had reviewed his record thoroughly. He did good work, but had more than one reprimand in his file, primarily for animosity toward local law enforcement. Matt had seen that firsthand during his OPR interview. Previously, Chavez covered for him. She smoothed things over with any local agency that complained about Thornton.

Thornton had changed squads multiple times within LA FBI. After digging around, Matt learned that no one liked working with him. Thornton was smart and closed cases; he was also arrogant and condescending.

Tom and Sloane were introduced as agents on Thornton's squad, here because they would be working any follow-up.

After introductions, Matt said, "I don't have a lot of time. I need to get to the courthouse. Please explain why I found out only last week that Agent Thornton hasn't been removed from the Chen investigation."

"There was no need to remove Bryce, who has been part of the investigation from the beginning," Rebecca said. "OPR was clear that it was up to the discretion of this office which cases we assign to which agents."

"And it was also made clear that Agent Thornton, who is still on probation, would not be allowed to work any case that included Detective Kara Quinn."

"She's not a detective anymore," Thornton interjected.

"Detective Quinn is employed by LAPD, on loan to my unit until after the Chen trial," Matt said. "She's testifying today, and thus is intricately involved with this case. Any prosecution is going to need Detective Quinn's assistance and testimony, including federal prosecution."

He looked pointedly at George Chandler, who appeared uncomfortable.

"Well, yes, most likely," George said, "but my office is waiting for the outcome of the state case before we decide which path to pursue."

"The state isn't prosecuting Chen for human trafficking, that's what our office is investigating," Matt said. "It's a federal crime. Are you telling me that there has been no investigation for the last eight months?"

Thornton opened his mouth, but Rebecca cut him off. "Matt, we didn't get the case until after LAPD raided Chen's warehouse. LAPD didn't consult with us, even after they realized that their suspected labor violations included trafficked workers. We need time to investigate, and witnesses haven't been cooperative."

"The primary witness was killed during the police action," Thornton said.

Matt kept his face as calm as possible. Thornton was referring to Soon Chi Chu, "Sunny," Kara's informant, who Chen killed at the beginning of the raid in an effort to get away. Or, as Kara believed, to punish Sunny when he realized she'd been talking to the police.

"Chen killed the witness," Matt said. "Are you telling me that in eight months you have no other women who are willing to talk?"

"We have some initial statements," Chandler said, "and we have a dedicated translator and social worker. But the women are scared. They fear for their families still in China. Finding anyone willing to openly cooperate has been challenging, but we're working on it, including pulling in resources from the State Department to see what recourse we have in bringing families to the US."

Matt was surprised at the compassion and understanding in Chandler's tone.

"That's why what happens today is crucial," Chandler continued. "My boss, Nina Radinovich, will observe the hearing. If the judge throws out Detective Quinn's testimony, our case is that much harder. We haven't been able to trace how Chen brought the women into the country separate from Quinn's knowledge."

If Kara's evidence was thrown out by the court, they would have to build the case from the ground up.

"The best case with clear physical evidence against Chen is the murder charge," Chavez said. "But everything Detective Quinn obtained while undercover is central to a conviction on all other charges. Thus, we need answers from the hearing today."

"That doesn't explain why Agent Thornton is still working this case. In fact, it confirms why he shouldn't. He has a personal grudge against Detective Quinn, which clouds anything he does with this case. That you didn't recognize this after the OPR hearing and subsequent reprimand surprises me."

Chavez bristled. Matt was being deliberately confrontational, frustrated by everything that had been happening with this squad. Chavez acted like Thornton had done nothing wrong.

"I assure you, Agent Costa, that should the FBI decide to prosecute Mr. Chen or anyone else based on the case built by Detective Quinn, Agent Thornton will not be the only agent involved, nor will he be the lead agent. That is going to have to satisfy you. No office appreciates national headquarters coming in and telling them how to manage their personnel."

"That is not my problem," Matt said simply. "My office is, in fact, watching this investigation very closely, and if anything goes wrong, you had better know the who, what, where, when and why. You have over five hundred agents in this building alone, and more than a hundred in regional offices under LA control. You should have picked a different agent for this case to avoid the microscope."

Matt rose. He was done with this conversation. "I didn't want to come here. You're the one who insisted on explaining why Agent Thornton was still involved with this case, and as far as I'm concerned, your reasoning is weak."

Matt took the elevator to the basement, where he would pick up a pool car to use, but first he stepped into a small office across from the elevator. Special Agent in Charge Brian Granderson looked up when Matt entered.

"Good to see you again, Matt," Brian said and shook his hand, motioning for him to sit at the small conference table. Brian sat across from him. "I have a car set aside for your use as long as you're in town."

"I appreciate it," Matt said. "I dropped the bomb. They all pretty much hate me now, if they didn't already."

"You're doing me as much a favor as I am you," Brian said. "Your suggestion to recruit Wagner and send her undercover in Chavez's squad solved my problem with using one of my own people to investigate. Did you have the same assessment I did of Chavez?"

Matt nodded. "She's defending Thornton, over and above what seems necessary. However, I'm an outsider telling her what to do, and if someone made an accusation about one of my people, I might respond the same way."

"OPR made it clear that Thornton wasn't to be involved in any of Detective Quinn's investigations," Brian said. "Chavez's reasons to keep him involved seemed weak, but I let it go because Wagner was already embedded."

Brian had flown out to DC for a meeting several months ago to discuss Thornton and other problems in his office with Tony Greer and Matt. Matt liked the man. Brian had come to the FBI via the military as a JAG lawyer, then starting as a field agent specializing in labor and employment investigations. Now he was the SAC of personnel.

"I discussed it with Chavez and she's taking lead," Brian continued. "Agents Schroder and Wagner are doing field work under her direction, and Thornton is involved only tangentially. There's nothing in her record to suggest there's a personal reason she won't remove Thornton."

Brian and Matt had discussed the possibility that there was something personal between Chavez and Thornton, but Agent Wagner ruled that out early on. Wagner said that Chavez appeared happily married and devoted to her family, and she could find no evidence that Chavez and Thornton were having an affair.

"Yet you and I both think something is wrong."

Brian nodded. "Agent Wagner has gone through all of Chavez's and Thornton's cases for the last two years, then asked me to request specific files from LAPD, though she didn't elaborate why. When the files came in, I glanced through them but I didn't see why she was interested."

"She mentioned the LAPD cases in one of her reports," Matt said, "though she didn't say what about them piqued her interest."

"Wagner is methodical and reports facts, but at this point, we need more."

"She may not be comfortable sharing theories, wanting actionable evidence instead," Matt said.

He had recruited Sloane Wagner out of Quantico specifically to go undercover in LA FBI. In addition to working given assignments, she was investigating Thornton and others in Chavez's division to determine who had leaked the identities of Colton Fox and Kara Quinn to the press. There was minimal evidence that someone in the FBI had leaked the information—a phone call to a reporter from an unassigned phone the day before Fox and Quinn were exposed. Brian Granderson had his own concerns about Chavez's division but his internal investigation didn't yield results, so he was happy to have a neutral party from DC.

"She may not realize she knows something important," Matt said. "Her reports are clear and concise, but a full debrief is warranted. I can come back tomorrow morning."

"Not here," Brian said. "I trust my staff, but no one outside of my AD and your AD know about this investigation. If you're seen here too often, people may start talking, asking questions that I would rather not answer. Plus, I don't want to call Agent Wagner up to my office and raise a red flag."

"We're staying at the Sheraton downtown."

Brian made a note on his phone. "It'll have to be early. I have a director meeting at nine."

"Seven?"

"Good. I'll let Agent Wagner know."

Matt would have to fill Kara in on this aspect of the investigation. Sloane Wagner's assignment was need-to-know—now Kara needed to know. He hoped she would understand why he kept her out of the loop until now.

"Wagner is good," Brian continued. "She'll get answers if there are any to be found. I'd let her stay in LA if she wanted, any division, but once the truth comes out about why she was here in the first place, it might be uncomfortable for her. Are you bringing her onto your team?"

The question surprised Matt. He needed another agent, but hadn't found the right fit yet. "She's a rookie. I don't know that my team would be the best fit for her."

"She has my recommendation," Brian said. "She's calm under pressure and in the four months she's been here, she has earned two commendations in her file. They're not easy to come by in this building—there's both a healthy and unhealthy competition fostered among the agents. She's quiet, but not silent. She's intelligent—smarter than most—but doesn't lord it over anyone. She does a good job whether she's given grunt work or something challenging. You know her test results at Quantico."

Matt nodded. "We recruited her primarily because she's loyal and disciplined—serving in the Marines will do that—and also for her ability to recognize patterns. It's a skill that is almost impossible to teach."

"She misses her family," Brian said suddenly.

"Montana, right?"

He nodded. "One of her brothers came to visit last month. She went home in July for her parents' wedding anniversary. She has already asked for time off in November. She said any four-day weekend—her family will change their Thanksgiving celebration for her. But then she made a point to say her brother—the one still in the military—is only on leave for a week, which happens to coincide with Thanksgiving."

"You gave it to her."

"I told Tony I intended to, but I haven't told her yet. Do you think this—" he waved his hand to imply the undercover investigation "—will be done by then?"

"I hope so," Matt said. "To be honest, now that Detective Quinn is in town, I suspect Thornton is going to make a move. He has a personal vendetta against her and I don't think he can stop himself."

6

Bryce Thornton ranted after Matt left the room. He was livid; Sloane kept quiet, listening intently for anything she might be able to use in her investigation, which was stuck.

"That guy is drunk on power," Thornton was saying, after hurling several insults at Costa now that he wasn't able to hear.

"We'll get through this," Chavez said. "He'll only be here for a few days."

"He has Quinn working for him! She's a stain on the LAPD and is going to be an embarrassment to Costa, the MRT and the FBI. Don't say I didn't warn everyone."

Chavez glanced around the room, realizing that Thornton's outburst was now fuel for the rumor mill. She gave Sloane a half smile, then looked pointedly at Thornton and said, "We have more important issues right now, so you need to let it go."

He watched her with narrowed eyes, then recognized what Chavez had: there were others in the room.

Not for the first time, Sloane wondered what they discussed in private.

The rest of their squad came in for a staff meeting. Thornton ran the meeting efficiently, the SSAs gave status reports, and cases were handed out. Chavez was in white-collar crimes, and they worked primarily fraud and money laundering investigations. Los Angeles and New York were the largest regional offices with multiple SACs, each managing multiple ASACs who each managed multiple squads. The bureaucracy was overwhelming and often redundant.

When Matt Costa approached Sloane two weeks before she graduated from Quantico, she thought she was being tested. It took two conversations with Matt, his boss Assistant Director Tony Greer, and the assistant director of the Los Angeles FBI for her to be comfortable not only with what they asked her to do, but her ability to do it.

She'd never forget how nervous she was when Matt Costa approached her while she was running on the track one afternoon, or how curious she was after he spoke to her. He'd been intimidating, but straightforward.

"On paper, I picked you, but I had to be certain," he told her.

"Picked me for what, sir?"

"I have to ask you not to repeat this conversation. Whether you accept or not, what I say needs to remain strictly confidential."

Matt explained that Sloane, a rookie, had no allegiances or loyalties. She could go into the LA office without preconceived notions. Plus, she was an older recruit: she'd gone to college, had twelve years in the Marines, and had both maturity and experience going for her. He'd even gone so far as to speak to her former commanding officer directly.

"Because of your background—family, military and FBI training—coupled with your psych evaluation, you are ideal for this position. It won't be easy. Not only is it emotionally stressful to go undercover and investigate your colleagues, but you'll also be a rookie agent and required to do the job. You are intelligent and resourceful, and I'm confident you'll be able to handle the pressure, but it will still be difficult."

Spying on your colleagues was never an easy assignment. She'd done it once before, in the Marines, and she vowed never to put herself in that position again.

Yet…there was something deeply immoral about a sworn agent forsaking their duties and obligations for personal gain or vendetta. It grated on her sensibilities as a Marine, as an American, as a law enforcement officer. So after hearing about what they knew and what they suspected, she agreed to report back to Matt Costa and Brian Granderson on not only the actions of Agent Thornton, but everyone else on Chavez's team.

Part of the problem was that Sloane had to observe and not ask too many questions. What seemed suspicious or unusual might have a logical explanation. So she simply reported what she learned.

It wasn't enough and she knew it.

Her personal phone vibrated in her suit pocket. She glanced down and saw the message from Brian Granderson.

Meet 7 am, full debrief w MC.

He'd included an address downtown.

She had nothing new to report and wondered if they were going to pull the plug on their investigation. She hoped not— there was *something* here, she just hadn't found it yet. She suspected whatever Thornton was doing involved the LAPD files she'd found on his desk, but there had been no opportunity to return to his office for more information.

When the staff meeting was over, she went to her cubicle and pretended to work. Mostly, she was listening to Thornton complain to Tom about Costa. Finally, they both left. Sloane soon found her chance when Brenda from Accounting came in looking for Thornton. Few people were in the office right now, so Sloane took the initiative.

"Hi, Brenda," she said, "he left, won't be back until this afternoon." She didn't know that for certain, but he'd turned off his office light, indicating he was leaving the building. If he was going to another office, he always left it on. "Can I help with something?"

"I need him to sign off on these expense reports by Friday. I swear, it's the twenty-first century but we still have too much paper. You'd think they could have streamlined expense approvals."

The expense reports were all submitted online, but then Accounting would process them by squad, print a summary report, and each supervisor would sign off. That was done on paper. Redundancy was built into the federal government, and the FBI wasn't immune to it. Brenda could have sent them interoffice mail, but she was one of the friendliest non-agents on staff and liked delivering files by hand.

"I can put them in his office," Sloane offered.

"Thanks, sugar. I have three more to drop off, then I have a dentist appointment. I hate the dentist. You have amazing teeth—must have cost you a small fortune."

"Genetics. My dad has good teeth, too. And I've never missed a six-month cleaning."

"Neither have I, but you wouldn't know it by the cavities I keep getting." Brenda smiled and walked away.

Sloane took the files directly to Bryce's office. She stuck a sticky note on top and scrawled that they needed to be approved by Friday, but held on to them while she looked around his office.

Bryce kept his office tidy, with minimal clutter. Files were aligned neatly on his desk in two piles. She pulled out her phone and quickly took pictures of each stack from several angles so that she could later enlarge the images to read the codes on the labels. Once she had the codes she could look them up in the system to find out what he was working on.

On his notepad was an impression from the last note he wrote.

She remembered him folding a piece of paper and putting it inside his jacket pocket when he left. She tore off the top page and put it in her pocket.

Once back at her desk, Sloane made sure she was alone, then held the note at an angle under the light from her phone. Scrawled in Thornton's sloppy penmanship was *Duncan, noon at his club*, followed by a phone number and a notation: *Mayor wants recent crime stats, talking points, rotary club.*

Theodore Duncan was the mayor's chief of staff. Prior to his probation, Thornton had been a liaison with the mayor's office. Why he still acted in that capacity was a question above her pay grade, but she made note of it. Granderson would want to know.

Duncan was a member of the Wilshire Country Club; why would Thornton be meeting with him there? It wasn't unheard of—FBI agents often met with key people in the community in order to maintain relationships, and these included elected officials, banking officials, local law enforcement, large employers, federal contractors, others. But this was written on his notepad, not in his official calendar.

She zoomed in on the photos she'd taken and studied the files. Each file had a code identifying the originating office, the date opened and the assigned squad. The information was available online, but could be printed in any office. One unfamiliar code stood out. She scanned her roster and identified the NOLA office. Odd that Thornton would have a file from Louisiana, unless it was a multistate investigation—but then she would have heard about it during a staff meeting.

She logged in to her computer and looked up the file online. Immediately, she realized that this was a case Matt Costa had worked on. His mobile response team had traveled to St. Augustine after a local detective filed a complaint of graft and corruption and a suspicious in-custody death of his informant. Matt and the bulk of his team had been there for a week and ended up solving multiple homicides.

Why was Thornton interested in this case? Because Matt had investigated it? Or because Kara Quinn had been involved?

She made a note to tell Matt about Thornton's review of the file. She didn't know what, if anything, might be important. She would also show him the photos—maybe he would see something she hadn't.

Her phone beeped—a message from the FBI emergency notification line.

1215. Shooting. Downtown Los Angeles outside Clara Shortridge Foltz Courthouse. Suspect at large. Two civilians down, status unknown. Briefing in auditorium at 1245.

7

For more than ten years David Chen had run a very profitable business importing Chinese laborers from the Shandong Province into the United States. He ran the operation out of Chinatown in Los Angeles, with business partners in San Francisco and Seattle who ran their respective operations. He didn't beat, starve or kill his laborers. They had Sundays off, a place to live, food to eat. They knew what they were getting into when they left Shandong: they would work for him, he would provide for them. They agreed to abide by his rules because they had a better life here, under his umbrella, than they had in their home country. A mutually beneficial relationship.

Until that *cop*.

He'd lost his human resources. He'd lost his property. It would take him years to rebuild, but he would rebuild. The state's entire case was dependent on one person, and she would not be alive much longer. He detested depending on others to handle these situations—he missed Xavier, who had been a loyal and dependable bodyguard. He'd also been a friend.

Kara Quinn would pay for murdering Xavier.

He wasn't concerned about the FBI—their case would go nowhere. He already had it on record that they offered him immunity in exchange for his cooperation; just because it hadn't been made official with the lawyers didn't mean that David wouldn't be able to hold them to it, should someone decide to go after him.

He had far too much dirt on certain FBI agents.

All these thoughts were on David Chen's mind as his driver took him to the courthouse on Monday. His lawyer texted him.

Meet in the lobby at 12:30. We'll discuss our options.

David frowned. What options? Detective Quinn wouldn't make it to the hearing and the case would be dismissed. That was the *point* of filing this motion.

Perhaps it was his lawyer's way of covering his tracks, the weasel.

I'm on my way, David responded.

David then called his FBI contact. There was no answer, but he didn't expect one. He left no message; his caller ID would be sufficient.

Five minutes later, his phone rang.

"Status?" David said without waiting for the caller to identify themselves. He knew who it was.

"Your timing needs work," the voice said dryly. "Everything is on schedule."

"Why isn't she dead now?"

"My timing is impeccable. You will not see her at the courthouse."

David hung up. He really detested not taking care of the detective himself, and he didn't like the way he had been treated, starting with the fact that there had been an undercover operation *for months* into his business. *Someone* should have known. They'd only given him *six hours*. Surely his contacts in the FBI had known before then! And if not, what use were they?

He had a backup plan. If they failed to put Quinn in the ground, and if the judge didn't dismiss the case, he would simply speak to the government lawyers. He had plenty of information to exchange for his freedom. It wasn't his first option, but sometimes sacrifices had to be made.

Reggie, his driver, pulled into the parking garage closest to the courthouse. There was no available parking except on the top floor. Reggie backed in, got out, looked around, then opened David's door.

They took the elevator to the bottom floor and exited on North Broadway. The courthouse was on the other side of the park. It was a pleasant day, though David would have preferred to be working. His business needed more of his time and attention since the raid in February.

His phone rang and he looked at the caller ID. Duncan. He almost didn't answer, but Duncan might have important information—he'd supplied valuable information in the past.

"David Chen," he answered.

"David, we've been in business together for several years now. We've made each other a lot of money. We've protected you. And yet…you would betray us."

"Fool," David said. "Why are you talking like this?"

"I have more friends than you."

David ended the call and looked around.

"We need to leave," he said to Reggie.

He turned to go back to the car and faced a man wearing a mask.

He had no gun because he was going into court.

Reggie pulled his gun too late.

Without hesitating, the gunman shot Reggie twice, then David three times.

David staggered back, fell to his knees, heard the screams of bystanders. Nearby he saw a girl, tall, skinny. She wasn't looking at him; she was staring at the man who shot him. He reached out to her for help, tried to speak. No words came out. Through his darkening vision, he saw her run, as if through a tunnel.

He couldn't breathe.

By the time he hit the cement, he was dead.

MAY

Five Months Ago

8

Traffic from Burbank to downtown Los Angeles wasn't much better on Saturdays than during the work week, but at least it was (mostly) moving.

The first Saturday of the month, Will and his First Contact volunteers cleaned up a homeless camp. He brought in the supplies, worked with the city as best he could to provide extra trash receptacles. There were two goals of the monthly program: First was of course to pick up the garbage and drug paraphernalia. The second was to work one-on-one with each homeless person to get them into the right program. Will always picked a location where he'd already spent many months getting to know the individuals, so they would be more apt to listen to him.

The city should be running programs like Will's, but they had their own way of doing things—and most of their programs failed. It made me angry, but I could do nothing except vent to Will, and he'd heard it all before. I wanted something to change; Will said he was making change and it had to be good enough.

I looked at the billions of wasted dollars—yes, *billions*—and Will looked at the people he could save, and not who he couldn't.

As Will always told me, the person needed to say yes. Some were homeless by circumstance; they were the easiest to assist. Some were homeless by choice. Some had tried to get clean before only to fail. Some had tried to get help, only to have hurdle after hurdle placed in front of them. Some had given up all hope and were just waiting to die.

Will was already there when I arrived at eight in the morning. He'd helped set up a table for juice and coffee, doughnuts and fruit—for both the volunteers and for the homeless. Will's strategy was to enlist the help of the homeless community, and most were happy to have something productive to do. It enabled Will to continue building relationships, to listen to their stories.

Will was my height—five foot nine inches—with wide shoulders and a narrow waist. He wore an army green T-shirt, the USMC tattoo on his bicep partly showing. He was talking to a small group of people, including Gina. I didn't see her partner, Fletch.

"I don't know what time the city will be here to replace the porta-potties," Will was saying as I walked up, "but they assured me it would be this morning. Hi, Violet. Glad you could make it."

I almost hadn't come, and Will would have understood if I'd bailed. I'd seen my mother only a few times in the last two months. She recognized me, but she was still angry about our last conversation and refused to speak to me. For a drug addict who had killed half her brain cells, she could hold a grudge.

Toby was watching from his spot, his shopping cart still tied to his waist. I picked up a chocolate-glazed doughnut and a bottle of water and walked over to him, squatted in front of him so we were eye to eye. "Hi, Toby, it's Violet. Remember me?"

He stared at me blankly.

"I brought you a chocolate doughnut. Do you want it?"

He stared at me, then slowly turned his head to look at the doughnut. He held out his hand and I placed the napkin on it, then the doughnut. I put the bottle of water on the ground next to him.

Toby didn't look well. He was a serious alcoholic and seemed to be withering in front of my eyes.

"We're cleaning up the park. We'd like you to help. Maybe I can help you organize your cart?" Mostly, I wanted to see if I could get Toby to talk to me, to tell me how he was really feeling. He needed a doctor. He needed to stop drinking. I feared he was going to die, that I was going to walk by one morning and see the coroner driving off with his body, just like Bobby and so many others.

Alone. Lost. Forgotten.

Toby leaned back against his cart and closed his eyes, clutching the doughnut.

I got up and went back to where Will was giving volunteers instructions. Everyone wore gloves and had garbage bags. Two people wore thick work gloves: one had long tongs to pick up needles, the other carried a biohazard box. Gina had engaged several people to help, though many ignored us. We worked around them. I avoided looking at my mom's tent.

"Something's wrong with Toby," I told Will. "I think he's really sick."

"I'll check on him. He's difficult."

By that, Will meant that he wouldn't accept any help or services, even a shelter.

Three men walked over to where we were standing. Two had been here on and off for the last year. They were veterans, but only talked to Will. I knew them as Dev and Jake, but that was it. Will told me that he'd get them to come around, but the VA had failed them and they were distrustful. Dev was addicted to painkillers, Jake an alcoholic, and both were dealing with severe PTSD.

A guy I had never seen before was with them this morning. He wore an army jacket over dirty tactical pants and three layers of shirts. His dog tags were around his neck. He was a vet, like Dev and Jake. But he was also different. He fit with them... but didn't quite belong. Most likely he was new to the streets, but there was something else I couldn't quite put my finger on.

I stood aside, admittedly a little intimidated. Will handed out garbage bags and asked the three to help. Dev and Jake took a bag and went to the far corner, but the stranger said he'd join them in a minute. Then he and Will talked quietly.

Will obviously knew the new guy. I gave them space, walked over to Gina as she slowly—very slowly—picked up litter. "Where's Fletch?"

"Talking to his brother," Gina said. "They haven't talked in years. But it's his brother's birthday and Fletch wanted to talk to him. They used to be close."

This was a positive sign. If Gina and Fletch could reconnect with family, that was one big step to getting them off the streets.

"Are you happy about that?"

She shrugged. "Sure. I met Jerry a couple times. He seems to be an okay guy. A mechanic. Fletch worked for him for a while, but..." Her voice trailed off and she didn't look me in the eye.

She didn't have to explain. Drugs. It was the common theme.

"Will has someone from the city coming here today to help people get their IDs updated, apply for transitional housing," I said. "Do you think you and Fletch might be ready?"

"Maybe," she said. "Fletch is still really depressed about Bobby."

It had been three months since Bobby had overdosed. "Talk to him. It's not easy, but it's better than this." *Anything* was better than living on the street. But I didn't say it. I didn't say what I really wanted to: that she didn't want to end up like Bobby. That she didn't want to wake up to find Fletch dead like Bobby.

Gina looked around as if seeing the filthy park for the first time.

"Maybe." She smiled at me, but her eyes were dull. "I'll see what Fletch thinks. It's just—I don't know if I can."

"I have faith in you," I said. "We'll help you every step of the way."

"Yeah." Gina nodded, then frowned. "We've tried before, but it just doesn't seem worth it."

I wanted to scream. What wasn't worth it? To have a home? To stop killing your brain cells? To not worry about being robbed, raped or beaten every night? Being homeless was dangerous. They were preyed on by other homeless people, those under the influence or so far gone they didn't know what they were doing or who they were hurting. This wasn't living—this was barely existing. It wasn't humane to let human beings live worse than a pack of animals.

"I think you're worth it, Gina," I said.

That was all I could do.

As I picked up trash, I looked over to the dirty blue tent with the zebra duct tape. It was still closed. My mom hadn't gotten up yet. Gina worked parallel to me, not wanting to talk, but fine with just hanging out with someone. "Have you seen Jane lately?" I asked.

She might know that Jane was my mother. Gina and Fletch hadn't been here when my mom and I got in a loud—on her part—fight a few months ago. But word travels.

Gina shook her head. "She keeps to herself, mostly. Saw her maybe Thursday night? Fletch and I tried to get into a shelter because it was raining, but it was women-only, don't matter that we're practically married, and I wasn't going to leave Fletch alone. And they weren't women-only last time we went there, so I don't know." She shrugged. "He doesn't do good when I'm not around."

Will had helped Gina and Fletch register as domestic partners so they could apply for benefits reserved for married people.

"I'm going to check on her," I said.

"I'll go with you."

Every step was filled with trepidation. I didn't want to do this. I didn't want to see how my mother lived. But I had to. What if she was sick? What if she needed help?

What if she's dead?

I stood outside the flaps. They had zippers, but they'd long ago broken and the tent was now tied closed from the inside. I couldn't get my voice to work.

"Jane? It's Gina. You okay? There's juice and coffee out here. Can I bring you something?"

I should have done that; I should have brought coffee and a doughnut. A peace offering.

The last time you brought her food she threw it in your face.

Silence. Maybe she wasn't in there.

Maybe she's dead.

It was frowned upon for anyone to enter another person's home. And this six-foot-square tent was my mother's home.

I almost turned away, but something in the back of my mind told me to check on her.

I pulled apart the flaps. Like many women who lived on the streets, she had a second tent on the inside, a means of protection, as weak as that was. Protection from sexual predators, drug addicts who didn't know what they were doing, thieves who would steal drugs or valuables. It was far more dangerous to live on the streets than most people were willing to acknowledge. Because no one wanted to look at the humanitarian crisis in their backyard.

There were pie tins around the secondary entrance, so my mom could hear if anyone was coming in. I intentionally stepped on one, hoping to just hear her shout, swear, tell me to go to hell. Silence.

"Mom?" I said, my voice cracking. "Mom, are you okay?"

A moan.

I tore open the second flap and the smell of urine and rotten food and marijuana and body odor hit me. And I saw her in the semidark, naked, her eyes unfocused, her body shaking. I gagged, stepped out, breathed.

"Will," I said, trying to get his attention. My voice was raw. I couldn't shout. I tried again. "Will, I need you."

Gina saw the look on my face and ran over to where Will was working.

I had to go in. Get my mom out, do something! But I stood there frozen, tears burning, and all the training I had disappeared.

I heard the pie plates crunch and then my mother crawled out of her tent. Her long blond hair was tangled and matted, her body bruised.

"Ah fa fuck fo."

"Mom," I said, squatting next to her.

She stared at me, but didn't see me. Her eyes were wild and bloodshot.

I looked around for a blanket, for anything. I reached inside and pulled out an old red wool coat I'd seen her wear. I put it over her shoulders. She screamed and threw it off as if it burned her.

Will ran up to us. "Jane, it's Will Lattimer. Remember me? Jane, can you hear me?"

"Fo ro aga fo!"

"What's wrong?" I asked, though I knew. She was overdosing. I'd seen it before, but not like this.

Not when I loved the person who suffered.

Then her eyes rolled back in her head and she began to convulse.

Will opened his backpack and pulled out a vial of naloxone. I watched helplessly as my mom's body convulsed. I saw the scar on her stomach from the cesarean she'd had to deliver me. She was my mother and she was dying and I could do nothing to stop it.

"Call 911," Will said.

I pulled out my phone and called.

Will administered three doses of Narcan before my mom started to respond. Narcan is short-lived, but needs to be spaced apart to be effective. By the time the paramedics arrived, she was stable, but hot, agitated and slurring her words.

She fought the paramedics, wouldn't let them touch her. I had to fix this.

"Mom," I said forcefully.

She blinked rapidly, then recognized me.

"Violet, what do you want? Go away. I told you over and over and over! Go away! Go away! Go away!"

I stepped forward, squatted in front of her, looked her in the eye. Her hazel eyes were pale and watery, but they focused on me.

"You need to go to the hospital. There's something wrong. They can help you."

"No. Don't wanna. You can't make me. Can't make me. Can't make me."

Completely ignorant that she was naked, she tried to get up, then fell down hard. She started to cry.

It took all my strength not to break down and cry with her.

I crawled back into the tent and found the backpack that I had given her two years ago, to keep her important papers. I had a copy of everything in case she lost her identification and Medi-Cal card. I had to make her copies three times already. Fortunately, everything was there in the front pocket, along with a large baggie of fentanyl, a baggie of marijuana and several rolled joints.

I handed the drugs to Will. He couldn't take her legal marijuana, but the fentanyl was illegal and he would destroy it.

I gave her ID and cards to the paramedics. They looked at me with pity, but I ignored them.

"Can you 5150 her?" I asked.

A seventy-two-hour psych hold might get her dry enough to comprehend what was happening in her life. If I could talk to her when she was sober—no drugs, no alcohol in her system—maybe I could convince her to go to a clinic. I would pay for it. I'd take out a second mortgage on my house to help my mother get clean.

She was going to kill herself if she didn't get off these damn drugs.

When I opened the tent, she could have already been dead. Luck, God, I didn't know what or who intervened, but she was alive and I wanted to save her. I didn't know if I could do this again. I didn't know if I could open the tent next time.

"We can't force her to come with us," one of the paramedics said.

"Bullshit," I said. "Can't you see she's dying?"

Will put his hand on my arm and said, "Let me try." He squatted next to my sobbing, naked mother. I walked away. Maybe seeing me had set her off. Did she hate me so much that she would rather die than get the help she needed?

I walked over to the food table, though I wasn't hungry. I felt dirty and angry and so deeply sad. I had done everything I could think of—and things I didn't think of but Will had—to get my mother off the streets. An apartment. ID. Drug rehab. Medical attention. I got her disability benefits and that just blew up in my face because she used the money for drugs. I didn't know what else to do.

But she was my mom. How could I just turn my back on her when she'd raised me? It wasn't perfect, but I had a house, food, school, clothes. She and my father fought all the time until he was killed. He was drunk, drove into a wall—thank God he hadn't killed anyone else. I'd been thirteen, thought without the fighting and drinking that everything would get better.

I was wrong. I just didn't know how bad things had gotten

until my mom lost her job because of her addiction, then our house.

I lived my life, went to community college, got a good job. All that time I tried to help her, even let her live with me for a time, until I caught her stealing from me and using drugs. I thought I had to kick her out, that it would wake her up.

It didn't.

Then I found her living on the streets. Lost, alone, drugged out.

I should have stayed. I should have fixed her.

The new homeless vet came over to me. "Here," he said, handing me a bottle of water.

I took it, mumbled a thanks, drank.

This guy wasn't like so many of the other homeless people. His clothes were dirty and he looked like he had slept on the street for a few weeks—his hair shaggy under a knit cap, layered shirts, boots old and scuffed. But I could tell his shoes were heavy-duty, durable work boots. Could have been name-brand. Maybe he'd picked them up at a thrift store.

But what stood out most was his eyes. They were very green, very sharp. He wasn't on drugs, at least not now, and he didn't seem to be drunk or coming down off a high. After working with the homeless for a few years, I could tell when someone was an addict—whether they were high, coming down or going through the early stages of withdrawal.

"How do you know Dev and Jake?" I asked, trying to forget about my mother. Out of the corner of my eye I watched as she finally allowed the paramedics to check her blood pressure and vitals. Will had worked his magic.

He shrugged. Didn't answer. He, too, was watching Will and my mom.

I finished the water. I didn't want to be here. I couldn't leave.

"It's not your fault," he said.

"Then whose fault is it?" I didn't mean to sound so angry, so aggressive. I bit my lip, but didn't apologize.

He shrugged again. "No one's? Everyone's? Your mom's?"

How did he know Jane was my mom? Had Will told him? Or had he heard everything?

"You don't live on the streets," I said suddenly. "Not regularly."

He slowly smiled. His teeth—they were clean and white. That was it, that's why I'd thought he looked different than everyone else, why he didn't quite fit in. He *looked* homeless on the surface. Clothes, attitude, walk. He smelled like stale beer.

But he didn't regularly use drugs, his teeth were too clean. His eyes were too bright and alert for him to be a serious drunk. Maybe something had happened, like he lost his house or was going through a divorce. Maybe he was suffering PTSD like Dev and Jake.

He was definitely different.

Will came over and said, "They're taking her to the public hospital. Her blood pressure is high, her pupils are nonresponsive, she has a fever and is acting erratic."

"So they'll get a 5150 hold?" I asked, optimistic.

"Doubtful," Will said. "I'll work on it, call a couple people, but chances are once she stabilizes they'll let her go."

"I need to talk to her."

"Do you expect a different outcome?" Will asked quietly.

I'd been through this with my mother over and over since I found her four years ago. Trying to help, only to have her reject my help every step of the way. I thought when I got her the apartment two years ago that it was a turning point...but she'd gotten worse since she'd lost the place.

"I have to try," I said.

He nodded. "We'll go this afternoon. I'll do everything I can."

Fletch walked down the sidewalk, watching the ambulance

pull away. Gina went to him, pointing toward my mom's tent. The stranger walked over to where Dev and Jake were working. "Who is that guy?" I asked Will. "He seems too clean, and not just his appearance."

"I don't know his story yet," Will said, but didn't look at me. Was he lying? Did he know him?

"What's his name?"

"Gunny. It's not his name, though. He was a gunnery sergeant in the Marines."

"So you do know his story."

"Some of it. You're right, he's not going to be around here long, will probably clean up his act pretty quick. If you want to go home, or take a break, I understand."

I shook my head. "No. I want to do this." I told him what Gina said about Fletch talking to his brother. "They're almost ready."

"I think I have a place for them. It's a halfway house, a lot of rules, no drugs, but they can come and go as they please from 6 a.m. to 9 p.m. Good counseling program—I know the people who run it. It's charity, not government. The best thing is they have a process to help them integrate back into society where they aren't just thrown back to sink or swim. If Gina and Fletch can quit the fentanyl, they'll make it. They are the perfect candidates."

Six hours later, the city swapped out the disgusting portapotties and replaced them with clean units. Will argued with the city employee that they needed to do this weekly, but the employee said to take it up with his boss, he was just the delivery guy. The three veterans had left, and I wondered where they had gone—if they were going to return here, or if they had a place. Legally, we couldn't touch my mother's tent without her permission, but I aired it out and removed the garbage and rotting food. Some people would argue that I couldn't even do that, but the people in this park knew me and Jane, and left me alone.

Over the course of the morning, Will had talked to everyone one-on-one, helped with paperwork as needed, passed out lists of nearby shelters and when they opened. And he had a long, private talk with Gina and Fletch. I crossed my fingers that they would take the help.

Then Will drove me to the hospital.

My mom wasn't there.

"We couldn't force her to stay," the nurse said, clearly annoyed that we pressed her for information. "We suggested she stay overnight, get fluids, have us run blood work, but she declined."

Will said, "I was working on getting a 5150."

"But you didn't get it," the nurse said bluntly. "They're rarely approved, and unless Ms. Halliday was showing signs of suicide, we aren't allowed to keep her."

"Where did she go?" I asked.

"She walked out."

"Can I talk to her doctor? I'm her daughter."

"Not unless she signed a HIPAA statement allowing us to share her private medical information with you, which she didn't."

I wanted to pull my hair out. "You allowed a sick woman recovering from a drug overdose to just walk away?"

The nurse bristled at my tone, but I didn't care. I knew her hands were tied, but that was always the problem. *Everyone's* hands were tied. *Everyone* passed the buck.

"Do I need to call security?" the nurse said.

"No." Will gripped my arm. "We'll leave."

"Can you at least tell me when you let her leave?" I asked, barely keeping the anger out of my voice.

"Please," Will added. "It would be helpful."

The nurse frowned, typed on her computer and said, "She left at 14:30 this afternoon."

That was only an hour ago. I looked at Will.

He nodded, understanding what I wanted without me even saying it, and we left.

We drove in ever widening circles around the hospital, but didn't see her. An hour later, we were back at the camp. Her tent was exactly as I had left it. Gina and Fletch said she hadn't returned. We looked until the sun went down, then Will drove me to my car. "Let me take you to dinner."

I shook my head. "I want to go home and take a hot shower."

He reached out and touched me. Gently. Kindly. Rubbed my arm with understanding and compassion.

He said, "She'll come back. She always does."

I wanted to believe him, but deep inside I knew he was wrong.

MONDAY, OCTOBER 7

9

The courthouse was on full lockdown.

Kara paced Craig Dyson's office. She itched to leave and find out what was going on, but Michael had made her promise to stay, then he went to get answers.

Craig sat at his desk reviewing the David Chen file as if there hadn't been a shooting half a block from them. Kara stopped pacing and stood in front of his desk long enough to catch his attention.

"We're stuck here," he said. "But the hearing isn't going to be canceled."

"You don't know that," she said. "If Chen can't get in, the judge will postpone!"

"We don't know what happened. It could be any number of things, and as soon as the sheriff's department clears the building, it'll be business as usual. We're the first case in front of Judge Hargrove after the lunch break. If the hearing is delayed, we'll still be the first case this afternoon."

She continued to pace. Craig was an experienced prosecutor

with a long history in the DA's office and a prestigious background in private practice. He had sacrificed a lucrative income to seek justice for victims after his mother, an investigator for the attorney general's office, had been killed while working a case. She respected him for his dedication to the job—he was noble, smart and beyond reproach. However much she admired him, they sometimes butted heads.

Craig admired her ability to communicate clearly on the witness stand, winning over juries with her likability. He appreciated how she meticulously built cases and gathered evidence for his team. He once praised her for remaining composed under cross-examination from the defense. However, he sometimes questioned her methods, fearing she walked a precarious tightrope where one misstep could jeopardize a case. Despite their differences, she had worked closely with both Craig and her boss Lex and brought him a solid case.

Until the feds put their fingers in the pot and started stirring up shit, taking the case from them and making Craig fight tooth and nail to get it back.

"Sit," Craig finally said, closing the file.

"I can't." She stood at the narrow window in his office and looked out. She could see nothing because they didn't face the park where the shooting had occurred. They'd only had confirmation that two people had been shot on Broadway in front of the park adjacent to the Clara Shortridge Foltz Criminal Justice Center.

He gestured to a chair. "Please."

She sat. Leaned back. Stuffed her hands in her armpits with a sigh. "I hate this."

"We're going to get Chen one way or the other. I can't share the details, but because of the work you did on the Chen case, I have another—bigger—investigation. I'm optimistic."

"You're going after the people who aided and abetted Chen." They'd discussed that early on.

"That's only a small part of it. Two inspectors have been fired and both made plea arrangements. They will be available to testify when this case goes to trial. I have a business owner willing to testify, but he's scared—he's left the area, though I know how to reach him. I'm confident he'll come in, do the right thing. The LAPD officer that I suspected was on the take has been transferred to the North Valley substation, and he'll cooperate."

"Asshole," Kara muttered.

"So far he's kept his nose clean."

"Who?"

"I'm not going to tell you that. I'm still working with him on his testimony."

"He'll lose his job." He should have already lost his job.

"Better to lose the badge and be free than lose it and go to prison."

She could get the information. All she needed was to dig around to find out who had been transferred from the downtown division to North Valley in the last eight months.

"But there's another, bigger investigation and I'm very close to going to the grand jury. I have a whistleblower in city hall and I want you to meet her—it's because of your raid that Violet started looking into records in the mayor's office."

Kara leaned forward. "The mayor? He was involved with Chen?"

Craig hesitated. "I can't talk about it."

"You said the mayor."

"I don't believe the mayor is involved, but—" He hesitated, probably trying to figure out what he could tell her. She wished he'd just spill everything. Who was she going to tell? But ethics and all that. Carefully, Craig said, "Someone in his office may be party to a broader graft and corruption scheme." He paused again, then nodded as if his statement was vague enough. "Violet called me last night and said she has something important to share, and I'm hopeful—her previous information has been very good, but I need a few more facts for the grand jury."

"Who is she?" When he didn't immediately speak, she said, "You already told me her name is Violet and she works for the mayor. I'm not going to spill the beans."

"I trust you, Kara, you know that. I want you to meet her. She works for the IT department in city hall. Very smart young woman. Quiet, observant, rather intense. She had a volatile childhood."

"I can relate," Kara said.

"Between the information Violet obtained and my investigation, I'm confident that a lot of people will be very unhappy next week." He paused. "I wasn't going to tell you this, but you'll find out after the hearing."

Her stomach sank.

"You're cutting him a deal," she said bluntly.

He didn't answer the question. "I contacted Chen's attorney. I am confident about the hearing today—there's no legal reason to toss your testimony or any of the evidence. I told him that I would be willing to negotiate a plea if Chen would answer detailed questions regarding the housing used for his laborers."

"What the fuck, Craig?"

"It's part of a bigger investigation, and again, I can't give you the details. I won't let him walk—you know me better than that. But I can negotiate time. This is a multimillion-dollar fraud scheme."

Something clicked. Violet—working in city hall. Chen—using housing that was what? Paid by the city? How would that work?

Kara was getting a headache. She hated public corruption cases. They were complicated and took thousands of hours to investigate and almost always ended up in a plea deal where someone lost their job and paid a big fine but rarely had to deal with the fallout from their actions.

"You're letting him plead. Damn you!" This was the part of the system she hated. Plea deals and letting bad guys off with a slap on the wrist. It sucked. "Sunny is *dead*. He killed her," Kara snapped.

Craig took off his glasses and rubbed his eyes. "I promise you, Kara, he will serve time." He retrieved a small cloth from his desk and cleaned his lenses, then put his glasses back on. "The reason I'm telling you this is because Chen's attorney contacted the AUSA. I have a good relationship with the AUSA on this case, and she's not going to let Chen walk, either, but she knows how to play the game. I want you to be prepared, because after this hearing, Chen is going to start negotiating. He knows that if the judge allows the evidence to stand, he loses."

She got up and started pacing again. Dammit! She knew this could happen—it had happened before—but she thought Chen was a big fish, too big for anyone to agree to plea.

A knock on the door gave her momentary relief that the courthouse was open and the hearing would continue as scheduled.

"Craig, it's Peter."

"My investigator, Peter Sharp," Craig explained. "Please let him in."

Kara didn't know the name, but recognized him when she opened the door. Tall, with lean muscles and smart brown eyes. There were dozens of criminal investigators in the DA's office to assist prosecutors by verifying facts, interviewing witnesses and researching cases. Investigators often interrogated law enforcement or verified reports before a case went to trial to make sure that there'd be no surprises by the defense.

"Detective Quinn," he said. "Glad you made it in before the lockdown."

"Lucky me," she muttered.

She secured the door behind him and he handed a file to

Craig. "The statements you wanted before court today, though I suspect all hearings will be canceled."

Craig glanced through the contents, nodded, placed the folder precisely on his desk. "You may be right, but Hargrove likes to keep a tight calendar. He may simply push everything back an hour."

"If Chen can't get into the building—his attorney is in the lounge, but Chen isn't—then his attorney would have cause for postponement."

Kara moaned. "That would really suck, Dyson. They'll send me back to DC." She hated this uncertainty. She wanted the hearing over, the trial confirmed, Chen in jail. Was that too much to ask?

"We don't know what we don't know," Craig said calmly. "Let's wait until we have more information."

Sure, she thought, that was the logical, mature thing to do. But right now she felt like she was waiting for the other shoe to drop. She suspected that had as much to do with her odd meeting with Lex this morning as being trapped in this office.

"Did Ms. Halliday make it in before the lockdown?" Peter asked Craig.

"I haven't seen her," Craig said.

"I'm curious to see why she was so insistent on coming in today," Peter said.

Another knock on the door interrupted Craig's response.

"Kara, it's Michael."

She let him in.

"Two men were killed in the park. One of them is David Chen."

Kara stared at him in disbelief. "Chen was *shot*?"

"Dead. Chen and his bodyguard, based on what I could glean. Matt's down there now, and we'll get more information soon."

Kara sat, stunned by the news. "I don't fucking believe this. He's *dead*."

Craig introduced Peter to Michael, then said, "What else do you know, Agent Harris?"

"Not much. Matt said there are conflicting witness statements, but that's to be expected. LAPD is all over the scene. One of the deputies in the lobby indicated that the lockdown has been partially lifted—the building is restricted, but people can come and go with an ID and badge through the main entrance."

Kara said, "He was shot and killed downtown in the middle of the day, there must be dozens of witnesses."

"The shooter wore a surgical face covering, no one thought twice about it. Most people concurred that he was a male, half said Hispanic, half said white. But two people said a white *female* in jeans was there and they hadn't noticed the male in a face mask, and a third witness stated they saw a white female running away from the bodies with something in her hand that may have been a gun."

"There are security cameras all over the place," Peter said. "Law enforcement should be able to pull together enough feeds to find out what happened."

Kara texted Matt and asked for an update. She was going to go stir-crazy if she had to stay in here.

Chen is dead, she thought. *I'm free.*

"You're thinking," Michael said.

"I'm always thinking."

"Act like there's still a threat against you until we can confirm that there isn't."

As reality sank in, Kara realized that her life was finally her own again. With Chen dead, she was free to go back to her old job. It didn't make her happy—she'd wanted him in jail for the rest of his miserable life. But death was the next best thing.

Though, Lex had been acting strange. That had bothered her all morning. He could simply have been worried about her, but he'd seemed angry that she'd come by headquarters.

Who wanted Chen dead?

Random violence didn't make sense—not downtown during the lunch hour. He had enemies, but there would have been a better time to take him down. Why here, with witnesses, on the block that housed the criminal justice center on one side and police headquarters on the other?

She wasn't sorry that he was dead. She was only sorry that he didn't expose others who were guilty.

But maybe...maybe with his death they would find the answers.

She texted Matt.

We need to be involved in Chen's murder investigation. Get access to his house, his files. He may have the names of everyone who helped him run his sweatshops, and I want to take them all down.

10

Matt had been minutes from downtown when he got word of the shooting. It took him nearly thirty minutes to navigate through multiple cops—LAPD, LA County Sheriff's, US Marshals were all on scene. Government buildings went on lockdown immediately as law enforcement made their initial assessment.

Matt found the woman in charge—Lieutenant Elena Gomez—standing next to a tactical van. She was a short, stocky woman with a command presence calling out orders with calm, stern efficiency.

He approached and introduced himself. "I know you're used to working with LA FBI, but I have an interest in this case."

She looked at him a beat too long, then nodded, said, "I know the name. Quinn was assigned to you."

"Yes, ma'am. Chen's hearing was this afternoon."

"Where's Quinn now?"

"With DDA Dyson."

"Since when?"

He immediately saw where she was going with this. "Since 11:45 this morning. One of my people has been with her all day."

"Good. I don't need the headache." She glanced to where he assumed the two bodies lay behind privacy screens. "This isn't her style."

"Are you her commander?"

"I oversee Sergeant Popovich's unit, among others. I recommended to the chief that he approve Quinn's attachment to your unit."

"I'm glad to meet you, then. She's been an asset."

"Quinn is a damn good cop, one of the best I've known, but also stubborn, reckless and will take ten years off your life because of the risks she takes. Never met a cop with more guts or empathy. Our loss is your gain."

Her brief commentary was spot-on, Matt thought.

"Who's running this investigation?" He nodded to the roped-off area. The street had been blocked at both ends by LAPD, and bystanders had been pushed to the opposite sidewalk or the east side of the park.

"Don't know yet. I just talked to the chief of detectives, told him I needed his best to drop everything and take over. You're not taking this." It was a statement.

"No, ma'am. But I would like to be kept in the loop, and I am happy to assist—and by assist I mean it. I'm interested only because it directly impacts my team, of which Detective Quinn is an important part."

"I'll hold you to that. The LA office is full of pricks."

"I've heard."

Gomez laughed, a deep, barking chuckle that started and stopped quickly. "Bet you have. They deserved everything Quinn dished out, but damn, I wish she would have steered clear of them. She enjoyed needling that asshole Thornton whenever she could."

"I need a threat assessment as soon as possible." He handed her his business card. "My cell number is on the back. Call or text. Quinn is under our protection, but she's not happy about it."

"What cop would be? I'll get you the assessment." She in turn gave Costa her card. "Whatever you need, let me know."

"I heard from one of your people that there are multiple witnesses."

"All of whom say something different."

That wasn't uncommon.

"But we have plenty of security cameras in the area," she said, "so we'll be able to see exactly what happened. Now, if you'll excuse me." She gave Matt a nod, then moved away to talk to three uniforms, instructing them efficiently. When they departed, she answered her phone.

Matt entered the courthouse. It was under restriction, but his badge and ID got him in. He took the elevator to DDA Dyson's office.

"Finally!"

Kara had clearly been pacing. She rarely sat still.

Matt looked around. "Where's Dyson?"

"He and his investigator went to talk to the judge," Michael said. "He wants us to wait until he gets back."

"Good." Matt sat at the small conference table. "Elena Gomez is in charge of the scene," he told Kara.

She sat across from Matt, an odd look on her face.

"She remembers you," Matt said. "Doesn't have any issues, seems to like you. Do you have a problem with her?"

"No." Kara slowly smiled. "She should love me. She was my training officer."

That surprised Matt. "A lieutenant?"

"She was a sergeant then. A total bitch half the time, and I thought she hated me. Lex said she could send me packing and to suck it up."

"Clearly, you must have."

"I wasn't going to let anyone stop me from being a cop. We

ended up riding together on and off for three years, between undercover gigs. I was her last trainee. We were effective together, and I learned more from Elena than anyone. Then she took over a squad, and a few years back was promoted to lieutenant."

"Then why the skepticism? Did you have a falling-out?"

Kara shook her head. "It's nothing."

"Not nothing."

"Command suits her." That was all she said.

Before Matt could get more out of Kara, Craig Dyson walked in. He seemed preoccupied and irritated.

"What happened?" Kara asked.

"Defendant is dead, case closed." He didn't sound happy. And by the look on her face, Kara wasn't happy about the turn of events, either. Dyson smiled wanly and extended his hand to Matt. "I'm sorry, you must be Matt Costa? I'm Craig Dyson."

"Good to meet you. Have you heard anything more about the shooting?"

"No, you probably know more than I do. Chen had a lot of information about a lot of people. LAPD has their work cut out for them."

"Then why not kill him before today?" Kara asked. "There are easier ways to take him out, without an audience and security cameras blanketing the area."

"He has good security—"

Kara snorted. "One guy? Walking down the street? Rather careless if he thought he was in danger."

Michael nodded. "One of the uniforms I spoke with said Chen had parked in the garage on the other side of the park. That's nearly two blocks walking in the open. If he thought there was a threat, wouldn't he have been dropped off at the courthouse entrance, or coordinated with his lawyer to park in the building?"

"Perhaps he didn't realize there was a threat," Craig suggested. "There were a lot of layers to his business model. The raid had repercussions across multiple avenues. I'm still working on untangling the threads, but we had him on murder and labor violations. That was the easy part."

Matt glanced at Kara. She said, "Don't look at me. I don't have any answers. But it's odd that a man like Chen didn't see this coming."

"Lieutenant Gomez promised to keep me in the loop," Matt said. "But at least for the next day we need to be careful with you." He turned to Craig. "Do you need Kara in court?"

Craig shook his head. "I'm prosecuting others involved with Chen, so at some point she'll need to be available to testify, but it won't be anytime soon."

"I'll be here," she said. "Matt—it's over. It's finally over."

His stomach twisted. He knew what she meant—the threat to her was over if Chen was dead—but he also took it another way. That their relationship was over. That she planned to come back to LA and reclaim her position in the Special Operations Unit and he wouldn't see her again.

He'd told her in August that if she returned to Los Angeles, he would move here. He didn't want to—but he could. He had a good relationship with the assistant director here, and while it would be uncomfortable once word got out that he was investigating one of their squads, he could make it work. He would do anything to be with Kara, even give up the Mobile Response Team.

But he loved what he was doing. He had built a great team. By the end of the year they would be fully staffed. Tony Greer said the Bureau might fund more teams based on Matt's successful model.

The team wouldn't be the same without Kara.

He wouldn't be the same without Kara.

Craig's cell phone rang. He answered, immediately frowned. "Where?" he said. Listened a minute. "Will...okay. I understand, but did she actually witness the shooting?"

Matt's ears perked.

"Call me when you pick her up," Craig said.

He hung up and looked at first Kara, then Matt and Michael.

"There may be a witness to the shooting, but I'm hearing this secondhand. It's someone who was meeting me today— but I don't know why she didn't immediately go to the police."

"Violet?" Kara said.

He looked surprised. "Yes. How— Oh. I told you about her."

"I'll go with you," Kara said.

Dyson shook his head. "I don't know where she is."

"Who called you?" Matt asked.

"A mutual friend. This is a sensitive situation."

He was gathering his briefcase together as he spoke. His phone rang again and he looked agitated, answered.

"Dyson." A moment later he said, "Now?" He listened, then responded, "I'll be there." He ended the call and said, "The DA has called an emergency meeting. I have to go."

Kara looked at Matt, tilted her head. He knew what she wanted. He didn't want to give in—he still wasn't confident that the threat against her was over. But she was safe in the courthouse.

"We'll meet you in the lobby," Matt said. "Don't leave this building without us."

"Wouldn't think of it," she said with a flash of a smile.

Michael followed Matt out. Kara stayed put.

Craig gathered files into his briefcase. "I have to go, Kara."

"Talk." She blocked his path to the door.

"I can't share details about my investigation. I plan on presenting my case to the grand jury this Wednesday. I have ethical and legal concerns. I need Violet's statement—it's key to my investigation, and she has valuable information."

"And she didn't tell you what information she had?"

"Not specifically, but I suspect it's the link we've been looking for that connects certain staff in government to nonprofits who have been benefiting from government contracts. I wasn't lying when I said this is going to impact dozens of high-ranking elected officials and staff."

He opened the door and started for the elevator at the end of the hall. Kara followed, saying, "This started with Chen."

"No. It started with the building he owns and a grant he received to use it for homeless Chinese immigrants." He paused, assessing how much to tell her. "He was paid by the city to house his laborers—it's insidious, but on the surface, not illegal. It was illegal for him to traffic the women and illegal for him to force them to work as indentured servants, but not to be paid to house them in his building. There's much, much more to the housing scheme—it's about grants and funding, who approved the grants, and who profited from them."

"And this Violet girl knows."

He looked pained, as if he'd already said too much. "I may need you—you are one of the few people who understands the structure of Chen's operation, and more important, I trust you. This case has shaken my faith in the system, but you've always been honest and I've never doubted your integrity."

Craig sounded genuinely upset. She didn't know whether to thank him for his praise, or push with more questions.

She opted to push.

"Do you think it's a coincidence that Violet witnessed the shooting?" Kara asked.

Craig pressed the button on the elevator. "I know you got rid of the feds because you think I'll talk to you alone, but I can't. I'm sorry, Kara. This is such a sensitive situation right now, and I need to talk to Violet, possibly get her under protection."

That comment surprised her. Craig thought the girl was in danger.

"I can talk to her, assess the threat level," Kara suggested.

"First, we have to find her."

"She's missing?"

"No, she is hiding—my friend is picking her up. Something really spooked her."

"Maybe seeing two men killed right in front of her?"

"Yeah, of course."

Her instincts buzzed. There was something more worrisome about the phone conversation than he'd shared. "I'll help any way I can."

"I know you will," Craig said. "I'll talk to my contacts and make a push to bring you into our investigation. We need you, especially now that Chen is dead."

Contacts? Not his boss? Not his investigator, Sharp? What was really going on here? Was Craig running an investigation outside the purview of the DA himself? Was Craig deep into something super serious—so serious that maybe Chen had been killed because of it?

Chen was going to talk…and that might make some people nervous.

If only Kara knew who these people were.

A man in a suit came from the opposite hall and as the doors to the elevator opened, he bumped into them hard enough to make her stumble.

"Excuse me!" Kara snapped, irritated.

The man kept walking without apology. Tall, slender build, thick facial hair, but that was all she could see as he turned away from them. He put something in his pocket and at the same time Craig slumped against her. He was clutching his side.

Blood dripped to the marble floor.

"Craig?" She looked down the hall. The man was heading for the east stairwell. She pulled her gun and shouted, "Stop! Police!" She couldn't shoot, there could be people on the other side of the wall.

"Find her. Save her."

"Save who? Violet? Save Violet?"

"Will. Call Will." He coughed, wheezed. He grabbed her blazer with a trembling fist, pulled her down. "Will Lattimer."

His voice was barely a whisper, and she wasn't certain she heard him correctly.

He was talking to a "Will" when he got that call. Was it Lattimer?

She knew a Will Lattimer.

His hand dropped as he lost consciousness. Two people came out of an office and Kara ordered one to call an ambulance, and one to take over for her and apply pressure to the wound. Without waiting to see if they complied, she pursued the suspect as the stairwell door closed behind him.

She called Matt as she ran.

"Dyson was stabbed. Caucasian male, dark suit, beard, east stairwell. I'm pursuing. Lock everything down!"

She pocketed her phone, picked up speed.

As soon as she entered the stairwell, she stopped, listened.

The man had gone up. He was taking the stairs two at a time. A smear of blood on the handrail… Craig's blood.

She ran as fast as she dared. Saw another smear on the wall as the staircase turned.

She didn't see him, but heard heavy footfalls as the attacker fled. Why up? There was no escape up.

She hesitated a half second before every turn in case the suspect planned an ambush. He was still moving.

They'd been on the tenth floor; the building was eighteen stories. There was nowhere to go from there. Places to hide, lots of courtrooms and offices, but there was no getting out. The building was on lockdown.

On the seventeenth floor when she stopped to listen, she heard an odd sound above—like a heavy metal door, not the typical fire door that protected the staircases. The roof?

She ran as fast as she could, past the eighteenth floor, and saw that the cage door leading to the roof was ajar. She didn't think twice and pursued with increased caution. She walked slowly up the final staircase, her heart pounding with adrenaline, trying to remain as silent as possible.

The door at the top was closed. She pulled out her phone, texted Matt.

He's on the roof.

Matt immediately responded.

Do not pursue! Backup coming.

Kara ached to go after him, but there was no place for him to go. She responded: I'm guarding the door, southeast stairwell.

She waited and watched for any sign that the suspect was coming back this way. A full minute later she heard several sets of footsteps on the stairs below her.

She identified herself and shouted down the stairwell, "Suspect on the roof."

"Sheriff's department," one of the men responded.

The door in front of her started to open.

Kara stood her ground. She kept an eye on where his hands would be, looking for a weapon—gun, knife, anything that could disable her.

He was silhouetted against the bright sky that partially blinded her.

"Freeze—LAPD!"

He threw something into the stairwell and slammed the door shut.

Smoke began to fill the stairwell. A foul, sulfuric stench hit her nostrils as the smoke entered her lungs. The two deputies called for a status.

"Smoke bomb!" she said. "Suspect still on the roof. I need cover."

No way was she running away and letting the bastard slip out and hide in the building.

"Backup is on the way," the deputy said. "Jones, you okay?"

His partner was coughing. "He's trapped up there," Jones said, coughed and spat. "Does he have a weapon?"

"He stabbed Dyson. I don't know if he has a gun."

Kara didn't like this situation. The guy on the other side of this door could be waiting to ambush them, take as many out as possible before he was killed, or he could have another plan, another idea. The ventilation system? Another way to get out?

Jones listened to his radio, then said, "All cameras are down, Newman."

Matt and Michael ran up the stairs, followed by two more deputies who each carried shields. Jones said, "Helicopter is on the way, ETA four minutes."

Matt identified himself but before he could say anything else, the power went out.

"Suspect took out the security cameras," Newman said.

The fire alarm rang, a piercing *whirl, whirl, whirl*. Emergency lighting powered on.

Michael asked for one of the shields.

"I go first, you follow," Michael said to Matt, taking over the tactical command. "Deputies, Quinn, behind us."

Matt took the other shield and the two cops went to the rear.

Kara's eyes watered and she held her breath as Michael passed by her and held his hand up. On three, he pushed open the door, the shield up to protect him from attack.

The roof was a smoke-field. They couldn't see anything. Michael motioned for Kara and Jones to stay on the door—the suspect could attempt to escape past them. Though the air was marginally better outside and the smoke was dissipating faster than in the stairwell, Kara's eyes burned. She and Jones stood sentry, alert for any movement. Almost immediately, the others disappeared in the smoke.

Jones said, "Fire suppression is on the side of this wall. I'm going to put out this smoke."

"I got your back," she said.

She could barely see him through the haze of smoke, but the fresh air was blowing it up and away.

Jones grunted as he worked to turn the spout for the emergency water. It gave way, and he grabbed the hose and sprayed down the area. The smoke bombs were extinguished almost immediately. There were five distinct "bombs" that provided ample cover for the suspect to hide.

Fully alert and finally breathing freely, Kara looked around for a threat, saw no one. She heard shouts of "clear," then a distinct "Aw, shit" from Matt.

She itched to find out what was happening, but held her post. Matt returned and said, "He rappelled down the roof. Hook is still attached to the building. Can't see anyone below."

Newman approached. He was talking on his radio, reporting what had happened. Deputies and LAPD were being dispatched on the grounds to search for Craig's attacker. "Description?" he asked Kara.

"Five foot eleven male, one-eighty, Caucasian or light-skinned Hispanic, dark curly hair, dark beard, glasses, wearing a suit—" She stopped talking. "Matt, what's that?" She gestured to a pile of what at first appeared to be rags by a roof vent.

Newman repeated the description to his commander then put on gloves and inspected the pile. Held up a suit.

"That's what he was wearing," Kara said. "Is that a wig?"

"Wig, fake beard, glasses, the whole nine yards," Newman said. "We might be able to get DNA or other evidence off it." He called for a crime scene investigator. "He left the hook and rope as well, might be traceable."

"Damn. Damn. How's Dyson? Is he going to be okay?" she asked Matt.

He turned and looked at her. His expression said it all.

"No," she whispered.

"I'm sorry, Kara. He was dead before the paramedics got to him."

11

Detective Lance McPherson with the sheriff's office debriefed Kara. The sheriff had jurisdiction over the courthouse and would be taking lead, which irritated Kara—if it was an LAPD investigation, she'd be able to get more information. Ultimately, the sheriff's office would work jointly with LAPD or turn the case over to a special unit, but right now, it was their crime scene.

She didn't lie to the detective who took her statement, just left a few things out. Though she reported that Craig had asked her to call Will Lattimer, she claimed she didn't know why, and she didn't admit that she knew him.

Will Lattimer—if it was the same person she remembered— ran a nonprofit organization. She'd met him through her partner Colton Fox, and the last time she'd seen him was at Colton's funeral in March. She wanted to track him down before McPherson.

She didn't say a word about Violet, the IT employee from city hall who may have witnessed Chen's shooting. If she had understood both what Craig said and implied, Violet was a whistleblower who could be in danger. Will Lattimer went to pick Violet up after she witnessed the Chen shooting, but Craig seemed very concerned about her safety. Therefore, Kara was concerned. Until she knew exactly what Will and Violet had to do with Chen—or Craig's bigger investigation—she would be careful who she told. Names went into reports, and keeping Violet's name out of the record seemed wise.

Though she didn't want a bodyguard, Michael stayed by her side while Matt was on the roof with the crime techs. It wasn't a coincidence that two people involved in the same trial had been killed. Her mind was whirling with everything she'd learned, but it came down to one key fact: Craig was running a close-to-the-vest investigation about corruption in city government, had called a grand jury, and he was now dead.

McPherson finished up with a few more questions, then thanked her and was about to cut her loose when his partner walked in. "We got the footage."

Kara leaned forward. "Can I see?"

McPherson motioned for her and Michael to follow him to a small security room on the ground floor.

The security chief had the feeds cued up and said, "I've already cut copies, but thought you might want to see it right away."

The wide angle was from the plethora of ceiling cameras that completely covered the halls, elevators and common areas. Staircases, individual offices and the roof were not covered.

She saw Matt and Michael exit Craig's office, bypassing the elevator and turning toward the west staircase. A minute later, Kara and Craig followed. Though the surveillance was soundless, the visual showed them in an intense conversation.

The killer came into view, followed Craig and Kara toward the elevator. She had glanced back at him—she didn't remember doing that, but the video showed she had, and dismissed him. He didn't walk fast or slow, just seemed to be heading for the elevator. The killer bumped Craig and Craig turned toward the man, a surprised look on his face. Did he recognize his killer? Or was the shock from being stabbed? The killer headed toward the east stairwell and didn't look back.

The guard replayed it in slow motion. It was only then that they could see the killer pull a small object from his right coat pocket and, without hesitating, stab Craig in his side. One deep thrust—the bump Kara had felt—and he pulled the knife out, put it back in his pocket and walked on.

"Four minutes later, all the security cameras in the building went out," McPherson said as they watched Kara pursue Craig's killer into the staircase. "IT is trying to figure out exactly what happened, but they think he damaged a router on the roof. It disrupts the system, forces it to reboot. It was down for twelve minutes."

"So we have no idea where he went after he rappelled off the roof," Kara said.

"There are plenty of security cameras in the area, and we're looking at all of them for a male of his height and weight, but it's going to take time."

McPherson asked the guard if he'd backtraced the path of the killer. A moment later, he brought up an image of the killer sitting on a bench at the far end of the hall from the elevator. "He sat here for six minutes before he killed the DDA," the guard said.

"He was waiting for Dyson to leave," Kara said. "Where did he come from?"

"From the opposite hall," the guard said. "We're still putting together the feeds."

"We'll check with door security and find out when he came in," McPherson said, "but I'd like to know how he got the knife past the metal detectors."

"Maybe he didn't," Kara said. "I couldn't tell if it was a knife or shiv, or if it was metal—which would show up in security— or plastic or ceramic, which wouldn't. A mechanic could have a

111

toolbox filled with screwdrivers and other tools that could kill a person, and virtually every office has a letter opener. He could have easily palmed one after he was in the building."

McPherson asked the guard to enhance and print out several images of the suspect, and send him the digital file. "Our people might be able to do more with it—this image of him on the bench is good. We can have computer techs take off his beard, glasses, maybe get lucky. When Forensics is done on the roof, I'll have them fingerprint the bench, bathroom, stairwell doors. The whole floor is sealed off, and I have guards posted at every entrance."

She itched to investigate. Talk to Will Lattimer. Find out more about Violet and what information she had intended to give Craig. Figure out what was going on with this grand jury. Maybe Craig's investigator knew more details.

She had to do *something* or she wouldn't be able to stop thinking about the pain and shock in Craig's eyes.

He knew he was dying.

A deputy walked down the hall and said to McPherson, "Detective, here's the list of pending cases for DDA Dyson, and his office is working on pulling everyone he put away who's been recently released—that's going to take more time. But the DA's office said they didn't call him for a meeting."

McPherson looked at Kara.

"I told you what he said when he got the call. I didn't know who it was from, but he said he would go down. Did you talk to his investigator, Peter Sharp? Maybe he knows who called."

"I'll track him down," the deputy said.

"Could have been a lure, to get him out of the office," McPherson suggested. "We're running his phone records—you said he took the call on his office phone, correct?"

"Yes."

"That helps. Thank you, Quinn. I know how to reach you. Are you heading back to DC tomorrow?"

"No," she said. She glanced at Michael. She hadn't talked to him or Matt about her status or plans. She didn't even know *what* was going on, and these murders were completely unexpected. "That's up in the air," she clarified.

"Where are you staying?"

She didn't know.

"The Sheraton, downtown," Michael said.

"Great. I'll call if I need you. It's always good having a cop as a witness."

But, Kara thought as she and Michael left, Craig Dyson was still dead.

12

Kara and Michael finally checked in to the hotel at five and she called Ryder Kim, the Mobile Response Team's analyst. She knew it was after hours in DC, but Ryder answered on the first ring. She asked him to find contact information for William Lattimer and Violet Halliday. She gave him everything she knew about Will, but it wasn't much.

Without a warrant, they could only access public source information, but an hour later Ryder sent what he'd found. She'd already left a message with First Contact on an answering machine but Will hadn't returned her call. Ryder gave her a personal number—a cell phone, based on the prefix—but again, no answer. She left another message and planned to track him down on foot tomorrow.

The police would probably be reaching out to him, too, but she wanted to know why Craig's last words were *Will Lattimer*. How did Will know Violet? Had he picked her up after she witnessed the shooting? If so, why hadn't he brought her to the police station to make a statement? That was the first thing Kara had checked on—she still had friends in LAPD—and Violet Halliday hadn't come forward.

Ryder had less luck finding anything about Violet. She owned a house in Burbank and worked for the City of Los Angeles. Only phone number attached to her was her work number. She could have a cell phone, but if it wasn't in a public database, they couldn't get it without a warrant. Kara wanted to go to her house, but first she'd talk to Will.

While waiting for Matt to return from the courthouse, Kara dug around on Google. Will Lattimer popped up immediately— quoted in articles about the homeless crisis, several op-eds critical of the government response and lack of oversight and transparency, extensive information about his work with homeless veterans. Nothing on Violet except for one article where she was photographed with Will at a homeless encampment in Venice Beach.

William Lattimer, President of First Contact "Empowering Not Enabling," speaks about what he calls a "humanitarian crisis." Pictured with him are volunteers Violet Halliday of Burbank, Anita Fuentes of Venice Beach and Mel Porta of Los Angeles.

Violet wasn't smiling. She had dark blond hair and serious eyes. Kara scanned the article, but there was no other reference to her. She was doubly frustrated that Will hadn't returned her calls. He would have answers to many of her questions.

She almost pounced on Matt for information when he walked into the hotel suite after seven that night, but hesitated when she saw how exhausted he looked. He took off his jacket and tie and sat on the couch.

She wanted information, but she also realized it was ten in DC and none of them had eaten. No wonder she had a headache.

"Hey, will the feds splurge on room service?" she asked. "I could eat a cow."

"I think tonight we can make an exception," Matt said. "Do you want to hear what's going on first?"

"Did they catch Craig's killer?"

"No."

"Let's order, then you can fill me in."

Matt knocked on the door to the room he and Michael were sharing. Michael came in looking refreshed after a shower and catnap. They ordered, and while they waited for room service, they split a can of ten-dollar nuts from the in-room bar.

"LAPD has a person of interest in the David Chen shooting," Matt said. "A woman named Violet Halliday, who works in the IT department of city hall."

Kara straightened. "What?"

"She was seen running from the scene. An LAPD officer was across the street, and while he didn't see the shooting itself, as soon as he heard the shots—there were five total, two in the bodyguard, three in Chen—he turned and saw her running. He knows her, identified her." Matt frowned. "Is Violet the woman Dyson was talking about this afternoon?"

"Yes. She's a volunteer for Will Lattimer's group. She was bringing Craig information for his grand jury investigation into a graft and corruption scheme. It involved Chen, but seemed to be bigger than that. He didn't give me many details, but said a lot of people in government wouldn't be happy." She paused, then added, "Remember that call he got, the one that upset him? I'm positive it was Will Lattimer telling him that Violet witnessed the shooting. When Craig was stabbed, he told me to find her, talk to Will. He didn't make complete sense, but putting it to-gether with what Craig said earlier in his office, I think that Violet called Will after the shooting and he was going to pick her up. Craig seemed very concerned about her safety. Is she a suspect or person of interest?"

"Right now, person of interest, but if they don't find her that'll change. Did you talk to Lattimer?"

She shook her head. "He hasn't returned my calls. I actually know Will."

"Personally?"

She shrugged. "Not well, but he and my old partner Colton were tight. The last time I saw Will was at Colton's funeral. I left messages on his work and cell numbers. I thought he'd call me back. I asked Ryder to find everything he can about Will and Violet."

"McPherson will reach out to him as well," Matt said. "Did you tell McPherson what Dyson said?"

"About Will? Yeah."

"And Violet?"

"He didn't *specifically* mention Violet to me after he was stabbed. Everything he mentioned earlier is sensitive and confidential. He didn't mean to share so much." She wanted to smile, but couldn't muster it. Craig was dead and she felt miserable. "I guess I just bring out the chatty gene in people."

"Put everything in your report."

"I know this isn't our case, but Craig was a friend. I need to be involved."

"LAPD is handling Chen, sheriff is handling Dyson. The FBI isn't involved."

"I'm LAPD," she reminded him. "I know, on loan to the FBI." She rolled her eyes. "What if the murders are connected?" She didn't see how, exactly, but what were the chances they were disconnected?

"Doesn't matter," Matt said. "I was friendly, didn't pull rank, so I think they'll share information with me. But this doesn't mean you're not still in danger, Kara."

"Chen is the one who wanted me dead, now he's in the ground."

"Until we know exactly what's going on," Michael said, "we have to assume the threat is still real."

"I do, but—" Kara began.

"You think that these two murders, less than an hour apart, are coincidences?"

"No, but—"

"I'm asking you to follow protocols. Michael is the tactical leader of this team and until he says there is no threat, we act like there is a threat. Don't go anywhere alone. Please."

He looked worried, so she agreed. "I have to find Will and figure out what he and Craig were working on. You or Michael can come with me, but I need to do this. It's the last thing Craig asked of me before he died, and I'm not going to let him down."

"I would do the same thing."

"We're on the same page," she said. "Agreed?" She looked at Michael.

"You haven't been a complete pain in my ass about the rules." Michael grinned. "I'm good with tracking down Lattimer tomorrow."

Kara thought the situation was resolved, but Matt looked tense and stared over her shoulder at the wall behind her.

"You have a look on your face. It's your *I don't want to tell you this but I have to* expression."

At that moment, room service arrived. Michael answered the door, signed the check and brought in the cart himself.

"I'm famished," he said.

Kara was, too, but she wanted Matt to talk. She stared at him. "What?"

"Let's eat."

She glared at him. "Fine."

She found her cheeseburger and fries, sat at the table and took a big bite. God, that was good. She chewed, swallowed, took another bite while Michael and Matt got out their food—Michael a burger, Matt a chicken sandwich.

"Okay, I ate," she said with her mouth full. "Spill."

Matt put a beer in front of her. He and Michael were drinking water.

"It's worse than I thought," she mumbled and opened the beer. She drained half of it in a gulp.

"It's not bad, just something I didn't tell you," Matt said.

"Just rip off the Band-Aid, Matt." Better than expecting the worst.

"With the cooperation of LA FBI, I have an investigator working undercover at their headquarters with the goal of finding out who was responsible for the media leak about you and Detective Fox."

She didn't know what she expected Matt to say, but that was not even close.

"Oh."

"Tony and I came up with the idea after Thornton's OPR hearing. We felt, along with one of the panel members, that he had been less than truthful."

"Meaning, he lied."

"Lied, or didn't offer information he knew would be relevant."

"Still a lie," she said.

"And so," Matt continued, "we recruited a rookie agent and had her assigned to Thornton in LA. There were some internal concerns—not necessarily criminal—about the overall unit that the director there wanted investigated, so we worked closely with LA to put together this operation. She's been there just over four months."

"And?"

"You're not mad?"

"That you didn't tell me?" She shrugged. "I get it. It's an internal personnel thing. I know how undercover operations work—the fewer people who know the better."

He stared at her, obviously having expected a different reaction.

She took another bite, didn't say anything.

"You're mad."

She drained her beer. "Did you get me two?"

Matt produced another, popped the top off for her. She couldn't help but smile. She stared at him; he didn't avert his eyes. This man…he drove her crazy half the time. But he had an uncanny way of knowing how she felt. Not always what she was thinking, but he seemed attuned with her emotions and that was just weird. And a bit endearing.

"I'm not mad," she said after a long pause, mostly because she wanted to get her thoughts together. She wasn't angry with Matt. This problem wasn't his fault. "Not about the undercover op," she continued. "It's a damn good idea. You have a couple bad feds, you need to get rid of them."

"Then what are you upset about?"

"That he wasn't fired when he lied to you. Or three years ago when he went after me and had me wrung through IA. Or seven years ago when we collided on another case and he nearly got me killed. Or ten years ago when he screwed with my investigation on the docks and put me in fucking handcuffs after I identified myself as a cop. He has never apologized, never accepted that what he did was wrong. He still has a badge, has been promoted, and I don't think anything is going to happen to him. He's going to keep his job because the FBI are a bunch of bureaucratic pricks. Present company excluded." She waved her hands at Michael and Matt.

She stuffed a fry in her mouth. Yeah, she was still angry about all the bullshit Bryce Thornton had rained upon her over the years. "He got Colton killed. No doubt in my mind," she said. "He'll never pay for that, and you know it. But I'm not mad at you. You didn't even know he existed seven months ago, and at least for the first time someone actually slapped his hand. He got reprimanded for lying to a fed, not for anything he did to me or others in LAPD." She drank more beer. "So why tell me now?"

"Our undercover agent is coming here tomorrow morning with Brian Granderson, one of the SACs in LA. We're going to debrief, and I want you here. She hasn't uncovered a smoking gun, but we think that maybe she doesn't know what she knows. She was a Marine, graduated top of her class at Quantico, but she's still a rookie. We want a discussion—something that has been hard to do."

That, Kara didn't expect. "Happy to oblige," she said.

Matt relaxed, finished eating his sandwich. "Sloane asked about several LAPD investigations that Thornton was interested in, but we can't figure out why. She also asked to look at some other files, and we've quietly obtained them. It would send up big red flags if the FBI asked for files without giving a reason."

That was true.

"I'll give you access to Agent Wagner's reports if you want to review them tonight."

"I'd like that. I might be able to get those LAPD reports without raising a flag."

Now Matt smiled. "I thought so."

"We could also bring in Lex."

"I'll think on that."

Kara glanced at Michael. He had been quiet. "Did you think I would get mad at you for keeping me in the dark?" she said to her partner.

"No. But you know me, I don't like secrets, and I don't like keeping them. I only knew about the operation, not the players. Now I do."

Matt's phone vibrated on the table next to his plate. He answered. "Costa... Sure, room 1050." He ended the call and looked at Kara. "Your boss wants to talk to us."

"Lex is here?"

"Elena Gomez."

13

Kara hadn't seen Elena since shortly after she took down Chen in February. Kara had been in the hospital with twenty-some stitches holding together the gaping slash in her back after Chen's right-hand man threw a knife at her.

Kara had known Elena Gomez for almost her entire career on the police force. She was divorced, had two kids, a surprisingly good relationship with her ex, and was a workaholic. She was five-six, with a round face, dark no-nonsense eyes, stocky build, and had passed on her love of tequila to Kara.

Elena looked nervous when she walked into the hotel suite with Matt. Kara wondered why. Kara couldn't remember a time when Elena ever looked unsure of herself. She'd told Kara more than once that command presence was the key to getting out of dicey situations, especially for female officers. *If the perp sees a weakness, they'll exploit it. Never let them see weakness.*

"It's good to see you," Elena said to Kara, breaking the awkward silence. "You look great."

Kara didn't know how to respond so she mumbled, "Thanks."

Matt introduced Michael, motioned for her to sit and asked, "What can I do for you, Lieutenant?"

Elena sat at the table across from Matt and Michael; Kara stood.

"Since you're not officially involved," Elena said, "I wanted to give you an unofficial report about today's shooting."

Matt offered water or coffee. She took neither.

"I don't have much time," Elena continued, "but you'd sent me a message about whether LAPD thought that Chen's murder was connected in any way to Dyson's. Right now, we're being cautious in what we publicly say—our official statement is that both homicides are priorities and under investigation, blah, blah. Internally we're running with the theory that the murders are connected. Based on the timeline Detective McPherson created, Dyson's killer was already inside before the courthouse went on lockdown. So it appears to be a coordinated attack against Chen and the prosecuting attorney with two different killers."

"Theories? Motives?" Matt asked.

"We have dozens, none that make sense. Chen had many enemies, so did Dyson, but who wanted both of them dead? We're still in the early stages of our investigation."

"What about forensics from the roof?" Matt asked.

"The lab has the grappling hook, clothing and trace evidence. It's a priority case, so they're working overtime. Hopefully we'll get something, but I'm not holding my breath. The wig and beard have the highest probability of getting DNA, but that'll take weeks. Several people saw a man in black scaling down the courthouse at the southeast corner, then on foot heading north on Spring. Once he went under the freeway, he disappeared. We haven't caught him on surveillance cameras, but the glitch in the park next to the Justice Center may have had a broader range."

"A *glitch*?" Kara asked sarcastically. "That's what they're going with?"

"Clearly, it was tampered with. Our techs are all over it, but I don't have a report yet. Once we have more details about the how and the when, we'll decide what we release to the public."

"No weapon yet?" Matt said.

"No," Elena said. "Likely took it with him."

"What about security footage?" Matt asked. "McPherson said he would nail down when he entered. We might get lucky, get a good image."

"McPherson and courthouse security have been reviewing security footage carefully, determining who entered but didn't exit. Unfortunately, it's a manual process and might take days, even narrowing the search to male adults under fifty and between five foot ten and six foot two."

"What about Chen?" Kara said. "Matt said there was a person of interest."

"Violet Halliday. An officer who knows her said she ran from the scene. She's a twenty-nine-year-old IT operator, been with the city for nearly five years, no record. We're treating her as a possible witness, but haven't been able to locate her at work or home, which is suspicious."

Kara considered telling Elena the little she knew about Violet but refrained, at least for now. Nothing she knew would help Elena find the woman.

"Chen was coming to the courthouse for a hearing that would decide whether he goes to trial or not. He's now dead," Kara said. "Craig told me he was going to offer Chen a deal if he ratted on who helped him keep his sweatshop in operation. Including a cop."

Elena didn't say anything.

"What do you know about the investigation?" Kara asked. "Were you working with Craig?"

She hesitated a fraction of a second. "I have worked with Craig on investigations before, but I don't know specifically what his plans were with Chen."

She was lying. Kara knew Elena well, and this woman—her mentor, her boss, her FTO—was lying.

"You know *exactly* what Craig's plans were," Kara said with cold calm.

Elena stared at her, her expression unreadable. Then she said to Matt, "Can I have a word with Kara alone?"

Matt looked to Kara. "You good?"

She nodded. Matt and Michael left for the adjoining room.

Kara didn't say anything. She leaned against the back of the couch and stared at Elena. She could wait her out as long as it took. She should tell her what Craig said about Violet Halliday, but right now she was trusting very few people, and she wanted to talk to Will Lattimer before she decided what to do and whom to trust.

"I saved your job," Elena said after several moments.

"What the fuck does that have to do with anything? What do you know that I don't?"

"Dammit, Kara! Do you know how many people were coming for *me* because I didn't send you to IA after the clusterfuck that was the Chen investigation?"

"The Chen investigation was no clusterfuck until he was tipped off to the raid." She stopped herself. This wasn't the time to argue about what happened in February. "That's the past," Kara said with forced calm. "Craig was killed *today*. What is going on, Elena?"

"That's Lieutenant to you."

Kara glared at her. "Okay, *Lieutenant*, what do you know that got Craig Dyson killed?"

"I can't talk to you about an ongoing investigation. You're not on my team."

"Bullshit!" Kara exploded. "I was standing with Craig when he was stabbed. I had his blood on my hands. We have no idea who the bastard is or why he killed Craig, but I'll bet my pension it's about this grand jury impaneling that he planned this week."

Elena's eyes widened in surprise, then she buried it.

"Fuck you, you know all about it!"

"You're close to insubordination," Elena said.

"You just said I wasn't part of your team, so I can say whatever the hell I want." Her anger was still rising. "I know it had something to do with an investigation that started *after* Chen's arrest—an investigation I know nothing about because I was sent away. An investigation that involved a dirty cop. You know it. I know it."

Elena couldn't tell Kara she was wrong, because Kara wasn't wrong.

"Who is it?" Kara demanded when Elena remained silent.

"I don't know."

"Bullshit. You suspect someone, I know you do."

"Suspecting someone means shit."

Kara pushed off from the couch and paced. She couldn't help herself, frustrated at her inability to do anything to fix this mess. Who was going to get justice for Craig? For Sunny?

"Let me explain something to you, Kara," Elena said, her voice edged with anger. "You have no idea the pressure LAPD has been under for the last few years. Don't get your hackles raised," she said when Kara almost interrupted. "I know uniforms have gotten the brunt of the public's rage, but my office is getting it from the top, from the politicians, the press, the feds. Intense pressure from every side. From our own people, from the fucking bleeding-heart DA, from the media, from people we are trying to serve and protect. I have worked my ass off getting every bad cop off the streets, even when I risked my own job to do so. Even when I got hate from my own people. I'm not going to fuel the fire. I have to know 110 percent that a cop is dirty before I go through it again. I take down bad cops quietly. You *know* that."

Kara did. She'd helped Elena. Sometimes forced retirement. Sometimes shifting to nonpublic positions like working the evidence locker or booking. Sometimes termination—though that was extremely difficult to do unless the violation was egregious.

"I have never doubted your ethics or your ability to get the job done," Kara said. "But Sunny is dead because someone tipped Chen off. If not one of our own people, then who?"

"Do you trust Costa?"

That came out of left field.

"Yes."

"Dyson decided we had enough to prosecute, which is why we pulled the plug on the undercover investigation."

"I remember. We decided to do it quick, first thing in the morning."

"Dyson held off getting the warrants until the last minute because he was afraid it would leak. But we had to put the SWAT team on call, and because we planned it for 7 a.m., before Chen's workers were on-site, we planned to call in the day shift an hour early to debrief. A lot of things had to move into place in a short period of time. We also had a team on Chen's house.

"After the fact, we discovered that the FBI had all our information through the interagency portal. Even though I had a lid on the operation and specifically ordered need-to-know, every single action is sent through as an informational memo to the FBI. It's a fucking nightmare and well above my pay grade. The portal was implemented after the FBI investigated the department for civil rights abuses years ago, of which we were cleared—though their bureaucratic procedures never went away."

"The FBI," Kara said flatly.

"I have no evidence that Bryce Thornton knew about the raid," Elena said quickly. "But someone there could have known. A fed, not a cop, may have alerted Chen."

"Why would anyone in the FBI want to tip him off, or even be able to so quickly? Thornton is a prick, but working with a human trafficker?" Kara had always thought of Thornton as a bad cop, not a dirty cop—and there was a difference. A bad cop is willing to bend rules and lie to get warrants and tweak evidence and sacrifice people in order to catch bad guys. He doesn't care if someone was the girlfriend of a low-level thug, he would turn the screws and destroy her life if he could learn something. Thornton in particular enjoyed the power that went with his position. A dirty cop worked *with* the bad guys. Took bribes, looked the other way, became an accessory. But Kara couldn't see him helping to facilitate a major crime.

"I can't say. I have investigated every single cop who knew about the raid, and it's not one of them."

Kara paused. "Dyson told me someone who knew about Chen's operation was transferred to North Valley. I'm thinking he took bribes to look the other way."

Elena shifted on her feet, a sign of discomfort or guilt.

"Who?" Kara demanded.

"I'm not going to tell you, but I suspected him before the raid and he was not in the loop. I made sure of it."

Kara mentally reviewed the teams that had been involved, and then it clicked: a cop who should have been there, but wasn't. At the time Kara probably thought he called in sick or was on vacation, but now it made more sense that Elena had purposefully cut him out. "Tom Lee?"

Elena didn't answer, but Kara knew she was right. Bastard. She would be paying him a visit before she left LA.

"So, if I get this right, someone in the FBI learned about the raid, tipped off Chen. Chen went to the facility before we could get there—maybe to shut it down, get papers, money, whatever he didn't want us to have. Sunny alerted me that he knew, but that still doesn't tell us who told Chen that *she* was my informant. There's no other reason that he would have killed her. And very, very few people knew that she was my contact. You. Lex. Craig. Anyone any of you pulled into the loop. Now Chen is dead. Craig—who was investigating everyone surrounding his operation and about to go to the grand jury—is dead. That sounds like someone is cleaning house."

"Go back to DC," Elena said.

"You said you saved my job. My job is *here*."

"You're not safe here. You've made a lot of enemies, Kara—in the FBI, in LAPD. You know I've always liked you even when you drove me crazy. And it's because I like you that I'm asking you to let me figure this out. Let me find the leak, let me find out who killed Dyson."

"You're a lieutenant. You haven't worked in the field in years. You need me."

"You're not the only good cop under my command," Elena snapped. "Don't ever think you're not expendable."

"I know I am," she said, bristling. "You asked if I trusted Costa—I do. I trust Matt and Michael with my life. I respect them. If the FBI has a traitor, Matt will find him. But this is bigger than a corrupt fed. Dyson was investigating multiple people in city government. He didn't tell me a lot, but I know he has a whistleblower."

Kara didn't tell Elena that she knew who the whistleblower was, and it was clear by Elena's expression that she knew. About Violet and more.

"You know exactly what he was doing. It got him killed, and you know it!"

"I can't." Elena walked around the room, motioned to Kara's empty beer bottle. "You wouldn't by chance have another one of those?"

Kara looked under the cart, saw there was a bucket of beers. She grabbed two, handed one to Elena. Elena opened it, took a long, deep drink. They stood in silence and stared at each other. Finally, Kara said, "You never called. I guess I felt like I was tossed to the lions and the one person I trusted to have my back didn't even care."

"I should have reached out, but I was pissed off. I was mad at

you, mad at the situation, at Lex, at the feds, and then Colton...
well, I just thought you shifting over to an out-of-town detail,
out of the damn state, was the smartest thing. I've been picking
up the pieces ever since."

"I'm going to call in Matt. You need to tell him everything
about that stupid portal, and he'll find the traitor in the FBI.
That, I promise you."

14

Elena Gomez left the Sheraton not feeling any better about the situation that she was in. Lying to Kara—even lies of omission—had made her stomach twist painfully.

Damn Craig for bringing Kara back to testify! *Maybe* they needed her for the Chen hearing, but bringing her back put the most sensitive investigation in Elena's career in jeopardy—and now her friend was dead.

What investigation? Without Craig, you have shit.

She drove to Hanks, a dive bar on Western, south of Third. It was far out of her jurisdiction, and didn't cater to cops. When she'd grown up not far from here in Van Nuys, the neighborhood hadn't been bad. Not great, but not bad. Now every storefront was a bar, dispensary or shuttered, every building covered with graffiti. She wasn't in uniform, but gangs smelled cops, so she kept her eyes and ears open.

Inside, Lex was already at a table drinking whiskey. Usually, it was Lex and Craig waiting for her. Craig—who looked so out of place here it was almost laughable—liked the joint, said the bar felt more real than the upscale places his fellow lawyers preferred.

Elena was going to miss him. They'd bonded years ago over common beliefs in justice and the law, and had become friends. She was a few years younger than Craig and Lex, but they were of the same generation with the same sensibilities.

Simply, they respected each other.

Hanks was never busy at nine thirty on a Monday night, but there were a few people sitting in singles or pairs at the bar, and a group of four men played pool. The bartender—Cindy—was six feet tall, close to sixty, with tattoos covering every visible inch of skin except her face. If she'd made them as cops, she never said. She could hold her own, and no one gave her shit.

Sometimes, Elena stopped here alone on her way home and sat at the bar feeling sorry for herself. Failed marriage, fucked job, a daughter that Elena had saved up money to send to college who was on her fifth year at UC Berkeley and wanted nothing to do with her because Elena was a "fucking cop." Her daughter had said that to her face and it hurt. A son who planned to enlist in the Marines as soon as he graduated high school, even though she pushed for him to go to college first. But Robby was stubborn. A lot like her.

Kara had listened to Elena practically cry over her daughter because there was no one else she felt comfortable talking to. The men on her squad didn't understand or thought she was too sensitive. Lex told her that Lizzy would "come to her senses" when she got out into the real world. Her ex had remarried and thought Lizzy was going through a phase. And Robby didn't talk to either her or her ex about much of anything. He had his friends, played football, and just waited for the day he could leave and fight other people's wars.

Kara listened and didn't offer platitudes.

When Kara learned the truth, she would never forgive Elena or Lex. Elena wouldn't blame her.

Without even asking, Cindy brought over a draft beer for Elena. Lex ordered another double whiskey.

"Well, fuck," Lex said when Cindy walked away.

"She's going to figure it out," Elena said.

"You told her about the FBI, right? The portal?"

"Yeah, and I filled in Costa. He's all over it. He has the reputation of a bulldog, he won't let it go."

"Still fucked," Lex grumbled and drained his whiskey. They were using the portal as a diversion to keep Kara out of their business.

"How long have you been here?" Elena asked.

"Long enough to be halfway to drunk. You can drive me home or I can Uber. Shit, shit, shit. Kara knows something's up. This morning, she gave me that *look*—you know the one she gets when she's twisting things around in her head because they don't fit."

"Gave me the same look," Elena mumbled and sipped her beer. "I can't believe Craig is dead."

"Makes no fucking sense. Chen had enemies. I can buy that someone would take him out. He was sniffing around both Craig and the AUSA talking about making a deal—he knew shit, and that shit got him killed. But why Craig?"

She had been wondering the same thing. "According to Kara, he planned to convene a grand jury this week. That tells me he was closer than we thought to finding out who's behind the nonprofits he's been investigating. Why wouldn't he have told us?"

"He's been unusually quiet lately. I called Peter, asked him to come by. Maybe Craig talked to him."

"Dammit, Lex, last week Craig said we didn't have enough for the grand jury. What's changed?"

Lex shook his head. "I was thinking about how Halliday's name came up today. What if she found the missing link in city hall records and told Craig?"

"Why did she run? She's in the wind. I was skeptical about

using her—even though Craig assured us there were precedents—she's too emotionally involved. She's edgy and ready to explode. And I don't know about the legality of what she's been doing in city hall."

"I trust Craig," Lex said. "He worked closely with her. Without Violet, we wouldn't even have known that there were deleted files."

Eight months ago, right after Chen was arrested, a huge swath of files had been wiped off government servers. It had made a big splash in the press for a day, then the story disappeared. At first, no one suspected anything other than a computer crash. But Violet had uncovered something potentially criminal—an admin code had been used to erase multiple files over a three-year period *right before* the system crashed. When they were able to rebuild the system and download backups, files were missing—all files that had to do with the Los Angeles City Housing Grant program.

As far as Elena knew, she had never figured out who had done it, and was still working on recovering the files. Craig had taken information Violet had uncovered and was using it to quietly investigate city officials—both elected politicians and city staff—to determine who, if anyone, had profited from grants that were supposed to go to homeless housing projects. Tangentially, he was reviewing all projects approved by the city council to build housing, and the costs incurred—that meant reviewing proposals, contracts, and finding out if there was fraud, nepotism or padding in any of the projects. It was painstaking work.

Why Craig was rushing this now, Elena could only speculate. Maybe there was a statute of limitations they were butting against, or maybe he finally found the smoking gun. That Violet was now missing was worrisome.

"Do you think she's okay?" Elena asked.

"Quinn?"

"Violet."

Lex shrugged. "I called Will, he's still looking for her. She called him this afternoon, told him that she saw Chen shot on the street. He was going to pick her up, but she wasn't where she said she'd be. Left her cell phone behind. One of the homeless women that Violet befriended told Will a couple of thugs she'd never seen before were harassing the homeless. They spooked Violet and she disappeared ten minutes before Will got there."

"Maybe she recognized the shooter."

"Why didn't she tell Will? Come to the station? She's been working with us for months, could have called any of us direct. She didn't, and that makes me suspicious."

Lex glanced up and Elena followed his gaze to the door. Peter walked in, looked around uncomfortably. Lex motioned for him to come over.

"When you said dive, you meant it."

"The good kind," Lex said.

"I didn't know there was a good kind."

Cindy came over and asked for orders. Lex nodded for more and Elena knew now for certain she would be driving him home. She got a second beer, Peter asked for Scotch on the rocks.

"I still can't get into Craig's office," Peter said after Cindy delivered the drinks. "I went there after I talked to his ex—she was in shock, I didn't want to leave her until her sister came over."

"They were still close," Elena said. "Not all divorces end in lifelong conflict." She also had an okay relationship with her ex.

"The desk guard said the floor will be open at seven tomorrow morning. I'll go through his files, messages, see what I can find."

"It has to do with our investigation," Elena insisted. "Kara said that Craig's dying words were to talk to Will Lattimer."

"Why not me? Or you?" Lex frowned, stared into his drink.

"You're missing the point," Elena said. "He told Kara enough about our investigation that she's going to sniff around. She was there when he was stabbed. She's not walking away."

"I told Will to avoid her," Peter said. "Buy us some time to figure out what we're going to do."

"We're fucked," Lex said. "And the only person with the power to take these bastards down is dead."

They might have something to their advantage. "No one knows that we're running an undercover operation," she said.

"No one?" Peter said, eyebrow raised.

"You know what I mean. We've kept this tight. Whoever killed Craig didn't want him opening a full grand jury investigation. No one else has the balls or seniority to do it, so they probably think the investigation will die with Craig."

"It does," Lex said.

"We need control of his murder investigation. We solve that crime, we get motive—motive is covering up public corruption, we just need to prove it. We dump it all in the open. The key is finding Violet, figure out what she told Craig or what she was going to tell him. Maybe she finally had the proof he was looking for about who in city hall was behind the computer purge."

Elena turned to Peter. "You need to get all of Craig's files first thing in the morning when they open the floor. Who can we take this to? What DDA will pursue this?"

"I'll think on that," Peter said. "But—I know you're going to hate this idea—but it is a public corruption case. Maybe we turn it over to the AUSA."

"No," Lex and Elena said simultaneously.

"Hear me out—the feds have the resources to get the warrants without pussyfooting around as Craig had been doing."

"The feds will take years to investigate," Elena said. "We have eight months in, and we're so close. I'm not giving it to them. Do you know how long it took them to investigate the last public corruption case, down in Long Beach? *Twenty-seven months.* Craig was adamant we keep this in-house. I'm going to honor his wishes. And don't forget—we all agree that it was a fed who leaked to Chen about the raid. They get this case, they could bury it."

"I agree with Elena," Lex said, "but even if we put this together with another DDA, I suggest we first talk to Costa. Kara is a good judge of character, and she wouldn't be working for his team if she didn't trust him. He's already looking into the raid— we can connect that with what we've been doing. Lay it out."

Elena wanted to argue, but Lex was right.

"Okay," she concurred, "but first, let's exhaust all other options. I know a few DDAs that might take it *if* we can get more information from Violet."

"We have to talk about the elephant in the room," Peter said. "All the cameras were out near the park. Violet has the skill to take out any computer system, and was seen leaving the scene by a cop."

"That's ridiculous," Elena said. "Violet Halliday? A killer? No."

Lex concurred. "The shooting happened fast, without hesitation. Five shots, none missed. The bodyguard barely had time to react and didn't get a shot off. What's her motive?"

"If she doesn't come forward soon," Peter said, "the lead detective will have just cause to get a search warrant."

"She's scared. She'll turn up tomorrow," Lex said. "I'll reach out to Will, see if he needs help."

"I don't think Halliday killed Chen," Peter said, "but the evidence is pointing there. In addition to her skill set, she was seen running from the scene, and she's now missing. Craig was worried that she wasn't being careful enough in her work at city hall. She's angry with the system and frustrated at the slow progress of our investigation. What if someone learned she was feeding us information?"

"And framed her?" Elena shook her head. "It would be an elaborate frame job. How did they know she would be in the park at the same moment that Chen was there? There are easier ways of taking her out."

"If they know she's a whistleblower, they can't fire her. If they stage an accident and kill her, they don't know where the evidence she might have is stored. Or even *what* she has. But if they know she's working with Craig, they kill him, and take her out by making her less credible."

"Possible, not plausible," Elena said. "I think she was in the wrong place at the wrong time. She could also be a target. Since she planned to meet with Craig today, maybe the killer was supposed to take her out as well."

Lex drained his whiskey. "Now, the *real* elephant in the room. What are we going to do with Kara? She's not going to be kept in the dark for long."

Seven months ago, she, Lex and Craig had debated telling Kara about the investigation that started after she arrested Chen. But with the threat on her life and the fact that there was a corrupt FBI agent in Los Angeles, they decided to lateral her over to the FBI and run the investigation with another detective. It had been a win-win.

Craig was the only one who had objected. He'd wanted to bring her in from the beginning, but Lex and Elena held firm: for her safety, it was best to keep her completely out of the loop. Craig reluctantly went along with them.

"Let's find Craig's killer before Kara realizes we lied to her," Elena said. "And hopefully, the information I gave Costa tonight will keep them both busy."

Lex caught Elena's eye and she knew exactly what he was thinking. Kara was not going to sit back and wait for answers.

Conrad sat on the balcony of the condo he had been using since arriving in Los Angeles nearly eight months ago when hired to clean up a nasty mess made by nasty people. He sipped a full-bodied cabernet and enjoyed the sights and sounds of the city. He'd been here before. He'd killed here before.

But he wouldn't want to live here.

He smiled as he closed his eyes and relived excellence.

He was a patient man. One had to be in his business. Planning each moment, thinking through contingencies, having an alternative escape route if the first failed. The murder itself was almost incidental. It was the whole that he cherished: plotting, waiting, killing, escaping.

That Detective Quinn chased him was quite exhilarating.

Conrad hadn't known she would leave with the target, but it was a possibility, so he had prepared. He saw them exit Dyson's office, talking urgently. Quietly. Quinn wasn't happy about something, and Dyson looked...troubled. Had he sensed the end was near? Did he fear his life?

Choosing the courthouse to kill him wouldn't have been his first choice, but if he wasn't dead before he met with Violet Halliday, then Conrad wouldn't receive the second half of his payment. His clients would fall and Conrad's reputation would be tarnished.

He succeeded in his business because of his untainted reputation, so failure simply wasn't an option.

Detective Quinn made the game more fun and exciting, but Conrad wasn't stupid. He recognized that both she and Agent Costa were skilled and perceptive. They wouldn't give up, so he had to be doubly careful.

His alarm beeped and he picked up his phone. Hit *Marie*.

"Daddy!" the happy voice said.

"I promised I'd call before bed. Tell me what you did today."

Marie, in her exuberant preteen way, chatted about everything, from snorkeling on the reef to having lunch with her friends to watching the sunset with her nana.

"When are you coming home?"

"Darling, I'm always home."

"You know what I mean."

The exasperated tone reminded him that his little princess was quickly becoming a teenager. "I don't make promises I can't keep, Marie. You know that. I hope to be done with my business by Friday. I will call and update you when I can. Be good for Nana."

"I will," she said, sullen.

He didn't spend enough time with his daughter. It was his greatest regret that his profession required him to be separated from his bright, beautiful child. But she was safe, she was well cared for, and because of the money he made doing dirty work for the rich, he could provide for her. And when he was done with this job, he would take a long hiatus. Perhaps even a year. Both he and Marie would enjoy the time.

"I love you, Marie."

"I love you more, Daddy." She kissed the receiver and ended the call.

No, darling, I love you more than you can possibly imagine.

He took a few moments to think about Marie and home, about what he could do to make up for this time apart. Perhaps an extended trip to New Zealand, where he had a home outside Queenstown. Marie hadn't been there since she was a toddler; she would enjoy exploring.

He would need to disappear for a few months when this job was over, and no better place than halfway across the world.

Conrad didn't allow himself to think too much about the upcoming trip. Violet Halliday was in hiding. The good news was the police hadn't found her and Detective Quinn didn't know her value. The bad news? He couldn't leave until she was dead and he'd destroyed the evidence she had uncovered.

With one last look at the view, he turned and went inside to get back to work.

15

Bryce Thornton worked late Monday night because someone had to prove that Kara Quinn was a danger to others and a disgrace to LAPD.

The cop was a menace and should never have had a badge. She arrived in town this morning and now David Chen was dead. Kara must have had something to do with it—she'd almost killed Chen during the raid in February, and she *did* kill his bodyguard. All she got was a slap on the wrist.

It physically pained him that the LAPD had so many bad cops who acted as if they were in the Wild West doing whatever the hell they wanted, damn be the rules. And he was still furious about the OPR investigation. It had been unnecessary and embarrassing. He was a twenty-year veteran of the FBI, had spent his entire career here in Los Angeles, and they should have taken him at his word.

He also blamed her for Craig Dyson's murder. She may not have held the knife that killed him, but *something* she was involved with had led to his death. Where Kara Quinn went, people died.

Rebecca walked into his office. "It's after nine," she said. "Go home."

"I will. Just reviewing the reports from LAPD on the two homicides."

"This isn't our case."

"Chen should have been our case."

She sat down. In a calm, maternal voice she said, "I agree, Bryce. We've been through this a dozen times. You need to stand down."

"Is that an order?" he asked.

"Nooo," she said slowly. "As your friend, not your colleague, I'm concerned that your obsession with Detective Quinn is clouding your judgment."

"You *know* she's behind this. She tried to kill Chen before on the roof. Just because we couldn't prove she pushed him doesn't mean she didn't."

"It was a he said, she said, and without evidence, LAPD rallied around their own. You need to let it go."

He couldn't. "That woman should be in prison, not walking around with a badge, and definitely not walking around with a badge working for the FBI."

"I quietly looked into that," Rebecca said, "and Greer is happy with her contributions. We need to be careful about how we investigate Quinn."

Bryce picked up the file he'd recently downloaded from New Orleans. "I read all of her assignments with Costa's team. This one—she went after a suspect and he was eaten by alligators. Alligators! And...and..." He sorted through files. "This case in Arizona? An innocent civilian was shot because of her, two suspects were killed, and another paralyzed. All the details are sketchy and vague. The woman is a loose cannon."

"Bryce, you know I agree with you," Rebecca said, "but you

have to stay away from Quinn. Not everything with Quinn and the FBI is wine and roses."

"What does that mean?"

She hesitated, then answered, "Like I said, I've been doing my own quiet investigation and I learned through a friend of mine that while Matt Costa has put two commendations into her file, a forensic psychiatrist has also submitted a letter that was less than glowing."

He leaned forward, excited. "Do you have it?"

"No, I couldn't access it without raising flags, but this tells me that she's already caused friction. She won't last."

"That's not good enough."

"Give it time."

That's what Bryce had always been told, that Quinn would dig her own grave, that she wouldn't last. But she'd been a cop for twelve years and Bryce had to be proactive and prove beyond all doubts that she was rotten to the core. "I'm going to dig into both the Chen case and the Dyson case. There's something there I can nail her with."

"I'll help," she said. "But tonight, I want you to go home, have a drink, relax. If you make any accusations against Kara Quinn while you're on probation, it's going to be a negative mark on your record. Whatever you find, give it to me, and I'll figure out how we handle it. Agreed?"

He appreciated that she was trying to help him, but sometimes he wondered if Rebecca was just placating him.

"All right," he said.

She rose, walked to his doorway. "For what it's worth, I think you're right."

"About?"

"Chen. She arrives and he dies the same day? Proving it—that's going to be difficult. Anyway, I'm going to walk you out."

"But let me—"

"I know you, Bryce. If I leave, you'll stay until midnight, and

ALLISON BRENNAN

that won't be good for you. You need a good night's sleep. Look at the details fresh in the morning. Maybe by that time, LAPD will have more evidence."

"Or maybe we can take over the investigation."

She smiled. "I'm working on it."

TUESDAY, OCTOBER 8

16

Kara liked Sloane Wagner.

She was smart, even-tempered and methodical in her presentation. Even though she was a rookie agent reporting to two SACs, she possessed a gravitas that held the room. She knew from Matt that Sloane was thirty-five and had served twelve years in the Marines after college. A woman in the Marines was badass, Kara thought. She was smart *and* pretty with long black hair, golden brown eyes, high cheekbones and light brown skin.

Last night, Matt had given Kara all of Sloane's reports, which she had read into the wee hours. The interesting points she highlighted—that Bryce Thornton had been looking at specific LAPD cases, even though there was no federal component.

Sloane didn't waste time. "I hope you have all read my reports. I know we don't have a lot of time, but if you have questions, please let me know. For now I am focusing on Agent Thornton's review of MRT cases, after discovering a copy of a file from the New Orleans office that Matt indicated was one of his cases."

"Not specifically mine," Matt said. "The Lafayette office ultimately took lead, but I'm in the paperwork."

"So am I," Kara said.

Matt nodded. "There's no reason for him to be looking at it. How would he even know we were working a case in Louisiana?"

Brian Granderson made a note. "I should ask him, or Rebecca, but I'd like more information before I bring either of them in for a discussion."

"I took pictures of all the files on his desk. I didn't have time to go through each one, but highlighted the case numbers."

"These are all MRT cases," Matt said, flipping through the enlarged photos that Sloane provided. "This is the Seattle jurisdiction, when we were in the San Juan Islands...the Patagonia case, the Liberty Lake case. These here?" He tapped one of the pictures. "Dammit, this folder is from when I ran the Resident Agency in Tucson."

Kara was also looking through Sloane's report. "He has some old LAPD cases here as well—but I can't see the file names."

"He printed out my case files," Matt said, clearly angry. "As if he's investigating me."

Kara looked at him pointedly. "Aw, now you know how *I've* felt for the last ten years."

She said it lightly, but she was just as angry as Matt. Because Bryce Thornton hated her, he now had Matt in his sights. She didn't want her problems to bite Matt on the ass.

"Honestly," Kara said, "he's probably doubling down on his investigation into me, and you were caught up in the net because you brought me onto your team. And filed the complaint that landed him in front of OPR."

Sloane said, "I can go back to his office and look—"

"No," Brian interrupted. "Too risky. I have legitimate reasons to walk through the office, so I'll stop by and talk to him about an active case, see what he's working on, and then find out what I can. What else do you have?"

"I've been monitoring the individual cases and physical movements of both Thornton and Chavez," Sloane said. "Last night, they were both in the office until 9:40 p.m. They left at the same time."

"How do you know?" Matt asked.

"Every agent logs in and out of the central database. It's easy to see who is in the office or if they are logged out as off duty or because they're in the field. Most agents don't track it or know the capabilities. They think it's simply a human resources tool."

"Is it unusual for them to stay so late?" Brian asked.

"Thornton regularly works eight to six. Chavez typically works eight to five. Half the agents on staff clock forty-hour weeks, most of them have children at home."

"I don't penalize staff that doesn't work overtime," Brian said.

Sloane's mouth twitched, but she didn't comment. Kara understood what she was thinking. Some cops could do the job in forty-hour weeks because they were organized, smart and worked when they were at work. Other cops just sat around waiting until the clock turned five, doing the minimum required. Probably that way in every profession.

"They both put in occasional late nights," Sloane said, "but after nine is unusual. In addition, Thornton left yesterday to meet someone named 'Duncan' for lunch at 'the club.' I believe that this is the Wilshire Club and that Duncan is Theodore Duncan, chief of staff to the mayor of Los Angeles."

Kara straightened. "Oh?"

"That isn't unusual," Brian said. "Our agents, especially SSAs and ASACs, often meet with key leaders—elected officials, bank managers, congressional staff, others. We have regular contact, though these meetings should be logged in the system." He made a note. "Sometimes they don't get logged until the end of the week, so I'm not going to assume he's being deceptive."

"Chavez has a standing lunch meeting every quarter with the members of the board of supervisors," Sloane said, "but that's a big deal in the office, several of us assist in putting together a presentation."

Brian concurred.

Kara said, "I read in one of the reports that Thornton has been reviewing specific LAPD cases. Do you have anything more about those? Copies? File numbers?"

"I have the file numbers, but I didn't have the opportunity to look into them." She shifted through her folder and extracted a sheet, then handed it to Kara.

There were seven cases, and Kara knew them all.

"They're all mine—but more than that, these are the cases I worked with my old partner Colton Fox."

"Is there a legitimate reason for Thornton to have these files?" Matt asked.

"Possibly," Brian said, "but I don't know what it would be." He made another note. "Agent Thornton was specifically told not to pursue any inquiries about you, Detective Quinn."

"Do you remember the details?" Matt asked Kara.

"One was an illegal guns investigation that we worked jointly with the ATF. Three were Narcotics. One was insurance fraud, one Vice—which was my case, and Colton backed me up. And this last one—well, I didn't work it with Colton, but I assisted. He went undercover in a homeless camp to locate a killer. I was in the middle of the Chen investigation when that went down, but because Chen was a lot of hurry up and wait, I backed him up when I could."

"I remember that case," Brian said. "The suspect was accused of killing six homeless men. I don't think it's gone to trial yet."

"The guy killed himself in jail," Kara said. "I don't know the whole story, but he was schizophrenic and self-medicating. Colton thought he killed himself out of guilt—once he was properly medicated and realized what he had done, he couldn't live with himself. He was probably the only killer I ever met that I thought shouldn't go to trial because of legal insanity." Someone should have helped him before he was that far gone, but Kara didn't have a lot of faith in the system.

Will had brought the homeless murders to Colton's attention. It was wrapped up about three months before Colton was killed. Was that how Will started working with Dyson? Was this whole case of improper grants, or whatever it was, coming from Will? Why else would Craig mention him in his dying breath?

"I feel I haven't found anything of importance," Sloane said.

"You have provided a lot of well-documented information," Matt said, "and proven that Thornton has an unhealthy fixation on Kara and is looking at my cases for an unknown reason. What I'd like to know—in the privacy of this room—is your opinion. What do *you* think is going on in your squad, Sloane?"

Brian looked a bit uncomfortable with the question, but he nodded to Sloane. "Nothing you say is going to get anyone in trouble, but it might help us refocus our efforts. For example, we still don't know who in the office leaked information to the media last March."

Kara bristled and ignored Matt's concerned glance.

Sloane took a moment to think before she spoke. "Rebecca Chavez is a competent manager. She doesn't micromanage cases, which I think is a positive, but at the same time she doesn't seem to be interested in what anyone else is doing. She offers advice when asked, and it's usually good advice—such as how to approach a witness or conduct an interview—but she doesn't get involved. However, there was one case related to group homes in Northridge that she personally looked at. I don't even know why it was brought to our attention, but she took it and I don't know the resolution."

"I can find it," Brian said and wrote it down. "Do you know other details?"

"Not many. It was brought to us—I don't know by who—the

first week of August." She turned to Matt. "I'd like permission to follow Thornton and Chavez."

Matt said, "We're all trained to spot tails, and we don't want you spotted. Our focus is finding the leak." He turned to Kara and said, "Sloane already ruled out more than half of Chavez's team over the last four months using a combination of access to information, knowledge of the system and personality assessment. Brian and I concurred with her conclusions."

"But that still leaves nearly a dozen agents," Sloane said.

"Including Chavez and Thornton," Matt said.

Sloane nodded. "I only mention it because there are times one or both of them leave the office without any log—usually, we log out and note if it's personal, such as a doctor's appointment, or work related, and what case. There are several instances where they weren't in the office but hadn't logged out. Everyone does it on occasion, but this has become a pattern. I'd like to know what they are doing."

"Together?"

"Sometimes, not always. I sent you a list of the days and times."

Brian said, "If there's an instance where you feel tailing someone would help, let me know first. It'll cover you, but we need a record."

"Yes, sir."

"There's one more thing to address," Matt said. "Last night, Lieutenant Elena Gomez of LAPD told me that there is a portal LAPD is mandated to use where every case is logged and sent to the FBI. It's mostly automated. It was put in place after an internal investigation a few years back."

"I'm aware of it, but we don't monitor it. It's used primarily if there are multijurisdictional cases or to generate comprehensive reports."

"Lieutenant Gomez made a serious accusation. She believes that Chen was alerted to the raid by someone in the FBI. The raid was kept so close to the vest that it was only hours before the scheduled raid that they pulled warrants and debriefed support officers. They had already reassigned any cop they had concerns about. Gomez isn't certain how the information got into the portal, but believes it was from the SWAT briefing that the information was inadvertently added."

"Does she have any other evidence that the FBI leaked information about the raid?" Brian asked. "Maybe one of those reassigned cops accessed it."

Matt shook his head. "On the LAPD side, the portal can only be accessed by specific people—for example, the head of a squad, but not the detectives on his squad. A lieutenant, but not her uniformed officers. I suppose it's *possible*, but Gomez did due diligence to clear her people. She firmly believes it was someone in the FBI."

Brian didn't say anything for several seconds. "That database is going to be next to impossible to analyze for any breaches," he said, "but I'll take a look, see what I can find in the logs."

"Thank you."

"I would appreciate that you keep this between us," Brian said. "Our relationship with LAPD is already strained. If these kinds of rumors get out among the rank and file on either end, it's going to further strain—to the breaking point—any hope of mending fences."

"It won't come from us," Matt said.

"If we learn that someone at headquarters was involved directly or indirectly in this leak, I'll take it to the assistant director," Brian said.

As Brian and Sloane were leaving, Matt added, "I'm sorry that we haven't been able to make much movement on this case."

"Don't be," Brian said. "This group home case makes me uneasy. Any case that any of my agents even looks at has to have a record. As you know, we look into a lot of things that go nowhere—but if we're spending time, even five minutes, on something, we assign a case number to it. This doesn't sound familiar. I might have missed it, but I've been doubly focused on Chavez's squad and I don't remember seeing it."

"Let me know what you learn," Matt said, "and I'll keep you up-to-date with what we uncover on our end."

Brian turned to Kara. "I'd like to see those LAPD files, if you can access them?"

"Not a problem." She might go around Lex. Charlie would pull them for her.

Once they left, Kara said, "Craig mentioned the mayor's office. Violet works at city hall, and now Thornton is meeting with someone on the mayor's staff? This rings *all* my bells."

"Brian said they meet regularly," Matt reminded her.

"What if this Duncan person found out what Violet or Craig were doing and called Thornton to put an end to it?"

"We need to be cautious with any accusations. I'll fill Brian in on the little we know about Dyson's investigation and remind him about Thornton's meeting. This could be one of those rare coincidences."

"Could be," Kara said, though *why* Thornton would be involved stumped her. Maybe her assessment of him was wrong. Maybe he *was* deeply corrupt.

"You disagree."

"I don't know what to think, Matt. But this?" She tapped Sloane's report. "He was investigating me, and you, and by default our entire team. Why? Just because he hates me? That seems thin."

"I'm following up with Gomez and McPherson this morning," Matt said. "What are your plans?"

"Michael and I are going to track down Will Lattimer," Kara said. "He might know what's going on, and at a minimum, I want to know why Craig Dyson's last words were about him—and Violet."

17

Kara convinced Michael to let her drive. After all, she knew the city better than he did, and GPS wasn't always the best guide in traffic, especially on side streets. She ignored his commentary about her driving as she headed from the hotel to the small office that housed First Contact, the nonprofit Will Lattimer ran that focused on park cleanup and individualized assistance to the homeless. He'd started it primarily to help veterans when he learned one of his Marine buddies was living on the street, but expanded it to assist anyone who said they wanted help.

Kara didn't know Will well—they'd only met a few times at Colton's place—but she knew he and Colton both served in the Marines, though not in the same unit. Will hadn't called her back, but even the FBI couldn't force someone to answer their phone, so it was time to track Will Lattimer down.

The First Contact office was a long, narrow space in a row of warehouses in Atwater Village off San Fernando Road. Most of the businesses weren't retail storefronts but destination businesses— computer repair, a nonchain auto-parts store, a mechanic, a paper supply company, and several roll-up doors with no signs. Half the places were for lease.

Because of the central location near four different freeways, volunteers met here to gather supplies for park cleanups, which was their primary activity. Will believed the key to getting people off the street was to talk to them one-on-one and connect them with services like drug rehab, transitional housing and job training. But the first step was to find out why they were on the street.

Will had a lot more patience than Kara.

Kara pulled up next to an unmarked cop car. "Damn. I assumed the detectives talked to Will yesterday."

"Tread lightly," Michael warned. "We're not here officially."

She smiled broadly. "Trust me."

Michael sighed, got out of the car, looked around. He was still acting the bodyguard. She walked next to him toward the door. "You look like a fed," she said. Michael dressed impeccably in a suit, shirt and tie. His shoes were always polished, and she wondered how he kept his clothes in such great shape when they traveled. She wore black tactical pants because they were comfortable, a white polo shirt and a lightweight black blazer to hide her weapon.

As Michael reached to open the door, it swung toward him and a detective walked out. He looked the part—slacks, button-down shirt, no jacket, badge and gun on his belt. He gave them a second glance and Kara said, "Detective."

He nodded, then walked quickly to his car and left.

"I know him," Kara muttered. "Damn, I don't know his name. I may never have known his name, there are a lot of cops in LA, but I've seen him before."

It would come to her, or she'd ask Lex. Caucasian, forties, five foot ten, about one-eighty.

"I got his plates," Michael said. He pulled out his small notepad and scribbled the numbers.

"You're awesome, partner," she said.

They walked inside and almost ran into a man who was coming to the door. He had a key in hand and appeared to be about to lock it.

"We're closing," he said, nervous and edgy.

Kara glanced around the space. Two small offices in the back of the long, narrow warehouse. The rolling door had been blocked off by a temporary wall that didn't reach the ceiling. A scarred conference table took up the middle of the floor where it appeared a mailing project was partly complete—stacks of letters, some folded, some stuffed. A woman in one of the offices was on the phone. She put it down when she saw Kara and Michael.

"Who just left?" Kara asked.

The man didn't answer. He was mixed race, short curly dark hair, a roughly trimmed beard, hazel eyes. The woman was Caucasian with light brown hair and blue eyes. They both were thin and neatly dressed, but Kara suspected they were recovering addicts. They were skittish, wary, looked ready to bolt.

Honesty would work best.

"I'm Detective Kara Quinn with LAPD, and this is my partner, FBI Agent Michael Harris. Who was the man who just left? I know he was a detective."

"He didn't give us his name," the man said. "Um, we have to go."

"You can give me a minute," Kara said. He didn't give a name? They were either lying or the detective wasn't following protocol. Or maybe he didn't identify himself as a detective, though he'd come in a city vehicle and wore a badge. "Do you work here?"

"I do," the woman said. "Gina Rocha. I work here mornings."

It was only nine. "You always quit so early?"

"I have errands to do for my boss."

"Is your boss Will Lattimer?"

She blinked rapidly, surprised. "Yes."

"Will is a friend of mine," Kara said. "I need to talk to him, but he's not answering his phone."

"When I see him, I'll tell him."

"Why are you so nervous?" Michael said.

Michael sometimes sounded too authoritarian, too much like a tough cop. He was a rock always, but he was also very law and order. Sometimes, situations—especially talking with people naturally nervous around authorities—required a little more finesse.

"I'm not," Gina said, clutching her oversize purse.

"Can we sit down and talk a minute?" Kara asked.

Gina shook her head. "You can call Will, or I can give him a message, but we have to go."

"Why was the detective here?"

"We couldn't help him, he wasn't happy about it."

"Why are you scared of him?"

The two exchanged glances.

"We haven't done anything," Gina said firmly.

"I didn't say you had," Kara said. "But from where I'm standing, you both look nervous. We're not here to jam you up for anything. I need to talk to Will—it's very important."

"I don't know where he is." Gina's chin tilted up, defiant. "I don't know why he won't answer your call, except that maybe he doesn't want to talk to you. And if he doesn't want to talk to you, then I don't, either."

She folded her arms across her chest.

Kara only had FBI cards labeling her as a "special consultant," so she asked for a piece of paper and pen. Gina walked back to the office and brought out a notepad and pencil.

She scrawled out a message to Will and left her number. She hoped it conveyed the urgency without giving away too many details.

"If he comes in or calls, give him this message," she said to Gina. "Like I said, it's very important."

"I promise to give him the message."

Kara left, and Michael followed her.

"They're addicts," Michael said as they got into the car. He clearly disapproved.

"Maybe. They're not using now."

"How can you tell? The woman was nervous, the man was jumpy and scratching his arms."

"I've been around enough addicts to know they're mostly clean. My guess? They're transitioning."

"Meaning?"

"They were homeless, now have some sort of semipermanent housing, maybe a group home. Colton always said that Will was a miracle worker, really good at getting people off the streets. He must trust Gina to hire her. I suspect in his line of work, he's a good judge of character."

As she spoke, she backed out of the parking space and drove down the alley, then stopped at the dead end where she could discreetly watch the building.

"What are you doing?"

"Waiting."

She didn't have to wait long. Two minutes later, Gina and the man left the building. They locked the door, had an intense conversation, then the man hugged her tightly and they stood close together, not talking. A few minutes later, an Uber pulled up. They both got in.

Kara followed.

"Maybe the detective intimidated them because they're guilty," Michael said.

"Of what?"

"Drugs?"

"Drugs are not going to get anyone jammed up. We're not allowed to arrest anyone for using. They have to be selling some weight, or committing another felony while in possession, and the paperwork is a nightmare." Michael knew as well as she did that most DAs didn't prosecute drug-related crimes anymore.

"If they're transitioning as you said, maybe they're nervous because they'll be kicked out of the program if they're caught using."

"Depends on the program," Kara said. "I don't think they were high, but I could be wrong."

"You don't think you are."

"Nope." Kara glanced at Michael. "Does this bother you?"

"What?"

"I don't know. The conversation? Addicts? Drug use? You seem uncomfortable."

He didn't say anything for a moment, as if gathering his thoughts. That's one of the many things she appreciated about Michael—he was thoughtful and rarely spoke off the cuff. Sometimes, she wished she had the same skill set.

"Maybe," he said slowly, "this all hits too close to home."

Michael rarely talked about his childhood. Kara knew that he'd grown up very poor in Chicago. She didn't know much— just that his father was out of the picture, his brother was killed in a drive-by shooting, and his mom died of a drug overdose before he turned eighteen. He'd been in foster care for a few years, which hadn't been pretty. Michael had told Kara more than once that the Navy saved him—he enlisted the day he graduated from high school.

Kara couldn't picture a desperate Michael—he was the epitome of the Great American Hero. Served his country with distinction. Went to college when he got out of the Navy, then joined the FBI. He'd always gone above and beyond, getting certified in SWAT, underwater rescue and more. He could be a flirt, and he dated quite a bit, but Kara had always thought that was because he was looking for "the one"—he valued his home, wanted a family. He didn't say it in so many words, but a few things over the months she'd worked with him had given her that idea.

"I'm sorry," she said honestly. "I had sucky parents, but I didn't have a rough childhood." Her parents were con artists and thieves, not violent or drug addicts.

"My experience has been most addicts don't change. With the addiction comes theft, violence, destruction of everything and everyone around them."

"It's not easy, and I certainly have no answers. As a cop? I want to arrest them all to get them clean. But that's neither viable nor realistic. They're breaking the law, but we can't arrest them except under very specific circumstances. The slippery slope of desperation where they are just looking for money to get more drugs, lose their friends, family, home… It's depressing. But I'm sure there's more to it than that. A lot of the vets Will helps suffer from PTSD and the VA is a bitch to work with to get help."

"It's a bureaucracy, but if you know how to work the system, you can get what you need," Michael said.

"Because you see the benefit. You're willing to do what it takes and fight for what you want. Other people see a mountain they can't climb. Will helps make that journey easier. But not everyone wants help, and the laws being as they are, we can't force them to do anything they don't want to do. I just wish we didn't make it so easy for them to continue down destructive paths."

Kara tried to see things as they were, not better or worse. She tended to be cynical, but mostly, she was a realist.

She slowed as the Uber carrying Will's two helpers stopped at the north end of Echo Park Lake. They got out and at first she thought she was wrong—that they were still using, in the park to buy drugs. There were dozens of homeless encampments along the semipermanent chain-link fencing the city had put up. She felt Michael tense next to her.

Then she saw Will Lattimer.

"Bingo," she said. "The guy in the dark green shirt with the blue baseball cap? That's Will."

She pulled over, parked illegally and jumped out before anyone could skirt away. Michael followed, letting her take the lead.

As she approached, Will glanced over, looked straight at her. Then Gina saw her and said something to Will. He handed Gina something—keys, Kara realized—and Gina and her friend walked away.

"Kara," Will said when she was within earshot. "If this isn't a blast from the past."

"You shouldn't be so surprised," she said. "I left you several messages."

"I've been really busy. I'm sorry." He turned to Michael, extended his hand. "Will Lattimer, director of First Contact."

"Special Agent Michael Harris, FBI," Michael said.

"FBI," Will repeated. "Well, Kara, I was surprised to get your call. I meant to call you, but—"

She interrupted. "You're avoiding me, and I don't know why. But two things you need to know. First, Craig Dyson is dead."

"I heard. It's awful."

"Yeah. I was there."

Will reached out, his hesitation gone. "Oh, God, Kara, I'm so sorry."

"Which brings me to the second thing. Craig's dying words. He told me to find Violet." Not in so many words, but Kara was clear on the meaning. "Then he said to talk to you. Why?"

Kara watched Will. He seemed confused, but she wasn't positive he wasn't acting. Then, he paled, as if just now realizing the scope of the situation. "I don't know—"

"Yes you do," Kara cut him off. "You know damn well what's going on. And I think it has to do with Violet Halliday."

"How do you know Violet?" he asked. Stalling.

"Craig wanted me to meet her because of something about my investigation into Chen and information she had. He said she was a whistleblower. I was irritated because I sensed that Craig was going to cut a deal with Chen. I remembered the name, and that she was bringing him a file but was locked out because of the shooting. Then, I heard from LAPD that she's a person of interest."

"She did not—" He abruptly stopped talking.

"You know what's going on and it revolves around this girl. Who is she, what does she know, did she kill Chen and why?"

"She didn't kill Chen. Dammit." He looked around, then said, "This isn't a good place to talk. People are watching me because they think I'll lead them to Violet. I don't know where she is. I wish I did. She's in danger, but I don't know what information she had for Craig. I told her to be careful. Look, I have people I trust searching for her, and when I find her, I'll call you."

She didn't know if what he said was the truth or mostly lies.

"The police are looking for her," she said.

"You can't trust anyone. There's so much money involved, I don't know who's dirty or who's clean."

"Money involved in what?" Michael asked.

"What did Craig tell you?"

"You're hedging," Michael said.

"Because I don't know you," Will said, defiant.

"You know *me*," Kara said. "Colton was my partner and your friend. If anything, you should come clean because of that."

He stared at her oddly. His mouth opened, closed. Then he nodded. "Yeah. You're right."

She waited, and Will finally started talking.

"Craig was about to impanel a grand jury to look into how the city and county allocates housing grants for the homeless," he said. "I have been fighting the city for years and getting no-where, but after you took down Chen, some new information came to light about *how* grant money is distributed and spent. The volume of corruption—the nonprofits within nonprofits with everyone getting a cut until less than 10 percent gets to the people who need it. We are talking billions—with a *B. Billions* of dollars.

"The thing is—nothing about the structure is illegal. It's immoral and unethical, but the way the grants are written, there's nothing illegal about it. I've tried to get the media to expose the waste, but they're not interested. Craig found something to hang his hat on—employee economic interest reporting violations. He was going to use that to segue into a larger investigation into how the grant money is spent under an old public fraud law he uncovered that has rarely been used. If he could prove that money was steered to the friends and family of those making financial decisions, then he had a case to open a full audit. But he needed the grand jury to do it."

Kara's head was spinning. "So you think that someone killed Craig because he was going to impanel a grand jury that *may* have issued an indictment against some politician?"

"More than one," he said. "And some of these people had ties to Chen, a known human trafficker. Some of these politicians profited from Chen's business."

"Are you suggesting that someone killed Craig to protect a damn *politician*?"

Will nodded. "And Chen."

"Because he was going to plea," Michael suggested.

"Craig told me the case against Chen was solid," Will said, "and he was going to use that to leverage him into turning state's evidence against multiple people. I don't specifically know who—Craig was keeping that information close to the vest until the grand jury."

"So someone kills Chen to prevent him from talking, then someone kills Craig so he doesn't pursue an investigation." She didn't see it. "Killing Chen—yes. No honor among thieves. But a prosecutor? These kinds of public corruption cases are held up for years because of motions and postponements and paperwork and bullshit. Murder is a whole other animal. Something else is going on."

Will shrugged. "I don't know what to say. This is what I've been working on with him. I planned to testify as an expert to the grand jury. We've been talking about it for months. I have research, documentation, facts to back up my statements, and more than a decade working with the homeless and navigating the city bureaucracy. I've seen the waste firsthand."

"Then it's this Halliday girl who has information," Michael said. "And no one knows where she is."

"I'm worried about her," Will admitted. "She called me yesterday in a panic, said that she needed to meet me, that she would be at the Fifth Street Park."

"Where's that?" Michael asked.

"A small downtown park about a mile from city hall north of I-10. It's a homeless encampment now, but she volunteers for me on the weekends."

"And she would go there?" Michael asked, surprised.

"Sure," Will said. "Everyone knows her. If she needed help or to hide in the open, that's where she would go. But when I got there, she was gone, and there were these thugs I'd never seen before going through the camp, harassing people, asking about her."

"Could they have worked for Chen?"

"They weren't Chinese—they were Hispanic. Three men, under thirty, looked to be gangbangers. Swaggered in, tossed a couple tents, all attitude. One had a neck tat, but I couldn't make out the details. They left when they saw me, but threatened me by 'shooting' their fingers."

"You need to watch yourself," Kara said. "Some of those gangs don't need a reason to kill you."

Will dismissed her concern. "When they were gone, I talked to the people at the park. Violet had been hiding in a tent, but when she saw the men looking for her she slipped away, leaving her phone behind."

"Where's her phone now?" Michael asked.

"In my office."

"Your office workers told me they didn't know where you were and yet came right here," Kara said.

"Don't blame them. I told Gina and Fletch not to tell anyone where I am."

"Even the police?" Michael said.

Will was growing irritated. "I don't know you, and I know Kara isn't with LAPD anymore."

"I am," she said, "just temporarily assigned to the feds until this Chen thing is resolved. A detective who didn't identify himself was looking for you, too," she added.

"Fletch told me he was an asshole. Thought Violet was there. Demanded to search. He walked around, looked in the offices—which are open, the doors don't even lock—and even searched the cabinets where I keep supplies. Fletch and Gina aren't confrontational, they only watched him."

"You're not telling us everything," Michael said. He was just as irritated with Will as Will was with them.

"Look, I'm done," Will said. "When I talk to Violet, find out what spooked her, maybe I'll call you."

"You *need* to call me," Kara said.

"First, I have to find Violet." He looked around, closed his eyes, shook his head. "Dammit, you both look like cops, and no one is going to talk to cops around here. Let me handle this."

Kara stepped forward and said in a low voice, "No matter what, you call me tonight and give me a report, even if it's that you found nothing. Do not avoid my calls. This fraud investigation Craig was running? There has to be more to it. We're talking about murder. Killing a DDA in the fucking courthouse. Violet is in danger, and you know it. If she really did find something, the smoking gun that she was bringing to Craig yesterday afternoon, then my team can protect her a whole lot better than you."

Will watched Kara and her partner walk away, then he swore and kicked the trash can next to him, hurting his foot.

He sensed before he saw someone approach him from the trees. Will whirled around, stared at his old friend who blended in so well with the homeless. Khakis, layered shirts, jacket, thick beard, hat, sunglasses. The sunglasses because some things—like being a drug addict—you can't fake if someone looks in your eyes.

"Goddammit, Colton, why didn't you tell me that Kara doesn't know you're alive?"

AUGUST

Two Months Ago

18

One of the best things about living in Los Angeles was the weather. Temperate all year, a little cold in the winter, a little hot in the summer, but mostly nice every day.

Except this week, I thought as I shut off my car and walked into First Contact to meet Will. The first week of August and LA topped one hundred degrees for the first time in five years and I was miserable. My tiny house didn't have air-conditioning but it had never bothered me before. The weather guy on the alternative rock station I listen to said it would be back in the nineties tomorrow and a reasonable eight-five this weekend when the Santa Ana winds kicked in. I couldn't wait. Nine at night and the air was still stifling.

I stopped just inside the door. Will had asked me to come over and meet someone who was investigating possible fraud in government grants for the homeless, but there were four people in the room. As soon as I entered, Will got up and locked the door behind me.

"Thank you for agreeing to come in tonight, Violet."

I didn't budge. Three people were staring at me from the conference table. I felt overwhelmed. Will had said *someone* not *three* someones.

A man came in from the back dressed in layered shirts and khaki pants. I immediately recognized him. He was the homeless veteran who had been hanging around with Jake and Dev. He'd been there the day my mother overdosed and Will saved her life; a week later he told me that he'd look for Jane and would let me know when he found her.

He hadn't found her yet, but I knew he was looking. The day I met him I knew he wasn't like so many of the other homeless people we worked with.

No one in the room paid him any attention. He helped himself to water from the refrigerator in the corner.

"Will," I said, my voice barely a whisper. I swallowed, tried to stop shaking. Groups of people made me nervous. "You should have prepared me." I do much better when I can anticipate a crowd. I did fine in regular staff meetings because I knew when they were, what was expected, and I didn't have to talk if I didn't want to.

"I'm sorry," he said quietly. "But we need your help."

Surprisingly, that simple statement calmed me. "Okay," I said, trying for a strong voice, but it sounded like a squeak.

Will introduced me to the people at the table. They all seemed to know me, though other than the homeless veteran who I didn't think was homeless, I had never met any of them.

I recognized the name Craig Dyson, a deputy district attorney. I'd been feeding information to Mr. Dyson through Will, specifically about the building owned by David Chen. He was in his early fifties with kind eyes. He wore a suit, the jacket hanging over the back of his chair. Will had a lot of respect for the man, and by extension, so did I.

The other two people were in law enforcement—Sergeant

Lex Popovich and Lieutenant Elena Gomez. Her sharp eyes filled with both suspicion and concern. About me? About the meeting?

My eyes drifted to the man in the corner who was eating an apple.

"Colton, sit," Will said, "you're making Violet nervous."

Colton smiled. A nice smile, revealing his perfect teeth—teeth that proved he was neither a drug addict nor chronically homeless.

"This is Detective Colton Fox," Will said. "He's a good friend of mine, and everyone thinks he's dead."

That was the last thing I expected to hear. I was still processing the information when Craig spoke up.

"Violet, I want to personally thank you for providing the information I need to investigate the city's grant process. As you know, the system is rife with waste, but it's very difficult to prove fraud. Nothing they are doing is illegal—on the surface."

The way he said it made me believe he had found something illegal—something that he could use to expose corruption.

"There's no accountability," Will said. "Fraud and waste are built into the system, which is a scam in and of itself."

Craig smiled, appeasing Will. "You're right, but it's legal. And that's where I'm having the problem in opening up a grand jury investigation. Something may be unethical, it may even be criminal, but if it's not against a law that I have the authority to prosecute, my hands are tied."

Will mumbled something I couldn't hear, then said, "I'm sorry. I interrupted."

"You're passionate about this issue, Will, and I agree with you. But we need to use what we have. Ms. Halliday, because of the information you provided about the crash of the city hall computer network, the evidence of deleted files and Detective Fox's own investigation, we *almost* have enough to go to the grand jury. But because it's a difficult case to prove, we need more time to put it together. And more facts."

"I'm sorry if this sounds clueless," I said, "but what investigation are you talking about? The police have an investigation? Into who?"

If people thought that Colton was dead, how could he investigate anything?

Craig said, "Will first reached out to me months ago about the housing project owned by David Chen, who was arrested for human trafficking and murder."

I remembered. "A podcast I listen to talked about it a lot. No one else was giving it much airtime." I didn't know how the Chen building connected to anything, other than it seemed odd to me at the time. But Craig had questions about it, so I answered them best I could. Unfortunately, most records regarding the city funding going to the building had been destroyed in the computer crash.

"I am the DDA assigned to prosecute Chen. When Will mentioned that Chen had housed his workers next to the warehouse, I looked into the building and there was paperwork missing. It appeared that the address was listed as a homeless shelter in one database, but I couldn't confirm the information and requested some documents from city hall. I was told the files had been lost in the computer crash and staff would research. I didn't think there was anything nefarious about this, just expected the information later rather than sooner. Shortly after this, Detective Fox was shot in the line of duty."

Elena Gomez spoke up. "We are still investigating the shooting—Colton's cover was blown by the media. We don't know who was responsible—the people he was investigating or someone else. While he was in the hospital, we devised this undercover plan, and put out that he didn't survive his injuries. We felt that going in deep cover would both protect him because the shooter was still at large, and give us an advantage in this investigation. Fox could go places as a homeless veteran and not arouse suspicion."

"What specifically are you investigating?" I asked. "You just said that how the city funds homeless services isn't illegal."

"The process may not be illegal," Craig said, "but how the grants are approved may be. There are very specific regulations about reporting income, the bidding process and more. If friends and family of those in charge of allocating funds have an unfair advantage, I may be able to open a larger investigation into the grant program and demand a full audit."

"Too much of this became political," Elena said. "Everyone arguing about the cause—drugs, mental illness, lack of housing, any number of things. The money kept coming. State money, city money, bond money, federal grants. No one seemed to be accountable for any of the services they were supposed to provide, passing the buck to this agency or that agency. But, because of the grant Chen was awarded, we realized there *was* a potential crime—how did a criminal who trafficked in humans and ran a sweatshop profit off a housing grant?"

"But more important, why can we find no evidence of the grant?" Dyson said.

"Because it was destroyed in the computer crash," I said, finally seeing what I had long suspected: someone in city hall had *intentionally* erased data that could get them in trouble.

"That's where I came in," Colton said with a smile and finally sat down at the table with us. He wasn't a handsome man, but he was alluring with intense green eyes and a strong jaw. He looked like someone who could both take care of himself and everyone else. "Will identified several nonprofits that seemed to receive a lot of money—millions of dollars—but had nothing to show for it. He gave me a list of their properties, what they claimed to do, who they claimed to help. I went to every location. Slept outside most of them for a few days, a week or so. Documented comings and goings. Took pictures. Tried to get into shelters. Talked to people inside. I was one of them. When you're homeless, you trust very few people—but you tend to trust your own kind."

"The primary problem," Craig said, "is that while Colton has been able to document that there is little sign of the money these nonprofits received, that isn't a crime."

That I knew. Will had told me over and over again and I still couldn't quite wrap my head around that truth.

Craig continued. "What *is* a crime is if the process is tainted. According to what you uncovered about the computer crash, it's only the housing grants that were lost, correct?"

"Yes, sir."

"We need those original proposals and approvals. You told Will that you might be able to recover the data, but that it could get you fired."

I cleared my throat self-consciously. I didn't know why I was nervous. These were Will's friends and colleagues, and they wanted the same thing I wanted—to fix the problem. Better, they had the power to do it. "I'm not afraid of being fired."

"That's honorable, but I might be able to give you some protection. Whistleblower laws have become convoluted over the years, but in general, when a government employee publicly reveals potentially criminal information about the health, safety or finances of a government agency, they cannot be fired. You may be removed from your current capacity, but you would receive a paycheck and be reassigned to another division. If you bring the information to me, as an officer of the court, I would be duty bound to look into the allegations.

"The concern I have is how you obtain the information. You cannot break any laws in gathering the data. But the information I want is public record. It's just been—possibly—destroyed. If you can recover it, I want to see it. That and all grants awarded since the crash. The who, what, where, when and why. How they are decided and who makes the decision. Who signs off. Is there a bidding process and has it been violated or suspended? If so, how? Is this something you would be comfortable doing?"

"Yes," I answered without hesitation. "I have been working on this for months." I glanced at Will, hesitant now because I didn't know how much he had told these people. Three of them were cops, after all.

Will said, "I've told them everything. We've done nothing wrong, Violet."

"How long do you think it'll take?" Craig asked.

"I didn't expect it to take this long," I admitted. "Someone intentionally went in and covered up the deleted files. I don't know who did it, but I know when it happened. February 18."

Why did everyone look like they knew that already?

"What's wrong? Is that important?" I asked.

"That's the day of the Chen raid."

I must have looked as confused as I felt, because Elena said, "Chen knew about the raid shortly before my team went in to arrest him. We had enough evidence to take Chen down and protect the women he'd been exploiting. That happened the same day that someone else—presumably someone in city hall—" she looked to me for confirmation, and I nodded "—deleted files then caused a computer crash."

"It's more complicated than that," I said. "They had to delete the files from the backup—either before the backup was installed, which was two days later, or after the backup—which means the files are still in an older backup, if I can gain access to it. Backup files are stored off-site at a data warehouse—data goes one way, unless we need a specific backup." I didn't go into more details. I'd found that nontechnical people didn't pay attention and ended up confused.

"But you believe someone did it on purpose," Craig said.

"Yes, I *know* it was intentional."

"Can you find out who did it?"

"I think so." Was I being too optimistic? I wanted to laugh—no one had ever accused me of being an optimist.

"Okay," Craig said. "That's what we want. Who did it, what they deleted and those deleted files if you can retrieve them." He looked at both Elena and Lex and they nodded their agreement.

I was getting excited. If these people—people in a position of power—believed they *could* do something to end the corruption, it gave me hope I never had before.

"I can do that." I sounded confident. And then, at that moment, I realized I *was* confident. This was my area of expertise.

"I'd like you to report directly to me as you gather information," Craig said. "I have a staff investigator who will be following up on what you learn. So if you get just a name or an entity, pass it along, and we'll do the background. Do not discuss this with anyone other than us in this room, and it would be best if you didn't even do that—you never know who might be listening."

"Violet is extremely trustworthy," Will said. "I would never have brought her this far if she weren't."

I felt my face heat up. Was I blushing? I hoped not.

After Craig and the two cops left, Colton came up to me. "You did good. Relax."

"You're going back on the street, aren't you?"

He nodded. "I'm heading out to Northridge. One of the entities you flagged is out there."

"Sunflower Group Homes."

"Yep. They have several facilities, some just for women, some for vets like me. I had to get fake documents, but I know the lingo."

"What you're doing—I couldn't do it. Living on the street is hard."

He shrugged. "What you're doing, I couldn't do it. Computers give me a headache."

I laughed.

Then, Colton said quietly, "I haven't found your mom yet, Vi."

I tensed. "You don't have to—"

"I want to. You're worried about her, and you should know how she's doing. As soon as I'm done in Northridge, I'll keep looking. A week ago, I met a woman—Army, serious case of PTSD, got hooked on oxy after shrapnel took out a chunk in her leg. I don't know how reliable she is, but she recognized your mom's picture. The one you gave me?"

I nodded, remembering. It was the most recent picture I had of her, one we had to get for her benefits.

"My friend thinks she went to Venice Beach. Something your mom talked about when she wasn't high."

My mom used to love the beach. When I was little and my dad had to work weekends, Mom would take me to the beach. Usually Santa Monica. We'd walk, make sandcastles, get snow cones, and sometimes we rented bikes. Before she started doing drugs. Before everything fell apart.

"So I'll check there next," Colton was saying, "but if you want to go out yourself, Will says there's a cleanup in a couple weeks."

"Thank you," I whispered.

He shrugged, gave me a half smile. "Anytime. Will knows how to reach me, if you need anything. Be careful over there at city hall. They might be a bunch of loafer-wearing elitist politicians, but some of them are dangerous."

TUESDAY, OCTOBER 8

19

After Michael and Kara left to track down Will Lattimer, Matt had a conference call with his boss in DC, checked in with Ryder Kim, took care of a lot of paperwork—the bane of his existence—and tried to reach Lieutenant Gomez. She didn't answer. He sent her a text message that he'd like a few minutes, then he headed over to the courthouse to meet with Detective McPherson.

McPherson and his small team had taken over a tiny office in the courthouse near the main security office, and welcomed Matt in with a wave toward a table of coffee and pastries. Matt helped himself to coffee. It was surprisingly good.

"What have you learned since yesterday?" Matt asked.

"We've learned a lot, but still no ID. I had teams working all night going through security footage. He came in—in the disguise we saw on camera—thirty minutes before the lockdown. Then we caught a glimpse of him on camera two blocks away—not positive it's him, but general build matches. Then poof. The image isn't clear."

"Can you send it to me anyway?"

McPherson nodded, made a note. "There's no cameras in the area he disappeared, near the freeway. Personally, I think he either had a car or someone picked him up, but I can't prove it. Either way, he's in the wind, and we just don't have a good image of him. Our artists are working on the camera footage and removing the beard, some weight, the hair. We have something, but no one is completely happy with it. It's a lot of guessing, nothing that will hold up in court. Still, we're showing it around to everyone who works here to see if they recognize the guy."

It's what Matt would have done.

"We're going through Dyson's current and pending cases, recent paroles, threats," McPherson continued. "The guy was well respected. The defense lawyers whined about him, but mostly because he didn't like to plead except on first offenses—they had no problem with his tactics in court. Judges said he was always prepared, professional. No one really knew him personally, though. He kept to himself."

"What about his investigator? Sharp? Does he have any information or theories?"

McPherson looked at his watch. "I'm meeting with Peter Sharp in Dyson's office in fifteen, if you want to sit in."

"Thank you," he said. "This feels like a professional hit."

"Yep. Reads that way for me, too," McPherson said. "Not a random crook who sees the lawyer who sent him away and goes ballistic. And what scumbag comes equipped to rappel off a roof? Plus, no one is getting that grappling hook through security."

Matt hadn't thought of that at the time, only about the knife. "You're right."

"Yep. Which is fucked, because this building is pretty damn secure. Of course, there are always ways to get in and out, but that hook was intact—it couldn't be broken down into harmless parts and snuck in. It wasn't concealed under his suit coat—and

I've watched the video a dozen times. He didn't have it on him. Which means it was in the stairwell or on the roof."

"Roof," Matt said.

McPherson nodded. "Yeah, my guess, too. He had a key to the roof—no signs of forced entry. Or, someone left it open for him—which says inside job. Those doors are solid—no one is breaking them down. They are accessed with a maintenance key—not everyone has them. So my guys are running down all the maintenance staff. Thing is? Every deputy has a key as well. And there's only two people who can come in and bypass security. Deputies and night janitorial staff. One of them could have put the grappling hook on the roof anytime in the two days before the murder."

"I assume janitorial is well vetted."

He shrugged. "City employees. Backgrounds, et cetera. But I'm pulling every janitorial staffer who has been in this building in the last forty-eight hours."

"Why forty-eight?"

"Because there's a lot of shit that happens on the roof—they have vents and control panels and other stuff I don't even know what it does. Someone is up there near every day. Sure, it could have been hidden someplace, but there's not a lot of places to hide a duffel bag with a grappling hook and rope."

"It could be one of your people." Matt didn't want to say it because he wasn't certain how the deputy would respond, but he had to bring it up, even if only to dismiss it.

"We have fifty to eighty deputies assigned to this courthouse every day. Some are here on rotation, some are here for light duty, some are here because they have a year until retirement and don't want to strain themselves. They're all seasoned."

"Bribes?"

"Maybe. But for murder?" He shook his head. "I don't see it. Anything is possible, but my money is on janitorial. Before you say anything—I am looking at my people. But *I'm* doing it, not the feds."

"I don't need to be involved but if you need my help—discreetly—just ask."

He looked surprised by the offer. "Appreciate it."

"My people believe Dyson's murder is connected to Chen's. Thoughts?"

"Hell if I know. Like I said, Dyson's respected. I've started digging into his private life, though the time and place of the murder tells me this is related to his job."

"I agree," Matt said.

"Still, we cover all the bases. Has an ex-wife, no kids. She's a high-priced lawyer, at the same firm he used to work at. She's now a partner, said they had an amicable divorce, still saw each other for dinner once a month or so. Except—he canceled the last two dinners they had planned, and that apparently was unusual. So I got to thinking, was he on a big case? Working something that took all his time? Worried about something? Threats?" He shrugged. "So far, nothing. He reported no threats to the marshals or to my office, but maybe his investigator knows more." He glanced at his watch and stood up. "Time to chat with Sharp, see what he's found in Dyson's records."

When Matt and Detective McPherson arrived at Dyson's office, Peter Sharp was sorting through stacks of files on the conference table. He looked up, acknowledged the men and said, "This is everything that Craig was working on. He had the Chen hearing, a plea conference this afternoon—that's been assigned to another DDA—and multiple pending trials in various stages of disposition."

"What about the grand jury investigation that he mentioned to Detective Quinn?" Matt asked.

"I don't know much about that. I primarily verify facts for the DDA—background checks, review witness statements, things like that. If the file is here, you're welcome to look at it, but I haven't seen it." Peter shook his head in frustration.

"What happens to the grand jury investigation now?"

"The DA will review the case, but I have no idea what Craig had or even who his witnesses were. He didn't talk much about it, and I don't see the DA pursuing it. Craig had a lot of leeway because of his seniority and record. The DA has his own pet projects."

"What was the case specifically about?"

"There was a public complaint about a transitional housing project. Craig thought there might have been fraud or at a minimum gross government negligence, but it was one of his side projects. Honestly, the first I heard of him impaneling a grand jury was late last week."

He handed McPherson a red file folder. "These are all the threats that Craig has received, most recent on top. They're copies—your office should have all the originals, but I made some notes that might help."

McPherson took the file. "Anything in here that we should flag?"

"The only one that sticks with me is Lamar Forsyth. He was very angry when Craig declined to prosecute after he was carjacked. There wasn't enough evidence and the case is still open, but Craig was blunt—without evidence, there's no prosecution. Forsyth won't let it go and blamed Craig."

"We'll talk to him," McPherson said. "If anything else comes to mind, please let me know."

Peter nodded. "If you need anything, please call. I want to help."

Matt followed McPherson out.

"I don't think that Forsyth is our guy, not like this, but I'll check him out," McPherson said.

"I'd really like to know more about the grand jury investigation," Matt said. "I thought Sharp would know more."

"DDAs all work differently. Some keep things to themselves, some talk to everyone. And a grand jury investigation is a whole other ball game. I'll ask the DA when I talk to him—I have a meeting this afternoon in his office. You're welcome to join me, but I don't think he has any details. Like Sharp said, Dyson was a senior prosecutor and had a lot of leeway. This is the third—maybe fourth—DA who's had the job while Dyson's been here."

"Text me the time and place, and if I can, I'll join you. Otherwise, if you'd pass on anything you learn?"

"Absolutely. You know, you're not like some of the dicks from LA FBI. No offense."

"None taken."

It wasn't the first—and Matt didn't think it would be the last—time he heard that comment.

20

Rebecca Chavez called Sloane into an unscheduled meeting at ten that morning. There were several people already in the room, including Bryce Thornton, Tom Schroder, two other agents and Rebecca's assistant.

"I'll make this brief. You're here because you are all working on cases that aren't priority, and we need to expedite an investigation," Rebecca began.

"As you have heard, David Chen, a suspected human trafficker, was shot and killed yesterday outside the Clara Shortridge Foltz Criminal Justice Center in downtown LA." Rebecca handed out a timeline printed on LAPD stationery. "Mr. Chen was on his way to a hearing his attorney requested to have evidence suppressed that may have been wrongfully obtained by the LAPD detective who led the investigation. We have our own investigation into Mr. Chen and his businesses, and the LAPD has been less than forthright in sharing information with us, both during their investigation and the prosecution, and now a murder investigation.

"Under normal circumstances, Bryce would be in charge of co-ordinating our involvement, but because of interoffice politics—which is, honestly, exhausting and rather ridiculous—Bryce has been removed from any investigations involving LAPD Detective Kara Quinn. He's here in an advisory capacity because he has historical information that would be beneficial for you to understand. I'll be coordinating our efforts."

Agent Schroder asked, "Are we now lead on the homicide?"

"I'm working on that. What I would like is a task force between our office and LAPD, but they rarely agree to coordinating efforts. However, we have an ongoing investigation into Mr. Chen and his business associates, and we need information from the homicide investigation to assist us in bringing all involved to justice."

Rebecca assigned tasks to everyone—background, media reports, reviewing LAPD documents and more. "I'm contacting the lead investigator and his supervisor and hope to expedite a joint task force, but I want to be able to go into this with information and an action plan. Questions?"

Sloane had many, but she asked only one. "What would you like me to do?"

"Agent Wagner, yes—I'll be calling on you to join me in any meetings today to take notes and follow up on action items. The next few days may go long, so be prepared."

Rebecca dismissed everyone but Sloane. "We're going downtown to talk to the AUSA and, hopefully, interview Detective Quinn. Bryce is certain that she is involved in Chen's death. She has an alibi, but I don't know how solid it is—I need to verify that myself. I don't think it's a coincidence that the day she arrives in Los Angeles a suspect she threatened and nearly killed is murdered. She's on record as having said she wished he'd broken his neck instead of his leg when he fell—or was pushed—from the roof."

"I'm confused," Sloane said. "Was Detective Quinn investigated for any of this?"

"Internal LAPD investigation," Rebecca said dismissively. She motioned for Sloane to follow her to her office, then closed the door behind them and motioned for her to sit. "You've done a competent job since you were assigned to my squad. I like that you had experience in the real world before becoming an agent. You don't act like a rookie."

Sloane nodded, not knowing if she should thank her boss or not. She was a bit nervous about being called in—especially in light of her meeting this morning with Costa and Granderson. *And Kara Quinn.*

"This whole thing is a mess, and if LAPD were smart, they would let us take over. They've spent countless hours protecting Detective Quinn from any real scrutiny. Bryce opened an investigation into her after the Chen situation because her actions were deplorable, but it got shut down before we could interview her, and then Bryce was pulled into an OPR hearing. It was, frankly, a complete surprise."

She paused, then said, "Between you and me, I think he's too close to this. He can't be objective when it comes to Detective Quinn. They've crossed paths before. LAPD Internal Affairs used to be competent, now they are very selective in who they reprimand."

"I feel a bit out of my depth, ma'am. Would you like to task another agent to assist on this?"

"No, you're perfect. Because you have absolutely no loyalties or previous experience with LAPD, you're a much-needed objective observer. I'm going to contact LAPD and request coordination with this investigation, and if they don't grant it, we might have to play hardball. It'll be a good lesson for you."

Elena Gomez slammed down the phone. "I don't fucking believe this!" she screamed to no one. She was alone in her office.

She was in command and her temper could get her in trouble. She took a deep breath, let it out.

Fucking FBI.

Was that why Matt Costa had called her earlier? Did he know they were flexing muscle? Was he involved?

She hadn't gotten that vibe from him, and she didn't think that Kara would have sung his praises if he was a prick. Maybe he had been trying to give her a heads-up. That still didn't calm her anger.

She strode down the hall to her commander's office. "Commander," she said as soon as Joe Campana waved her in, "I just got a call from the FBI that they want Chen's investigation— well, she said she wanted to 'coordinate a task force'—" she used air quotes "—but you know damn well that means she wants to be in charge."

"What's their reasoning?" Campana asked calmly, a telltale pulse in his neck the only outward sign of his frustration.

"That *we* have a conflict of interest. Our office initially arrested Chen, our detective is the primary witness, Detective Quinn made a verbal threat against him and there had been a *pending* federal investigation, other assorted bullshit."

"A threat?" Campana looked confused. "Quinn? I don't remember that."

"The press played it nonstop for a couple news cycles, when Quinn was caught saying on another officer's body cam that she wished he'd broken his neck when he fell off the roof."

Campana couldn't stifle the smile that rose on his hangdog face. "She was slapped for that, I remember now. I also remember that she'd been stabbed in the back, was in pain and lost a lot of blood. I don't think it should be held against her now."

"The FBI will hold anything and everything against Quinn," Elena said. "They also want a formal interview."

"About what?"

"Where she was. I told those pricks she had a solid alibi. I did not give in to their request, but they're going to push."

"Push back. I'll talk to the chief. They should have called me, not you. Who was it?"

"ASAC Rebecca Chavez."

"She's not in violent crimes, is she?"

"No, something in White Collar. Her squad had been investigating Chen for the feds."

Though the FBI was divided into squads that each had their own specialties, there was a lot of overlap. If a suspect in cyberterrorism, for example, committed a violent crime, the cyberterrorism unit would still handle the investigation. Elena had never figured out how the FBI office worked—all she knew was that they were a huge bureaucracy and seemed to have unlimited funds to make LAPD's life miserable.

"Keep working it," Campana said. "And Quinn might have to go in and give a statement, but it's our case, the FBI is *not* getting it. Clear?"

"Very."

"Close the door," he ordered.

She did.

"What's the status of Operation Sunshine?"

Other than the chief of police himself, Joe Campana was the only senior officer who knew about their deep undercover operation into the homeless grant process at city hall that had benefited David Chen and others. Because there was at least one bad cop involved, they all had to be extremely careful with who was read into the program.

It had been Campana's call to use Colton's shooting and fake his death—Colton had no family and he was at risk of someone else coming after him once the FBI had, allegedly, exposed him and Quinn to the media. Colton knew this would most likely be his last undercover investigation. He didn't care. If they could prove what they suspected, it would rip apart Los Angeles government at the roots.

In fact, this might be the last case for all of them. They were not only investigating a bad cop, but corrupt politicians. If they didn't get each and every one of them, their heads might be on the proverbial chopping block—and they knew it.

"Violet Halliday is missing. Colton is looking for her, Will is waiting for her to call again. Detective Caprese, who's running the Chen homicide investigation, wants to talk to Violet as a witness. The longer she's missing, the more they are going to look at her as a suspect or accomplice." She didn't have to state the obvious: if Caprese attempted to pull a warrant, they'd have to read him into the investigation.

"Why would she run?" Campana asked.

"Fear," Elena said. "Craig worked with her more than anyone, but he's been quiet the last couple weeks. Maybe she heard that he was killed and she's scared for her life. The girl is a computer nerd, this has to be completely foreign to her."

"What's happening now with the grand jury?"

"I don't know," she admitted. "It's up to the DA. I didn't know until yesterday that he planned to impanel the grand jury this week. I didn't think he had enough, but now? I'm pretty sure he was holding something back."

"Why would he shut us out? We've given him some of our best people, our resources, *months* of time in this investigation."

Campana was angry. She didn't blame him, but she also suspected they didn't know the whole story.

"I think," she said cautiously, "that he may have been worried about a mole in the DA's office."

"And he didn't give you any idea who it might be?"

"If I knew, I'd bring them in for questioning." She didn't want to put Colton on the hot seat, but her undercover asset had also changed over the last couple months. "Two months ago, we met with Halliday. She proved that the computer crash was deliberate and that specific files were extracted and then when the backups were installed, those files were gone. It takes a lot of skill to remove data from backups. Someone as good as Halliday, at a minimum. I think she found those files, and that's why Craig called the grand jury."

"Yet he didn't tell you or Lex."

She shook her head.

Campana swore. "This is a clusterfuck, Elena. Did you read Quinn in?"

"No. She and Matt Costa know that I was working with Craig on an investigation into housing grants, but she doesn't know about the undercover operation. I did, however, tell them that we believe someone in the FBI alerted Chen to the raid through the interagency portal."

Campana leaned back in his seat, looked at the ceiling quietly for ten seconds. Then he said, "Okay, this is what we do. We find Halliday, put her in a safe house, debrief her. What she knows, we know. When you feel Quinn and her feds need to know about Operation Sunshine, read them in. I know it'll be difficult, considering, but we might need help to wrap this up."

"And," Elena emphasized, "keep the Chen murder investigation in-house."

"No way am I turning that over to the feds, not when their own house is dirty. I need to talk to the chief."

That was the signal for her to leave. She did, relieved that Campana had her back, but worried about the state of their investigation with Craig dead and Violet still missing.

Elena pulled out her private cell phone and called Colton. He didn't answer.

She ended the call without leaving a message.

SEPTEMBER

One Month Ago

21

The park cleanup in Venice Beach was a disaster.

Protesters from a harm reduction advocacy group launched a verbal assault against Will and First Contact, accusing us of stealing from the homeless. Will countered that he had permission from the people who lived in the park to help them clean up their garbage. The protesters opposed Will's nine-step plan to end the homeless crisis, but mostly they objected to interfering with what they called "free will."

The first step in Will's plan was to make contact—find out who each person was, their name, their background. Basically—what was their story. The second step was to find out where they were at—if they used drugs, how long, if they were on medication, if they needed medical care, if they had identification (necessary to get into virtually any housing program), if they needed help to fill out government forms for disability or Medicare.

Everyone was different, but the stories were remarkably similar. The majority of the people living on the streets had been abused as children. Depending on which statistics you read, up to 67 percent were addicted to drugs or alcohol or were mentally ill—but working with them every day, Will put the number closer to 90 percent who had a history of addiction. The only way to get them off the streets permanently and teach them to become self-sufficient was to address their problems head-on and help them take ownership over their lives. Will had done it over and over and over again, but it wasn't easy. It was time-consuming and frustrating. The government put more hurdles on success than anyone.

It was especially frustrating when I looked across the boulevard from the park we were cleaning and saw the four-story, 170-unit transitional housing project that was being built with a grant to Angel Homes.

Each unit, once completed, cost $1.1 million to build. Subsidized housing would be available for the homeless and those living below the poverty line—benefiting only 170 people. Two hundred million dollars wasted.

All I could think about was how far two hundred million dollars would go if the city spent it on actual affordable housing, real rehabilitation to help people not only get clean but stay clean. Job training, mental health screening, teaching people who had been living on the street for years real skills so they were empowered over their own lives. It was clear that the city could construct a far greater number of units at a much lower cost, but doing so would not benefit the personal interests of campaign contributors, politicians, contractors and the bureaucrats who served them.

It made me sick. I knew what was happening and felt like David battling Goliath, but I didn't even have a rock for my slingshot.

I was doing *something*, but it never seemed to be enough. Each week I came closer to figuring out how to locate the files deleted in the computer crash. I *would* find them, but would it be soon enough? I feared that Craig Dyson and the others were becoming frustrated at how slow and laborious the process was. I had given them details on the nonprofits involved, but didn't have the financial documentation between the city and the nonprofits.

Craig assured me that his office was digging into the publicly reported financial records of each entity and that everything I had provided was a piece to the puzzle. But we still couldn't see the whole picture.

Will was talking civilly to one of the protesters who started swearing at him. I didn't know how he could remain so calm, so reasonable. How he could tolerate being yelled at by people who disagreed with his solution. I didn't see them picking up trash; I didn't see them talking to the homeless. I doubted they even knew the name of one person who lived on the streets.

I continued to pick up garbage. I didn't like confrontations. Will came out here often, but I didn't. I didn't know most of the people living in this park. I introduced myself, asked them if they had any garbage they wanted me to take away. Some ignored me. Some helped me.

"Do you have an extra bag?" a familiar voice said.

I turned to face Colton Fox. He was filthy, but his teeth were still too clean. He got away with it because he didn't smile, didn't show people he had a complete set of straight, white teeth. Sunglasses shielded his eyes.

I handed him a bag. "I haven't seen you all month."

"Busy," he said. "I gave some stuff to Will when he got here. Good stuff. Go through it. Pictures. People I don't know. Some documents I found in the trash."

Somehow, I didn't believe that. Not that he hadn't found documents, but I wondered what rules—what laws—he might have broken to get them.

I realized then that I didn't care. I didn't care if Colton Fox broke every law if he found evidence of what these people were doing.

"The woman in the blue tent over there," he said and jerked his head to the right, "between the two palm trees?"

I glanced over. "Yeah?"

"Her name is Sissy. She knows your mom. She won't tell me anything, but she knows her. Maybe you can find out where she went. I've been here a week and haven't seen her."

I swallowed nervously. "Thank you."

I waited until the other volunteers left, then told Will what Colton said. He was tired, angry with the protesters, frustrated that they had impacted his work. But he still went over to the tent with me, and I was grateful.

"You talk to her," Will whispered as we approached. "I'm here for you."

Sissy was sitting on a broken chair next to the tent in the shade of a short palm tree. She watched us suspiciously. She appeared to be in her midthirties, wore heavy pants and a flannel shirt over a T-shirt. Her short, frizzy red hair stood up in tufts, her scalp mostly visible.

"Hi, Sissy?" I said. "My name is Violet, and this is my friend Will."

She eyed us, chin up. I could hear her breathing, a raspy, shallow sound. Her pupils were pinpoints and she had hollow cheeks, as if she were malnourished. Several square foils littered her space, all of them burned through the center. A fentanyl addict.

My heart broke. The drug was going to kill her if she didn't stop.

"You from the gov'ment?"

"No, ma'am," I said. "We're with First Contact, a volunteer group. We helped clean up the park today, helped some of your friends here with whatever they needed."

"You have some blues?" Blues, fenty, dragon, jack, TNT—fentanyl went by dozens of different names.

"No, I don't."

"Then I don't need your help. Come back with blues."

"One of your friends here—"

"I don't have no friends. No one here is my friend. You lyin' to me."

"I won't lie to you. The white guy with the beard, wears an Army jacket with a flag patch?"

"Colt. Yeah. I know him. He's not a friend. You with the gov'ment trying to fuck him over?"

"No. I'm trying to help him like we're trying to help others here." I was losing her. Her eyes darted around, and she was on the verge of bolting.

Will whispered, "You got this, Vi. Speak the truth."

He said that often, to "speak the truth" because so often social workers or volunteers lied to the homeless. Promised one thing, didn't deliver. Came by with food, but no real help.

I squatted next to her. She smelled of urine, but I resisted stepping back. "I'm looking for my mother. Her name is Jane. She's in her fifties, has blond hair but it's mostly gray. Hazel eyes like mine." She looked like anyone, I thought. "She had this really heavy fake fur coat, dark red, she always has it with her. And a scar on her cheek." I traced my finger along my cheekbone to mimic where my mom had been cut by a junkie two years ago.

"Jane," Sissy said, scratching the back of her neck.

"Yes. Colt said you knew her."

"I remember her."

"She was here?"

Sissy shrugged. "Here, gone."

I blinked back tears I didn't want to shed. "Did she say where she planned to go? She doesn't have a car. Maybe she went down the beach?"

"No, she's gone gone. Forever gone."

"No," I said before I realized the word came out of my mouth.

"Sorry," she said and closed her eyes.

I didn't move. I wanted to shake this woman and scream at her to tell me what happened to my mother.

Will pulled me up, and I whirled around and pushed him away. "What does that mean? What the fuck does forever mean?"

"Let's go."

"I have to find her!"

"Please," he said quietly.

I looked at Will and saw compassion, not pity. Understanding, not frustration. I followed him.

Will didn't take me home. Instead, he drove to the Los Angeles County Morgue. I didn't want to go in.

"All the dead pass through here," he said. "Either she's here or she isn't. If you'd rather not know, I'll take you home."

I got out of the car without saying anything. Followed Will to the main entrance. He rang a bell before someone opened the door. "Thank you, Shelley," Will said to the woman who answered.

Shelley was in her fifties, petite, with short gray hair and eyes to match. She wore scrubs. I realized then that the morgue was closed to the public on Saturdays, but Will knew someone who worked here—someone who was willing to do him this favor.

"We're looking for Violet's mother. She may not have been identified."

"What's the name?" Shelley asked as she walked around to a desk and sat in front of a computer.

"Halliday," I said with a croak. I spelled the name. "Jane Elizabeth Halliday."

"No one by that name here."

"Do you have an unidentified homeless female in her fifties?" Will said. "She wouldn't have been here longer than two months." They kept John and Jane Does in the crypt for one year before burying them in a county plot.

She typed. "I have four that meet that criteria."

"Can we look?"

"Give me a few minutes, okay?"

"Of course."

I sat heavily on one of the two plastic chairs in the small lobby. "Oh, God. I can't do this."

"Yes you can, Violet. I'm here for you. You know that, right?"

Tears burned but didn't fall.

"You did everything you could for your mother."

"I should have done more."

Will sat next to me. Took my limp hand. "There was nothing more you could have done," he said. "You can't force people to get help. If you can't accept that truth, you can't work with me."

"Everyone else? I accept it. But she's my mom. My *mom*..."

I jumped when Shelley returned. "Follow me," she said and led the way down a long, cool corridor. We turned once, then at the end of that hall Shelley used her card key to unlock wide double doors. They swooshed open. "Is your mother white?" Shelley asked.

I didn't answer her. I looked at the huge room filled with stainless steel drawers that held the dead. They were eight high, and a rolling ladder was used to access the higher levels. There were rows and rows of bodies on gurneys, covered with sheets.

"Yes," Will answered for me. He took my hand, held it tight. "That eliminates two of the four. We'll start here."

She pulled out a drawer on the bottom near the middle of the first row. I stared and my bottom lip quivered. A strangled sound escaped; I couldn't speak.

Will said, "That's Jane Halliday."

I turned and buried my face in Will's chest.

Shelley let me wash in the employee's bathroom. Then we sat down in her cubicle and she brought up the file. She changed the records to confirm identity and next of kin, and asked what I would like to do.

I didn't know what she meant. "Do what?"

"I can give you a couple of days to make arrangements. You should contact a funeral home—they will claim the body. You need to decide if you want her remains cremated or buried. You can talk to the funeral home about costs of each and what kind of service you'd like."

"I don't know," I said.

"Like I said, I can give you some time to make these decisions. I know it's difficult."

"How?"

"I can give you a list of funeral homes."

"I mean, how did she die?"

Shelley looked at the file. "She was found unresponsive on the beach in Venice Beach. Medics were called, but they were unable to revive her. The autopsy showed she died of hypoxia. That means—"

"I know what it means," I said with more anger than I wanted.

Opioid users who overdose don't get enough oxygen, go into a coma and die. Narcan can save them if administered soon enough, but when you're riding high or with others who are too high to notice, you simply lie down and die.

Addicts that have been resuscitated even once by Narcan and go back to using have a thirteen times greater chance of dying within a year. My mother was now part of that statistic.

"When?" I asked. "When was she found?"

"Her body was brought to us August 20. Two and a half weeks ago."

I should have looked harder for her. I should have done more. I should have been a better daughter, a better friend, a better person.

Now she was gone. Forever gone.

The system had failed her.

I had failed her. No matter what Will told me, I would never accept that I couldn't have done more.

She was my mom.

TUESDAY, OCTOBER 8

22

Kara had convinced Michael that she needed to track down Tom Lee. Something was very strange about how he was still on duty when the other known officials who'd been bought off were out of the picture. Now was the easiest time in the history of LAPD to get rid of a corrupt cop, so why let him stay?

She'd been thinking about it all night.

It didn't take her long to learn Lee was on shift from 5 a.m. to 3 p.m., so they waited outside the precinct, arriving at two thirty.

They sat in silence for a while, then Michael said, "You never told me what happened the day your informant was killed. Did you suspect the FBI had leaked it to Chen?"

"I knew someone had leaked to him, but I didn't even think it could be the FBI. I assumed it was someone in LAPD."

"Like Lee."

"Yeah. Except I didn't suspect him. He wasn't there. Apparently, Elena had doubts so moved him before the raid, but I didn't know that until yesterday."

"What happened that day?"

"You really want to know?"

He nodded.

Kara didn't like talking about it, but this was Michael, her partner. And if you couldn't trust your partner, who could you trust?

So she told him everything.

Kara had built the case over nearly a year, spent eight months undercover with a big-box store and finally had enough to nail David Chen, his asshole bodyguard and a half dozen others who were complicit in keeping human beings as slaves. What else would she call the nearly three hundred girls and women—and a few old men—he'd illegally trafficked from China to work in his sweatshop? They were not free to leave—they lived in an apartment building Chen owned—and they weren't free to find work elsewhere. They worked fourteen-hour days in a business he ran, and based on the books Sunny had obtained for her, it would take each person eighty years to "pay off" what Chen said they owed him.

Chen's tyranny would end today.

Knowing she had to be up before five in order to stage with SWAT and a dozen cops, she stayed at Colton's small house in Echo Park, much closer to Chinatown than her Santa Monica condo.

The sex was an added bonus.

For the last two weeks Colton had helped with the case by playing the part of a homeless drunk sleeping in an alley with line of sight on the shipping doors. He'd put the final pieces together—documenting shipments, individuals, schedules. So, they were having an early celebration. They didn't work together often, and they hadn't hooked up in months, so it was a nice evening.

He woke her up at 4:30 a.m.

"I have to bolt, need to build my next cover," he said. "I made coffee."

"You're a god," she muttered, stretching.

He chuckled, kissed her. "Hardly. See you when I close the next case." And he left.

Kara didn't know then that it would be the last time she saw him. He'd be murdered three weeks later after his cover was blown by the media.

She drank coffee, ate a banana that was a couple days over-ripe and was heading to the precinct when her cell phone rang. It was her undercover cell, and she glanced at the number.

Sunny.

She answered. "Yep," she said neutrally. Sunny knew it was happening today. She was supposed to stay in her apartment until Kara got her.

Kara tensed when she heard machinery in the background. What was Sunny doing at the factory?

"He knows," she whispered, and the phone went dead.

Kara pressed the gas and called Sunny back—no answer. She then called Lex. "Kara, I'm on my way, sh—"

"Chen knows we're coming. My informant is at the ware-house. She's in danger."

"Fuck. Okay, meet me—"

"No! Activate SWAT now. We can't wait."

"Dammit, Kara, you can't go in alone!"

"I'm going to stake it out, see what's going on, try to make contact with her. I'm not going to be reckless, Lex, but I can't wait two hours!"

The plan was to stage at 0600, raid at 0700, based on the intel that Kara and Colton had put together.

"Don't get dead."

"No plans to die today. Me, or Sunny."

She ended the call, sent Lex her tracking information so he could see her movements in real time and headed to Chinatown.

Chen owned two square blocks in Chinatown. Street-side he ran shops that catered mostly to tourists; in the back was a network of warehouses where his slaves worked. All trafficked from Shandong in China, all threatened that their families would be killed if they disobeyed, talked or ran.

Except Sunny. Sunny learned from a new arrival that her only relative, her mother, had died, and now Sunny had no one. When Kara approached her, at first she didn't want to help. Terrified for her life. But she was sad, lonely, desperate and angry, and Kara pushed.

Kara had a way of getting people to work against their own self-interest. And over time, she turned Sunny, pulled her in. Without Sunny, Kara would never have been able to build the case against David Chen.

Kara parked her beat-up undercover car in an alley. She was dressed in tactical pants and a Kevlar vest over a black T-shirt. She pulled a larger T-shirt, this one dark gray, over her vest as she walked.

She knew the secret way into the main factory where Sunny worked. Down the alley, through a nondescript door that had no outside knob, but a hidden panel revealed a code box. Sunny had uncovered the code six weeks ago, and that was when the case began to steamroll.

Before Kara entered, she texted Lex and informed him of her plans. She pocketed her phone before he responded, knowing he'd order her to stand down. If she didn't see the order, she wasn't disobeying.

Most of the workers hadn't yet come in. In fact, while she heard the machines, Kara saw no one.

The facility made clothing—designer knockoffs that were sold in the shops on the street, and generic brands sold to big-box stores. Stamped with a big fucking *Made in the USA* but nowhere did the stamp also admit that the clothes were sewn by trafficked Chinese nationals who made no money for their labor.

Kara headed down narrow metal steps into the basement, where a hall led to the main floor. With the help of Sunny, Kara had been here before to take photos and copy documents. Sunny knew how to avoid or temporarily disable the security cameras. She was a smart girl who deserved more than life had handed her. She had to be okay.

Over the hum of the old machinery, Kara heard no voices. As she proceeded down the faintly lit corridor, glancing into each dark room as she passed by, she still saw no one. Empty. Empty. Empty.

She walked briskly but cautiously, all her senses in tune with her surroundings. Sounds. Movement. Smells. She heard voices in the main factory room, followed by a stifled scream.

Then silence, except the damn machines.

Kara stopped. A plastic sheet blocked the doorway, obscuring her view. She listened, wishing she knew who was in there, what they were doing, if it was Sunny and if she was in danger.

A clamoring sound of falling metal had Kara running onto the factory floor, gun drawn.

At first she didn't see anyone. Machines took up the center of the building—she had no idea what they did. More than a hundred sewing machines were set up in rows along the far wall, though no one was working now.

Keeping her gun close to her body to avoid someone jumping out at her and grabbing it, she ran down a narrow hall toward where she heard the sound. A scream echoed in the cavernous room followed by two gunshots.

Kara ran around the machine and saw David Chen racing down the hall opposite from where she'd entered.

"Stop! Police!" Kara shouted.

He didn't stop.

On the filthy cement floor, Sunny lay in a pool of her own blood. She was gut shot and at first Kara thought she was alive.

She ran over, pulled off her shirt and pressed it on the wound. "Stay with me, Sunny!"

Kara pressed on the wound with one hand, pulled out her phone with the other and called 911. As she demanded an ambulance she saw the blood in Sunny's hair.

He'd shot her in the head. She couldn't find a pulse. She couldn't feel Sunny's heartbeat.

Sunny was dead. Kara didn't hesitate—she jumped up and ran after David Chen, biting back a scream of rage bubbling in her lungs.

He would not get away with murder.

He'd gone up a staircase that she had seen on the map Sunny had drawn for her. The stairs went up three stories to the roof. As she pursued, a metal door clanged against the wall.

She took the steps two, three at a time, never slowing. She burst out of the door, barely hesitating except for her training telling her to pause, assess.

Chen was near the edge of the roof. She heard sirens all around, but Chen was here because he had an escape plan.

"Police!" she shouted. "Stop, keep your hands where I can see them!"

Chen didn't stop, and he didn't turn toward her. He ran, jumped from his roof to the adjoining building. It was only a ten-foot gap. She pursued, rolling as she landed, then popped up and followed.

Shoot him. He killed Sunny!

She couldn't shoot him in the back. If he turned to her, she would fire. If he just turned to face her, she would kill him. He was evil, a monster who didn't deserve to breathe the same air as the women he exploited.

Turn and face me, you coward!

He ran, leaped to another roof, this opening narrower than the one before, and she followed, gaining on him, but not fast enough. The sun was just starting to break through the morning. Security lighting on the street barely reached the rooftops. The sirens were louder, and she could see whirling lights—the cavalry was almost here...

But Sunny was dead.

One more roof and he would be able to disappear into the heart of Chinatown. There were dozens of ways he could escape. She couldn't let that happen.

She'd been slowly gaining, now only twenty feet away. He spared a look over his shoulder and then everything happened so fast.

He tripped over a vent and went sprawling...down, over the edge of the roof. She sprinted, her breath labored, and saw him spread-eagled two stories below, his leg at an unnatural angle. She was about to pull out her phone and call it in when a burning pain in her back had her grunt out a scream.

She turned and fired her gun at a large Asian man as she saw him reach into his waistband. Xavier Fan, Chen's bodyguard. She fired three times and he went down.

She fell to her knees. She hadn't heard a gunshot—but the pain told her she'd been hit. She turned her head best she could and saw the hilt of a knife that had barely missed her vest.

She called Lex as she lay down on her stomach. She didn't dare pull out the knife.

"Quinn! Where the fuck are you? Quinn!"

"Roof. Three buildings south. Chen tripped, fell to the street. Officer down."

"He shot you? Dammit, talk!"

"Fan—knife. I'm woozy. Fan is down. I need, fuck. Damn fucking hospitals."

She was losing consciousness. "Sunny," she muttered. "Chen killed her. I was too late."

Michael didn't say anything when she was done with her story. She didn't tell him everything—he didn't need to know, for example, that she'd been sleeping with Colton or that it was the last night she'd seen her partner before he was killed. But she told him about finding Sunny dead, chasing Chen, wanting to kill him but not being able to shoot him in the back.

"You did the right thing," he said.

"Did I? All this would have been over eight months ago if I had killed him."

"Shooting a man in the back as he's fleeing—"

"Fleeing? Running because he killed a woman in cold blood."

"You're lucky the knife didn't kill you."

"Yeah. And for my trouble, the FBI almost let Chen walk because I apparently violated his civil rights. He claimed I targeted him because he was a Chinese American, and Bryce Thornton was happy to believe it." She paused. "Sorry. I guess I'm still angry about the whole thing."

"I would be, too."

"And there he is," Kara said, watching Lee's patrol vehicle drive through the gate. They were sitting across the street. She would wait until he came out in his personal car—a late model Acura—and then she'd call him. "This is going to be fun."

Michael groaned. "Really, Kara, you and I need to discuss your definition of fun."

Tom agreed to meet with them at a pub well outside of his precinct. Though he was twenty minutes late, Kara didn't doubt that he would come. She'd told him she'd show up at his house and make a spectacle if he bailed on her.

Tom Lee was a short, stocky cop of Chinese heritage. Kara had known him, but not well—they didn't run in the same circles, didn't work the same cases.

He eyed Michael with suspicion.

"Michael Harris, my partner."

"You're not LAPD," Tom said.

"FBI," Michael said.

"Shit."

"Sit," she told him. "This is off the record. For the next ten minutes, you have immunity. Besides, we haven't read you your rights."

Michael was obviously uncomfortable, but she ignored that. She knew she couldn't offer Tom Lee anything official, but she could offer him the freedom to walk away tonight.

She needed answers.

She said to Tom, "I know why you were transferred, what I don't know is why you aren't sitting in prison right now."

Suddenly, Michael got up. "I'm going to sit at the bar," he said and walked away.

She was surprised, but grateful. He sat at the end where he could watch both her and the door.

"I thought it was just for show, you going over to the FBI," Tom said, looking over at Michael. He gulped his beer.

"Nope, I've been working my ass off for them. The real deal."

"Is DC as bad as LA?"

"I wouldn't know. My boss runs the Mobile Response Team, so we've been all over the country. My team is solid. I don't care about anyone else."

Still, Tom had one eye on Michael.

"I had a long talk with Lieutenant Gomez last night," Kara said. "She didn't confirm or deny that you were on Chen's payroll, but you were. And then you were transferred here right before the raid. I thought about this half the night, and my guess is you're still on somebody's payroll and feeding Gomez information."

"Why don't you ask her? Didn't she train you? Aren't you two besties?"

The snide comment had no place in this conversation, so Kara ignored it.

"I'm asking you."

He didn't say anything. She leaned back, sipped her beer.

"Craig Dyson is dead," she said conversationally. "I was there. It was a professional hit, no doubt about it. Chen? Not quite as professional but the killer took out the security cameras before he shot Chen on the street and walked away. It was a bold attack downtown when it would have been a hundred times easier killing him in the parking garage or his house or in the middle of a fucking restaurant. That tells me the killer wanted the splash to send a message or to force the courthouse into lockdown or any number of things. There had to be a reason because it was stupid."

"It's not stupid if he gets away with it," Tom commented.

True, she thought. "So when Elena confirmed, more or less, that you were feeding her information, I was trying to think why. Here's my guess. You were caught taking bribes from Chen while I was undercover. You were moved to the north division only a week before the raid. Tell me why I should believe you're not the one who leaked the raid to Chen. You must have suspected something."

"I saw you on-site months before. If I wanted to fuck with your operation, I would have told Chen you were a cop when you were pretending to be a clothing buyer."

"Why didn't you?"

He didn't answer right away. He sipped his beer, looked down at his napkin as if something super interesting was written there. Then he looked her in the eye. "I took money from Chen to ignore what he was doing. To make reports disappear, to stay on that beat. To look the other way, you'd probably say. But I'd never set up a cop. Chen would have killed you, and I couldn't live with that. So I kept my mouth shut."

There were so many problems with Tom's attitude, but Kara didn't comment. She forced herself not to think about the women trapped in servitude, or Sunny murdered in cold blood. She blocked out the pain and suffering and inhumanity of Chen's actions, which Kara placed firmly on Tom's shoulders.

"How did Elena find out?" she asked.

"Not exactly sure. She might have been fishing, just suspicious, but when she confronted me, I admitted it. I suspected the raid was going to be coming down sooner rather than later. She told me she was moving me to the north division and for me to keep my mouth shut. That I would be called upon to testify against Chen and anyone else they caught during or after this investigation. If Chen reached out and asked why I had been transferred, I was to say that North Valley was short-staffed and I had no say about it. If anyone else reached out to me, I was supposed to call Gomez. After the raid, she fully debriefed me—I told her everything I knew. I kept expecting the shit to hit the fan, but it never did.

"Then, a couple weeks ago, Gomez and Dyson came to my house. Sunday night, my wife was making dinner. I thought this was it, I was being arrested in front of my family. I felt sick and disgusted with myself. But they didn't arrest me. They said that they were in the middle of a major undercover investigation stemming from Chen and wanted to know if I had seen any specific people with Chen at any time. They showed me a bunch of pictures."

"And?"

"I pointed out several people I recognized. I only knew the name of one—an inspector for the city named Connie. I didn't know her last name. She came by the warehouse several times over the years. But I also recognized a man—didn't know his name—who had been to the apartment building where Chen's workers lived. He came by several times. I had no idea why, never asked."

Elena had withheld a lot more information than Kara had thought.

"Then what happened?"

"They told me to just keep doing what I was doing and I would be called in front of a grand jury to testify within the next few months. If I kept clean and told the complete truth to the grand jury, I could keep my pension. If I lied, I would be prosecuted." He finished his beer. "I don't expect you to forgive me, Quinn. I don't really care if you do. I did what I did, and there are cops who do far worse than me. I was just riding out my time in a thankless job and making a little green on the side. I have fifteen years on the force. I won't get my full pension—they'll make me leave early, after the hearing—but at least I'll have something for my wife and kids, and no black marks on my record so I can get another job. Until then? I'm doing what Gomez ordered—staying clean, keeping my head down and telling her everything I know."

23

Kara drove straight to LAPD headquarters. She'd told Michael everything Tom had said, and he didn't think she should confront Elena right now. She considered his advice, dismissed it. There were too many things kept from her about *her* investigation. Why shut her out? Had she fucked up and no one wanted to tell her?

Nothing made sense and it wouldn't until she knew everything, and that started at the top.

"You can come with me," she began.

"I'll wait here. I'll call Matt, let him know what's going on."

"Thanks."

He reached out, touched her arm. "Take five minutes to calm down, okay? More flies with honey."

"I'm fine," she said.

Still, she took several deep, cleansing breaths in the elevator and felt calmer when she reached Elena's office.

It was the ten minutes she had to wait for Elena that had her anger building again.

One look at her and Elena swore under her breath. "Come in." She picked up her phone and a moment later said, "I need you in my office."

"Lex," Kara guessed.

"Sit."

"No."

"Kara—"

"I want the truth. All of it. Starting with why you didn't tell me Tom Lee, a dirty cop, knew I was undercover with Chen."

"Lee didn't rat you out. He knew almost from the beginning—"

"He knew about Chen's operation—all of it—and looked the other way for a price. He's a liar who sullied the badge, and you believe that he didn't tell Chen about the raid?"

"There are a lot of reasons why I believe him, including information he has passed on to us over the last few months."

"You've kept me in the dark—"

"You weren't even here."

"Before I left you knew about Lee and you didn't tell me. Before I left, you knew that the FBI portal may have been the leak and you didn't tell me. Craig had investigations into multiple people stemming from my operation *and you didn't fucking tell me!*"

Lex walked in, quickly shut the door.

"I had no obligation to tell you anything, Detective," Elena said. "If you have a problem with my command, you can take it up with your union rep."

Kara wanted to hit something; she didn't. She looked at Lex, saw the guilt in his eyes before he turned away. "So I should just turn in my badge and walk away from all of you?"

"Sit."

She didn't want to. God, she wanted to pace, hit something, slap her boss. That wasn't going to get her anywhere, so she sat.

Elena walked around her desk and sat at the small table across from Kara. Lex took one of the guest chairs, turned it around to sit. None of them seemed comfortable with the silence. But Kara waited. She stared at Elena and waited for words. She didn't know if she could believe anything her boss said, but she waited.

Elena spoke first.

"I'm not going to tell you all the reasons why we decided to keep Tom Lee in uniform, because they are complex and layered and confidential. I will tell you that he has performed satisfactorily since he was confronted with evidence of his crimes, and he has provided much-needed information about Chen's operation that has helped Dyson build a case against multiple people—all of whom have either pled or been given conditional probation. Several are in jail today. Lee wasn't privy to any of the inner workings of Chen's operation, but he saw a lot, and he has identified key people for us, people we've continued to investigate. Lee is required, under the terms of his sealed agreement, to testify in front of the grand jury and be available at trial. Provided that he is truthful, he will not be prosecuted."

"Whoop-de-do," Kara muttered.

Elena bristled, then said, "Craig's death has hit all of us hard. He'd been dogged in his pursuit of the truth, and he felt we had enough to go to the grand jury—"

"Against *who*? Who are you trying to get indictments on?"

"It was a grand jury to open an investigation into the city's grant approval process, specifically grants for homeless services and housing."

"So, not against a person, just a loose entity of government bureaucrats?"

"We believe that the grant and contracting process is corrupt, that it's used to benefit the friends and family of government officials. Craig believed he could prove fraud to the tune of hundreds of millions of dollars. The city spends one billion dollars a year on the homeless crisis. One billion a year, every year, with little to no accountability."

Kara was now confused. "What does that have to do with

Chen? Is this about the apartment building he owned? Craig mentioned he got government money for it."

"That's what jump-started his interest. Chen applied for and received a ten-million-dollar grant to house immigrants from China."

"Wait," Kara said, "Chen illegally brought hundreds of Chinese women and teenagers into the country and the city gave him money to put them up in housing so they could work for him for free?"

"Yes."

"And that's not enough to go after whoever approved it?"

"There was nothing illegal about the application or the process. What would be illegal is if the individual approving the grant application received a kickback, or if they knew that the apartment was going to house trafficked women. But it's bigger than Chen. This money isn't tracked well, it's handed out to nonprofits who have no requirement to document success. No transparency. Some may be doing good work. Others could be pocketing every dime and we wouldn't know."

"And this is what Violet Halliday was helping with? Because she works for the city, knows these things?"

"Yes, in part," Elena said. "She's a computer expert who rebuilt the crashed city hall system and intended to testify to the grand jury about what happened and prove—at least, that's what we hoped—that the crash was intentional in order to hide corruption at the highest levels of city government."

"I have no idea what you're talking about. What computer crash? What does that have to do with human trafficking or housing grants or anything?"

"Someone intentionally crashed city hall the same day as our raid on Chen," Lex said. "Violet is the one who figured it out—and she has been working on rebuilding the destroyed system and finding the files that disappeared when the system was rebooted."

Kara hated computers and technology, but she understood the gist of the issue. Violet was smart. She knew things. Information that Craig needed to prosecute.

"And now she's missing," Lex continued. "We're looking for her, Will Lattimer is looking for her. With Chen and Craig dead, she's the only one who knows those files exist and the only one who may be able to find them."

"Then she's in danger," Kara said. "She could already be dead. You had her working for you? She's not trained, and she's not a cop. She's a computer whiz, that's it. And you put her undercover?"

"She's a whistleblower. Works for the city and reporting on fraud and corruption," Lex said.

"And she witnessed Chen's murder! She's hiding or already dead." Kara couldn't believe that they sounded so nonchalant about what they had Violet Halliday doing.

"This is getting us nowhere," Elena said.

"I want to know what else is going on. Who are you investigating? What happened after I left LA? Who do you have undercover?"

"I can't tell you that," Elena said. "And even if I could, I don't know that I would. You came in here accusing me of letting a dirty cop walk, and I resent that. Craig's murder might jeopardize every single case stemming from Chen's arrest. Every one of them! Eight months of work—undercover, investigatory, field work, grunt work. We've put in hundreds of man-hours since the raid. Do you think I don't feel like the weight of the world is crashing down?"

Kara had never seen Elena this upset about anything. Angry, sure, but she was truly upset.

"Then read me in. Bring me into the operation. Fresh eyes—you know me, you know I'm an asset."

"I can't—not now."

"Bullshit."

"I can't because the FBI is tugging on the Chen murder investigation and they want to interview you. If you're under suspicion of a crime, any case you're working could be tossed."

"That's bullshit. I was nowhere near Chen when he was killed. You know it."

"Apparently my verification of your alibi isn't good enough for the feds."

"You can't be serious." Kara itched to pace; she forced herself to remain seated.

"They think LAPD has a conflict of interest," Elena continued, sounding calmer, "and they mentioned your comment that you wished Chen had broken his neck when he fell."

"Is this Bryce Thornton? This is a joke—he can't come after me. I know for a fact that the FBI's IA, whatever they call themselves, told him he couldn't investigate me for anything."

"ASAC Rebecca Chavez. I don't know her, but she's the one pushing. Called me, Campana talked to her, now the chief thinks we need to play nice. We're not giving her the Chen homicide, but I have to sit down and tell her what I know."

"Which is?"

"The cameras weren't working. We have multiple witnesses with conflicting stories. We have a cop who was across the street, didn't see the shooting itself, but saw Violet Halliday running from the scene. Multiple people saw her—she was carrying something. One person thought it was a gun. One person thought it was a briefcase. Another thought it was a phone. Two blocks south, we caught her on camera—she was indeed running—and she had nothing in her hand. We spent hours scouring the area and didn't find anything she may have dropped—no gun, no phone, no briefcase. She had a messenger bag crosswise over her body, where she may have hidden something."

"What would her motive be to kill Chen?"

"Anger at the system?" Lex offered.

Kara dismissed the comment. "I have far more anger than most people, but I have never killed anyone in cold blood."

"I don't believe she killed him," Elena said. "Another witness stated that she saw a man wearing a face mask covering his mouth and nose walking away from the bodies. People still wear them sometimes, and no one gives them a second look anymore. She gave a decent description—white male, about forty with brown hair and maybe six feet tall. But that could fit any number of people. She didn't see a gun."

"I want in. Let me help find Violet."

"Go for it," Elena said. "Tap into any resources you have in the FBI and if you find her, great."

Kara was surprised that Elena gave in so easily. Was she missing something? She asked, "Where does Will Lattimer fit into all of this?"

"After Chen's arrest, Lattimer heard about the housing scandal and went to Craig, who he'd met through Colton."

At the mention of Colton's name, her stomach twisted. "Why Craig?"

"Because he didn't know who else to go to," Lex said. "Craig looped us in and we put together an operation. And here we are."

"You're leaving a lot out between then and now," Kara said.

"I'll talk to Campana," Elena said quietly. "Until I do, this is the best I can do. I hope you find Violet."

"Where was the last place she was seen?"

They both hesitated.

"Really? You tell me you hope I find Violet and then clam up?" She stood. She was done with this runaround. Elena and Lex were hiding something from her, as if they didn't trust her. It hurt. Damn, it hurt. "I talked to Will today," she said. "He told me that Violet called him and he was supposed to meet her at a homeless camp off Fifth. But she disappeared and left her phone behind because some thugs scared her off. Has she been seen since?"

"No," Elena said.

"Neither of you are telling me the truth. Maybe parts of the truth, but not everything. I don't know why, but I *will* find out what you're hiding."

"And I will remind you, Detective Quinn, that we are your superior officers," Elena said.

Kara walked out without responding.

MONDAY, OCTOBER 7

24

There's a safety rule you're supposed to follow—don't wear both earbuds when you're driving or riding a bike or jogging so that you can hear potential danger.

But walking? I always wore both my earbuds. Partly because I didn't want to talk to anyone, partly because I enjoyed being lost in my thoughts. Or, in this case, listening to *LA with A&I*. Their latest podcast was about the housing project in Venice. With Will's blessing, I had sent them everything we knew about the project—the cost, the contractors, the financing, and what the city was getting for two hundred million dollars. Basically, taxpayers were paying $1.1 million a unit to house .002 percent of the homeless in the city. I had also included information about Angel Homes, the organization that received a three-million-dollar annual grant to manage the facility. Angel Homes had two full-time employees and were already managing three other transitional housing buildings that served a total of 410 homeless people. For those projects, they were paid $4.5 million a year. Add the new grant? That made $7.5 million a year.

Sure, they could be contracting out services and hiring staff on-site and any number of things, but no one knew. Why didn't the city know how they were spending the money? Because the grant didn't require any documentation, paperwork or transparency. They didn't have to prove they did anything for the money. As Will always told me, nearly every city operates the same way, from Seattle to Portland, to here in Los Angeles.

But Amy and Ian went one step further for their podcast: they started digging into Angel Homes and learned that Los Angeles County Supervisor Lydia Zarian's sister, Muriel Coplin, ran the nonprofit.

I hadn't known that. I don't know if Craig knew, either, though he had been investigating all the nonprofits that Will and I had identified. I was excited to tell him...because this new information about Zarian and Coplin fit extremely well with what I found yesterday when I went into city hall.

One of the benefits of working in the IT department is that I can come and go anytime of the day or night and no one paid much attention, even on a Sunday afternoon. I told the guard that I had to run a virus scan and he pretty much ignored me. I had finally worked out the coding problem and used my administrator access to reverse engineer the virus that had taken down the entire system.

I learned far more than I expected. And what I found both excited me...and scared me.

Someone much smarter than me had written a program that was ingenious. The files weren't deleted in the backups. When the backup was run, the files were deleted at the point of download. I would never have figured it out except for nineteen missing gigabytes of data. The backup drive from the day before the crash was nineteen gigabytes bigger than the data that was uploaded to the system after the crash. The virus was in the boot code. Every time someone tried to re-create the problem, they would never find it.

The only way I could access the missing data was either to go to the data warehouse and retrieve the drive there—and they would never let me leave with it—or install the backup without any security protections into a brand-new drive. But because of the size of the backup, I couldn't handle it on my own computer.

I wrote out the plan, but I would need access to a large network to be able to replicate the city hall mainframe. It was very illegal for me to do, so I wanted to talk to Craig about it first. The easiest thing would be for him to get a warrant for the original backup, which would have the missing files. But I worried that if he got the warrant, someone would have time to destroy the data on-site.

I was thinking about all of this, half listening to Amy and Ian discuss what they called "the biggest scam on Los Angeles taxpayers" related to the Angel Homes project in Venice Beach, and walking diagonally through the park on my way to Craig's office when I heard a loud backfire, so close I thought a car was going to run me over.

I stopped, stood on the edge of the path that merged onto the main sidewalk. Looked toward the street. I pulled my phone from my pocket to pause the podcast when I heard another backfire— and that was when I realized it wasn't a car. It was a gun. A man fell onto the sidewalk not twenty feet from me.

Three more gunshots hit another man—I recognized him. David Chen. The human trafficker that Craig Dyson was prosecuting.

He fell, blood spreading across his white shirt.

I turned to run and saw the shooter.

He wore a black face mask covering his nose and mouth, and sunglasses blocked his eyes. He was taller than me—six-one at least. Brown hair. He saw me.

He turned the gun toward me.

I stared at his hands.

I knew him.

I ran. I had never run so fast in my life. I didn't hear a gunshot but my heart was beating so fast I didn't know if I could hear anything else but the rush of blood in my ears. I ran all the way to the Fifth Street park, where I surprisingly felt safe.

"Miz Violet?" Toby said. "You okay?"

I shook my head. I would never be okay. "I need... I need..."

I called Will. "Will. Will—I saw... I saw David Chen. Shot. Come here. Fifth Street. I... I've seen the killer. I think. I know him." I couldn't catch my breath.

"Stay there, I'm on my way."

Relieved, I walked slowly through the park. I saw Midge, who'd been living here a few months. She was in her fifties, close to my mother's age. She was petite and skinny, but with a bloated stomach, a sign of heavy drinking. I didn't know her story yet—she was wary of everyone—but when she saw me, she asked, "What happened?"

"Can I—can I sit in your tent for a minute?"

"Go ahead, sweetie."

Her tent was stuffed with plastic bottles. She collected them from trash cans all over downtown and turned them in when she had a shopping cart full. Then she would buy as much alcohol as she could and drink until she passed out. When she woke up, she'd start collecting again and repeated the cycle.

The tent smelled of urine and alcohol and vomit. But I felt safe here for now. Will was on his way. He would come for me.

I sat there for five minutes when I heard someone shout, "Hey, that's mine!"

There was a general disturbance and rustling in the park, a titter of voices, an angry yell, a woman's scream.

Hands shaking, I parted the opening of Midge's tent.

Three men wearing sagging pants and angry expressions sauntered through the park ripping open the tents. The homeless here were both mad and scared at the intrusion. They retreated to the edges of the park, letting the men storm through. One of the thugs pushed Toby; he fell down and lay there. Was he hurt?

"Where's the girl? She ran in here. Are you hiding her?"

How did they know? Why were they looking for me?

I stared at the phone in my hand.

I knew who killed David Chen. He was a cop.

And he tracked me here because this was where I first saw him. But since he was a cop, he might also be able to track my phone.

I couldn't risk it.

I stuffed the phone under Midge's blanket and crawled out of the tent. I ran between two buildings, past sleeping men and women who littered the alley, under blankets and sleeping bags and jackets. I exited on Sixth Street and saw a bus coming toward the stop.

I made it. I didn't know where the bus would ultimately take me, but I knew where I was going.

I stuffed my hand into my pocket and felt my key ring.

After I buried my mother, Colton said the investigation was heating up, and if I was scared or worried, he had a safe house for me.

My fingers circled around the key Colton Fox had given me that day.

TUESDAY, OCTOBER 8

25

At six that evening, Matt knocked on Kara's door, then entered without her saying anything.

"Everyone's ready," he said.

She didn't budge. She was sitting at the window, staring out into the city she once loved, wondering when and how everything had gone wrong.

He stepped inside and closed the door.

"You're not alone," he said. "Michael and I will be with you the entire interview. You didn't kill Chen, and the faster we get through this bullshit, the better."

"They want to interview me about everything," she said. "The investigation, the arrest, shooting Chen's bodyguard, the whole nine yards."

"You don't have to answer those questions," Matt said. "Elena Gomez is here as your LAPD representative in case they stray too far off course."

"But if I'm adversarial, they'll just dig deeper. Taking up my time—and yours—when we could be out looking for Violet."

"Thirty minutes. That's all we'll give them."

"I have nothing to hide, but you damn well know that Chavez is doing this because Thornton pushed her to."

"Chavez may be in trouble herself," Matt said cryptically.

"Oh?"

"Sloane called me earlier. Chavez is leading this investigation into Chen's murder. In the four months Sloane has been in the office, she has never seen Chavez get so passionate about any case she was involved with, and she's rarely taken the lead."

Odd, Kara thought. "What do you think that means?"

"I don't know, but I have Ryder digging deep on her, deep and broad. Family, associates, old cases."

"Maybe she just doesn't like me."

Matt walked over to where she sat, held out his hand. "We need to get this over with. Sloane's here, too."

"And no one else knows she's working for you."

"Correct."

She took his hand and he pulled her up, kissed her lightly. "It's going to be fine," he said. Then he frowned, rubbed her shoulders. "Why are you so tense?"

She'd already told Matt about confronting Elena that afternoon. "Elena and Lex have been lying to me for months," she said. "And I think they lied to me today, but I can't put my finger on what's wrong. It was... Damn, it just keeps slipping away. But I'll figure it out."

"Promise me one thing, that when you do, you'll come to me before you do anything. I'm your partner in more ways than one—never forget that."

"I won't," she whispered. "Okay, I'm ready."

They walked out and Kara stared at the group assembled at the small conference table in the hotel suite. Elena was sitting at the head of the table. Matt motioned for Kara to take a seat in the center, next to Michael. Then Matt sat, flanking her, and she felt emboldened by her team. She'd get through this. Even though it was an "informal" interview, it was being recorded. Kara didn't like that. She didn't like anything about this interview, but Matt said it was in her best interest to cooperate, and he would protect her.

She trusted him. He slid her a cup of coffee and she smiled her thanks.

"Detective." A trim, attractive woman with flawless brown skin and sleek hair styled into a chic bob started the meeting. "I'm Assistant US Attorney Nina Radinovich. This is Assistant Special Agent in Charge Rebecca Chavez—" she gestured to the woman on her right—late forties, dressed just as impeccably as the AUSA "—and Special Agent Sloane Wagner, both from the Los Angeles field office. You of course know Lieutenant Gomez. We appreciate you taking the time to talk with us."

Nina Radinovich was straightforward and to the point. Kara noted the bright red four-inch spike heels she wore. She hadn't even kicked them off under the table, which Kara would have done if forced to wear the ankle-breakers.

Even though she was petite, Nina Radinovich commanded the room. "First, I want to share my condolences about the murder of Craig Dyson. Craig was a good man, an outstanding lawyer. I had great respect for him."

"Thank you," Elena said. "He was a good friend."

Kara glanced at Elena. It was true, but Kara hadn't acknowledged it when she spoke to Elena last night or today in her office. Elena kept her emotions even closer to the vest than Kara.

"As you know," Nina said, "my office has been looking into one aspect of Mr. Chen's alleged crimes. We have been working to find evidence of his trafficking. And we've made, thanks to ASAC Chavez and her team, some inroads there. I have witness statements that are compelling, but unfortunately—as I know you have encountered in your investigation—some people remain silent out of fear. These cases are difficult to prosecute because of that.

"However, we've traced much of Mr. Chen's finances. We have payments to dockworkers and after some negotiations, we may have an eyewitness willing to go on record."

"Isn't that a moot point because he's dead?" Kara said. She didn't need to know what might have happened should Chen have lived.

"No, because there were other people involved. Craig and I spoke briefly about this, and we had a meeting scheduled for today—to fill me in on the grand jury investigation he intended to launch, and he wanted some legal advice."

"About what?" Elena asked.

"He didn't say."

Motive, Kara thought. It had eluded her, but it all came back to the grand jury investigation. He was killed because someone—whoever was going to be exposed because of the investigation—didn't want the jury looking into them. And the only way to stop it was to kill Craig. Even Elena said he was keeping information from her and Lex. Why would he do that? Because he didn't trust someone? Because he didn't trust Elena? Someone close to her? Was it another dirty cop?

According to Nina Radinovich, Craig wanted to talk to her.

"How long have you known Craig?" Kara asked Nina.

The question surprised Nina. "Eleven, close to twelve years. I came here from the Seattle office when my husband took a teaching position at UCLA. Craig and I had a case that intersected, and we became friendly. He was very easy to work with, tough but fair. That particular case was a fraud investigation—a contractor had defrauded both the federal government and the City of Los Angeles related to inflated bids. We both wanted the case, and he turned it over to me because he felt the federal case was stronger than the state case."

"Was it?" Kara asked.

"No—but it was clearer, if that makes sense. Both cases were good, but the federal case was straightforward, and the state would have had to prove multiple points. Craig's primary concern was for the individual affected in the state case, so we worked together to ensure they were included as part of the restitution award in my case. A win-win."

Elena turned to Rebecca. "How's your family, Rebecca? If I remember, you have a son and daughter, right? Grown now?"

Rebecca blinked. "Yes, they're fine, thank you." She turned to Nina and said, "I know your time is valuable, Nina, so maybe we should continue?"

Kara looked at her pointedly. "I would say my time is also valuable, Rebecca."

Chavez bristled and shot Kara a narrowed glare before hiding her irritation. Kara bit back a smile, then added, "So is Elena's time, and Matt's, and everyone else at this table. So let's get to it."

Nina looked momentarily confused at the tension, then said, "According to your statement, Detective, you were in the courthouse with DDA Dyson and FBI Agent Michael Harris at the time of the shooting, correct?"

"Yes."

"What time did you arrive?"

"Approximately 11:30 a.m."

"Do you concur, Agent Harris?" Nina asked Michael.

"Yes."

She made a note.

"Were you both together the entire time you were in the building?"

"No," Kara said.

"When did you separate?"

"About twenty minutes after the shooting. While we were in lockdown in Craig's office, Matt called and asked Michael to meet him in the lobby."

Nina made a note.

"Are we done?" Kara said. "It's been a long day and I'm really hungry."

Rebecca cleared her throat. "We're in the process of getting warrants for your banking records, Ms. Quinn—"

"Detective Quinn," Kara said. "And you have no cause for my bank records."

"On the contrary, you threatened Mr. Chen and have the contacts and expertise to hire a professional."

Nina cleared her throat.

"You are accusing my detective of a serious crime," Elena said. "As her advocate, I'm going to recommend that she stop this interview and you can talk to her with her lawyer present."

"We are not accusing Detective Quinn of any crime," Nina said diplomatically.

"Ask me," Kara said.

"This doesn't need to be adversarial," Nina said.

"Tell that to your fed there."

Rebecca reddened.

"Detective Quinn," Nina said, "did you hire anyone to kill David Chen?"

"No."

"Would you be willing to voluntarily turn over your banking records?"

"No."

"If you have nothing to hide…" Rebecca said, holding her hands palms up, "you should cooperate."

Kara didn't say anything. She wasn't taking the bait. Rebecca Chavez was just like Bryce Thornton, only with a prettier face and higher rank.

"There is no need for this," Matt said. "Lieutenant Gomez already verified Kara's alibi, and jumping through these hoops is only further damaging the already tense relationship between the FBI and LAPD."

"I apologize," Nina said and sounded like she meant it, "but if the FBI is investigating Mr. Chen's murder, we need to interview all witnesses and verify alibis for the record."

"You don't have this investigation," Elena said. "This is an LAPD homicide investigation. Out of the kindness of my heart, I agreed to share information with Agent Chavez, but that's it."

Now Nina looked confused, and a bit irritated. "I apologize. I was under the impression that Agent Chavez was building a case and I needed to be present for the interviews."

"I am building a case," Agent Chavez said. "This is a joint investigation."

"Take that up with my boss," Elena said, "because this is *not* a joint investigation. Senior Detective Caprese is lead, under my command. I will give you a copy of all his reports because of your interest in the case, but if you interfere with our process, I will have my commander take it up with your director. We're done here."

Elena reached over and shut off the recorder. "You're a piece of work, Chavez. You think you can just muscle your way in and take over a legitimate LAPD investigation?"

"That wasn't the intent," Agent Chavez said, jaw tight.

"Bullshit," Elena said.

Kara enjoyed watching her lieutenant go off on the fed.

Matt rose and said, "I think we're done here tonight. Nina, nice to meet you. Agent Chavez, we'll talk tomorrow. Agent Wagner," he acknowledged with a nod. He walked to the door and waited for the three women to rise, gather their notes and exit.

Nina looked like she wanted to say something, but simply said good-night to the group and followed Chavez and Sloane out.

Matt closed the door and came back to the table.

"Wow," Michael said. "You really know how to make friends and influence people, Kara."

"She's taking direction from Thornton," Kara said.

"Maybe," Matt said, "but we don't know for certain. I'll go over there tomorrow and demand some answers. She already doesn't like me."

"Join the club," Elena mumbled. "That was a fucking waste of time. What is her game? I sent her everything we had. But we didn't give the feds the case. My boss said play nice, share information, don't budge on jurisdiction." She frowned. "Why did Craig want to meet with the federal lawyer?" The abrupt change of subject had Kara's instincts twitching.

"Maybe there was a federal component to his grand jury investigation," Michael offered.

"Or maybe he wanted advice," Kara said. "Like when you go to a colleague and bounce ideas around as you work through things. I think the question is, why didn't he tell you, Elena? Is there another bad cop in LAPD?"

Elena stared at her, but Kara didn't back down. Elena must have thought the same thing. Why was Craig keeping information from the already small investigative team?

"I gotta go," Elena said. "Let me know if there is any fallout from this, and if they want to talk again, don't do it without your department rep or a lawyer. I don't like the look of this. It's as if Chavez wants you to be guilty."

"I'm sure she does, but I'm not, so I'm not worried."

Elena left, and Kara stared at the door when she was gone. Something was bugging her about Elena, had been all day, and Kara would damn well figure out what it was.

26

Kara was exhausted but couldn't sleep.

When she went to bed after dinner, telling Matt and Michael that she was tired and had a headache, she hadn't been lying. But she'd sat at her laptop and started researching. She read more about Will Lattimer and First Contact. Will was quoted criticizing some of the government programs that were supposed to help the homeless. He called sixty thousand homeless in Los Angeles a "humanitarian crisis" and claimed he had a nine-point plan that would virtually end homelessness in less than three years for a fraction of the money that the city had already spent but, "The homeless industrial complex will never initiate my program because they would lose billions of dollars. They care more about the money than they do about the people they are supposed to help."

He was also quoted as being critical of harm reduction programs that didn't provide rehab options. "Most homeless outreach programs funded by the city aren't even allowed to offer treatment."

Kara didn't know if that was true, but she'd seen enough city employees giving away the "tools of the trade"—pipes, clean needles, foil, Narcan—that she wouldn't be surprised.

She searched Violet Halliday and found a bio on a website for a computer company that she helped start up ten years ago at the age of nineteen. The bio indicated that she was attending community college while working for the company, which streamlined some sort of online form system. The description went way over Kara's head, but apparently it was a good program because the company sold to a bigger company, and Violet was one of four people credited with the technology breakthrough.

Impressive. Probably. Kara still didn't know what the program did, but other people seemed to appreciate it.

There wasn't much online about Violet, and everything she found about Will she already knew. She was about to shut down and try to sleep when she saw an obituary that mentioned Violet. It ran three weeks ago.

Halliday, Jane Elizabeth, 54. Died in Venice Beach on August 20 of hypoxia. She is survived by her daughter, Violet Halliday, 29, of Burbank. In lieu of flowers, donations should be sent to First Contact, an organization that seeks to empower the homeless so they can become self-sufficient.

Kara frowned. Hypoxia was almost always caused by a drug overdose.

Was there a more personal reason for Violet's involvement in Craig's investigation?

She closed her computer and lay back on the bed. She fell into a deep, heavy sleep and dreamed about a woman overdosing on fentanyl, then it morphed into Colton being shot over and over and over...

Kara woke up suddenly. She looked at her clock. It was just after midnight; she'd slept for two hours. But something had been bugging her about her meeting with Lex on Monday, then yesterday with Elena. After reading the obituary, she realized what it was—she had never been informed about Colton's will.

She was in it. She knew because Colton had joked about it.

"'And to my partner, Kara Quinn, I leave my Harley, which is far superior to her wimpy bike.'"

"My bike is not wimpy."

"It's for girls."

"I am a girl."

"The Harley is better, and it's one of the lighter, faster models."

She laughed, finished her beer, grabbed two more for her and Colton. They'd just finished a very successful investigation together and were relaxing at his place. "Don't tease me. I might really want it."

"I'm not teasing. I have a will. Don't you?"

She shrugged. "I don't have anything of value."

"Your bike. Your condo."

"It'll go to my Grams."

"Your gun collection?"

"So you're saying if I start pushing up the daisies, you want my guns."

"That Colt .45 you have is pretty damn sweet."

"It's not practical to carry, but yeah, it's nice to have around."

"You need a will, Kara," Colton said, now serious. "We're cops. More than that, we take the dangerous cases because we have no family."

"Hey, my grandma is my family."

"You know what I mean."

She sipped. "I take the dangerous cases because someone has to, and they're more fun."

He touched his bottle to hers. "True, that." He drained half his beer. "I'm serious about the will. The union has a template and you can use the staff lawyer, might as well take advantage considering we pay dues. You should go see him, have it written up. I did."

"Damn, Fox, I don't like talking about dying. You or me."

"Then promise me you'll write a will. You can leave everything to me or to charity or to your grandma. But you need to do something, or the courts and government will get involved and probably screw it all up."

Or worse, she thought, my parents will try to get it.

"Deal." She drank while Colton got up and flipped the steaks. "Do you really have a will?"

"Yep, and I'm leaving you my Harley. You can sell it if you want, but it's a nice bike. And you get my badge."

"Don't."

"Seriously. We make a good team. If I bite it, I want you to have something to remember me by."

Maybe it was nothing. Maybe Colton lied to her about his will. Or he changed it and wrote her out of it.

Something itched in the back of her mind and she would never get back to sleep if she didn't scratch it.

She opened her computer and went to a real estate search engine, typed in Colton's address in Echo Park. The last time the house had been sold was ten years ago—that was when Colton bought it. It wasn't for sale now.

Might mean nothing.

Might mean something.

Will has been avoiding you. He avoided you Monday, you had to practically hunt him down yesterday, and he hasn't even tried to get back to you about Violet—and she's still missing.

Colton and Will were close. Will had brought Colton into the investigation when homeless men were being murdered, maybe he brought him into *this* investigation.

Elena said there was an undercover operation still going.

She wouldn't tell Kara who.

It could be...

It could be Colton, and if it was, he wouldn't stop until he found Violet. And if he did, and she was in danger, what better place to hide her but in the house of a dead man?

Her heart raced. Could Colton actually be alive?

No. No, he wouldn't do that to her. Lex wouldn't do that to her. She'd blamed herself because she hadn't been in town to watch his back. She blamed the FBI for outing him, Lex for benching her, the world for the unfairness of his murder.

She'd gone to his funeral. She'd cried.

Yet...something was off. Maybe...maybe he wasn't alive—the thought seeming ridiculous now. Maybe he left his house to Will, and Will was hiding Violet there. And she didn't get word about his bike and badge because she was out of state...

But she didn't know. She didn't *know* if Colton was dead or if he could be alive. She had to know for certain.

Kara almost left then and there, but Matt would be furious.

She felt very uncomfortable. Colton had once been her lover, now Matt was her lover. She and Colton were friends with benefits, but they were still friends, and they shared a lot of benefits. Matt was...more. She didn't know what yet, but *more*, because she felt different with Matt than with anyone else she'd been with. She wasn't certain how Matt felt about her previous relationship with Colton. He was very old-fashioned about some things.

Yet...she didn't know what she was going to face, and she needed backup. She could ask Michael, but she wanted Matt.

She dressed all in black, left her room, crossed the living area of the suite and knocked on the door of the room Michael and Matt were sharing.

"Matt, it's Kara. We need to talk."

It took him a minute, but he got up, opened the door. He'd

obviously been sleeping hard—his face was still splotchy from where he slept on his cheek. "Sorry," she said.

He glanced behind him, closed the door, looked at what she was wearing. "What's going on?"

"I think Colton's alive."

He blinked once, twice, still waking up. "Why?"

"A lot of little things, but tonight I found the obituary for Violet's mom. She was a drug addict, died of an overdose this summer. I fell asleep and woke up remembering Colton's will. He had one, and he left me some things. We had this conversation a few years ago… Anyway, that's not important. No one contacted me about his will. And then I looked up his house—it's never been sold or even listed, not since he bought it. And Will Lattimer has been avoiding me. Will was Colton's best friend. He was at his funeral…but then I remembered the funeral. Will was there, but he left early. He said all the cops were making him antsy. Will doesn't have issues with cops, so that didn't really make sense. But I dismissed it because I was in shock—and Lex got me out quickly because he was afraid Chen would come after me.

"And then, the final tipping point—one of Colton's last cases. A killer was targeting homeless men. Colton went undercover and tracked him, found him. I remembered how seamlessly he had disappeared, how he had worked closely with Will…and how they always met at Echo Park Lake to exchange information. That's where I found Will on Tuesday—at the lake. I didn't put it together then, but now? It's all I can think about."

"Why would LAPD fake his death?"

"That's not the question I have. I know why—they want him so deep that no one knows he's looking. This explains why Elena wouldn't tell me anything, not even a hint about the undercover operation. And if everyone thinks Colton is dead, he's the best to do it." She paused, considered. "I don't think they faked the shooting—that was real. I think he lived—maybe he was injured, maybe he had a vest—but I think they took advantage of the op-portunity. I don't know! Maybe I'm wrong about everything."

"Kara—" Matt reached for her, but she stepped away.

"Matt, I appreciate your support, but I need to do something. I'm going to go to Colton's. He lives in Echo Park. It's not far."

"I'm coming."

"I have to do this by myself. But that's because of me, not you. I don't know how to explain. I'm sorry if this makes you mad, I don't want to make you mad. I trust you. This is just… it's my past, and I have to know the truth."

Matt stared at her. "I appreciate you coming to me, and I understand that you think you need to do this alone. I don't know that you're right, but there is definitely something going on with your boss and your lieutenant. We're a team, Kara— you, me, Michael, the others. You need to use your team even when you want to be a maverick. You have always had my back, every case we've worked. You have to know I have yours."

"If I'm right about this, my judgment about everything is wrong. And if my judgment is wrong? I'll never be able to do this job because I'll always doubt myself."

"No," Matt said. "Whether you're right or wrong about Colton, your judgment has never been in question. Don't start now."

"I won't be long," she said. "I'll call you—"

"No."

"Matt, I have to! Please understand."

"I'm going with you. I'll let you confront him alone, but I'm going with you to watch your back. I need to tell Michael. Give me five minutes. Please."

She didn't want to—she wanted to leave now. She wanted to do this alone. But Matt was right. It was better to have a part-ner. A partner she trusted.

She said, "I'll wait."

WEDNESDAY, OCTOBER 9

27

Colton Fox had owned the thousand-square-foot two-bedroom in Echo Park for as long as Kara had known him. The roughly two-square-mile area where four freeways came together had a lot going on—Dodger Stadium, the LAPD Training Academy, parks, hiking trails, a lake, houses both expensive and cheap. Echo Park was a microcosm of Los Angeles itself and all that the city offered, while also boasting a view of downtown from the hills that led up to the baseball field. Colton had loved living here because it was centrally located to everything he cared about—a rarity in Los Angeles when most people spent hours in their cars every day.

Colton's modest house stood on the corner of two narrow streets. The surrounding properties included a dilapidated three-story Victorian and a two-story postwar house next door that had been expertly renovated to its full 1950s glory. Colton's own house had been constructed during the same era, but was smaller and located on an irregularly shaped lot. It was set back farther from the street compared to the other houses, and two towering trees in the front provided ample shade and privacy. Though minimal natural light was able to filter through, Colton had cleverly installed skylights in each room, which greatly brightened the interior. He'd done most of the work himself and enjoyed the process.

Kara remembered when he was refinishing the floors in the living and dining room. She wanted no part of it, but sat on a stool in the kitchen, drank beer and watched, telling him he missed a spot, that he should sand harder.

"Nice plumber's crack," she said with a laugh.

He glanced over his shoulder at her. "Watch it, Quinn. Or I'm going to smack your plumber's crack, but good."

"Oh, I'm scared."

She'd been thinking a lot about Colton lately. Not just since she'd returned to Los Angeles, either. She'd done a lot of comparing her former relationship with Colton and her current relationship with Matt. That wasn't smart—they were two different men. It wasn't fair to either of them. And Colton was dead.

Or not.

She glanced over at Matt in the passenger seat. He looked straight ahead, a little angry, a lot worried. Matt told her he loved her, and she believed him, but was still twisting that information around in her head because she didn't know what to do with it. She had nothing to compare it with.

Colton was comfortable. She knew exactly what to expect, exactly what he gave her and what she gave him, and they never pushed each other to give more. There were months when they didn't even see each other, then they'd spend a weekend in bed as if they did it all the time. They sometimes worked together, they argued a lot, but in the end, their relationship was about trust. They trusted each other. Love? That she didn't know. They each went out with other people, never talked about moving in together or anything that couples do.

Kara hadn't wanted more…neither had Colton. Yet…the last

few months before she was forced to take leave and Colton was killed, they had spent more time together *not* working.

She hadn't wanted to read anything into it. She couldn't ask him—hell, they *never* talked about their relationship. And now he was dead.

Maybe.

She drove past his house; it was dark. There was no *For Sale* sign in the yard. It looked pretty much exactly as she remembered the last time she was here.

When there was a baseball game, the community felt alive as people roared from the stadium and bright lights illuminated the skyline, but tonight it was dark, the only sound the constant hum of the freeways.

She pointed out the house to Matt, kept driving by, circled around the block, parked on the opposite side of the street. The rear corner of Colton's house was visible.

"How do you want to do this?" he asked.

"I know where Colton hides his extra set of keys, in a lockbox under a rock behind the garage. I don't think he's here—he could be, but I should be able to tell pretty quick. I'm going to let myself in and look around, see what I see. I'd like to do it alone."

"And if he is there? And shoots you as an intruder?"

"He's too well trained to shoot first. Please, Matt—I need to talk to him one-on-one. He's not going to be straight with me if you're glaring at him."

"I don't glare."

They sat in silence a moment, watching the house. Then Matt asked, "Do you love him?"

"No." Then she added, "I don't know if I ever did. I never told myself or Colton that I loved him. I've never used those words, but I don't think so. I wouldn't even know what it feels like." She winced. She shouldn't have said that, because clearly Matt had feelings that she didn't understand. But it was the truth.

She didn't know how she felt about any of this…she didn't like thinking about it. The emotions she had were complicated.

Fortunately, Matt didn't say anything, and if she hurt him he didn't show it. Damn, she didn't want to hurt him.

"I never lied to you that we had a relationship," she said. "It was casual, but I've known Colton practically since I graduated from the police academy. So I guess it's a little more complicated than I want to admit. I'm angry and hurt that he let me think he was dead. I missed him, Matt. It hurt deep inside that he was dead." She pounded her fist twice on her chest.

"You don't know that he's alive, Kara."

"Maybe I don't have proof, but I know in my gut that he's alive. Will Lattimer will tell me. He might be a Marine and trained not to give up secrets, but he can't look me in the eye and tell me Colton is dead if he's breathing. Do you think I'm wrong? Do you believe that Colton is dead, just like everyone told me?"

Matt looked at her. "I don't know," he finally said. "But I know you, and you don't believe in fairy tales."

Kara didn't know why that simple statement, that simple faith in her, made her chest swell. She leaned over and spontaneously kissed him. "Thank you."

"Go. I'm right here. Keep me updated every step of the way or I am going in, and I'm not going to be subtle."

There were no free newspapers or advertisements on the doormat.

Kara remembered Colton was always irritated by what he called "littering on private property" because every day people left junk on his small porch. The yard was maintained—the trees dumped a generous amount of leaves no matter what the season, but the lawn was trimmed with few scattered leaves, meaning someone had hired a gardener to take care of the place.

Probably Lex. Keeping an eye on Colton's place like he kept

an eye on her place. Like he kept an eye on every home of his detectives who were working undercover and might not get to their house for several nights...

Or whoever Colton left the house to in his will was living here. Maybe she was wrong.

You're not wrong.

The long driveway went to the back of the house. There was no vehicle in it. A one-car garage, detached, used to house Colton's bike. Like her, he only owned a motorcycle. Much easier getting around traffic on a bike than in a car. They'd gone riding together a couple of times, through the Topanga Canyon or up to the Angeles National Forest.

The single window was dark, a thick canvas blind pulled down, so she couldn't see if his bike was still there. It wouldn't mean anything if it were, though she could inspect it, see if it had been sitting inside for a while.

The door was manual; Colton had never put an automatic door opener on it. She squatted to the handle on the bottom right—it had a new lock on it. He'd never locked his garage before. Maybe the new owners...

Kara was having second thoughts about her plan, but decided to just do it. She was 70 percent positive that she was right.

She walked around behind the garage to a large rock that was wedged between the corner of the garage and the side fence.

She and Colton had been on their first joint undercover assignment when he brought her here.

"If the shit hits the fan, go to my place. It's clean, safe."

He walked her down the driveway and to the back of the garage and pointed to the rock.

"You keep a key under a rock. Original."

"More than a key." He grinned.

The rock was heavy but rounded. He heaved it over on its flattest side. Underneath was a lockbox.

"It would be pretty easy to break that open," she said.

"Yep," he agreed. "The code is my badge number."

"You're full of originality."

He rolled the numbers into place.

Inside was a set of keys and a plastic bag with a thousand in cash and a small notebook.

"Now I know where to get bankrolled for a trip to Vegas."

"Help yourself, just replace it. I have another stash in the house, but if I think I'm being followed, I can get here through the alley and hop the neighbor's side yard, grab the stuff and disappear with no one knowing I was here." He held up the keys. *"Keys to the house, to my bike, and to my uncle's cabin in Big Bear."*

"I didn't know you had an uncle."

"He died, the cabin is in a trust that I now control. Uncle George lived there for the last twenty years of his life, was kind of a hermit."

"Well, if I need a hideout, it would be nice to have the address," she teased.

He pulled out the notepad, wrote it down inside. "Just in case."

"Overkill."

"It's never overkill to be prepared for every contingency."

"Who else knows this is here?"

He looked at her and shook his head. "No one. Not even Lex. Just you and me."

Colton had trusted her. And now she felt sick. Because if she was right, he had hurt her more than he could possibly know.

"I grieved for you," she whispered and picked up the keys.

The cash was still there in the box, along with the notepad. She pulled out the notepad and looked at the address he'd written years ago. The ink had faded. She flipped through the notepad and saw in Colton's small scrawling handwriting several other addresses, all local, but no indication why he wrote them down. They were all written on three pages in what appeared to be the same pen—and not the black pen that was in the box.

She pocketed the notepad, left the money sealed in the box

and spun the numbers. She put it back and took the keys to the back door.

She listened, blocking out the freeway traffic, the sound of nearby music. Listened to the sounds of the house. Silent, except for the hum of the refrigerator.

"Dammit," she muttered. "Just do it."

She sent Matt a text message.

I'm going in.

As silently as possible, she unlocked the door—both the dead bolt and the regular lock.

She closed the door behind her, listened again, using all her senses. Smelled something...hamburger? Yep. A distinct greasy fast-food scent.

The skylights above provided some ambient light in the house, so it wasn't pitch-black. She was in the kitchen. The new refrigerator Colton had bought when his old one croaked hummed. The '50s-era tile counters that were original to the house were wiped clean and in near-perfect condition. The retro kitchen table with red top and red vinyl seats and silver legs stood in the corner where it had been since the first time Kara came here. Colton had always been a neat person, never left dishes in the sink, never left garbage that needed to be taken out. She smelled a hint of garbage.

She opened the door under the kitchen sink. A wrapper from In-N-Out Burger, which was only three blocks away and open until 1 a.m. As quietly as possible, she retrieved the bag and looked at the receipt.

Last night, 9:47 p.m.

Her heart skipped a beat. She closed the door and walked down the hall to Colton's bedroom.

A figure lay in the bed.

Dark blond hair. Female. Certainly not Colton.

Violet Halliday was a blonde.

For a split second, Kara considered that maybe—maybe—
Will Lattimer was using Colton's house, that he had put Violet here to protect her, that Colton wasn't alive and she hadn't
grieved for nothing.

There was a gun on the nightstand. A mighty snub-nosed
Smith & Wesson .357. Colton had the exact same gun that he
usually kept in the kitchen drawer.

Kara walked over, picked it up. It was a heavy gun, but one of
the best for self-defense. Easy to shoot, as long as you expected
the kick from what Colton called his "hand cannon."

She put the gun in one of her tactical pockets, then stepped
away from the bed in case Violet had another weapon.

Using the door as a partial shield, Kara said quietly but firmly,
"Violet, wake up."

The woman bolted awake, eyes wide and terrified as they
adjusted.

"Colton?" she said, scared and groggy.

Kara's heart sank even as she was flooded with relief that
Colton was very much alive.

Violet fumbled for the gun that was no longer on the nightstand.

"My name is Detective Kara Quinn. I've been looking for
you."

28

Staring at the woman in the dim light, I reached for the gun Colton had given me, but immediately realized it wasn't there.

Kara Quinn.

I had heard that name several times over the last few months, knew she was a cop, knew she was the one who had arrested David Chen and then had to leave because of a threat on her life.

But most recently, I heard her name from Colton on Monday night when he found me here.

"Kara still thinks I'm dead."

Then he'd said that Kara was a dog with a bone, that she would be looking for me.

"I can't stay. Now that Craig is dead, I have to go deep until I have everything."

"What if she finds me?"

"You can trust her. Tell her everything. She'll be mad at me, but she'll understand."

Trust was hard for me, and it hurt to learn that Craig Dyson was dead. He had listened to me, even when I got emotional and upset. He gave me directions on what to look for. Without him, I would never have found out that Theodore Duncan, the mayor's chief of staff, was profiting on the backs of people like my mom. That he had made a deal with David Chen and helped that evil man exploit all those Chinese women.

Colton didn't trust people, either, but he said he trusted Kara Quinn. I needed to try.

"Let's talk," Kara said.

I got out of bed. As I slipped on my flip-flops, I realized I towered over Kara. But I looked at her and knew she'd be able to hurt me if she wanted. She motioned for me to lead the way to the kitchen. I did. I sat at the table, in the dark, because I didn't know what to do.

Kara made coffee. She knew where everything was. She waited, watched the pot brew, as if she didn't need to talk. I didn't need to talk, either. I was scared and defeated and just wanted this to be over.

But I didn't think it would ever be over. Even if the police arrested all the people involved in killing Craig Dyson, the system would still be broken. Craig was the only one who could fix it, and he was gone.

Kara put a mug of black coffee in front of me. She pulled out her phone and sent someone a text message; my heart skipped a beat. Could I trust this cop? I didn't know. But…she'd been Colton's partner, and I trusted him.

She said, "From the beginning."

I told her everything. About how I became suspicious after the computer crash at city hall. How I'd suspected that the crash was deliberate, and then Will introduced me to Craig. How I figured out that someone had overwritten files from the backups and they all related to homeless housing grants. I learned that David Chen had received government money to house the women he'd trafficked, and Craig wanted to know how the system worked, how he got away with it, and so I got him the files and records he needed. We uncovered hundreds of millions of dollars of waste, possible fraud. I explained how there were non-profits within nonprofits and how whoever was in charge prof-ited off the system.

"None of it is illegal," I told her. "But Craig started looking at who worked at each nonprofit. He brought in his investiga-tor, Mr. Sharp, to do deep background checks on everyone. And then I found it."

"Whatever you were bringing to Craig at the courthouse on Monday afternoon."

"Yes. I found the original files. I can't get to them, but I know where they are and knew that Craig would be able to get a war-rant. The virus deletes specific files when the backup gets loaded into the city hall system, but the files are still there in the back-ups. The city by law has to keep them for a year. So we only have until the middle of February before they're gone forever."

"Do you know who is responsible? Who erased the files to begin with?"

"I know whose computer it was done from—the mayor's chief of staff. And that makes sense because Theodore Duncan had created the commission to review all grants when the mayor won his first election. Duncan put his brother-in-law in charge. At least, that's what Craig and I figured out. After that, things started clicking into place."

"I don't understand what clicked into place," Kara said.

"The city spends nearly a billion dollars every year on the homeless. But nothing gets done. It costs the city over eight hundred thousand dollars to house *one person*. The money that's supposed to go into transitional or permanent housing? By the time it gets to the end point, it's a fraction of what the grant was originally for. The city doesn't actually *do* the work—they have the money, and then private contractors and nonprofits apply for grants to do different things."

"Don't they have to like, I don't know, give a report? Show what they've done with all this money?"

"No. Built into the grant itself is complete autonomy. There are no checks and balances. That's why the system is so lucrative to people who know how to exploit it."

I paused, needed this woman to understand even though it was complex. I said, "For example, Angel Homes applied for a twenty-million-dollar grant to provide temporary shelter for women and children escaping abuse. They didn't provide one bed. Instead, the director made a salary of $650,000, and the treasurer made a salary of $250,000. The director is the sister of LA County Supervisor Lydia Zarian.

"Angel Homes also gave a ten-million-dollar grant to Sunflower Homes, a nonprofit that runs group homes for homeless women and children. Each group home has a huge overhead—rent, supplies, staff. The houses are owned by an LLC that is controlled by the *brother* of Supervisor Lydia Zarian. Not only the houses, but the transportation, the food service, everything. All told, each homeless family that is served through that program costs between two hundred and five hundred thousand dollars a *month*."

Kara frowned. "Wait—that's like what? Fifty families? That has to be illegal."

"It's not illegal, but as Will said, if it got out, it could destroy Zarian's career, and public watchdogs might have sway to effect change in the process. Unfortunately, it's difficult to explain to the average person because like you, they'd look at the dollars and say, no, this can't be happening, someone would have noticed. Will has gone through the public filings for each entity, and Colton investigated every property owned by the group home—in the last year, sixteen women with between one and three children have been housed in Sunflower Homes, and they are already approved for even more money next year. This isn't one house for one family, these are group homes, so multiple families in one house.

"This is just one of many scams. There are multiple nonprofits working multiple angles, and half of them are controlled by the Zarian family—Lydia's name isn't on anything, but her brother, her sister, her daughter even! And we've been wondering how they've been getting away with this, while hiding the supervisor's involvement, and Colton recently learned that Duncan's brother-in-law is the son of a federal agent and on the housing commission."

"What's the brother-in-law's name?"

"Jonathan Avila. Do you know him?"

Kara shook her head. "You have all this documented?"

I nodded. "And more. Most of it is shuffling money—moving a couple million dollars into one nonprofit, taking a salary, then moving it into another nonprofit where a relative or friend takes a salary, then moving it to another, and so on. But Craig thought he caught them at something that he *could* take to the grand jury. That's why I was bringing over the documentation where I prove how the computer system was crashed and identify the specific files that were deleted."

"Do you have the files?"

"No, I have the file names, size and when they were created, but not the actual records. As I said, we have to get the backup drive—the physical drive from the data center."

"Where is your documentation?"

"Colton took everything for safekeeping." My voice cracked. "I'm so sorry about Craig. I really liked him. He was the only person other than Will who listened to me. Listened to my theories. He believed me about the computers. I tried to tell my boss months ago, but he said it was a server crash and we didn't lose anything, only time."

"Do you think your boss is involved?"

"No, I've never suspected my boss. Though I think Craig looked into him to make sure he wasn't living above his means."

"What is Colton doing? Where is he working?"

"Everywhere. He was in Venice Beach last month, the Valley after that, Echo Park Lake recently, but he moved—I don't know where, but he's been taking photos of people, buildings, contractors, that sort of thing."

"As what? A journalist?"

"As a homeless vet."

"He's been living on the streets for how long?"

"Um, about five months?"

Kara frowned.

"He told me to trust you," I said.

She didn't say anything.

"What more do you want to know? I don't think I forgot anything, but maybe. Ask me anything. I want this to be over."

"I thought he was dead."

"I know. I'm sorry."

Her head jerked up. "You knew? Well, shit."

Kara got up and paced. I didn't say anything. Then she turned to me and said, "Why did you run?"

I started to shake and grabbed the coffee mug to steady myself. "David Chen was shot in front of me. I know who killed him. Steven Colangelo. He's an LAPD officer. I've met him a couple times—he patrols downtown."

"You're telling me that a cop killed Chen." Her voice and eyes were flat. Did she not believe me?

"I didn't recognize him at first—he had a face mask on, sunglasses—but then I saw his hands and I knew... He has this watch. It looks expensive, has a distinctive yellow face. I'd seen the watch before, when he was responding to a call at the Fifth Street Park. He looked at me, pointed the gun at me, and I ran. I thought he was going to shoot me, too."

"When did you end up here?"

"Here? Um, late Monday night. After midnight. I didn't come directly here because I was afraid someone might follow me."

Kara frowned. What was she thinking? She looked upset and worried. Maybe...angry. But then her face cleared and she said, "And Will and Colton know you're here."

"Yes."

"Colton knows that Chen's shooter is a cop."

I nodded.

"Where is Colton *right now*?"

"I don't know," I said. I wasn't lying, though I don't think she believed me.

She stared at me. "I'm going to get you someplace safe, then—"

"No. Please, Colton said I had to stay here."

"He also told you to trust me, right?"

I nodded, but started shaking again. Everything had gotten so far out of control I didn't know what to do or who to trust.

"Billions of dollars, you said?" Kara said. She was typing on her phone.

"Yes. There's an entire business that will end when we solve the homeless crisis. That's why it'll never be solved."

"I don't know about fixing this kind of problem," Kara said. "That's way above my pay grade. But murder? That I can solve. We're going to get you out of here, someplace safe, and then we'll take down every single one of these people and find justice for Craig."

"But I'm safe here," I pleaded.

She stared at me, then said, "Maybe you are. But too many people are lying, and you are the only person who knows exactly how to extract the evidence."

"Yes, but—" I stopped talking when I saw the look on her face. It wasn't violent, but close to it.

Kara looked at her phone. "Okay, my boss is going to check

the area, make sure there's no one watching the house, then we'll go out and meet him."

"I don't know..."

"My partner Michael was a Navy SEAL and my boss Matt was in FBI SWAT and I have street smarts, so between the three of us, you'll be safe. Do you have anything here?"

I shook my head. "Colton loaned me these clothes," I said, gesturing to my sweats and T-shirt, "but I'd like to change into my own clothes if I can?"

She looked at her watch. "Okay, you have five minutes. And I'm going to watch. My patience and my trust are wearing thin these days."

29

Matt read Kara's message.

Colton is alive. Will Lattimer knew Monday night that Violet was here but didn't tell me when I talked to him yesterday morning. Violet said the shooter is a cop named Steve Colangelo and that Colton has this information. Did he tell Elena and she's keeping that information from me? Or did he not tell her and why? Violet is getting dressed. We'll be coming out in five minutes.

Matt forwarded the message to Michael and then to Ryder in DC so he could follow up on background for everyone involved.

Driving around the block twice, he looked for anyone sitting in a car, walking along the street, acting suspicious.

He was upset for Kara and what she must be feeling. She kept so many emotions bottled up inside that she had never learned how to process, so they came out in anger. She was a bundle of tension, and all he wanted to do was give her some peace. There were times when he felt her truly relax, especially after sex, when she fell asleep in his arms. Sometimes, when they were alone at his place, chatting about work or movies.

She didn't relax enough. He wanted to change that. This deception by her old team was going to tear her apart. It would hurt for a long time. He didn't know how to fix it, other than to just be there for her when she needed him.

It was near the end of his second trek around the block, when he was driving the street parallel to Colton's, that something caught Matt's peripheral vision.

Two men dressed in black walking down the side of a house. From here, they could go through two backyards and be in Colton's backyard.

He called Kara.

"Yep."

"Two men are approaching from the back. I'll be out front in thirty seconds. Watch yourself and keep the line open."

"Copy that," she said.

He lost sight of the men as he drove down the street toward Colton's corner. He sent Michael a quick message alerting him, though it would take him too long to get here.

A van pulled up in front of the house and cut Matt off at the intersection. One man wearing a ski mask jumped out and held a semiautomatic rifle on Matt while two others ran to the front of the house.

"Kara! Men are approaching front and back! I'm pinned down."

The gunman hadn't yet fired his weapon, but he had it pointed in Matt's direction.

"Don't get dead," Kara said. "I got this."

"I'm not leaving you."

Matt slammed the car into Reverse. The gunman opened fire, aiming at his front tires and grill. A bullet ricocheted off his hood and shattered part of his windshield, the safety glass cracking, but not breaking. Yet. One more bullet would do it.

"Matt!"

"I'm okay, they're shooting at the car."

"I have a ride. Get out of here."

"What ride?"

His car was rolling backward. Steering was tight, and he fought to maintain control. Over the car speaker he heard a motorcycle start up.

"Kara—"

"Trust me. I got Violet. Go." She ended the call.

He backed up, hit another car, did a one-eighty and drove away.

They didn't pursue.

He called 911.

Kara had Violet out of the house as soon as Matt told her that two men were approaching. She knew as well as Matt that they'd have two teams coming for them. Whether they were after Kara or Violet, she didn't know, but she wasn't taking chances.

She didn't want to tell Matt how much of a risk she was taking, because he wouldn't have left her, and she didn't know what these people had planned. Kidnapping or murder? Or kidnapping, torture, then murder? None of the options appealed to her because every idea she had ended in her being dead.

She broke the lock on Colton's garage. She had to believe with all her heart that Colton kept his bike in top running order like usual, even when he was in deep cover. She had to also have faith that it was still here, in his garage.

Because if it wasn't, this was going to be a short-lived escape.

The garage door rolled up and there was his bike in all its glory. Kara owned a Kawasaki 800, but she'd driven Colton's heavier—and more powerful—Harley V-Rod. The best thing about Colton's bike was that it was fast.

She threw a helmet at Violet and put one on herself because there was no shield on the front of the bike to protect her from debris and bugs. She needed to see clearly. She ordered Violet to climb on.

"Hold on tight because I'm going to be moving fast and not slowing down. You fall off, you're going to break something and those guys are going to grab you."

She heard gunfire and screamed, "Matt!"

"…shooting at the car."

"I have a ride. Get out of here."

"What ride?"

She started up the bike. Colton hadn't let her down. He loved his bike, and would never let it stay idle for long.

"Kara—"

"Trust me. I got Violet. Go," she said before ending the call.

As long as the men were going to the front door, she was okay. If they were coming down the driveway, she was toast.

She turned the bike and floored it. Riding a motorcycle was literally like riding a bike—you never forgot.

But she *had* forgotten how much she loved it.

Violet gripped her tight and Kara practically flew down the driveway. The men were coming out of the house in the back—they'd already busted the front door—and she thought she heard a gunshot, but she felt nothing, and Violet's grip didn't waver.

The van blocked the intersection, so Kara turned left, up the hill. They would pursue, but she was faster on the bike. And motorcycles could go where vans couldn't.

At the top of the hill, the road curved around and went down toward the Hollywood Freeway. She went through a red light—slowing only briefly to make sure there was no cross traffic—and merged onto the 110 heading north.

She debated for two seconds about heading straight for the Sheraton, but she didn't know what was going on, how these men had found her, if they'd followed her and Matt from the hotel or if they might be waiting for her there. She needed to get Violet to safety, and that meant getting her out of town.

Like to Colton's Big Bear cabin.

It was a two-hour drive—maybe less on the bike. When she felt they were safe she'd pull over and figure out exactly where in Big Bear she was going.

Violet repeatedly tapped on her leg. Kara glanced in the rear-view mirror, didn't see anyone pursuing or gaining on her. Still, she didn't want to pull over just yet.

She waited until she got through the I-5 interchange and was heading more east than north, then pulled over in South Pasadena where there was an easy on/off-ramp next to a dog park.

She pulled into the parking lot and throttled down the bike, looked at the gauges. Nearly full tank of gas. Everything appeared in good working order.

She took off her helmet and looked at Violet. "What?"

Violet struggled but removed her own helmet. She was pale and wide-eyed. She said, "Your phone. You have to get rid of your phone. It's how they found me. That's the only way I can think that they found you, unless they followed you."

Kara was good at spotting a tail, but she thought she'd missed it. Her phone? Damn.

She called Matt.

He answered immediately.

"Status."

"We're good. I'm getting Violet out of town."

"Bring her to the hotel."

"No. Not until I know every single cop who's part of this. She has valuable information, Matt—we need her safe."

"Where?"

"I can't tell you over the phone. Violet thinks someone tracked her on her phone, that they might be tracking my phone. I'm wiping it and dumping it before I take her."

"I'll meet you—tell me where you are."

"Once she's safe, I'll get a disposable phone and call you.

There are millions of dollars at stake, and people will kill for far less money."

"Okay," he said quietly. "Do not die on me."

"Ditto. And, Matt? Find Will. He knows where Colton is, and he has been playing some game with me."

She ended the call, erased the phone, restored it to factory settings, dropped it, then ran over it with the motorcycle. She turned to Violet. "Good?"

Violet nodded.

"Are you okay?"

She nodded again.

"It's a nearly two-hour ride to where we're going. Just hold on, we'll be there sooner than you think."

If you wanted something done right...

Conrad quietly fumed that the men he hired couldn't do a simple job. He wouldn't trust Theodore Duncan's recommendations in the future. That man was, frankly, a pompous asshole.

He was, however, greatly impressed with the ability of Detective Quinn to extract herself from the dangerous situation. She was resourceful, a valuable attribute he admired. The cop's tenacious reputation had been accurate and well-earned. Everything he'd learned about her in preparation for this job had been spot-on.

Now, he suspected the other bit of gossip he'd stumbled upon was also true: the detective and Agent Costa were involved. That tidbit could come in handy now...or in the future.

He had been correct that Quinn would find Ms. Halliday. Quinn would have been collateral damage; his job was to find Violet Halliday, extract what information she knew about the deleted files and any documentation she had, then dispose of her.

Conrad didn't like killing innocents. Not Quinn—he wouldn't like to kill her, and he may let her live depending on how things played out—but Ms. Halliday. The girl was just a computer nerd, a smart young woman who became nosy. In this case, there was no other option. She knew too much, she had to die.

He would charge more for his discomfort.

Conrad dialed the secure number of his FBI contact. It was late; he didn't care.

Two rings later. "What happened?"

"Detective Quinn has Ms. Halliday. Where are they?"

"I need to get to my computer."

"Your plan failed."

"It wasn't mine! I told you not to listen to Theodore—"

"You don't pay my bills."

Silence.

He didn't like where this assignment had been going. Too many people with too much information. There was always a weak link.

He put half his money on this fed, the other half spread evenly around to the other conspirators.

"One minute, I'll find her."

He would have smiled if he wasn't so irritated at the failure tonight.

Chen was dead, because of his plan. Dyson was dead, because of his hand. Both perfect murders because *he* had orchestrated both.

As soon as he brought in others? Failure.

"Her phone isn't transmitting anymore. I have the last location..."

"She destroyed it. You know what to do. And so do I."

He ended the call, then called the woman who originally hired him to fix the avalanche of problems created after David Chen was arrested.

"I need an additional one million in my account by noon tomorrow or I'm walking. I'm not in the mood to negotiate."

30

Bryce Thornton knew Kara Quinn was a bad cop from the minute he'd met her. She'd been allegedly working undercover as the whore of some drug runner, and she certainly acted the part. He'd documented her committing crimes, but apparently, that was allowed in LAPD when you were working undercover.

She'd been belligerent and cocky and had a mouth on her he wanted to slap.

He hated how she made him feel—hot, tense, angry. She was everything he despised in a bad cop. The rules didn't apply to her. She could do anything she wanted and apparently got away with it. LAPD shoved her bullshit under the rug because she was their golden girl, all because early in her career she had shut down some major high school drug operation and saved some prima donna's life.

He might have given her *one* pass, but she was a rebel, a maverick, and he didn't like mavericks. He believed in law and order, with the emphasis on *order*. If they didn't have a civil society, what did they have? Anarchy. And cops running around pretending they were in the Wild, Wild West.

Every time he was close to nailing her for serious violations, something happened and her violation just disappeared. She'd be suspended, or reprimanded, but she still had her badge, and she still had her gun.

If he had his way, she'd be sitting in federal prison for the next ten to twenty. But apparently, she'd been cleared of wrongdoing every single time she'd been called into Internal Affairs.

He had the body cam footage of her threatening David Chen, stating that she wished he'd broken his neck. There were no witnesses to confirm that he fell off the roof, and Chen himself said she threatened him and he backed away, fearing she would shoot him, and he fell. Quinn denied it, but Thornton believed Chen.

Unfortunately, no one else did. Just because someone is a killer doesn't mean they lie about everything.

He went to bed Tuesday night thinking about all these things, and how he was going to catch Kara Quinn breaking the law. His phone woke him at two thirty. It was an unknown caller, but he answered.

"Thornton." He cleared his throat.

An unfamiliar voice said, "Check your messages. I have the dirt on Quinn."

The caller hung up and Bryce turned on his bedside lamp and looked at his phone messages. He had one text.

I have proof that Quinn orchestrated the hit on Chen. I'll be at the South Pasadena dog park off the 110 at 4 a.m. if you want it.

He responded.

Who is this?

There was no answer. He got up, dressed, looked down at his phone when it beeped.

The gun used to kill Chen is registered to Quinn. She may not have pulled the trigger, but she gave the killer the gun. You want it? I have it. It'll put Quinn away for life. You know where to find me.

He was in his car heading to South Pasadena when he called Rebecca. It took her several rings before she picked up. "What's wrong?"

"Quinn's gun was used to kill Chen. We're going to get her."

"How do you know?"

"An informant. I'm meeting him now."

"Now? You can't—we need to put together a team. Do not go alone."

"I'll get there early, make sure it's safe."

"Where?"

"South Pasadena dog park off the 110. I'll be there in fifteen minutes, a good twenty minutes early. This is it, Rebecca. This is how she goes down."

"I'm up, getting ready. I'll be there. Wait for me. Dammit, Bryce, wait for backup. Don't confront anyone, it could be a setup."

"She's not that smart, Rebecca."

31

It was five in the morning and Matt watched as both LAPD and FBI crime scene teams went through Colton Fox's house. The shooters had left quickly, but were inside long enough to toss the small house.

He had a headache. Tony, Matt's boss, was livid that Matt hadn't brought Michael with him.

"That's why Michael is on the team! He's a tactical expert, and you left him in the fucking hotel?"

Tony Greer rarely swore, so Matt knew he was truly angry.

"Michael was monitoring the situation. We didn't know what we'd face, and—"

"You didn't know what you would face so you should have had him with you, Costa! You know better than this."

"You're right."

"Of course I'm right!"

Matt told Tony everything he knew, and Tony said he was calling the chief of police and to expect a full debrief as soon as he and Michael arrived at the police station.

"Maybe the LA office has a reason they don't trust LAPD if the department is pulling bullshit like this," Tony said.

"The witness indicated that one of the individuals Craig may have been investigating is the son of an FBI agent."

"Who?"

"Last name Avila. Ryder is on it."

"I'll follow up with Ryder, and I want this Colton Fox in a room answering questions."

"Yes, sir."

"This is bullshit, Matt."

"Yes it is."

"Is Detective Quinn ours or theirs?" Tony asked.

Matt knew exactly what he meant. He hoped he was right when he replied, "Ours."

Lieutenant Elena Gomez showed up just after five while Matt stood to one side watching the scene. Michael was his eyes and ears now, working with the teams.

"You took over my crime scene?" Elena said.

He stared at her. "I need a face-to-face with Colton Fox. Now."

She didn't say anything, but he gave her credit for not denying the truth.

"Where's Kara?" she asked.

"Not here."

"Dammit, Costa, we're on the same team."

"Are we? You have been lying to her for months. She mourned his death. She still struggles because she blames herself—that she wasn't here to have her partner's back."

"There was a threat on her life and she wouldn't leave if she knew Colton was in deep cover. I have more considerations than Kara's feelings. I have a corrupt cop on my staff," she said, her voice very low, "and I don't know who the fuck it is."

"You don't?"

"No!"

He didn't believe her. He was about to confront her when she said, "No one knows Colton is alive except me, Lex and my commander. I need him to stay deep as long as possible."

"Dyson didn't?"

"In LAPD we kept it from our own people, but Dyson helped put together the investigation."

"So other people *did* know."

She didn't say anything.

"Did you know that Violet was here?"

"No."

"So you didn't even know that your own detective had a key witness staying in his house?"

She hesitated.

"Do not lie to me, Gomez."

"I didn't know she was here, but yes, Lattimer told me yesterday afternoon that she was safe."

"Kara has been busting her butt trying to find her!"

"I didn't even tell my boss."

"You don't trust your boss? This is a mess, Gomez."

"I trust him, but Violet identified a cop as Chen's killer. A cop! We've been trying to figure out how to work this, because everything has gotten out of control."

"A cop by the name of Steve Colangelo."

She blanched.

"You lied to me. Yesterday, then just now, not two minutes ago. This is when you should have brought the case to the FBI," Matt said. "The FBI investigates public corruption."

She laughed. "Trust me, they would have fucked everything up. You know how Thornton went after Kara. She wasn't the only detective on the FBI hot seat. Half the men and women I know have had to deal with asshole feds who fucked with their cases, treated them like shit on their shoes. And don't pretend you don't know there are feds just like that. It's the culture here. LA FBI pisses all over us and tells us to be grateful for the rain."

She was on a roll, and Matt didn't interrupt. When Elena was done ranting, he said, "Colton Fox. He has evidence that an FBI agent may be compromised. Violet Halliday gave it to him."

"So Kara has Violet?"

Matt didn't want to trust this woman—she had lied to him, lied to Kara, but she was his access to Colton.

"She has her someplace safe. Don't ask me where, I don't know."

Elena relaxed. "That's okay. Kara will keep her safe."

Michael approached, looked at Elena, then said to Matt, "Not many prints, likely the ones here aren't the suspects'. Don't know if they found anything. Documents in the desk show a Harley-Davidson motorcycle registered to Colton Fox. It's not in the garage—the lock was broken."

"Kara took it. I heard it, but didn't see her." He turned back to Elena. "I need to talk to Fox now. Not tonight, not tomorrow, but as soon as you can bring him in."

Quietly, she said, "I don't want to break his cover, not now."

"Don't you think that people are going to know he's alive by now?"

"No. Even if they suspected, they'd never know where to look for him."

"I don't want to pull seniority, but I need to know everything you know, everything Dyson suspected, and I need the fucking evidence Violet Halliday gave to your detective."

She looked at her watch longer than necessary, then said, "Okay. Three hours. I'll try to find him."

"Where?"

"First Contact office."

Matt motioned for Michael and they left.

Elena waited until the feds were gone, then she called Will Lattimer. "Bring Colton in, 8 a.m., your office."

"What happened?"

"Clusterfuck. Just do it, and if he balks, tell him Code Three."

Cover may have been blown, mandatory debrief, don't come into the station.

Colton Fox played by his own rules, but so far, he had never ignored a direct order.

Then she called Lex. "Kara knows everything."

Matt and Michael went to the hotel and Matt took a shower. It was only five minutes, but when he got out he had four missed calls and a text from Tony to call him immediately.

Still dripping, Matt called his boss first. "What?"

"Bryce Thornton was found dead," Tony said bluntly. "Shot in his vehicle. LA FBI put a BOLO out on Quinn."

"What the hell happened?"

"Thornton drove to a dog park in South Pasadena. A cell phone was found a hundred yards from his body, smashed, but Kara's prints were on it."

"Which proves nothing."

"They know she's driving the motorcycle that's registered to her allegedly dead partner Colton Fox. A text came in from an unknown number to Thornton to meet at 4 a.m. at the park for proof that Kara orchestrated the hit on David Chen. The text claims that her personal gun was used to kill Chen. Thornton contacted his boss Chavez, and she told him to wait for backup. He didn't. Their theory is that Kara killed him because she believes he outed her and Fox, getting her partner killed."

"That's all bullshit," Matt said.

"I know," Tony concurred, but Matt barely heard him.

"Not least of which she has known since late last night that Fox is alive and well," Matt said. "I was with her until two this morning. She called me at two thirty and said she was destroying her phone because Violet Halliday believed someone had tracked her on it. She's taking Halliday to a safe location, and she was nowhere near South Pasadena at four."

"You don't know that for a fact."

287

"I know that Kara would never ambush anyone, even that bastard Thornton. You can't possibly believe she's guilty."

"I don't. But Kara has to come in for questioning."

"How was he killed?"

"Shot point-blank from the passenger seat while he was sitting in his car. It appears that he met someone there, they got into his vehicle, shot him, got out. No prints on the door. No witnesses. There are some security cameras in the area, but none in the lot. The FBI is going through them, and Sloane is going to verify everything they find."

"This is no coincidence."

"What?"

"We just learned that an FBI agent may be compromised and now they're going after Kara. Which puts my investigation in jeopardy."

"Remember what I said—get Kara to come in on her own, before this blows up."

"She hasn't called me yet." It might be one of the missed calls, but Matt didn't tell Tony that. "As soon as I talk to her, I'll tell her what's going on. I'm pulling the plug on this undercover LAPD investigation. Lieutenant Gomez is bringing Fox in to talk to me."

"To you and Michael. Where you go, he goes. Too many people are dropping dead out there."

The missed calls were from Granderson, Sloane and an unknown number, who didn't leave a message. He called Granderson, who was cordial but not forthcoming. He insisted they wanted to interview Kara about what Thornton claimed his informant said, and verify her alibi because her phone was found at the scene of Thornton's murder. Matt said he was working on it, but she was on assignment protecting a witness and not reachable for a couple of hours. "Brian, please don't put a BOLO out on her. She'll come in and talk, but if it leaks that she's sus-pected of killing an FBI agent, it puts a target on her back."

"That ship has sailed, but it's just a BOLO for information. Nothing about Thornton's murder."

"She didn't kill him. I stake my reputation on it."

"I hope for your sake that you're right." He ended the call.

Matt called Sloane. She sent the call directly to voice mail, and five minutes later, after Matt was dressed, she called back.

"I had to find an empty office," she said quietly.

"I talked to Tony and Brian. What do you know?"

"Brian is upset. He's inclined to think that Kara is involved in some way, but I think that's based on his guilt over investigat-ing Thornton. But that's not why I needed to talk to you. I read your report about Jonathan Avila—he's Rebecca Chavez's son."

Matt froze. "From a previous marriage?"

"No—she's been married for thirty years. She has always used her maiden name. The only reason I even know this—she never talks about her family, never brings anyone by—is from the research I did on Chavez and Thornton when I first got here. Rebecca's husband is Paul Avila, and I documented that she had two adult children, a son and daughter. She has one photo of the four of them in her office on her desk. After some research this morning, I learned that Jonathan Avila works for the city. I don't know in what capacity, but I can find out."

"According to Halliday, he's on the housing commission re-sponsible for approving grant money. Can you verify that, find out how much he's paid and how much money he's responsible for allocating? Anything else you think is important. And any-thing about Avila's wife. I'm hoping to get actionable informa-tion in an hour. I'll let you know what I learn."

Five minutes later, his phone rang. Unknown caller.

"Costa," he answered.

"Hey, Matt, I'm alive and well," Kara said.

Relief flooded through him. "Where are you?"

"Colton's uncle has a cabin in Big Bear. There's a gas station a mile down the road, and I'm using their phone."

"Is it safe?"

"Yep. Violet is tucked in. I even slept for two hours. Honestly, I haven't ridden a bike in months and I'm feeling the pain in my thighs, needed a couple Tylenol. I'm getting her some supplies, then heading back. I'll call on my way out with my ETA."

"Stay put."

He hoped Tony didn't fire him.

"Explain."

"Bryce Thornton was killed. Your phone was found at the scene, there's a BOLO. They know you're on Fox's bike."

Silence.

"Kara? You there?"

"What time?"

"At 4 a.m. He received a text from an unknown number who claimed to have evidence that you orchestrated the hit on Chen—that your personal gun was used."

"If my gun was used, someone took it from my condo. I have a lockbox in my closet with three handguns—a .45 Colt, a .40 Glock, and a .38 revolver. I have my .45 SIG on me. The box is basic, someone with minimal skills could pick the lock, or with minimal tools, break the seal on the box. Four a.m.?"

"Yes."

"Good. I have a gas receipt time-stamped 3:56 a.m. from a twenty-four-hour gas station in Big Bear. I also bought Tylenol, beer, water and junk food inside the mini-mart. The clerk would remember me because he was admiring my Harley. Not many girls ride Harleys."

"Send a copy of that receipt, and I'll get them to drop the BOLO."

"You didn't think—"

"Of course not! I don't want the cops to get itchy fingers thinking you killed a fed."

"I'm coming back, Matt. Someone is setting me up. Two hours, tops. I don't have a phone, they didn't sell any at the mini-mart, and nothing else is open right now."

Matt looked at his watch. It was seven.

"Hold off on sending the receipt," he said. Tony was definitely not going to like this. "I don't want anyone knowing where Violet is. Do you think she's safe there?"

"Yes. But I don't want to leave her alone for long. Where are you going to be?"

"First Contact."

32

The world Rebecca Chavez had painstakingly built and protected for years was being challenged from all sides. But she
would overcome. She would fix each problem, one at a time.
The situation she found herself in wasn't her fault; in fact, had
everyone just listened to her and stayed the course, this would
have been over months ago.

She'd been right. Then and now. But fear was a powerful
emotion, and everyone else reacted instead of just doing exactly
what she told them to do.

The FBI should have had the Chen case; if not for Bryce's
obsession with Detective Quinn, she could have taken the case
and dragged it out until she could make it disappear. But Bryce
had tunnel vision when it came to Quinn. Once DDA Dyson
insisted on prosecuting, Chavez knew she would have to take
care of Chen before he could plea and provide information that
might come down on her people.

Then she learned what Dyson was really investigating—the
apartment building that Chen owned and the money the city

gave him for housing his women—and she realized Dyson was the bigger problem.

All because of Kara Quinn.

By that time, she started fueling Bryce's hatred of the detective to the point where he would do anything to take Quinn down. He wanted to arrest her, interrogate her, reopen all her cases.

That would have been no good because if Bryce looked too deeply into Chen's business, he might uncover the connection to Jonathan—and that was unacceptable. Rebecca had buried it deep, but it was there.

Still, she had it under control until information started leaking out. She had no idea how, but suspected that LAPD had an undercover operation. It was exactly something that Kara Quinn would do—pretend to be one place, but actually be infiltrating another. The only way some of the information could have been leaked—like the documents on Sunflower Homes— was if someone knew what they were looking for. And then that ridiculous podcast discussing Angel Homes and Muriel and making the connection that she was Lydia Zarian's sister.

That didn't directly impact Rebecca, but anything that damaged Lydia could potentially come back on Rebecca.

Her own contact confirmed the undercover operation, but could find no information as to who the operative was, other than a male detective out of Lieutenant Elena Gomez's squad. Then he learned there was a whistleblower who worked in city hall.

That was nearly a month ago, but it explained almost everything that had gone wrong.

It was eight in the morning and Brian Granderson had called her into the office. She would be late, but he would accept her excuse. She had an exemplary record and being a few minutes late for a meeting when one of her men had just been killed in cold blood was justifiable.

She and Lydia needed this heart-to-heart before Lydia put into play one of her insane plans.

Lydia was at home in her opulent estate above the 210 not far from the Glendale Freeway interchange. The view was spectacular, but Rebecca had always thought Lydia's taste was on the tacky side. Ornate statues and columns were bad enough, but she'd painted her house *pink*. A light pink, but still pink.

Rebecca parked her sensible, older Mercedes in front of the wide staircase that led to the portico. Ivy grew along stone fences—the stone did *not* match the Mediterranean-style mansion. And gargoyles standing sentry on the top of Greek columns on either side of the door? Just…no.

Rebecca would never say anything to her oldest friend, but clearly money didn't buy taste.

She rang the bell, irritated. Lydia knew she was here—Rebecca had to be buzzed in at the gate—and she should have been waiting with the door open.

Lydia opened the door. "Becca," she said, giving her a kiss on the cheek. Rebecca would never let on that she despised the nickname. The only person who called her *Becky* (not Becca) was her husband, when they were in the privacy of their own home. In public she was Rebecca; her friends and colleagues all called her Rebecca. Except Lydia.

"Please tell me you have coffee," Rebecca said.

"Of course." Lydia led Rebecca to the nook off the kitchen, which had a full coffee bar, and poured a cup for each of them, put cream and sweetener on the table. Rebecca added a dollop of cream and honey into her cup and stirred with a small spoon. Sipped. Watched her closest and longest friend.

Lydia Zarian was an attractive fifty-four because she paid to be an attractive fifty-four. Her hair was professionally done weekly, her makeup flawless, her designer clothing stylish. The nose job and lip job and face-lift were top dollar—if Rebecca hadn't known the woman for forty years, she wouldn't be able to tell.

LA County Supervisor was a powerful position in a power-ful city within a powerful state. In fact, the county board was the largest government entity within a state, serving nearly ten million people. Each board member represented the equivalent of 2.5 congressional districts, making them more important than the House of Representatives—at least here, in Los Angeles.

Lydia had served eight years in Congress, but quickly real-ized she would have more power as one of five than one of over four hundred. When the longtime supervisor of her district re-tired, she ran in a very crowded field. She owed her election to Rebecca and a few others—people who were happy to support Lydia because of what she could do for them. People who were happy continuing to support her, provided certain truths re-mained buried.

"Lydia," Rebecca said, putting her cup down, "we have several problems and need to get everyone on the same page quickly."

"I spoke with Theodore this morning," Lydia said in a dismis-sive tone, "and he *assures* me that the little computer girl didn't find anything important."

"He's lying to us."

"That's a bit harsh, don't you think?"

"Someone is sniffing around Jonathan *and* Sunflower *and* Angel Homes. That puts both of us in the hot seat."

"My campaign has polled this issue. No one cares about it. The complexity alone of any potential conflict of interest is nearly impossible to explain in a thirty-second sound bite, and there is nothing illegal in the grant process. *Nothing.* Dorothy has personally reviewed the legal paperwork, and the nonprofits all abide by state and federal law. You and I do not directly bene-fit, and therefore, we are above reproach." Lydia smiled, leaned back and sipped her coffee as if her analysis put an end to the conversation.

Lydia looked at every issue through polling. It drove Rebecca up a wall. She'd always been that way. In high school, it was the perception more than the truth that Lydia cared about. That was how popularity contests were run, and Lydia was the most popular person wherever she went.

But Rebecca knew the law; she would most certainly be brought up in front of the Office of Professional Responsibility. And while she might be able to feign ignorance about what her son was doing, or what her sister was doing, say that she was completely hands-off on all of their businesses, she couldn't walk away from murder. She may not have pulled the trigger—or in this case, plunged in the knife—but she would still go to prison.

The thought terrified her.

"Theodore overstepped this week," Lydia said without sounding at all concerned, "but *something* had to be done about David. He was going to talk."

"It's not David I'm concerned about. I had a plan for him from the beginning..."

"Which your agent screwed up."

Rebecca was not going to play this game with Lydia, but she couldn't help but remind her that it could have been much, much worse. "Ben was supposed to monitor David, but *your brother* dropped the ball. I was the one who found out about the raid."

"Only hours before it happened," Lydia snapped. Then she sighed. "Why are we sniping at each other, Becca? We have been friends and partners far too long to bicker over this minor setback."

Minor setback? Rebecca wanted to grab Lydia by the shoulders and shake sense into her. There was nothing minor about murder. "You're right," Rebecca said, trying to be conciliatory. "But I need to know what our exposure is. What did that girl take from Theodore's office?"

"I don't know for a fact that she has anything but theories, but she may have been able to re-create deleted data."

"We paid a lot of money to have that information wiped. And a low-level IT drone was able to find it? How?"

Lydia dismissed her concern with an arrogant flip of her bejeweled wrist. "Even if she has it, there's nothing illegal. A computer glitch. We'll ride it out. I'm working on a statement to shield everyone."

Lydia was *technically* correct that the grant process wasn't illegal, but funneling money to friends and family through the grant process was unethical and *could* be seen as a conflict of interest. While there were a lot of people involved in different aspects of their enterprise who all had a reason to want to keep the process quiet, if word got out that Craig Dyson's murder was connected to them, someone would talk.

Lydia couldn't have *all* the potential threats killed off. She might control the media spin, and she might have high polling numbers, but her support would disappear if she was suspected of a capital crime.

And she was completely ignoring David Chen's involvement. The city had paid him millions of dollars for use of his building—the building where he housed his employees.

Employees? They weren't paid. You're believing your own lies, Rebecca.

She really didn't want to be in this position, but here she was.

"You're forgetting I'm an FBI agent," she said. "I don't have idiot voters with short attention spans to manipulate. I will be held accountable by my office."

She had three years until retirement. Three years, and then she would begin to collect the profits she had to defer for the last decade because she didn't want to report them. The money was just sitting there, waiting for her—she and Paul could finally enjoy their lives rather than working so hard for everything they had. She had done everything in her power to set up her children to have comfortable lives. It wasn't Jonathan's fault that this got screwed up. He shouldn't have to pay for it.

"You've done nothing," Lydia said, sounding exasperated. "You have plausible deniability. Jonathan has done nothing wrong, and even if some intrepid reporter exposes him, his pedigree and good works will save him. In fact, I'm working on a statement he can give. It will start with his call for a full investigation and audit of the grant program. That he is shocked that anyone would cheat the system that is set up to help so many of the unfortunate. My office will coordinate it. We'll find pockets of waste and clean it up. Anything that our detractors find later will appear like nit-picking and sour grapes. It's a win-win."

"You're forgetting one important fact. Murder does not get brushed under the rug so easy."

"We have no connection to anything so unsavory."

Did she really believe that?

"Theodore has made several very bad decisions," Rebecca said. "And your daughter is in the middle of it."

Now, Lydia bristled. Of course she did; no one could say a negative word about her perfect, beautiful daughter.

"Nothing can be traced to him," Lydia said haughtily. "He's too smart."

Rebecca was done. Sometimes, talking to Lydia was impossible. "Someone needs to find and deal with Ms. Halliday, and that means dealing with Detective Quinn, who apparently has her under wraps. I'm working on discrediting Quinn, but if Halliday told her anything, the detective will be a pit bull in ferreting out and exposing our business. She doesn't let go." Rebecca stood.

Lydia walked her to the door. "I'll remind you, Becca, that I did put out a hit on Detective Quinn after the media exposure didn't take care of her in March, and the person *you* recommended failed. So I will do this my way."

Rebecca didn't have a response. She walked away and wished she had never met Lydia Zarian.

In the car she made a call she was dreading. It was a bell that couldn't be unrung.

"Dorothy," she said firmly, "your son has made a huge miscalculation, and I think you know exactly what I'm talking about. The repercussions are starting to steamroll, and Lydia is in complete denial. She has a plan and she hasn't shared it with me—when Lydia starts thinking, that's when we always get trouble."

"I'll take care of it," Dorothy said and ended the call.

33

It was eight fifteen by the time Matt walked into the First Contact office. He'd sent Michael to Kara's condo to check on the status of her firearms and any sign of break-in, then talk to the neighbor who had the key. They needed to get in front of this.

Lex, Elena, Peter and Will were there. Colton was not.

"I told you to have him here," Matt said.

Elena stared him down. "I don't answer to you, Agent Costa."

"He'll be here," Will said. "Please, sit."

Matt glanced at Peter. "You were in on this, too? You told Detective McPherson that you had no idea why Craig was killed."

"I'm his investigator for the DA's office. I do background checks and interviews. It wasn't until I met with Elena and Lex on Monday night that we started thinking the grand jury investigation might have been the trigger. He hadn't even planned to impanel them until late last week."

"It's water under the bridge," Lex said. "Let's focus on the now. I hope you told Kara to stay away."

"Kara is on her way here," Matt said. "I have proof she was

nowhere near the dog park where Thornton was killed. I will submit it to Granderson once Violet is safe." He and Kara realized that if there was a mole in the FBI—or more than one—and they shared the receipt, Violet could be tracked to Big Bear.

"How solid?" Peter asked.

"Receipts and witnesses."

"Why was her phone at the park?" Peter asked, curious. "It seems odd that her phone would end up at the same place where Thornton was killed."

"Violet believes that someone tracked her through her phone, and since Kara had an FBI-issued phone, GPS is always on." Matt remembered how hard it had been to get Kara to switch over to the FBI phone, but she'd finally agreed.

But someone would have to have her FBI phone number to track it, and they would have to either be a really good hacker, or in law enforcement.

A cop killed Chen. He could have tracked her, set her up, killed Thornton.

Matt turned to Elena. "Did you know Monday that a cop killed Chen? Did you lie to me?"

"I didn't know until Tuesday morning."

"You had plenty of time to tell me."

"We've been through this, Costa," Elena said. "All I had was Violet's statement to Colton that she thought it was Colangelo. He was wearing a mask. I need her official statement, and we were going to do that today, once Colton finished putting together evidence. This was a seven-month-long undercover investigation—we couldn't shut it down in five minutes."

"That cop could have killed a federal agent. And that's on you."

She bristled. "He didn't," she said through clenched teeth. "I'm not reckless, Agent Costa. Colangelo and Officer Perez—who saw Violet running from the scene and is on the same shift as Colangelo—have been under twenty-four-hour surveillance since Violet reported to Colton. They were transferred to jail duty for the week, pulling twelve-hour shifts, on camera the entire time. When they leave, I know, and they are both tailed."

Colton Fox sauntered in through the rear of the building.

Matt stared at the man who had once been an important part of Kara's life, professionally and personally. He was average height and build, lean and muscular. His unshaven face was darkly tanned from being outdoors, his brown hair sun-bleached. He had a small scar on his face. He wasn't handsome, at least Matt didn't think so, but he did have the dangerous good looks that attracted some women. Rough and confident.

Matt hated this man. Did he hate him because he had faked his death and caused Kara pain? Or did he hate him because Kara had once been involved with him?

Maybe both.

Matt suppressed his emotions and said, "Everything on the table. Now."

"You must be Special Agent in Charge Mathias Costa," Colton said with a cocky half grin as he pulled a chair out. He wasn't dressed like a homeless man, but was clean and in jeans and a black T-shirt, his gun and badge on his belt. Clearly, the undercover operation was over.

He sat, leaned back, casual.

Matt sat across from him. "I need to know what you know. All of you. Whatever is going on here, it's over. We have a dead prosecutor and a dead FBI agent. We all want answers."

No one spoke at first, then Will threw up his hands. "For shit's sake," he said. "This guy is right. No one was supposed to die—you were investigating graft and corruption, fraud, white-collar crimes where people aren't killed. Now Craig, who we all liked and respected, is dead. Violet is in danger. I told her I would watch out for her. She's been through hell. She lost her mom not two months ago. She has done everything we've asked, things we didn't ask but she knew we wanted. She found the truth and now she's in hiding, terrified. So no more bullshit."

When no one said anything, Will turned to Colton. "Colt, everything. For Violet, and for Craig."

Colton gave an almost imperceptible nod, then Will turned to Matt and said, "I was the catalyst for this investigation."

Matt turned his attention to Will. "Because of Chen's building."

"Yes. I didn't know at the time he owned it, but I had been tracking a group of nonprofits used as pass-throughs for grant money. It's a legal scam. However, if Chen was a criminal—and if he used this grant program to profit off human trafficking—then maybe we could expose the system and effect change. Craig agreed. Once we had enough evidence, he could take it to the grand jury. At the same time, Violet came to me about a suspicious computer crash in city hall. She's been instrumental from the beginning, first working with me, then working with Craig."

Lex said, "While Kara was on leave—when you first met her—she and Colton were outed by someone to the media. We believe it came from the FBI, so you can see why we were skeptical of everyone in the LA office. Kara was out of town in Washington, as you know, but Colton was shot by a gangbanger while he was undercover in another operation.

"It was while he was in the hospital that Elena, Colton and I decided a deep cover operation into the housing grant scandal was warranted. We took it to our boss, he agreed. There were too many facilities, too many people potentially involved, and the issues are complex. We needed solid evidence to build a case of massive government fraud and corruption. Without layers of proof, we'd never get it through the DA's office. Letting everyone think that Colton died gave us the time and freedom to work the case as long as it took."

"The homeless are invisible," Will said. "Most people walk by and either intentionally ignore them or just don't see them.

Colton was able to get physically close to every facility that is operated by these nonprofits. He has thousands of pictures of how the money is spent—or not spent. He has gone through the shelter process and documented what they do and don't do. Craig intended to launch a grand jury investigation into the finances of the nonprofits under an obscure law related to public monies. While on the surface there is nothing illegal about how these nonprofits are set up, they are ultimately pass-through accounts that enrich the people running them. Craig believed he found a loophole by which the grand jury could issue indictments for fraud."

"He said it was threading a needle," Elena said. "But he was the master."

"It is clear to me that this grand jury investigation that was supposed to start today is the reason he was killed," Matt said. "And you kept that information from me from the very beginning."

"Not intentionally," Elena said.

"Yes, intentionally. You should have come clean Monday night when you came by the hotel. Instead, you sent me on a wild-goose chase pointing fingers at the FBI for alerting Chen to the LAPD raid."

"They did!" Elena snapped. "It came from the FBI, just like leaking Colton and Kara's identities to the press back in March."

"We have no proof. Neither do you."

"I wasn't going to risk Colton. Not when we were so close."

Matt turned his attention to Colton. These people were getting on his last nerves. "Where is the evidence that Violet uncovered?" he asked.

"Safe."

"I want it."

"This isn't your investigation, Costa."

Matt wanted to punch the smirk off Colton's face.

"What did she find?"

"Evidence that Theodore Duncan, the chief of staff to the mayor, intentionally installed the virus that crashed city hall."

"He could argue that he wasn't aware of the virus," Matt said.

"He could," Colton said. "Yet his sister is married to the head of the housing commission overseeing all grant writing for homeless, transitional and permanent housing. His sister is married to Jonathan Avila, the son of FBI agent Rebecca Chavez."

He was grinning, as if he had won some unknown game. Matt didn't care. Let him take the win on this.

Matt remembered what Elena said to Rebecca last night. She was asking about her family, and it had seemed out of place. "You knew last night."

"I knew as soon as Colton found out. He reports regularly. I wanted her to know that we were closing in. That I knew about her family. But we have to tread carefully."

"You tipped your hand."

"I needed her to make a mistake," Elena said.

"That mistake may have been what got Thornton killed."

"You have no evidence of that," Lex said. "Let's not start casting blame for every little thing. We had legitimate reasons to keep Colton's involvement secret. We have a lot of little pieces, but no smoking gun. That's what the grand jury was for—to put all these pieces into one clear indictment."

Matt understood that—white-collar crimes were a bitch to prosecute—but that ended when Craig Dyson was killed.

He said, "We have cause to bring Duncan and Avila in for questioning."

"Duncan's mother is Dorothy Duncan."

"I don't know who that is," Matt snapped.

"A criminal defense lawyer for the top firm in Los Angeles," Elena said. "She'll eat us alive if we don't have impeccable evidence of wrongdoing. Jonathan may be the son of an FBI agent, but he's also the son-in-law of a powerful attorney."

Matt had a headache. He switched gears.

"Colangelo, according to Violet, killed Chen. He didn't kill Dyson, but the two murders must have been coordinated. Someone had to have planted the rope and grappling hook on the roof. It was top-grade equipment. Someone had the skill. Dyson's murder was professional and well executed. Chen's murder was quick and bold. But they were orchestrated by the same person." Or people. Considering how many people profited from the grant program, it wouldn't surprise Matt that a criminal cabal was running the entire operation while he and the LAPD were chasing the wind.

"Who?" Peter asked. "Because proving it is going to be next to impossible. You're not going to get warrants for a fishing expedition."

"Who loses the most if the grand jury investigation begins?" Matt asked.

The others considered. "Numerous nonprofits may lose their funding. Some of the directors make a million, more, a year. Travel is paid for, cars, perks," Peter said.

"Contractors," Lex offered. "The Venice Beach project, which is costing the city over two hundred million dollars, might be halted. That would rack up costs, contractors would lose money, financing. Potentially go bankrupt. The Sunflower Group Homes is also on the list—they might be shut down or audited."

"Exposure," Will said.

"Excuse me?" Matt said.

"Violet has been leaking information about our investigation to a podcast, *LA with A&I*. They don't have a huge audience, it's mostly tech people and gamers. But when the press wouldn't pick up when I leaked information about Supervisor Lydia Zarian's sister, Muriel Coplin, profiting off Angel Homes, Violet gave the documents to the podcast. It's all public record, but not only do you have to look deep for it, the connections aren't at first obvious. Violet and I drew the lines to make the connection easier to see."

"That was when?"

"It aired Monday morning."

Matt shook his head. "Not enough time to orchestrate Craig's murder."

"It was enough time to target Chen," Elena said. "Chen had information—maybe information that would hurt Zarian or people close to her. And he'd only recently been making noise about cutting a deal. If he lost the motion in court on Monday, he could have immediately talked to Craig. Craig felt that Chen had potentially explosive information that could prove criminal intent to defraud the taxpayers of Los Angeles."

"We need to pull in Colangelo and Perez separately," Lex said. "We don't know if Perez is involved. They'll call their union reps, but if we can turn one or both of them, we'll have some answers."

"Violet is the only witness to Chen's murder," Will said. "That's why they went after her."

"They," Matt said. "Who are *they*? Are you talking about some vast conspiracy with the Zarians and Duncans and an FBI agent and a cop? That's a lot of people and I haven't heard any proof, just theories."

"Well, I have one more theory," Elena said, clearly angry with either him or with the entire situation. "When Dyson started the process to impanel the grand jury last week, someone panicked and had Chen and Dyson killed."

"*They* went after Violet," Colton said, "because she's a computer genius and can prove the data was intentionally wiped from city hall. Better, she knows how to get it back. They've been running this scam for years, making millions. They got cocky and greedy, and when they were faced with losing their gravy train? They resorted to murder. And," he said with a smirk, "I have the proof that Zarian's brother, Ben Kaprielian, runs Sun-flower Group Homes."

He pulled a flash drive from his pocket and slid it across the table. It landed right in front of Matt. "Consider it a gift for keeping an eye on Kara for us."

He snatched it up. "Elena, the cops. I need to talk to them."

"I'll arrange it, but you're not doing it alone. I'll be there."

"Pick them up separately, take them to your headquarters, we'll interview them. I'm also going to inform Granderson that Chavez may be compromised." He got up to step out and make the call, but before he could leave, Kara walked in.

Cheeks flushed from her ride down the mountains on the motorcycle, Kara was windswept and vibrant.

Her eyes settled on Colton.

Matt followed her gaze.

Colton smiled sheepishly, his eyes lighting up.

Colton was in love with her.

Matt stepped out and called Granderson, then he called Tony and told him the plan.

Kara knew that Colton was alive, but seeing him rattled her.

"What did I miss, other than a resurrection?" Kara walked over to the coffeepot and poured herself a cup mostly because she needed something to do with her hands. She willed them to stop shaking and wished Matt hadn't left.

They had all lied to her. She felt hollow inside, so she focused on murder. Craig's murder.

"How's Violet?" Will asked, breaking the awkward silence.

"Good," Kara said. "Safe."

"Where?" Peter asked. "If we need her statement, can she be here quickly?"

"Sure," she said, noncommittal. "I recorded her statement, just in case. She can do it all official once I know she's no lon-ger a target."

"Peter," Elena said, "can you check with McPherson and see if he has any new information about Dyson's murder? Lex and I are going to bring in Colangelo and Perez and set up the interviews. Kara, tell Costa I'll text him the time and location."

"Can't wait," Kara said. She stared at Elena. She had trusted her, believed in her, admired her.

Elena had lied to her about Colton's death.

Lex's deception hurt just as much, if not more. He'd been like a father, a mentor, more than a boss…and he let her believe that her partner, her friend, had been murdered. Let her believe that it was because of Bryce Thornton's obsession with her that Colton was dead.

She would never forgive them.

Elena averted her gaze first, but Kara felt no pleasure. She was too raw, too sad. They left with a mumbled goodbye. Will noticed the tension, went to his office and closed the door.

Kara was alone with Colton.

Damn, the emotions threatened to tear her apart. Betrayal, guilt, relief, regret, grief, but she settled on the anger because she and anger had always been on good terms.

"Hit me," he said.

She wanted to. She wanted to pound his chest for making her hurt, for making her grieve.

She didn't move. He sat at the table looking all cocky and confident, as if all he had to say was *I'm sorry* and she would forgive him.

"With the hit Chen put out on you, it was safer for you to be three thousand miles away, and we all knew you would have wanted to back me up."

He was right, in part. She was safer three thousand miles away. But she didn't have a death wish. She wouldn't have been happy about it, but she would have stayed away. Maybe she didn't know it at the time, but now as she thought on it, she realized she was a good cop; she would have protected herself—and the integrity of the case.

And not ended up hating the man she had so many conflicting and complex feelings for.

"I get it," he said. "I'd be mad if the situation was reversed."

"You think I'm mad." Her voice was calm. She didn't expect the calm, but right now it soothed her.

Now he looked confused. "You should be. It was fucked, but someone really tried to kill me. I was shot in the back—I can show you the scar. It could have happened again. It was safer for me and you if everyone thought I was dead."

"Huh." She shook her head. "Whatever." She tossed him his keys. "Take your bike. Do your job."

He caught his keys in one hand. "Come over tonight. We'll talk, work everything out."

"Talk? Is that what we do?"

Now he smiled, got up and walked over to her. "I've missed you, Kara." He reached out for her, touched her arm, leaned in toward her, his head tilted just a bit, his lips crooked, his dimple barely visible under his three-day growth of beard. He was so sexy and she'd always been hot for him. They'd had something… she thought. Once. It seemed like a million years ago.

She punched him in the gut and turned to leave.

"See, you feel better now, K. Come over tonight. I'll make it up to you."

Slowly, she faced him. She was surprised she could speak. "I don't feel better, Colton."

"You want to do it again?"

But his tone had shifted a bit. Wary. Worried.

"No."

"Kara, forgive me. Please. We had something good, let's find it again."

"We had something," she said. "Good? I don't know. Maybe sometimes it was. It's lost now, and I don't want to find it."

"You don't mean that."

"Then you don't know me at all."

She walked out.

34

One thing that Sloane had learned from her parents growing up on a ten-thousand-acre ranch in Montana was to treat everyone with respect. Ranch hand or cattle buyer, farrier or banker, be kind and it would come back to you in spades.

She'd taken that mentality to college and then the Marines. She never used her rank unless required for her job, she never treated the enlisted as inferior just because they didn't have a college degree. Here in the FBI, she was surprised by how some agents treated civilian staff as borderline servants. Polite, sure, but few agents cared to make personal connections with the people who supported them.

Sloane knew every civilian who worked in or with her squad. She knew the guards at the front desk by name. It was a skill her mother had instilled in her and it served her well.

Especially this morning.

She went to the IT department and asked to see Vikram Mehta. Vik had helped her with a computer problem she had the first week she was on staff, and she'd come to him multiple times to learn more about the FBI system. He was smart and knowledgeable, and had worked in the IT department for years.

"Hey, Agent Wagner, what can I help you with?"

"Is there a private office where we can talk?"

"Sure, is there a problem?"

"No, but I need some help, and it's confidential."

They took a small office and Sloane said, "Do you know how the LAPD/FBI portal works?"

She knew he did. He'd helped develop it years ago.

"Sure, what do you need?"

"Is there a log of who accesses the portal on either end? For example, if I were to review cases in the portal, does it generate a log of my access, badge number, time, date?"

"Yes, but it's not used for anything. It's just a log file."

"But you have it."

"I can run a log under any parameters."

"Is it possible to access the portal and *not* have the visit logged?"

"No. I mean, it's technically possible to be unknown—use a 999 code instead of your employee number. But the computer IP, time, date, request is all logged. Now I'm curious. Especially since the portal is rarely used except in joint investigations."

"I need to see the log for February 17 and 18 of this year. Every access into the portal—who, where, when. Is that possible?"

He hesitated.

"If I need permission, I'll get it." She could have Granderson approve it, but she hadn't wanted to reveal she had a direct line to the SAC.

"No, of course not. You said confidential, right?"

She nodded.

He motioned for her to follow him. Without talking, he logged into his extensive system and typed rapidly. Screens flew by, then he typed in the dates she'd given him and hit Print. A second later his printer spat out a page. He handed it to her.

It was a log of one access to the portal on February 17, at 2215 hours. And it was indeed a 999 code, so the individual didn't put in their badge number or their ID.

"Whose IP address?"

"ASAC Rebecca Chavez. It's her computer."

Sloane didn't know for certain that this was the Chen raid, but the time and days matched.

"Thank you, Vik. I appreciate this."

"Anytime, Agent Wagner."

"Call me Sloane," she said.

She went to her cubicle and, after glancing around to make sure no one paid her any attention, sent the information about the log and IP address to Granderson.

There had to be a reason. Her son worked for the city, was involved in housing grants that were the subject of Dyson's investigation. Was there another connection? How deep did they go? Sloane had already looked into her husband and immediate family. But what about extended family? Friends?

She might tip her hand. Now, however, was the time.

Sloane dug deep into everyone who touched Rebecca Chavez's life.

As Matt drove back to police headquarters, he didn't push Kara to talk. She was sullen after leaving First Contact.

Michael called when they were halfway to LAPD headquarters.

"Michael, you're on speaker with me and Kara."

"Kara's Colt is missing. There are signs that the lockbox was picked—it's a standard metal box with a keyhole. Nothing else appears disturbed."

"How did they get in?" Kara asked.

"I don't know. No sign that the condo's locks were tampered

with, but I could be missing something. He could have had a key. **Your** neighbor said he hasn't seen anyone suspicious. Some-**one should** print the place."

"I'll call Popovich," Matt said. "But whoever took it likely **wore gloves**. Secure the place and meet us at LAPD."

"Copy that. Sorry, Kara," Michael said.

"I'll live," she muttered. "You know what this means. That my gun was used to kill Chen, and probably to kill Thornton."

"Don't jump to conclusions," Matt said. "We don't have ballistics back yet."

"We'll know by the end of today," Kara said. "Clearly someone lured Thornton out to kill him, using my name and gun. That was a big fucking bread crumb for the FBI to follow right to me."

Michael said, "Traffic was miserable coming out here, so it'll be at least an hour before I'm back."

Matt hit End and glanced at Kara. "We'll find the gun and the killer."

"None of this helps us solve Craig's murder. Different killer, different method. All because he was going to expose corruption?"

"They aren't thinking," Matt said. "A public corruption case like this can take months—even years—to prosecute. It's extremely difficult to prove. But murder *is* a major crime."

"Politicians don't like their dirty secrets being exposed. It could cost them an election, right?"

Matt paused. "There is an election in five weeks."

"See? Something like this comes out now as people are sending back their ballots? People might pull their heads out of the sand and look around."

"You don't have a lot of faith in the system."

"I vote in every election. I do a little research and end up skipping half the races because I think they're all bad."

"Some people vote because of issues, so the person might not be the best, but voters agree with the issues they represent."

"When has a politician not flipped on an important issue? The last time I voted because of an issue was a guy for mayor because he was supported by the police union and he talked a good game about making sure cops had the tools to do our job. I was a new cop, I thought yeah, I want tools, I want a good partner, I want more training, better guns, the whole nine yards. He wins, great! Not six months later he fucks us all over jumping on the media bandwagon about a video taken out of context where two cops tasered a suspect. First zap, the guy keeps coming, so second cop gets in on it, guy goes down hard. The prick turns against us, apologizes, gives the guy money for his injuries and rehabilitation and pain and suffering. When the truth came out—full body cam footage, witness statements, drug screening to show the guy was wired on meth, and proof he'd hit a cop with his car—did he apologize? No. Then he screwed us over in the next budget."

"You hold grudges."

She shrugged. "About some things, I guess I do. So I skip most of the races—does that make me a bad citizen? Maybe it's the people who vote for these idiots who are bad citizens, because if no one put up with the bullshit, maybe better people would want to get involved."

"I see your point."

"You probably vote in every election for every race."

"I vote using the lesser-of-two-evils philosophy."

Kara laughed. He was happy to hear the sound. He parked in the garage and turned off the ignition. "We're going to find Craig's killer."

"I want the killer, but I *really* want the person who hired him."

35

By the time Matt and Kara arrived upstairs, Elena Gomez had Juan Perez and Steve Colangelo in separate rooms, each with their own rep.

"What's your take?" Matt asked Elena.

"Steve is angry, belligerent, wants to leave. Juan is confused."

"Is it fake?"

"Genuine." She handed Matt their files. "Juan graduated from the academy five years ago, has several commendations in his file for going above and beyond, was on graveyard until eight months ago when he requested and was moved to days after his wife had their first child. His wife is an elementary teacher in Santa Clarita, where they live. The shift moved him from one precinct in the division to another. They don't ride with partners on day shift—we don't have the numbers to double up—but if they're responding to certain calls, they wait for backup.

"Steve," she continued, "is a ten-year veteran of the force. He and Juan have worked the same precinct and shift since Juan's transfer. Steve is divorced, and his ex-wife and daughter moved out of state. He has a couple of commendations in his file early in his career, but several dings in the last two years."

"Since the divorce," Matt guessed.

Elena nodded. "The divorce rate is high—it's a stressful job, as you know. None of the dings are serious. They were all off-duty related—but he drinks, then he fights. Last time he was suspended for two weeks without pay. That was six months ago, and he's been clean ever since."

"Can I see?" Kara asked.

Matt handed her the file. She skimmed through it, frowned, tapped on the report. "This bar, where he was suspended for fighting? It's a known gambling spot. Colton and I—" She hesitated a second, then said, "We worked an undercover gig nearby, learned about it, sent it up to Vice. Don't know what they did with the intel."

"Could he have a gambling problem?" Matt asked Elena.

"Something to ask."

"Maybe something to ask Juan," Kara said.

"Kara, do you mind watching from observation?" Matt asked.

She shook her head. "If Steve used my gun, I don't want to jeopardize the case by being in the room."

Kara watched through the glass as Matt and Elena took Juan's room first.

Juan's rep was seasoned, tough but reasonable. They set some ground rules for the interview, and Matt and Elena gave in on most everything.

"Lieutenant, I want to cooperate," Juan said. "I don't know what you think I did, but I will answer any and all questions to the best of my ability."

"I appreciate that, Officer. You have an outstanding record with the department, and I hope we can resolve this quickly," Elena said. "You gave a statement on Monday after the shooting in the park that you saw a woman running from the scene that you identified as Violet Halliday, who is known to you."

"Yes."

"You stated that you did not see her with a gun, and you did not see her shoot anyone, correct?"

"Yes, correct."

"Where was she when you noticed her?"

"Can I bring up a map on my phone?"

Elena nodded.

Juan pulled out his phone and brought up a satellite image of the park and sidewalk. "I was here, across the street on the side-walk. I was leaving early because of a dentist appointment—I asked for the time off last month."

Kara couldn't see the phone but she had already read Juan's report and pictured his description.

"That's not under review, Officer. We're all entitled to use our sick leave or personal time as we wish."

"I was walking from the department to the dentist, which is a couple blocks away, when I heard two gunshots in rapid suc-cession. I was already out of uniform, didn't have my service weapon, but I knew it had come from the park and I thought someone would need help. I didn't see anyone down at first, but I was looking farther south, toward the edge of the park." He pointed to the map, and Kara knew he was referencing a spot near the parking structure. "Then I heard three more shots and that's when I saw Violet running. I noticed her here—" he in-dicated a path that went diagonal through the park toward the street "—and she was running through the park, toward the southeast corner."

"You recognized her, though she was fifty yards away?"

"Yes. I've seen her often at the Fifth Street Park where there is a homeless encampment. She volunteers there, and—" He hesitated.

"And?"

"Her mother used to live there. I kept an eye on her, when she was around."

"Where is her mother now?" Matt asked.

"She died. Drug overdose. Will Lattimer told me last time I saw him."

Kara felt for Violet. She'd really been through the wringer this year. But she was tough, and she hadn't backed down, even when she saw Colangelo kill. That took guts.

"You volunteer for First Contact?" Elena asked Juan.

"Not a lot, not like Violet, who's out every weekend, but a few times. Will has a good group, his approach makes sense. He's a veteran, I'm a veteran."

"Did you see anyone else fleeing the scene?"

"No. I'm kicking myself. I was watching Violet. She was running fast, I thought she was terrified—most people are when they hear gunfire. A lot of people were running, some dropped to the grass. Then I turned to see what she'd been running from, and that's when I saw two men down on the sidewalk."

"Did you see the shooter?"

"No, ma'am, no one was standing near them. I went over to the two fallen men while I pulled out my phone to call in the shooting, but ultimately I didn't call because several cops in uniform were running my way." He paused. "I stated all this, twice. I know what I saw and what I didn't see."

"We're not doubting your statement, Officer," Elena said. "How long have you worked with Officer Steven Colangelo?"

"For the last eight months, since I transferred to days."

"And you often respond to calls together?"

"Yes."

"How often?"

"At least once per shift most days."

"Do you socialize outside of work with Officer Colangelo?"

He looked at his rep, who asked, "Is this relevant?"

"Yes," Elena said.

Juan replied, "No, we don't."

"Do you socialize with anyone in the department outside of work?"

"Yeah, all the time. Most of my friends are cops. My dad was a cop, my mom was a dispatcher, my sister is a deputy sheriff. We rag her about that," he added with a nervous smile.

Elena smiled. "I would, too. But not Officer Colangelo?"

"I don't see why that's important."

Kara did. They weren't close, they weren't friends. It was very important.

"Were you aware of his suspension six months ago?" Elena asked.

"Yes."

"Did he discuss it with you?"

"Not really," he said with a shrug.

"But?"

"He wasn't happy about it."

"Most cops wouldn't be. Did he feel it was undeserved?"

"He said he should have been docked three days, not two weeks."

"If it was his first offense, it would have been three days."

"Oh." Juan looked contrite. "I didn't know."

"No reason you should have," Elena said. "Do you know why he was suspended?"

"He got in a bar fight. That's what he told me. Defended himself."

"It was at a bar that has an illegal betting room."

Juan didn't say anything. Did he know? He did, Kara thought. He knew about Colangelo's gambling, or at least he suspected.

"Do you know if Officer Colangelo has a gambling problem?"

"Is that why you really called me in here? To rat on him? For gambling?"

"No. I wouldn't do that to you, or to him. I will lay it out for you if you can answer my question."

"I do not have personal knowledge of Officer Colangelo's gambling."

"But?" Matt said when Juan didn't continue.

Kara could see that Juan was wrestling with his conscience. She would, too, without knowing why her boss was asking the questions. No one wanted to talk shit about other officers, not to the brass.

After a brief conference with his rep, Juan said, "I am aware that he travels on his days off to Indian gaming casinos. He's single, he seems to spend most of his disposable income there. He complains a lot, so I don't think he wins much."

"Have you ever gone with him?"

"I have a ten-month-old baby, Agent Costa. I don't have money to throw away." He turned to Elena. "You said you would lay it out for me. What's going on?"

Elena turned off the recording.

"This stays between us, Juan."

He nodded.

"Violet Halliday has come forward and identified Steven Colangelo as the shooter on Monday. She was less than twenty feet from him. She ran because he turned the gun toward her. She went into hiding, but one of our people found her and is keeping her in a safe house."

He stared, shook his head.

"We're taking her statement seriously."

"There's a rumor that Violet shot Chen," Juan said.

"I'm aware of the rumor," Elena said. "We do not believe there is any validity to it, but I can't go into any more details. You may go home, and I'm giving you the rest of the day off. Report back to the jail tomorrow to finish that rotation, then you'll be back on your regular squad next week. And, Juan? Do not discuss this conversation with anyone."

Steven Colangelo wasn't as pleasant or forthcoming with Elena and Matt, Kara noted through the one-way glass. His rep tried to keep him calm, but Steve was belligerent.

"I've been sitting here for two hours twiddling my thumbs," Steve said. "There's no reason! You need to tell me if I'm being written up for anything, but you're treating me like a suspect, not a cop. I have rights."

"Yes, you do, which is why your rep is here," Elena said. "I need to know where you were Monday between noon and twelve thirty." She glanced at his wrist. "Nice watch." It had a yellow face.

He scowled. "Check my logs. I don't remember specifically, but it'll be in my logs."

Elena pulled a paper from her file. "You clocked in at 0600, took your seven at 11:48, and went back in service at 12:35. Where did you eat?"

He shrugged. "I don't remember."

"I have the security footage from the precinct that day. You took your seven in-house, went down to the gym."

"I often work out during lunch."

He flexed, and Kara knew the type. Thought he was tough when he was simply a bully.

"You left the building in civilian clothes at 11:55. Returned at 12:25."

"If you know where I was, then you know where I was. This is tedious, Lieutenant." But he had lost some of his rage. He glanced at Matt, assessed him.

"I have a witness who claims they saw you shoot David Chen and his bodyguard on the sidewalk late Monday morning. So if you tell me you were somewhere else, I can verify your alibi, and you can go on your way."

He didn't say anything. He stared down at his hands. At his watch. He was thinking. Kara could see him working through everything in his head, trying to figure out what to do. When the truth became evident, that there was no way for him to lie his way out of this mess, his entire body shifted, his face fell and he looked at his rep. "I'm not going to jail. No way. I need an attorney. Someone who is a damn good negotiator. Until then? I'm not saying another word."

36

By the end of the day, they had very little from Steve Colangelo, but enough to generate small leads for Matt to follow.

Colangelo was being blackmailed.

A halfway decent cop goes through a rough divorce. Starts gambling, loses money, gets in fights, doesn't care about himself or the job, takes bribes. But going from bribes to murder is a big jump.

Matt didn't want to deal with the asshole, but he didn't have a choice. Steve Colangelo was just one cog in a much larger wheel, and if they didn't figure out how this conspiracy worked—and who ordered the murder of Chen and Craig Dyson—Kara would never be safe.

The DA granted Steve partial immunity provided that he served ten years in federal prison and fully cooperated. If he lied, the deal was off and he would be tried for killing Chen and his bodyguard, and as an accessory to Dyson's murder.

Steve admitted that he had been working for David Chen for several years. "Minor" work, like intimidating business owners, relocating a meth lab in Chinatown that was too close to Chen's business, moving problem girls to other jurisdictions. When Chen was arrested, he expected Chen would turn on him, but he didn't. Steve waited it out and believed nothing would happen to him until last week when a man approached him at a casino in San Diego. Steve had just lost; he was angry and bitter.

The man identified himself as Conrad and said Chen needed to die. If Steve wanted the evidence of his crimes to go away, he needed to kill Chen before he entered the courthouse on Monday. If Chen was alive, the files would be on Commander Joe Campana's desk before Chen exited the building.

Conrad gave Steve a Colt .45 and information about where Chen would be and when. The cameras would be disabled on Spring Street from the dog park to the corner of the courthouse, and as long as he killed Chen on that block, there would be no evidence.

Steve did everything according to the plan outlined for him, then he saw Violet out of the corner of his eye. She looked right at him. He didn't think she recognized him because he wore sunglasses and a face mask, but he had a gun in his hand and she ran. He pocketed the gun, mask and glasses and walked briskly through the park, then circled around, heading back into police headquarters. But he told Conrad that Violet had seen him.

When Matt asked about the gun, Steve said he left it where Conrad told him to: under the seat of his personal vehicle. When Steve went home that night after work, the gun was gone and his file was there. Steve burned the file.

"I figured Conrad planned to frame someone," Steve said, "but I didn't think about it."

Of course not, Matt thought as he silently fumed. Steve didn't care who got hurt as long as he was in the clear.

"You will work with a sketch artist," Elena stated.

He shrugged. "Whatever."

His attitude grated on Matt. He asked, "What did you know about the apartment building where Chen housed his workers?"

"Nothing."

"You knew where it was."

"Sure."

"Did you know that Chen received a government grant for the building?"

"Really? What a great scam." He grinned. "The guy had friends in high places."

"Who?" Matt asked.

When Steve hesitated, Matt said, "You agreed to fully cooperate. Ten years is nothing for two cold-blooded murders. Who are his friends in high places?"

"I didn't *socialize* with him," Steve said dramatically. "The guy was a prick. But, he claimed to have a politician in his pocket. I thought it was the mayor for a long time, but I overheard him talking with his bodyguard once about 'she' in context of a land deal he was trying to get approved through one of his shell corps. He also had a fed." Steve smirked. "That probably irks you, doesn't it, Costa?"

"Do you have a name?" Matt said, keeping his voice calm.

He shook his head. "All I know is that he thought she was a bitch and he told Xavier—the bodyguard Quinn killed—that he would have to remind 'the bitch' that they had 'a partnership, not a dictatorship.'"

"How do you know the comment was about a federal agent and not the politician or someone else?"

"Context. This fed had wanted him to postpone a shipment of women coming in because of a planned FBI raid in Long Beach. Chen didn't want to, but agreed to hold them out at sea for three more days. She wanted ten. He said it was a partnership, and this was his compromise. Apparently, they worked it out, because there were a lot more—and younger—women who came in a week later. Older teens. They work hard, aren't sick, still believe they're going to earn enough to get out in a few years." He shrugged.

Matt barely restrained himself from hitting the bastard.

"When was this shipment?"

"Late February."

"Before the raid?"

"A year before. I don't remember the exact day, but it was the last week of the month."

Matt made a note. That would be easy to verify with FBI records.

Elena said, "Do you know who killed Craig Dyson?"

"No. Look, I may have broken a few laws, but I wouldn't take out one of my own people. Chen was a criminal, no one cares that he's gone. Dyson was a good guy. I'm sorry he's dead."

"So this Conrad didn't mention anything about Dyson or a grand jury investigation?"

"No. Just Chen. I kill Chen, the file is mine. I did, it was. If I knew who killed Dyson, I'd tell you."

Elena read an incoming text message. "The sketch artist is here."

The lawyer said, "My client has been in custody for nine hours straight. He is entitled to a meal, sleep."

"He can have a meal while the sketch artist sets up, then sleep when he provides us with a face."

"I will have to object—"

"It's fine," Steve said. "I don't care. It's not like I have anywhere else to be."

The sketch artist was good. An hour later he had a sketch Steve said was near perfect.

Elena had Steve taken to the jail. He would be in solitary until he was transferred to federal prison next week. They'd debrief him again before then, but Matt didn't know how much more the cop knew, and he didn't think Steve intentionally held anything back.

Matt made copies of the sketch and they met in Elena's office—him, Elena, Lex and Kara. Matt had earlier sent Michael to stay with Violet in Big Bear, and Kara had been relieved. She'd planned to drive back, but was exhausted after a couple long nights.

Conrad was thirty-five to forty-five with cropped brown hair, dark eyes, a high forehead, square jaw. His ears were narrow and lay close to his head, his lips thin and tilted down. Faint acne scars dotted his cheeks.

Kara stared at the drawing for a good two minutes.

"Do you know him?" Matt asked.

"Wait," she said. "Just...wait."

She sat down at Elena's computer and logged in. A minute later, she brought up the courthouse security footage from Monday. She found the best view of the killer, when he was sitting on the bench down the hall from Craig's office.

"He was wearing a disguise—hair, beard, cheek fillers, glasses. But...it's him. I can't swear to it in court, but I'm eighty percent positive. What did Colangelo say his height was?"

"Five-ten to five-eleven."

"That matches. Eighty percent certain."

"That's good enough for me," Matt said.

"I'll get this to McPherson and my boss," Elena said. "Go home, sleep. It's going to be a long day tomorrow."

It was ten o'clock when Matt and Kara returned to the hotel. Michael called and said that Violet was good, that he'd checked out the property and everything was secure.

Matt had concurred with Kara to keep the receipt from Big Bear to themselves, but he'd sent it to his boss Tony and explained why he didn't want to give the receipt to anyone at LA FBI. He didn't have to say it twice: if there was a bad agent, Violet could be in danger should her location leak. Tony talked to Granderson and while Granderson wasn't pleased that Tony was withholding proof of Kara's alibi, he agreed to remove the

BOLO, though he expected the FBI to make Kara available for questioning.

Kara didn't want to go in for questioning. She planned to avoid it as long as possible. She didn't kill Thornton, and she wasn't positive that Rebecca Chavez was the only corrupt fed in the building.

She collapsed on the couch. She wanted a beer, but was too tired to get up and call room service.

Matt sat next to her and took her hand. "I know you want to keep it platonic when we're working, but I need to hold you."

Matt sounded unusually tired and sad. "What's wrong?"

"I'm tired, I'm depressed, I'm angry. We learned so much… and still don't know enough."

She leaned into him, tucked her feet under her; he wrapped his arm around her, held her to his chest.

It felt right to be here with Matt. Kara didn't do romance well. She liked sex, she liked to have fun, but she wasn't a romantic "flowers and chocolate" kind of girl. She never wanted to get too close to anyone, for a lot of reasons she didn't always understand. Sure, her childhood was a mess. She'd been raised by con artists, kept everyone at arm's length because she didn't know who her parents would con next. Getting to know your mark, *liking* your mark, was a recipe for disaster. By the time she escaped that life and moved in with her grandmother—when her dad was in prison and her mom was running around with her "boyfriend" who was a total dick—she didn't know how to shed her wariness of intimacy.

She didn't particularly like people, as a general rule. They usually disappointed you, or they expected more from you than you could give. They lied. They manipulated. But living with her grandma Emily for three years taught her that there were good people, and those people were worth fighting for. She loved Em. Unconditionally, without reservation. Em was the first, maybe the only, person she could say that about.

Over the years she had befriended people. Mostly cops, because hey, that was her life. She was a cop, she hung with cops. She had grown to admire many of them—like Elena, her training officer. Lex, her boss. Colton, her partner.

And they all lied to her.

Romantic relationships were nonexistent. Sure, she had sex. Colton wasn't her first or her only. He was, though, the only cop she'd slept with before Matt Costa. Easier to not get involved with people you worked with. She kept her love life simple, focusing on casual relationships with interesting men who didn't want commitment. When they started sniffing around at something permanent, she turned away.

There was a firefighter she dated awhile. They'd met on the job. He was tall, firm, sexy and fun. That didn't last long because it was clear he was looking for a wife.

Then there was a bartender. More laid-back, definitely not looking for a wife, but she didn't like his serious marijuana habit. It wasn't illegal, and she didn't care if he used occasionally even though she didn't, but she'd always found excessive pot smoking made people unmotivated and dopey.

And there was one doctor—she'd been shot in the line of duty, it wasn't serious, but the bullet was stuck in her shoulder and she had to go to the hospital and have it removed. Dr. Nick Mendoza. She didn't care that he was eleven years older than she was; he was a walking cover model, smart but humble and as skilled in bed as he was in surgery. She really liked hanging with him, even if he owned an expensive house and drove a BMW and spent far too much money on her.

Then she found out he was writing scripts for opioids and other drugs for the wealthy women of Hollywood. He made more money pushing pills than he did as a surgeon. How did she find out? They were out at dinner at the Odyssey, an amazing restaurant with an incredible view of the Valley, and one of his "patients" came over and asked for a refill. She was drunk, and he brushed it off as her intoxication—he told her to call his office to set up an appointment—and Kara had played along with him. Then she contacted a friend of hers in Vice, learned that Dr. Mendoza had been under suspicion for years but there was no active investigation, and she volunteered to work undercover and take him down.

Three months later, he was arrested. He avoided jail time, but lost his license and paid a hefty fine.

In between her varied relationships, she would hang with Colton. The whole "friends with benefits" thing. She liked Colton. More, she trusted him. A kindred spirit. They spent more and more time together, and she stopped dating other men. They never talked about being in a relationship, but it had developed into a comfortable habit.

And then he was dead.

And now he wasn't.

She felt Matt's heart slow under her hand. Heard his even breathing and knew he was asleep, his arm still holding her close.

Matt was different from everyone who came before. He was honest and honorable. At first, it was just mutual attraction. Lust. But her lust hadn't been satiated after a night in bed. For months, she tried to convince herself that they weren't anything special, that one or both of them would realize it wasn't going to work, even though they both played hard and worked hard.

She was a street cop, rough around the edges, a lot of baggage she sometimes dealt with by drinking too much, a chip on her shoulder that was sometimes pretty darn big. She was hardly girlfriend material. And Matt could be so rigid about some things. Too damn traditional. He had a temper that he worked hard to control. He was a federal agent, not someone she was inclined to trust or even like.

Look where her trust had gotten her in the past. Parents. Elena. Lex. Colton. All lied to her. Betrayed her. Tried to convince her their deceit was necessary for her own good. For the greater good.

Deep down, she knew that Matt would never hurt her like that. She didn't hurt easily, to be honest, because she never expected people to live up to her expectations. They never did.

But so far, Matt had.

You've known Lex and Elena for twelve years. You've known Colton for more than a decade. Give Matt time; he'll disappoint you.

The thing was...he had done some things that hurt, but he hadn't done them on purpose. And when he realized how she felt, his apology was sincere. He never made her feel like she was to blame for his mistakes. She certainly wasn't perfect—she'd had to do her own amount of groveling when she screwed something up.

Kara liked things the way they were. She didn't want to mess this up.

She probably would. She didn't understand how relationships were supposed to work.

But for now...now she could lie against this man and accept that he was one of the good guys. That he truly cared about her, he cared about justice, and he would do what it took to honor his commitments. She didn't know what he saw in her, other than they were good in bed. But with him, she liked herself more.

She feared, deep down, that it wouldn't last because nothing lasted with her. That she would do something Matt couldn't forgive or forget—or that he would realize he wanted more than she could give him. That he wanted a forever commitment, kids, a house and picket fence and minivan.

A wife.

The thought terrified her. But she pushed that aside as he shifted in his sleep, his arm tightening around her before relaxing.

She drifted off.

THURSDAY, OCTOBER 10

37

Matt walked into FBI headquarters at seven o'clock Thursday morning, greeted by both Brian Granderson and Sloane Wagner.

Brian had pulled the plug on their undercover investigation even though Sloane had only found part of what they had been looking for. But in light of Thornton's murder and Chavez's suspicious behavior, he wanted to now be straightforward with his internal review. After Sloane uncovered evidence that Rebecca Chavez's computer had accessed the LAPD portal the night before the raid on Chen's factory, Granderson's approach was best.

While they didn't have solid proof that Chavez had been the one to leak info about the raid, they had enough to question her. Coupled with the information about her son, Jonathan Avila, and his grant program being under investigation by the DA's office, they would push hard and hope something shook loose. In the meantime, she would likely be suspended while they looked into her actions.

Brian led Matt and Sloane to a secure room where a video conference was set up. To keep leaks and gossip to a minimum, only Vik Mehta from IT was in the room to handle the equipment. Vik looked a little nervous, but Sloane gave him a warm smile and thanked him for coming in so early.

Brian said, "We appreciate your diligence and confidence in this matter."

"Yeah, of course, anything you need, Mr. Granderson, sir." He cleared his throat. "I have Assistant Director Greer, Special Agent Heller, and FBI Analyst Ryder Kim on a video call."

"Bring them on, thank you."

Once they had realized there was a possible white-collar crime and public corruption case at the root of Craig Dyson's murder, Matt had brought in Zack Heller. Zack was a genius when it came to tracing money and uncovering financial crimes. While Matt found him annoying and difficult to work with, there was no doubt of his brilliance.

A moment later, the large wall screen was split between the three men on their respective computers.

"I've read your report, Matt, and I talked to Brian this morning," Tony said without preamble. "What approach have you decided with ASAC Rebecca Chavez?"

"She'll be brought directly to my office when she arrives this morning," Brian said, "and Matt and I will interview her. Unless she makes a startling confession, I intend to suspend her with pay and refer the matter to OPR."

"Make sure Chavez understands that she must make herself available for questioning," Tony said. "Not only by our department, but LAPD. She can and should have a representative during any LAPD interview."

"Of course," Brian said. "Also, we confirmed that the ballistics match in the Chen homicide and murder of ASAC Bryce Thornton. The report arrived early this morning, and Matt and I discussed the implications as he drove in."

"What is your take?" Tony asked. "That Officer Colangelo lied about giving the gun back to the man he calls Conrad?"

"No, sir," Matt said. "He seemed relieved to share and there was no sign of deception. We haven't disproven anything he told us, and what we could prove shows he told the truth. Detective Quinn observed the interview from another room, and she has advanced training in interrogation. She concurs with my assessment."

"I'm aware of Detective Quinn's credentials, Matt. And what's the status of her missing firearm?"

Brian straightened. Matt hadn't told him that Kara was missing one of her personal weapons, though he had informed Tony as soon as Michael confirmed.

"LAPD sent over a crime scene tech to go over Kara's condo. She indicated that one of her personal firearms, a Colt .45, was missing from a secure lockbox she kept in her bedroom. She has no knowledge of when it went missing. She went on record that the last time she saw the weapon was when she left in March of this year. She hasn't been to the condo since. Agent Harris interviewed her neighbor, who had nothing to add, and a detective is following up with others and checking building security."

"Keep me informed."

Matt said to Brian, "I intended to tell you as soon as we had the theft confirmed."

"You can see why this looks bad," Brian said.

"Yes," Matt said, "but Kara didn't kill Chen or hire his killer. This is a setup."

"With all due respect," Brian said, "we need to follow the evidence. She shouldn't be anywhere near this investigation."

"Brian," Tony said, "you and I will discuss this later. I understand your concerns, and we'll address all of them. For now, let's focus on identifying Conrad. Matt, Kara believes that the sketch matches the man she saw kill Craig Dyson?"

"She won't swear under oath as she's not one hundred percent positive, but his key features match. Colangelo believes that Conrad retrieved the gun between twelve thirty and when he left work at six. Colangelo parks in the structure next to LAPD main headquarters. There are security cameras at the entrances and exits. Detectives Caprese and McPherson have partnered and are in the process of reviewing the footage. We have a good description of Conrad and we may be able to identify his vehicle, if he drove in. If he walked in, we can confirm Colangelo's statement and possibly get a better image of our suspect."

"If the statement is accurate," Brian said, "it means that either Conrad gave the gun to someone else to kill Agent Thornton, or he killed my agent."

"Brian, do you believe that ASAC Chavez has any culpability in Thornton's murder?" Tony asked.

The question carried a lot of weight, and Brian took a second before he answered.

"She has already stated that he contacted her at two forty-five Wednesday morning and informed her that he would be meeting with an informant regarding evidence that Quinn may have ordered the hit on Chen. She ordered him not to go, and said that he agreed and would wait for another contact from the informant. She claimed she didn't know that he went to the park without backup."

"You don't sound like you believe her."

"I don't know what to believe at this point," Brian said, his voice showing the first real sign of stress. "Phone records confirm that Bryce called her and they had a four-minute conversation. We know that his body was discovered at five ten that morning by city maintenance. The autopsy puts time of death between three and four."

"He was set up," Tony said.

"It seems plausible he was," Brian said. "Still, while Bryce had a blind spot when it came to Detective Quinn, I don't see him flaunting procedure in such a fashion or lying to his superior."

No one said a word for a good ten seconds. If Brian's assessment of his agent was correct, Chavez lied about what Bryce had said during their phone conversation. If she knew he was going to the park even without backup—or expecting backup to be provided by his superior—she may have been party to the setup.

Matt didn't like her, but he hoped he was wrong about his suspicions.

"Keep me and your director in the loop," Tony said. "On the allegations of fraud and public corruption, Agent Zack Heller is one of our top white-collar crimes experts, and Mr. Kim and Agent Wagner have been assisting. They have information."

Zack had been fidgeting on-screen, and now he seemed relieved to be able to speak. "So, yes, this is a very interesting case," he began. "I have reviewed everything sent to me—the statement by Mr. Lattimer, the public records that Agent Wagner and Ryder have uncovered related to the grants and nonprofits in question, press reports, and the file that Matt obtained from Mr. Dyson's office.

"Mr. Lattimer is correct that on the surface there is nothing illegal about any of these grants or expenditures. However, the nonprofits being used as pass-throughs are certainly suspicious and I can see why Mr. Dyson felt that they warranted a grand jury investigation. There are some state and federal statutes regarding *intent* that may come into play. Since this is not my area of expertise, we would need to consult with the AUSA to determine what recourse the federal government has here.

"For example, there appears to be a comingling of federal and state monies with the city monies. This is not a crime. The money is given to local governments for the purposes of assisting the homeless, and comingling that with local money could be justified if it's used for those purposes."

Zack was certainly in his element here, Matt thought. He hadn't warmed to the white-collar crimes expert, no one on the team had. But when it came to following the money, Zack was the best.

"But the grant process itself is rife with the potential for fraud,"

Zack said. "There is no mechanism in these grants I've reviewed to account for the funding. Meaning, there is no built-in accountability. The entity receives five million dollars, they file the proper reports, and they have done their job. They do not have to prove *based on the contracts* where the money went or justify why they passed the money through to other nonprofits after taking a cut of the funds."

Brian asked, "Is this common or an outlier?"

"Apparently, this is common in the homeless grant process, but it would be highly unusual in the private sector. Cities contract with nonprofits to provide services and yet don't demand transparency or reports, such as who they helped or how many meals they prepared or individuals they housed. On the surface, this seems unethical but not illegal, as several people have said. Yet there are both federal and state laws that may have been violated regarding the fiduciary responsibility of state and local governments in approving the grants as written."

"So while the grants themselves or the actions of the non-profits may not be illegal," Tony said, "the city's lack of oversight could be a legal violation."

"Yes." Zack nodded. "And if it was *willful* or, as Mr. Lattimer suggested in his interview, individuals in government profited from the grants, then it's certainly illegal. However, Mr. Dyson's files are incomplete. Based on his reputation and the witness statements from Ms. Halliday and Mr. Lattimer, plus the reports from Detective Fox, he should have extensive information that was fed to him by those three individuals. I don't have it."

"You're saying," Matt began, "that the grand jury files we retrieved from his office are not sufficient to open a grand jury investigation, and that someone may have removed records."

"Removed them, or perhaps he didn't keep the records in his office. His notes refer to facts that I can't verify from the files."

Heller was very good at his job, but long-winded and talked around everything. It annoyed Matt, but it was hard to overlook the results, and if Heller said that files were missing, then files were missing.

"Briefly, from Dyson's notes, even though you don't have files to reference, did he believe he had cause for an investigation?"

"Yes," Zack said, his voice both increasing in speed and intensity as he spoke. "Based on his written notes, I suspect he planned to use the grand jury process to force an audit. Considering that the city spends one billion dollars a year on these grants, plus receives extensive federal and state money that they also distribute, a grand jury investigation could spur more fiscal responsibility and make the distribution process more efficient. In an audit, every dollar would be accounted for, and the pass-through accounts would be heavily scrutinized. If half of what Dyson claims can be proven, I would think the investigation would force change in the system."

"But you need those files," Matt said.

"Yes."

"What about the flash drive Detective Fox gave me? Or the files from Halliday?"

"The flash drive is documentation about Sunflower Homes, the CEO, the grants, the houses they own. There's nothing criminal there. It's one piece of the puzzle. The files from city hall are more of the same, but there's a lot more and we're still going through it. It's clear from the note Ms. Halliday included that she has identified specific missing files that she believes are stored in an old backup at the city data center."

Matt made note. "Is the information Fox provided useful or not?"

"It could be, once we can compare his evidence with the missing files. I don't know what's in those until I see them."

Brian said, "One of the issues is that the homeless crisis is a political hot potato, and to launch this investigation five weeks before an election makes it problematic."

"Sometimes, it's just the way the case lines up," Tony said.

"We're damned if we do, damned if we don't. We don't do anything, and one side says we held back until after the election to favor one political party. We do something, and the other side says we did it to favor the other political party. It doesn't help when some of our own people have been caught making ill-advised and inflammatory political statements. Believe me, it's one of the biggest headaches of my career, and it's only gotten worse."

"For what it's worth," Matt said, "I don't think that Dyson had politics in mind when he started this. The timeline is clear—he assisted LAPD in the research and the undercover operation stemming from the arrest of Chen back in February and the revelation that Chen received government funding to house the women he trafficked. It's a legitimate case. That it took seven, nearly eight months to build the case is par for the course, that he was ready to bring it to the grand jury in October before an election is just the way the timing worked. Besides, the grand jury could have taken months before issuing any report."

"Okay, we're going to assume his motives were noble and apolitical," Tony said, "as he wasn't running for office and has no family running for office. Zack, what is the government's interest in federal money being used in these pass-through accounts?"

"We have an interest, but the way the grant process works we have given the money to the city to use as they see fit. This limits us. However, we can demand an accounting of all monies spent. Then the government can decide whether to give more or less to the city. Fraud is going to be hard to prove, but these missing files may speak to that. Ryder also has information."

Ryder was much calmer than Zack. Matt wished he could clone his analyst. The MRT wouldn't exist without him.

"Agent Wagner and I have been working together since yesterday afternoon," Ryder said. "We've reviewed all nonprofit tax filings for entities listed by Detective Fox and Mr. Lattimer. There are several nonprofits that have received substantial sums of money and do not appear to do anything other than pass through the money to other nonprofits."

"But that's not illegal," Zack quickly said.

"Not on the surface," Ryder said. "But let me finish. The principles receive hefty salaries, and one thing caught my eye. Some of these people are the same. Muriel Coplin is the CEO of Angel Homes. Angel Homes is the nonprofit that's building a city-approved 170-unit project in Venice Beach. She has allocated grants to other nonprofits for different aspects of the project, such as construction, supplies, environmental reports and more."

"Which is pretty standard," Brian said. "One organization doesn't have the skill or expertise to handle all aspects of a multimillion-dollar project."

"True," Ryder said, "but it depends who is getting these contracts and if there is a bidding process. But I'm jumping ahead. The CEO for Sunflower Group Homes is Ben Kaprielian. Sunflower has received tens of millions of dollars over several years. It funds group homes for transitional housing, and has received funding from Angel Homes as well as directly from the city. Kaprielian is Coplin's brother. Agent Wagner?"

Ryder nodded and Sloane spoke. "I worked primarily in public databases to confirm identities and run backgrounds on all the key names in the grants process. Lydia Zarian is a member of the board of supervisors. She is also a sister to Kaprielian and Coplin. She has decision-making authority over many of the projects that benefit these nonprofits. Kaprielian and Coplin, along with several other people I've identified, run other nonprofits. They profit through contracts in building, housing, food, supplies, et cetera. Ryder and I are putting together a matrix of how this works, but it's going to take more time. Halliday and Lattimer have extensive documentation we're still culling."

"If you need more people, you have them," Brian said.

"Thank you," Sloane said. "The other thing we uncovered is

that the individual responsible for approving all homeless-related grants is Jonathan Avila. He was appointed after the election of the mayor four years ago, and answers directly to Theodore Duncan. Avila is married to Duncan's sister, Annabelle. Avila is also the son of Rebecca Chavez, as I informed you yesterday."

Hearing Sloane lay out the bread crumbs so clearly put everything in perspective, Matt thought. Clear, concise, to the point. He could visualize now how the entire operation worked—who approved the funding, who benefited and why.

"Since then," Sloane continued, "I have learned that Agent Chavez is Duncan's godmother, and Chavez, criminal defense lawyer Dorothy Duncan, and Supervisor Lydia Zarian all went to the same private Catholic high school in Glendale. They've all been married for more than thirty years and only Chavez kept her maiden name, so the connection wasn't obvious until I started digging.

"And—this is one more connection—Krista Zarian is the live-in girlfriend of Theodore Duncan. They haven't registered as domestic partners, so there is no economic interest statement required."

"Which means...?" Matt asked.

"Most city employees, including Duncan, are required to file a statement of economic interest regarding income outside of employment, property other than primary residence, investments, those sorts of things. Similar, but more extensive to economic statements we are required to file as federal employees. They also report half of their spouse's holdings as California is a community property state. But not being married or registered as domestic partners, none of Krista Zarian's economic interests are reportable."

"Okay. Do you think that was deliberate?" Matt asked.

"I'm not comfortable assigning a motive," Sloane said, "but they appear to have lived in the same residence for at least three years. Krista is the treasurer of *every* nonprofit we've looked at—

nine of them so far. The listed treasurer is 'KZ Accounting.' Research confirms that Krista is the sole owner of KZ Accounting LLC. She earns $250,000 a year per nonprofit, which totals at two million, 250 thousand a year for the nine we've found."

"Accounting pays well," Zack interjected, "but not that well."

Sloane said, "Krista is twenty-six, and she graduated from UCLA four years ago with a degree in graphic design. KZ Accounting LLC filed as a business with the state a full year before she graduated. The law firm that drew up the paperwork is Duncan, Young, Lee—which is Dorothy Duncan's firm."

"And that's just what we've found so far," Zack said. "There could be more. It's a matrix, a spiderweb of nonprofits within nonprofits, but the names are repeating. And this is what I think Dyson was looking for and may have found. These connections may be in the files we know are missing. Even if there is no law against what these people are doing, if someone in the city is directing contracts and money to friends and family *even if those friends and family are doing something legitimate*—it's suspicious. But this doesn't look legitimate. I don't see how a twenty-six-year-old graphic designer makes more than two million as an accountant."

"The homeless industrial complex," Matt muttered.

"Excuse me?" Tony said.

"Something Will Lattimer said the other day. So, what you're saying, Zack, is that Dyson may have found a law under which to prosecute someone on this list for fraud?"

"Fraud, maybe. But California has a very specific and obscure law that has never been used, that I know of, regarding nonprofits and how they spend their money. Meaning, if they receive state money they are required to open their books at the request of a grand jury. Because the city comingled city and state money, that means *any* of these grants could have state money—they can't retroactively say, 'oh, no, this was only city money.' Well, they could, I suppose, and then it would go to court. So it's a potentially sensitive issue, and that's what Dyson was focused on."

"This is hard to prove," Brian said.

"These cases always are," Tony concurred. "What we have are two unsolved murders that may have been committed by one person we know as Conrad. And the solved murders of Chen and his bodyguard by a cop who was blackmailed by Conrad. Zack and Sloane, you both focus on the money. Anything you need, let me know. And Brian? You and Costa focus on homicide. I want the killer—or killers—in prison."

So did Matt. He was glad he and Tony were on the same page.

"And," Tony continued, "anyone who is involved after the fact will be prosecuted as an accessory to murder. I'm taking no prisoners. The first person who spills gets a deal, but everyone will get jail time."

Rebecca Chavez sat in Brian Granderson's office, her hands firmly clasped in front of her, glancing first at Matt, then at Brian. Brian sat behind his desk; Matt had pulled over a chair next to his desk so he and Brian would appear united against Chavez. He wanted her to sweat.

"Brian, this is highly unusual," she said, her voice clipped and formal. "Do you have news about Bryce's murder? Were you able to prove what he suspected? That Detective Quinn orchestrated the assassination of David Chen?"

Matt kept his face blank. She was trying to bait him, knowing that Kara was on his team.

Brian said, "Agent Chavez, this is a formal interview regarding information that has come to light. The same gun was used to kill David Chen and Agent Thornton. A Colt .45. We know that there are two different killers who used the same weapon."

He slid over a photograph from the parking garage where Steve Colangelo claimed he left the gun in his car. The man in the photo closely matched the sketch Colangelo approved, and resembled the image captured in the courthouse.

"We have a confession from the individual who killed Chen and his bodyguard. He gave the gun to this man after the shooting. Do you know him?"

Rebecca looked, shook her head. "No. Did Quinn hire him?"

"No," Brian said.

Rebecca was holding her own, but she shifted a little in her seat, seemed to finally realize that she was under suspicion for something.

Brian slid over the log that showed her computer accessed the LAPD portal the night before the Chen raid, and an employee log that showed she was in the building at the time her computer was used after hours.

"Did you access the LAPD portal on February 17?"

"I don't remember."

He slid over the LAPD case file. "The accessed file related to SWAT authorization for a raid on David Chen's warehouse scheduled for the morning of February 18."

She didn't say anything.

"Do you remember now?"

"No."

"You were in the office at eleven that night and your computer was used to access an LAPD report during the time you were here."

"I am unaware."

Matt said, "Coming in late at night you may have been alerted to something suspicious, some activity at LAPD, and you wanted to see what it was."

"That's conjecture."

"Who did you tell about the raid?" Matt asked.

"I didn't access the report."

Brian said, "I will remind you, Agent Chavez, that as a sworn

FBI agent you are required to answer all questions of a superior truthfully and without obfuscation."

"I answered your question. May I leave?"

"No," Brian said. "Did you contact any member of the press regarding the identities of Colton Fox or Kara Quinn and their position within LAPD?"

Rebecca glared at Matt, then said through clenched teeth, "No."

Matt looked at his phone. Michael had texted him to call ASAP. Matt showed the message to Brian, then left the room and called Michael.

"There's a press conference right now on the steps of city hall," Michael said immediately. "The mayor, Lydia Zarian, Dorothy Duncan and Jonathan Avila. There's a lot of media, it might be live, but it's nearly over. I'll get a recording, but Kara is there now. The gist? It has come to the attention of the mayor that there may be improprieties in some of the grants allocated to help alleviate the homeless crisis, and a joint task force between the city and county has agreed to hire a law firm to conduct an audit, led by Dorothy Duncan."

"Well, shit," Matt said. If what he had learned this morning was true, at least three of those people were involved in the grant process itself—and may have profited. What were they up to?

"When a reporter asked what specific improprieties were discovered," Michael said, "Duncan herself answered that the matter was under investigation by her office and a full report would be made available when complete. The timeline for that report is expedited and will be available in ninety days."

"Ninety days is after the election," Matt said. "Both the mayor and Zarian are up for reelection."

"Correct," Michael said. "She took no more questions because of attorney-client privilege, and allowed no one else to answer questions. The mayor, then Zarian, ran through how much they care about people and taxpayers and the whole nine yards, but it reads phony to me."

"Someone tipped them off."

"Violet is with me at LAPD headquarters." Matt had asked Michael to bring Violet in this morning to give her statement, but not to let her out of his sight. Not until they knew she was safe. "Violet blames herself. She leaked information to a podcast and she thinks that jump-started this 'Cover Your Ass' audit by Zarian and the others."

"I want the podcast recording and the tape of the press conference. We'll compare, but tell her this isn't on her. That woman has been through hell this week. I don't want her taking any of the blame from anyone, including herself."

"I already told her."

An armed guard and an FBI agent approached and stood outside Brian's door.

"I have to go, but stick to her like glue."

"Roger that," Michael said.

Matt ended the call and watched as Rebecca and Brian left his office. Brian said to the guard and agent who had just arrived, "Please process Agent Chavez's credentials, secure her weapon, and escort her and only her personal items from the building." He handed the agent a cell phone. "Log the phone into evidence as well as her computer, seal her office and no one goes in without my permission."

"Understood," the agent said.

Rebecca looked pale and terrified. "You're making a mistake, Brian." Her voice quivered and Matt noted her knuckles were white as they clung to her purse.

"I really hope I am, Rebecca. Because if you lied to me just now? You will be prosecuted."

38

Dressed in jeans, oversize jacket, sunglasses, and a generic black ball cap, Kara listened to the press conference outside city hall. Damage Control 101, she thought, watching the crowd, looking for any sign of Conrad, the man she believed killed Craig Dyson. She hadn't seen him yet, but she had his face etched in her mind and wouldn't miss him.

As person after person spoke onstage, Kara realized they weren't saying anything of value. It was hollow, empty, a lot of acronyms and platitudes and concern about taxpayers and the homeless. They said the exact same thing in different ways. They were conducting an audit. Concerned about waste. Cared about the poor. Apple pie and Uncle Sam, whatever. It was like each sentence had been crafted to be a sound bite alone, then strung together to make it seem they had a plan. But the plan was clear to Kara: cover our asses.

Kara didn't understand many of the details in this case. Violet had laid everything out to her yesterday, but she barely followed. Even after talking with the group yesterday at First Contact, she didn't *exactly* know what was going on. Fraud that might not be fraud, corruption that might be legal, grants given to friends and family that appeared to be part of the system and everyone said *nothing to see here, folks.*

But Kara understood murder. One of these people—or all of these people—had conspired to kill her friend Craig Dyson because he was going to expose them. Which told her that there *was* something deeply wrong with what they had been doing with all the money they funneled to the nonprofits that Violet, Colton and Will had identified. You don't kill someone unless you fear exposure for a crime. Or if someone was threatening your payday.

Her gut told her they killed for greed and power. People in power never wanted to give it up. Once there, they would do anything to keep control. But murder? Murder was about greed and fear. The exposure Craig threatened would shut off the free-flowing spigot of dollars going to these organizations that profited their brothers, their sisters, their sons and daughters. And, by extension, themselves.

She would end it. Not alone, but with her team. She would get justice for Craig…and justice for Sunny.

The press in the audience threw out questions that the people onstage answered by simply rephrasing from their previous comments. Her phone vibrated and she stepped farther away from the crowd to answer it.

"Quinn."

"It's Costa. Rebecca Chavez has been relieved of duty and Brian is sending everything to OPR for a full investigation, but we have her."

"Good. Sloane really went above and beyond."

"She's smart."

"But Chavez didn't admit to anything."

"No. She's still pushing the 'Kara Quinn is behind the curtain' card, but it's not flying. Now that Violet is safe, I turned over the receipts to Granderson, just for the files, so you're officially cleared. And Michael interviewed the clerk at the gas station who admired the Harley—got him on record as well."

"Good thinking," Kara said.

"Everyone is on this. Michael just called me about the press conference. This isn't going to end our investigation."

"Nope," she said.

"Are you still there?"

"It's wrapping up, but—"

Colton approached her. Even though he wore a low-brimmed Dodgers cap, big Army jacket and mirrored sunglasses, people who knew him well would know it was him. Bold, right in front of police headquarters, when most of your friends and colleagues thought you were dead.

"Kara?" Matt said because she'd gone silent.

"Give me one sec." She muted the phone and turned to Colton. "What?"

"Will wants us to come to First Contact. He has something."

"He should bring it to headquarters."

"He says there's a leak and he trusts you and he trusts me. That's it. He sounds worried."

She turned her back on Colton and unmuted Matt's call. "Matt?"

"I'm still here."

"Will has some info he says is important. I'm going to First Contact."

"I can be there in thirty minutes."

"I'll meet you there," she said.

"Be careful."

"Right back at ya." She smiled, then ended the call and said to Colton, "Costa will meet us there."

He scowled. "Costa."

"If Will trusts me, he trusts Costa."

"The leak is probably from the fucking feds. I can't believe you trust those people, and after everything Bryce Thornton put you through?"

"I trust Matt and my team. *They* have never let me down."

She let the unspoken truth hang between them: Colton and everyone else she once trusted had disappointed her.

"Forgive me, Kara. If there had been another way—"

"There was another way."

"I love you, K."

She couldn't believe he was doing this now. Here. "Bullshit," she said.

"We have something."

"We *had* something. But it wasn't real."

"What wasn't real? I know you, Kara. Better than anyone."

Last year she would have believed him. Hell, three months ago she would have believed him, been so relieved that he was alive and well that she might have forgiven him. But now? Kara was finally beginning to know herself. And that was because of Matt—not Colton. Matt saw her—not the woman she wanted people to see, but deep down to who she actually was. He saw who *she* wanted to be. No one had ever needed her like Matt.

She had never needed anyone, until Matt.

Need was the wrong word. They had a symbiotic relationship. They were stronger together.

With Matt, she felt like she had someone standing for her: standing behind her in support, standing in front of her to protect, standing at her side to join her in the fight.

For the first time, she had a hint about the true meaning of love.

She said to Colton, "We're not having this conversation. Not now, not ever. I'll get the keys to the rental car and—"

He gestured with his thumb over his shoulder. "I have my bike."

The Harley was parked illegally on the street. She couldn't help but smile. That was so much like Colton.

But if he thought reminding her that sometimes they had fun together, that sometimes they were good together would bring her back to him, he was wrong.

That part of her life was over after she thought he had been killed when she wasn't there to protect him. She might be able to forgive him, but she'd never forget the deep, painful guilt, sorrow and rage she harbored when she thought he was dead.

They walked around the diminishing crowd and he said, "Campana is sending out a memo to everyone that I'm alive and kicking and have been in deep cover. My part is over and done with."

"Scheduled, or because of all this bullshit?"

"It would have been out after I testified in front of the grand jury," he said. "But now that they—" he waved toward city hall "—are closing ranks, I won't be able to get much more even if I stayed on the streets." He slipped onto his bike, handed her the extra helmet. She put it on, climbed behind him.

"I missed you, Kara," he said and, without waiting for a response, started up the bike and pulled into traffic.

Will was pacing the First Contact office when Kara and Colton arrived. Gina and Fletch were sitting at the table drinking coffee and looking nervous.

"You didn't tell anyone you were coming down?" Will said.

"She told Costa, the fed," Colton said wryly.

"Oh. That's—okay. It's not him. But he can't tell anyone."

"What's got you so stressed?" Kara asked.

"This morning, I was at LAPD headquarters and realized that almost all your reports," he said, nodding toward Colton, "weren't there."

"I sent them directly to Craig because Gomez was concerned about a potential leak or if someone saw my name, they'd realize I wasn't dead."

"But after Craig was killed, everything from his office was

sent to the sheriff's—the detective running the investigation, I talked to him." He snapped his fingers trying to remember his name.

"McPherson," Kara said.

"Right. McPherson. He said he had the files and would be looking through them, but he was working closely with this detective Caprese from LAPD. I went today because I wanted to check on Violet, make sure she was okay after everything that happened, and saw the box from Dyson's office. It was open there on the table and it had hardly anything in it. Someone stole your files—specifically, all the pictures you took outside the group homes and nonprofits."

"You're jumping the gun, buddy," Colton said, trying to calm Will down. "Gomez could have ordered copies made, or she sent them to someone else for analysis. This was a tight case until now."

"No. There were no photos listed in the log of files taken from Craig's office. I know he had them—I saw your reports in his office last Friday. Pictures with names, organizational charts, financial statements."

Colton frowned, and Kara said, "Could he have taken them home? Put them somewhere for safekeeping?"

"Maybe," Will admitted, "but that's not the only reason I'm suspicious that someone might have destroyed them."

"First," Colton said, "I have copies of everything. You think I would send my only copy?"

"Yes, but your house was tossed, and the police were here. Gina, tell them."

Gina was biting her thumbnail, but she spoke clearly. "I came in early this morning with Fletch. As soon as I opened up, that detective who was here Tuesday? He walked right in. Said he had a warrant to search the place. Showed me a piece of paper that looked official, but didn't let me keep it. He was with another guy—the guy from the sketch."

Kara tensed. "Conrad."

"Yeah. I guess. Will showed us the sketch and told us to call the police if we saw him. But… I was scared."

Fletch took her hand and squeezed it. "It's okay, baby. Finish it."

"This place isn't big, but they went through the offices, they looked in the cabinets and they took the computer. Gave me a receipt, but…it was weird. I called Will as soon as they left."

Will put his hand on her shoulder. "You didn't do anything wrong, Gina."

"I'm really sorry," she said.

"You and Fletch, go home. Stay clean—okay? You need a meeting, go to a meeting. But lie low and I'll call you later."

"Are you sure?"

"Yes," Will said and walked them out. He locked the door behind them.

Kara asked Colton, "Where is your copy?"

"Safe."

"Tell me."

"You can come with me to retrieve it."

That told Kara nothing, but before she could argue with him, Will said, "That's not all. I listened to the press conference and something bothered me. So I listened again to the podcast that exposed Lydia Zarian's sister as running some of these nonprofits. And it clicked."

"Explain," Kara said. "Clearly, as if I'm a child."

"The press conference was clearly damage control, but they talked specifically about Sunflower Group Homes. The podcast didn't mention Sunflower at all. Violet had never given them the Sunflower information. That was all Colton's theory, one of the tipping points for Craig. But the Sunflower files aren't in Craig's documents."

Colton tensed. "I gave him everything on Sunflower last week."

"Let me get this clear," Kara said. Her head pounded trying to put the information together. "You think that they knew Craig was investigating this Sunflower group and because none of those files were in his office, that they somehow destroyed them because they have someone on the inside? Anything could have happened, including Craig hiding them himself, especially if something in there was explosive."

Colton said, "Sunflower ties Angel Homes and all the other group homes together. It shows how Zarian's brother and sister used the system to make millions of dollars. And I had pictures—pictures of every person going into the Sunflower offices over the last six weeks. If they are concerned about something I found, why would they put it out there at all?"

"I don't know," Will said, "but why bring it up if they didn't know we were looking at it? And the only way they could have known we were looking at it is if they had access to Craig's files."

"I see your point," Kara said. "So who had access?"

"Just Craig," Will said.

"And Peter Sharp," Colton said. "I'll be damned."

"His investigator?" Kara asked. "Why would Sharp be working with these people?" As she said it she knew it could happen. Steve Colangelo was a bad cop. Tom Lee was a bad cop. Why not a bad investigator in the DA's office? She felt angry and sick to her stomach.

"Craig brought Peter in well after the investigation started, and he didn't know I was undercover—few people did. Craig, Lex, Elena, Will, Violet. That was it. All Peter knew was that Elena had someone in deep cover."

"Could he have found out it was you?" Kara asked.

"Not until this week. I'm good, Kara. Just like you." He shot her one of his charming smiles, but she didn't smile back. "Anyway, Peter met with Elena and Lex on Monday night. I don't know what he learned at that meeting, but Elena and Lex trust him."

"We still don't have proof that he took evidence," Kara said, but she was thinking.

Will ran both hands through his hair. "This is fucked."

"He won't get away with it," Colton said.

"The FBI—my team, not LA FBI," Kara said, "believe the files from Dyson are light. That there are things missing that are referenced in his personal notes. They are operating under the assumption he may have locked up the files or hid them for safekeeping, but Sharp had access to Dyson's office immediately after the murder and was the first to access it Tuesday morning. He could have hidden the files, destroyed them, taken them. But so could anyone who had access to Dyson's office."

"The simplest explanation is usually the correct one," Colton said. "Sharp knew about Violet's role *and* about Chen talking about a deal. He knows about Violet's history, her work with First Contact, her mother—and that she was working on the computer crash."

"Why didn't he have city hall fire her?"

"It's not easy firing a civil servant, and she's in the technology department, not working directly for the mayor's office. But he could keep track of what she knew and what she fed to Craig."

Kara remembered what Craig told her on Monday. "She had something for him, she was bringing it to him Monday when Chen was killed. But we now have it. So whoever had Chen and Dyson killed only delayed the inevitable."

"What she had was evidence of *how* the crash happened and *why* the deleted files could never be recovered except at the data storage facility. It's the original backup drive that she needs. And we're waiting for a warrant to get it. Dammit!" Colton pulled out his phone, pressed a button, frowned. "I can't make a call."

Kara grabbed her phone, looked at it.

No signal.

"Someone is jamming our phones," she said.

She had the awful feeling that they were trapped.
The door rattled, then the glass broke.
There was nowhere to hide.

39

"You doing okay, Violet?"

Michael Harris, the FBI agent who stayed with me in Big Bear last night and kept me in sight since we returned to Los Angeles, sat across from me in the bustling LAPD conference room. He was a large man—not overweight, just big. It didn't intimidate me because I was tall for a woman, and if I was being honest? I felt safe with him. Safe for the first time since I found my mom living on the streets. It wasn't that I thought I was in danger. It was that I kept waiting for bad things to happen because they kept happening.

People died in filth and garbage and the city kept running. My mom wouldn't stop doing drugs and none of the programs were designed to truly help people quit. More people came to the streets and fewer people were leaving. And then my mom was dead and I felt...lost and alone.

But now, for the first time in years, I had hope. This roomful of people were all working to help me. Well, not specifically me. The police wanted to solve a murder. They cared about

Craig Dyson and wanted justice for him. I talked to two FBI people on the phone, who worked with Michael, and explained what I had learned in city hall. They actually seemed to care and understand what I said. Even better, they thought my information and analysis would go a long way into exposing the fraud and corruption in the housing projects. They asked smart questions and listened to my answers.

Other than Will and Craig, no one had ever really listened to me. Maybe because I never had much to say.

That was then. Now I realized I needed to use my voice, join Will in speaking up.

"I'm okay," I said to Michael. "Thank you for staying with me."

"That's my job." But he didn't smile.

"Are you okay?"

"I heard what happened to your mother. I'm really sorry."

I didn't want sympathy and automatically mumbled, "Thank you."

"My mom died of a drug overdose," he said quietly. "I was fourteen."

I hadn't expected that. Michael seemed to be so...levelheaded. Smart. Organized. He didn't look like he'd grown up in a house full of ups and downs and chaos.

"Oh." What else could I say? "I understand how you feel."

"I don't understand it. Logically, I do," he said. "Logically, I see how people fall down the self-destructive path. But in my heart, I don't get it. I've been angry with my mother for my entire life. I don't like that in myself, but I can't stop hating her for what she did to our family, what she did to herself."

I reached over and took his hand. It surprised me—I don't really like touching people. But he gripped it like a dying man and I realized he needed help. He was in pain. It didn't show on the surface, but he hurt like every other survivor on the planet.

"I never hated my mom," I said quietly. "She always had ups

and downs, but it wasn't until after my dad was killed in an accident that she started seriously using. She blamed it on her pain, but that was an excuse. Everything in an addict's life is an excuse to keep using. I blamed myself—sometimes I still do. If I could have found the right words or the right treatment center, if I could have just let her live with me one more time…" I stopped. This wasn't about me, this was about Michael. He'd been a child. Alone. Angry.

"It's okay to be angry," I told him. "I am. I just turn it to the people who cause the problem. The doctors who overprescribe. The drug dealers who push fentanyl. The people profiting off the homeless crisis. Yes, I blame my mom. Because I gave her every opportunity to get clean. I did everything in my power and it wasn't enough." For the first time, I believed it. For the first time in my life, I believed I did everything I could. Failure wasn't on me.

"I admire you," Michael said.

"I'm not anyone special. You're the big, tough FBI agent," I said with a little laugh.

He smiled. "I am. It helps, being able to do something good in the world. Like protecting supersmart computer nerds."

I laughed for real and he smiled wider. "Thank you."

"I just wanted to share because watching you and how you've handled what happened with your mother has helped me. You didn't try, you didn't even know, but I think for the first time I'm beginning to understand my mom better. I don't know that I can forgive her, but I don't want to hate her anymore."

"Good," I said. "Because hate is exhausting."

Michael frowned and pulled his phone out of his breast pocket. "It's my boss. Don't leave the room, okay?"

"Roger that," I said as he got up and walked to the corner for semiprivacy while he talked.

Lex, Peter and two cops were going over stacks of files on the table. Elena walked in and sat with them, motioned for me to join her at the table, so I did. "I just finished debriefing Campana and the chief of police." I didn't know who Campana was, but assumed this was someone high-ranking. "Campana himself is making the argument to the judge for the data center warrant, and as soon as it comes in, we're rolling. I need you with us, Violet. You're the only one who knows what we actually need, according to everything I've heard."

"It's more I'm the only one who knows how to retrieve the data without reinstalling the virus that destroyed it in the first place. But I'm ready. This will prove everything I've been saying from the beginning, and we'll finally know exactly what was removed from the server."

"That's what we hope," Elena said.

I didn't hope; I knew. This was my world: computers and data. I knew what files had been removed, I just didn't know what was in those files.

Now I would. Once and for all. Not only me, but the police, the DA's office, the people of Los Angeles.

Everyone would know what was hidden…and who did the hiding.

"Something's missing," Lex said. "Look." He pulled out Craig's notepad. "He talks here about the photos Colton took, but there are no photos. Nowhere in these files are photos."

"He could have emailed them," Elena said.

"Colton only submitted physical files," Lex said. "He was paranoid about leaks, considering that everyone thought he was dead."

"We're going to get so much shit when Campana sends out the memo about the investigation," Elena said.

"There's a lot of things missing," Lex said. "Costa's team was right—Dyson references information that isn't here. Peter, what do you make of this?"

Peter glanced at the notepad Lex held up. I couldn't see what was on it. Peter said, "We looked through his office, none of that was there."

"It has to be somewhere."

"Maybe he locked it up," I suggested. "Does he have a safe or something?"

Will had been here earlier. He said something similar, that something was missing. He seemed worried, but left before I could talk to him about it.

"No one knew about this investigation except us," Lex said.

"Not exactly no one," Peter said. "Campana knew, probably his admin. Dyson's legal secretary, even if she didn't know specifics, she could have figured it out. The DA knew the goal of the investigation and he would have had to sign off on the grand jury and wouldn't do that without more information. And don't forget, even though the courthouse was locked down on Monday, people were still inside the building."

Lex swore and shook his head. "Something is wrong. I just can't put my finger on it. Elena, get Colton in here. Where is he?"

"He said he'd be here at noon," Elena said with a glance at her watch.

I looked at the wall. It was twelve fifteen.

"I'll bet he came in and made a big splash about not being dead," Lex muttered. "Shit, I need him. He'll know exactly what's missing." Lex pulled out his phone and dialed. A minute later he slammed the phone down. "Voice mail. I'm going to throttle him."

"I'll call Kara," Elena said. A minute later she, too, said, "She's not answering. Where the hell are they?"

Michael said, "Who are you trying to reach?"

"Colton and Kara aren't answering their cell phones. They were at the press conference, but that was over thirty minutes ago. They should be here by now."

Michael put up his finger and listened to whoever he was talking to on the phone. Then he ended the call and said, "Costa says they were going to First Contact to meet with Will. He's on his way there, but still ten minutes out. We're closer."

"Not by much," Elena said and pulled out her radio. She asked for a patrol to be sent to the First Contact office. "Something is wrong," she said. "The closest patrol is more than ten minutes. They're headed in, but I'm going, too. I don't like this."

"I'm joining you," Michael said. He looked at me. "Violet, stay here. You're safe in this building. I need to make sure my partner is okay."

I nodded. "Go."

Elena said to Peter, "Call me as soon as the warrant comes through."

"Of course. And let me know what's going on. There must be an explanation."

Everyone left the room and I was worried. About Kara and Colton and Will. I wish I could have gone with them, but I wasn't a cop. I didn't want to be a cop, but I had a lot more respect for them now than ever before. I had never met anyone who cared so much about justice until I met Colton...and then Kara and Michael. They wanted justice as much as I did.

Two minutes after the room cleared out, Peter said, "We need to go."

"I'm good here." Michael had told me to stay, so I was staying.

Peter pulled a gun. I didn't even know he had a gun, but why shouldn't he? He was an investigator for the DA's office. They probably all had guns.

"Violet, on my word, Kara Quinn and Colton Fox will either live or they will die. If you come with me now, they live. If you stall, they die—and so will you."

I stared at this man. A man that Craig had trusted. Yet Peter Sharp had betrayed his boss. He'd betrayed everyone. I believed him in that moment when he said he would kill me; and I believed him when he said he could have Kara and Colton killed.

Colton, who had helped me find out what happened to my mom. Kara, who had saved my life and gave me hope. They would be dead because I was scared.

My voice sounded off, but I whispered, "What do you want from me?"

"I have the warrant." He grinned and looked evil. Like he was enjoying this. Except...his neck pulsed and his hand had practically crumpled the paper. "Took it right off the computer before Elena saw it. You and I are getting the drive from the data center and then this will all be over."

"They'll figure it out. They'll know you took it. They'll find you."

"Doesn't matter. I have an escape plan as soon as I get these files. They have no idea what's in those files. They might suspect, but they don't know, and as long as they never know, that's all that really matters. Now, Violet. Walk. And if you try anything, you're dead. Don't test me."

40

After the glass broke in the main door, Kara and Colton went into action. Together, they pushed the large conference table on its side. A hand reached inside the new opening and tried to unlock the door but couldn't because the lock required a key on both sides, and the key was in Will's pocket. Thank God there were security bars on the door, but they wouldn't hold for long.

Kara ordered Will to secure the back door. It was a fire door and would be near impossible to break down, but Kara assumed that someone would be waiting for them to escape that way.

Will ran into the back office where the door was and made sure it was locked, then pushed a desk against it.

"Stay low!" she commanded, and Will dropped to the floor, behind the half wall. She didn't like that the top half was all glass, but he was safer there.

Colton pulled out his Glock and fired three shots at the intruder, then they both squatted behind the table.

The hand disappeared and there were voices, but Kara couldn't hear what they were saying. She drew her SIG and said, "We're sitting ducks here."

"We just need to hold them off. Costa is on the way, right? We just need a little time."

"I have two guns, twenty-eight bullets between them. You?"

"Now I have fourteen."

"You're only carrying one gun?"

"I have a knife."

"So do I, but I don't want this to come down to hand-to-hand combat."

A series of bullets hit the table and Kara made herself as small as possible. Then they stopped and a male voice shouted, "Fox! All we want is your phone with the pictures. You can walk away."

Colton called out, "Won't do you any good, I already sent everything to my boss."

"I know that's not true," the voice said.

Who is that? Kara mouthed.

Colton shrugged.

"You don't have the only copies, do you?"

"No, but… I think…" His voice trailed off.

"Talk!"

"Yesterday morning I was at the Sunflower main office and took pictures of people I didn't recognize. I don't know how they could possibly know I was there."

"But Peter knew—he knew you were still out in the field yesterday, before we met here. He must have suspected something."

"Aw, shit."

"Send them now. Send them to me, send them to Matt, to everyone. There's something important there and—"

More gunfire made Kara yelp. Someone started hammering at the security screen on the door. It was only a matter of time before they got in. Kara looked to Colton. "I'll cover you, just get those photos out in the wild right now."

Colton pulled out his phone and Kara brought her gun up

and fired her entire clip at the door. She hit someone, heard a grunt and lots of swearing. They moved away and he said, "My phone isn't sending anything. There's no service."

"Give me your phone," she demanded.

He hesitated, so Kara grabbed it out of his hand and gave him her phone. Matt had given her a backup after she destroyed hers at the park. She then put Colton's phone in her boot. It didn't completely fit, but she pulled her jeans down over it.

"This isn't going to work," he said.

"We're buying time. Tell them."

She didn't believe that whoever was out there wouldn't kill them when they got the phone, but Matt would be here any minute. She needed to hold them off until then.

She glanced back to the offices and saw Will under the desk. He looked a little scared and a lot angry. Exactly how she felt.

"Okay!" Colton shouted to the attackers. "How do I know if I slide out my phone you won't try to kill us?"

Silence.

"Hello?" Colton said.

"Slide your phone to the door," a voice said.

"How many do you think are out there?" Kara asked. She thought two, and likely one in the rear. "Did you see Conrad?"

How many people were involved in this damn conspiracy? Politicians and staff and the son of an FBI agent? Enough people to hire these assholes to steal Colton's phone at gunpoint in the middle of the day?

Did the gunfire draw attention to the area? Had someone called the police? Response time had gotten worse over the years. She glanced at her watch. Only four minutes had passed.

"Slide the phone now!" the man shouted. "Do it!"

"He sounds panicked," Kara said.

As if to emphasize her point, three more bullets hit the table. There were voices outside—two, maybe three.

"Colton Fox, goddammit, you slide me the phone now or I'll blow your brains out all over the fucking room."

"Definitely panicked," Colton said.

"Do it. They have to come in and retrieve it. We'll at least see who he is. He knows you. Look at him—be careful," she added quickly.

"It's coming!" Colton called and slid Kara's phone as far across the floor as he could without it going out the door. It rested three feet inside.

No one moved.

Staying low, Colton and Kara peered around opposite sides of the conference table and watched.

A man stepped in through the broken security screen and fired two rounds at the table as he bent down and grabbed the phone.

"Doug Meyers? What the fuck!" Colton jumped up.

She knew the name, but didn't have time to think about why. Colton was going to get himself shot.

Meyers fired at Colton at the same time as Kara pushed him down. They ended up sprawled on the floor without the protection of the table. Kara fired her weapon toward the door as Meyers fled.

"That prick! He's a cop."

It was the same man Kara had seen on Tuesday morning when she was looking for Will, the man she thought she recognized.

"Are you hit? Tell me!"

"No, I'm going after that bastard—"

He scrambled up and Kara said, "Don't be stupid, he's leaving."

"I'll destroy him."

A crash outside had Kara and Colton diving back behind the table, then there was more gunfire.

Matt, Kara thought.

She jumped up and ran to the side of the door, then cautiously looked out into the small parking area.

Meyers had crashed his car into Matt's. She didn't see what

happened, but Matt was behind his driver's door, gun out, and Meyers was stumbling from his car, clutching his side. Blood streamed from his head. He aimed at Matt but Matt fired and Meyers fell to the gravel, unmoving.

That's when she noticed a man collapsed outside the broken door, unconscious and bleeding.

Kara saw no one else. Had there really only been two men?

"Quinn!" Matt called.

"We're okay," she shouted back and waved to him.

She walked over to the prone shooter and searched him, removed his gun, found his wallet. No ID. She cuffed him. Matt went to Meyers, kicked his gun away and cuffed him.

They met at the end of the small row of warehouses.

"No one could reach you."

"They jammed our phones. They wanted this." She reached down and handed Matt Colton's phone. "Colton must have gotten something good yesterday for them to go through all this."

Matt ran his hand up and down her arm. "You're really okay."

"Promise." She touched his cheek, wiped away a small amount of blood. "You're bleeding."

"From the glass. I'm fine."

He looked over her shoulder and saw Colton.

"He's a cop," Colton said and motioned to Meyers. "Is he dead?"

"I don't know," Matt said. "Ambulance is on its way."

Will came out of the building at the same time two unmarked police cars with grille lights roared onto the street. Elena, Lex, Michael and a uniformed officer jumped out, looked at the two unconscious men. Michael immediately started first aid on Meyers, then stopped. "He's dead," Michael said.

"Meyers?" Lex said, incredulous. "Colton, what happened?"

"He wanted my phone. Shot up the place, we gave him Kara's phone, he ran."

"He hit my car and shot at me," Matt said. "I returned fire and he went down."

Elena was on the phone calling for more cops, an ambulance and the coroner. Kara didn't envy her right now—sometimes, command sucked. Because after all this, there was a dead corrupt cop and Elena would have to go to the brass and explain everything.

"What did you have that he wanted?" Matt asked, opening Colton's phone.

"Can I?" Colton asked, and Matt handed him the phone. "These are the photos I took yesterday morning at Sunflower. I don't know what's important here, because nothing stood out to me. This person? This is Muriel Coplin, Zarian's sister. What's she doing at Sunflower? She's there because she and her brother are conspiring together," Colton answered his own question. "Ben showed up immediately after, then four other people came in, about the same time, and I figured for a meeting. But I didn't know any of them."

They were all well-dressed. Two Asian men, a white man, and a Hispanic woman.

They scrolled through photos. "I know this person," Kara said, tapping the screen. "I don't know his name, but he was at Chen's factory many times. He would come in, take several women, leave."

"For the sex trade?" Matt asked.

"I don't think so, they weren't always young women. Sunny said Chen worked with other businessmen in the same line of work—smaller factories in different cities. We didn't have a good handle on that end of the business, but hoped to build it up once we had all his files. But when he found out about the raid, he destroyed his files, so we only stopped his operation."

"The woman," Will said. "She's familiar, but I don't know her name. The old white guy? I know him. Larry Klein. He's Lydia Zarian's biggest donor. Owns a shipping line, lots of property."

"Want to bet his property is making money the same way Chen's was?" Colton said.

"Why are they meeting with Muriel Coplin?" Matt asked.

"Muriel is Lydia's campaign manager. This is damage control, my guess—yesterday, twenty-four hours before the press conference. Damage control and strategy meeting. Damn them," Will said. "I'll bet as we dig deeper into the finances of Sunflower and the other nonprofits we'll find that Zarian's donors are all profiting. God, I hate politics."

"We don't know that they were doing anything illegal," Matt said.

"Then why would Meyers want my phone?" Colton countered. "There must be something here we're not seeing."

"Where's Peter Sharp?" Kara asked.

"Headquarters," Lex said. "Why?"

"Colton, Will and I realized that Peter Sharp is the only person who could have taken Colton's reports out of Craig's office. Everything we got from his office was light—you said it, the FBI said it. Files are missing, specifically Colton's photos."

"We still don't know," Lex said, glancing at Elena, who was still talking on the phone.

Kara shook her head. "We know. Craig had everything in his office when I was there. I remember glancing at stacks and stacks of files. Will said there was only one box logged into evidence. Where are the missing files? Where are Colton's pictures? Sharp knew on Friday that Craig was impaneling the grand jury. That gave him more than enough time to put together the hit, then take or hide the files during the chaos after Craig's murder, before his office was sealed."

"That's a serious accusation," Lex said.

Will started to explain about the podcast, but Michael cut him off. "Violet's not returning my text messages."

"Where is she?" Kara asked.

"At headquarters. When we couldn't reach you, we left her and Sharp in the conference room." Michael looked stricken.

Lex got on the phone and walked away. Michael tried calling Violet; no answer. Matt said, "Violet's the only person who knows how to retrieve the deleted files."

"And Sharp knows that," Kara said. "Did we get the warrant?"

"We were waiting for it when we left," Michael said. "If anything happens to her..."

"We're going to find her," Kara said. She didn't want any more innocent blood on her hands.

Lex came back. "I talked to security. Peter left twenty minutes ago. Violet was with him."

"Can we track them? The car? Phone?" Matt asked.

"They're going to the data center," Kara said. "This is the big 'cover your ass' move. The press conference. Getting Colton's phone with pictures of Zarian's donors. But if they don't get that backup drive and destroy it, they're all toast."

"Let's go," Matt said. "Lex, I need your car."

"I'm going with you, the lieutenant has to stay here and deal with the fallout," he said. "Peter." He practically spat out the name. "That bastard. Craig was my friend. Why, dammit!" He climbed into the driver's seat. "Why the fuck did he do this?"

Kara slid into the seat next to him. Though it was a rhetorical question, she answered: "Money. It's all about money and power."

Matt and Colton got into the back and Kara glanced at them. They glared at each other, both suspicious, wary. Matt caught her eye and she winked. "We're going to stop him. No one else is going to die today."

"I think I have a plan," Matt said. "I need to make a call."

"What?" Colton demanded.

Matt ignored him, and Colton looked at Kara as if to say, *See? All feds are pricks.*

Kara said, "I trust Matt."

Colton stared at her. She didn't avert her gaze as Lex picked up speed as they headed to the freeway.

Colton looked away first.

41

Peter gave Violet strict guidelines about what to say and not say when they went into the data center. She obeyed him. Fear did that to people, and Peter knew how to use it. He wouldn't have brought her at all except the warrant was specific: that Violet would verify that the backup was uncorrupted. He had to bring her or the manager might get suspicious.

Everything had fallen apart in the last two days, but Peter had an escape plan.

That included retrieving the backup drive and using it to extract a whole lot of money from Lydia Zarian and Dorothy Duncan. Rebecca Chavez didn't have access to her money yet—trying to stay clean because of her job. It was layered in shell corps and trust funds so deep that she couldn't get to it quickly. But Zarian and Duncan? They were made of money, and they would pay handily to protect their children.

And themselves.

He had his brother's passport—they looked enough alike that no one would think twice—just in case the FBI caught wind before he could get out of the airport. He was flying to Mexico City tonight, then tomorrow to Brazil, then he would lie low in a house he'd bought when he first started working for Zarian on the side. With the money he'd get from Lydia, he could buy a new identity and use that to move anywhere he wanted. Maybe Australia. If he liked Brazil enough—he spoke Spanish well and could pick up on Portuguese with a little practice—he might stay there.

But first things first: get the backup drive, exchange it for money wired to his offshore account, and disappear.

"Ms. Halliday stated that the drive was undamaged and from the correct day," the manager said. "I don't know how a virus could have gotten into our system—we have the best cyber-security out there."

"Your security is good," Violet said. "It was on our end."

Peter didn't want her talking *too* much. "Here's your copy of the warrant, and a receipt for the drive. I think we're good?"

The manager glanced at Violet. He was assessing her, and Peter couldn't have him paying too much attention—not until they were gone.

"Violet is our computer guru. She'll get to the bottom of the problem," Peter said with a smile. "Is this it?" He gestured to a silver box the size of a large briefcase.

"Yes, we secured the drive in the case to protect it."

"Great. Thank you for your cooperation."

And the manager walked them out.

"You could have been friendlier," Peter said as they walked to his car.

She didn't say anything.

"You've been a pain in my ass since you started talking to Craig."

"You killed him."

"I didn't kill him."

"You might as well have."

"I didn't want it to happen. I told Duncan he was being paranoid. But when you figured out how to locate the deleted files, we had no other choice."

"Craig was doing the right thing and he died because of it."

"Oh, please. You can't be that much of a Pollyanna. People are making money. If not Zarian and her lackeys, someone else. The system is fucked, it's never going to work the way people think, and I'll take my slice of the pie, thank you very much."

Peter stopped when he reached his car. He didn't believe this.

Conrad James got out of the SUV next to his. "Why are you here?" Peter asked. "We're meeting in an hour."

"Just making sure everything is in order," Conrad said.

"All is good. We need to go. I don't know how much time we have before the feds put it together."

"Give me the drive."

"You know how this works, Conrad. Don't pull this bullshit with me."

"Meyers is dead."

"Oh, fuck."

"Time is running out. Hand me the drive and walk away."

Everything clicked right then. Conrad was here to clean up. If Meyers was dead, that meant Colton Fox was still alive, and he had the photos that would take down Zarian.

Peter reached out for Violet, but she stepped away, as if sensing exactly what he sensed.

Conrad pulled out his gun faster than Peter could get to his and pulled the trigger.

Violet screamed.

Conrad James watched Peter drop to the ground, still clutching the briefcase. The bullet had gone through the center of his forehead. A perfect shot, if he did say so himself.

Hard to miss when you were less than five feet away.

He turned the gun to Violet, who had started backing away.

"Freeze," he said.

She froze.

"Get the briefcase."

She didn't move.

"Now, Ms. Halliday."

Her hands were shaking as she pulled the briefcase from Peter's dead fingers.

He heard the SUVs before he saw them.

This was certainly inconvenient.

He grabbed Violet by the arm and held her close to him, turned and faced the FBI as they screeched into the parking lot.

FBI Agent Matt Costa jumped out of the back of the car, gun out, aimed at Conrad. He hadn't expected them to arrive so quickly; he had some quick thinking to do.

He had no intention of dying today, but he wanted to see how this played out and what he could learn.

Information was always his trump card.

Matt immediately assessed the situation as he held his gun on Conrad. The data center was thirty feet away; they were on lockdown. Matt had his people contact the manager and told him to lock down as soon as Peter and Violet left. If they tried to stall, Peter could have become nervous and taken everyone inside hostage. Having one hostage was bad enough.

Lex stayed in the vehicle, door open. Kara had gotten out and flanked Matt. Matt wished Colton would stay in the car, but he got out as well, taking the other side.

Michael and two officers pulled up behind them. Conrad watched everything with cool eyes. Matt had to be careful how he played this. This man was a cold killer. But cold killers were, by definition, dispassionate. Matt had to believe he didn't want to go out in a blaze of glory. It was rarely as cinematic and exciting as the bad guys thought.

"Conrad, it's over. Let Violet go and no one else has to get hurt."

"Agent Costa," he said. "I've been impressed with your team. You have lived up to your reputation."

Matt didn't know what, if anything, Conrad knew about him. He could just be playing with his head, stalling, distracting him.

"The FBI has already launched a full investigation into Lydia Zarian and Dorothy Duncan, and everyone associated with them. Rebecca Chavez has been suspended. If you hurt Violet, you will die. I promise you that."

Matt sensed more than saw Michael take a position to the right of Kara. Now Conrad couldn't keep them all in his sight. Michael was the best shot. He could take Conrad out with a clean head shot, but Violet was nearly as tall as the man. There was no guarantee she wouldn't be caught in the line of fire, and Michael wouldn't put her at risk.

Matt had to talk Conrad down. Convince him to turn himself over.

"You're hired help," Matt said. "You roll on who hired you to kill Craig Dyson and FBI Agent Bryce Thornton, death penalty is off the table."

Conrad laughed. "It's funny that you think it was ever on the table."

"I've seen too many dead bodies this week," Matt said. "I don't want to see another."

Conrad didn't say anything. He still held the gun to Violet's head, clutching her arm. He was calculating. Matt could see it in his eyes.

"Are you willing to die for these people? Do you actually believe that the drive in that briefcase is the drive with the evidence? We spoke to the data center before Peter Sharp ever walked into the building. No way in hell was I going to risk the files—the proof of all the crimes that Zarian and her people committed—getting into Sharp's hands."

Conrad looked surprised, then he smiled. "Bravo, Agent Costa. Bravo. You win this round."

He let go of Violet's arm, slowly squatted and put his gun on the ground, knelt and put his hands on the back of his head.

"Violet," Kara commanded. "Come here."

Violet walked slowly toward Kara, still carrying the briefcase. Then she ran and Kara immediately escorted her into the SUV.

Matt and Colton Fox approached Conrad. "Cuff him," Matt ordered Fox as he holstered his own weapon. Michael still had a clear shot if Conrad tried anything.

Fox complied, sparing only a glance at the dead Peter Sharp.

"Who gets him?" Fox asked Matt.

"We'll let the lawyers fight over him, but he killed a federal agent so he's mine first."

Conrad laughed.

"Shut up," Colton told him and pulled him to his feet.

Conrad looked right at Matt and said, "I live to fight another day, Agent Costa."

He didn't look worried, but Matt expected that to change. Once he realized he wasn't walking free again, he would be very worried.

Colton led Conrad to the rear vehicle so Violet wouldn't have to ride with him.

They had Conrad James on murdering Peter Sharp in cold blood and they had him on hiring Colangelo to kill Chen. And likely enough evidence to convict him of killing Craig.

But they had better find more evidence or he wouldn't go away for killing a federal agent.

They needed the gun.

Matt called Tony Greer and laid out his plan.

FRIDAY, OCTOBER 11

42

Conrad James wasn't talking, but they had the disk drive.

It took all night and half the morning to analyze the data that Violet, with the help of Vik at the FBI, extracted from the backup drive. What they found was every file that had been deleted the day LAPD raided Chen's factory, exactly as Violet had predicted. The files were a series of contracts and memos outlining how grant money was steered to twelve different nonprofits, all of which were run by relatives of Rebecca Chavez, Lydia Zarian and Dorothy Duncan. Krista Zarian, Lydia's daughter and Theodore Duncan's live-in girlfriend, earned a cool three million dollars every year as the accountant for each nonprofit even though she had no accounting degree. She was the figurehead; Dorothy Duncan's law firm filed all forms and taxes for the nonprofits.

Brian Granderson was leading the formal investigation into the city's grant finances.

All the players had lawyered up. They probably thought that they'd get away with it because a complex white-collar crime case would be hard to prove. But Brian felt confident they would be able to build the case with the evidence they had from the data center and from Colton Fox's investigation.

"We're going to get them," Brian said to Matt. "Why the sour face?"

"Because Conrad James isn't telling me who hired him. He killed Craig Dyson on the orders of one of those people. I want them on murder."

"You have James dead to rights for killing Peter Sharp. We also have a good case for Dyson."

"I agree," Matt said, "and there's enough evidence that a jury would buy that he was the one in disguise. But I want his boss. I want the person trying to keep their hands clean. I want to know if he killed Bryce Thornton and why."

Brian frowned. "You think James killed Bryce?"

"Yes. I know men like Conrad James. He isn't a man who kills for himself. He takes pride in his work, he even enjoys it, but he kills because that's his job. He killed Thornton because someone hired him to. I want that name."

"Okay. Tell me what you need from me."

"Right now, we don't know where he lives. We don't know who paid him. We have his name, but I don't even know if Conrad James is his real name. His prints aren't in the system, but this isn't the first time he's killed. He's too experienced and too disciplined. We don't have the gun that killed Chen and Thornton, but we suspect someone—James, most likely—took it from Kara's condo. I need to talk to him and have some leeway on what I can offer. Not freedom, but some carrots that he might grab when he realizes he's not getting out of prison for a long, long time."

"What incentive does he have to talk?"

Matt considered. "We can take first-degree murder off the table. I don't want to—I don't want him to walk ever—but we're not going to put Zarian or her cronies in prison for years. It'll take at least a year to investigate, then another year before the trial—more because they have the money to postpone and play games. White-collar crimes take forever to prove, and this one is doubly complex. But murder? We can nail them."

"I'll call Nina Radinovich and see what we can do."

"And, Brian? Rebecca Chavez needs to talk. I don't think I'm the right person to convince her of that."

He sighed, forlorn, then he nodded. "I'll talk to her."

Matt entered an interview room in the federal detention facility and faced Conrad James.

His lawyer was a public defender who looked nervous. "I, um, advised my client that he doesn't have to speak," the lawyer said.

"What's your name?"

"Webster. Ethan Webster."

"Thank you."

Matt kept his focus on Conrad. Ryder had learned some important information about Mr. James since he was arrested last night and Matt hoped he could parlay the information into answers.

"Mr. James, thank you for agreeing to meet with me."

He smiled. "Conrad. Everyone, friend or foe, calls me Conrad."

"Conrad, we have the drive, we have the information on the drive and we have launched a full investigation as I told you yesterday. Better, we have people who have come forward with pieces of information that are helping us find the truth—the entire truth. We will get all of them on something."

"That has nothing to do with me, Matt," Conrad said informally.

"I know you were hired."

"Do you? Do you have evidence that I was hired? For what?"

"Either you killed Peter Sharp, Bryce Thornton and Craig Dyson for your own personal reasons and, if so, you will be tried for first-degree premeditated murder, or you were hired to kill them."

"Objection," Webster said.

Conrad ignored his lawyer. "You're stretching everything, Matt. I know what you have and what you don't have. You can prove Peter—there were cameras. A witness. Peter was a liar and a thief and of no concern to anyone. You might—and I'm being generous—be able to prove Dyson, but it's a weak case and you know it. You'll bring Detective Quinn up to testify—I know she plays very well for juries—and you'll bring in the video and set everything up, but it's still thin. No prints, no weapon, vague resemblance on tape—even if the jury goes for it, it would be appealed. And Agent Thornton—you have nothing tying me to his murder." He leaned back. "And you know why you'll never have anything tying me to his murder? I didn't kill him."

Matt didn't want to believe him, but he wondered. "I have a clear line on Officer Colangelo killing Chen, putting the Colt .45 in his vehicle, and you retrieving it from his vehicle at 3:43 that afternoon. Thornton was killed just over twelve hours later with the same weapon. I have evidence it was in your possession. Unless you tell me where it is or who you gave it to."

"I know how this goes, Matt," Conrad said with a half smile. "You play tough, I hem and haw, you make me an offer, I pretend to confer with my rather unintelligent—no offense, Ethan—lawyer, and I give you something for something. I like you, Matt. From the minute I saw you at LAX Monday morning, I knew everything I'd learned about you was true."

Matt tensed. How had he known Matt and his team were coming in on Monday?

Rebecca Chavez? Peter Sharp? Or was there another leak?

Conrad grinned. "Don't be surprised. It's important to know your adversary. As soon as Detective Quinn went off with your unit, I knew you'd be here with her when she came back. At least, I was reasonably confident once I learned you and the hot-blooded cop were sleeping together. I did my research, just like I'm sure your brilliant analyst Ryder Kim did his research on me."

Suddenly, Matt felt like he was in well over his head. Conrad James was not who Matt thought he'd be. He expected the arrogance and the cockiness; he didn't expect the intelligence and games.

He reminded himself that Conrad would be in prison for a long, long time…even if they didn't get him on everything.

"I want the person or people who hired you. You tell me what I need to know and agree to testify, I am authorized to offer you thirty years in federal prison."

Conrad laughed. "Thirty? No."

"You killed three people."

"I've killed a lot more than three people."

"Mr. James," Webster interrupted.

Conrad put his finger in front of Webster's face to silence him, without taking his eyes off Matt.

"I know what you want, Matt. You want to know who killed your agent. An agent you didn't even like. No one liked him. He was an arrogant, mightier-than-thou prick. There is nothing more distasteful than a man with a badge who thinks he's better than everyone else."

Conrad stared at Matt for a long minute.

"I'll give you the name of the person who hired me, how they paid me and how you can prove it. I'll give you the name of the person I gave Kara Quinn's beautiful Colt to after I retrieved it from Colangelo's car. I don't know if that person killed Agent Thornton, but I imagine it'll be easier to prove if you have the information that I have."

"What do you want," Matt asked through clenched teeth. He was trying not to show his anger, but it was difficult with this man. Conrad knew and understood him in a way that made Matt very uncomfortable.

"I want to walk out of here a free man, but I know that's not on the table?" He said it as a question, but his voice was mocking Matt, so Matt didn't respond.

Conrad said, "Ten years."

"No."

"Okay. Then I'll go back to my cell. This isn't going to be an easy slam dunk for you, Matt. And I think you know it."

"Maybe your daughter will have some insight into how I can persuade you to cooperate."

A flash of anger so intense washed over Conrad, then it was gone...except for a slight tick in his jaw.

Ryder did it again, Matt thought. He held Conrad's gaze and didn't flinch, regaining control of the conversation.

In a low voice, Conrad said, "If you ever speak to my daughter, I will kill you, Mathias Costa."

"Do not threaten me, Conrad. I am a federal agent."

"Ten years. Take it or leave it."

Matt rose and left the room.

Nina Radinovich and Brian Granderson stood on the other side of the one-way mirror. "He creeps me out," Nina said. "Damn."

"We're not giving him ten years," Matt said.

"No," Nina agreed. "My boss would never agree to it, and he's usually the first to want to plead down."

"I think he gave the gun to Chavez," Matt said.

Brian shook his head. "I don't believe it. He killed Bryce. He's playing us."

"He's playing, but he's not lying. He has no reason to lie. He enjoys the game."

"Why would Rebecca kill Bryce?"

"To frame Kara and divide us. Have you found out whether Chavez tracked Kara's GPS?"

"She wiped her computer. We're rebuilding it now."

"My guess is she found out Kara dumped her phone near the

dog park and then Chavez sent Bryce there. Knowing he would go to meet an informant with dirt on Kara. We need the origin of the messages to Bryce Thornton."

"Eighteen years," Nina suddenly said.

"No. Thirty. We agreed to thirty." Matt didn't want Conrad James to ever get out of prison. He had a feeling the man would hunt Matt down just to fuck with him. "We'll make the case. We need Rebecca to talk. I changed my mind, Brian. I want to go with you."

"Good cop, bad cop?" Brian said without humor.

"Yes."

Reluctantly, Nina and Brian agreed.

Matt went back into the room. Shut the door, but he didn't sit down. "Thirty, or no deal and we prosecute you to the maximum allowed by law."

Conrad nodded. "Yes, I do like you, Matt. Very much. Good luck."

Matt turned to leave.

"And, Matt? If you think I'm going to be in prison for five years, let alone thirty? You're lying to yourself."

Matt walked out.

While Kara waited for Matt to be done with Conrad James and the FBI, she headed to LAPD headquarters and ran into Charlie Dean outside of Lex's office. She hadn't had a real conversation with Lex or Elena since everything went down, didn't know if she wanted to.

Colton walked in. Charlie glared at him. "You're a fucking bastard, you know that?"

"Hey, it was the job."

"No, it wasn't the fucking job. You and Lex can both go to hell. I pulled my papers today. I'm outta here."

"Charlie, I really am sorry. It was important—"

"Do you know how many friends I've lost in the line of duty?

Two. It used to be three when I thought you were six feet under. Each one is still with me. It hurts. I never want to see you again."

Kara put her hand on Charlie's arm. "I'll come see you before I go, if that's okay?"

"Can we maybe meet up at a bar? Dinner? Here… I'm not going to be here long. I can't do it anymore." Charlie glared at Colton.

"I'll call you this weekend," she said to Charlie, then gave him a hug.

When Charlie left, she turned to Colton and motioned for him to follow her. They went into an empty office across the hall. "You hurt a lot of people."

"We've both followed orders we didn't like. It's the job."

"This wasn't. This was cruel."

He reached out for her; she stepped back. "Babe, I really missed you. I know you said you're still mad, but after everything that happened yesterday? I can't just let you walk away. What do I need to do to get you back?"

She stared at him. "You never had me."

"That's not true." He grinned. "We were *really* good together. It was wild, Kara. I want you. I haven't been with anyone since that night with you, before the raid. There's no one else for me. It took me a long time to realize it, but it's you."

"It's not me, Colton." Had he said that eight months ago, would she have had a different answer?

She didn't know. But she knew the right answer now.

"It's that fed, isn't it? You're sleeping with him."

The way he said it was cruel. Not the words, but the tone. She didn't want to talk to Colton about Matt, as if somehow that would taint what she had with him.

She didn't always know what she had with Matt, but the one thing she knew—the one thing she was grateful for—Matt Costa was nothing like Colton Fox.

"Goodbye," she said and left.

★ ★ ★

Kara listened to Elena offer a promotion, a raise and the choice of any precinct she wanted.

"You've always been one of my best people, Kara. Even though you drove me up a wall sometimes, you are a great cop. I'm proud of you."

Last year, those words would have made Kara happy. All she had wanted was to make Elena and Lex proud of her. To be the best cop she could be and have the people she cared about most recognize her skill.

Now she saw what she had done to herself: she'd put her superiors in a parenting role. She had wanted to please them because she could never please her own mother and father. She never was the kid her parents wanted her to be. They had trained her to be a con artist, just like them. They didn't understand that she wasn't like them, that she couldn't be like them.

But to have the respect of people she respected had been her goal—a driving need.

She didn't need their respect anymore. She didn't need anything from them—because they were diminished in her eyes. That might not be fair, but she didn't care. They had lied to her, manipulated her, hurt her. That it was for the mission, for the greater good, that it was "just part of the job" made no difference.

Lex and Elena exchanged glances because she was quiet. She wasn't angry, and they didn't expect that; she was certain. She had always been one to speak her mind and when things were fucked, she was the first to point it out.

"I've read all the reports from Tony Greer," Lex said, clearing his throat. "You served us well with the FBI, and apparently have a knack for solving homicides. Major Crimes would love to have you. West Bureau, Pacific District? It's a choice assignment, close to your condo. Major Crimes is run by Detective Sergeant Leon Jackson. He's a good guy, real good guy, you'll like him."

"No," she said.

"Just name what you want. Anywhere."

"I want to go back seven months to when we sat here, Lex, and you told me Colton was killed. I want you to say, 'Colton was shot, but he's going to be okay. Everyone else is going to think he's dead, because he's going deep cover to nail everyone who helped Chen get away with keeping three hundred women in servitude. We have to do it this way because there's a cop involved and there may be a dirty politician.'"

"I know—" he began, but Kara cut him off.

"I *cried* for Colton. I blamed myself for his death because of my feud with Thornton. I was positive Thornton outed him because of me and I got him killed. Now we know it was probably *not* Thornton but another fed. I physically hurt. I can't even put words to the pain I felt. I don't trust you. I don't trust *either* of you," she repeated, looking from Lex to Elena. "You lied to me, betrayed my trust. I will never work for either of you."

"Kara, we fucked up," Elena said, "but there were legitimate reasons for us making the decisions that we did. I don't blame you for feeling the way you do, and I understand you won't work here anymore. That's why I'm giving you these options."

They would never understand. Hell, Kara didn't even understand these overwhelming emotions running through her so hot that she thought she'd explode. She pulled her badge from her pocket and threw it at Elena. Surprised, Elena caught it.

"You don't want to quit."

"If you think that, you have never known me."

She walked out.

43

Matt and Brian were heading to Rebecca Chavez's house in the West Valley when Sloane called. "I'm conferencing in Ryder Kim. We found something you need to know."

"We're listening," Matt said. They needed a break—any break.

"We don't have anything more on Conrad James," Ryder said. "But we were able to restore Rebecca Chavez's computer and phone. You were right. She's been tracking Kara since Kara received her FBI-issued cell phone."

"That was in July."

"And," Sloane said, "we have pages of text messages to everyone involved in the grant scheme. Nothing blatantly illegal, but there are a lot of suspicious conversations and text messages that say, for example, 'call my private cell.'"

"Okay." Interesting, but not completely helpful.

"There's also a password-protected file that Vik in IT was able to break. It's documentation of Bryce Thornton's obsession with Kara. It goes back more than ten years. Initially, Rebecca had been concerned and watchful, but over the last few months she was clearly fueling his rage."

"To the point where Bryce outed her and Colton?" Matt asked.

"No," Ryder said. "We have documentation that Rebecca sent Kara's and Colton's files to a television station, acting as a confidential whistleblower and pretending to be Thornton."

"I'll be damned," Brian muttered. "She used him. And killed him. I didn't want to believe it, but I can't stop thinking about it."

"We still need to prove it," Matt said. "Anything else?" he asked.

"There is one more thing, and it might give you the motive you're looking for," Ryder said. "Sloane, tell him."

Matt and Brian listened to Sloane as they sat outside of Rebecca's house. When she was done, Matt knew they had enough.

"Outstanding," Matt said. "Both of you." He ended the call. "Are you ready?"

Brian nodded.

Matt let Brian explain to Rebecca everything they knew in detail. Brian did a terrific job speaking calmly, without anger, even offering hints of sympathy. Brian talked about her life-long friendships, the love for her family, how things spiraled out of control.

"I might be able to let this all pass," he said. "Terminate employment but not prosecute. Because you have done some great things in our office. You were a good agent. But I can't walk away from murder."

"What do you mean?"

Taking the role of bad cop—one he didn't have a hard time pulling off in this case—Matt said, "Conrad James gave you the Colt .45. The same gun used to kill Bryce Thornton."

"No. No! He's lying."

That she went so quickly to that denial told Matt they were on the right path.

"We have your computer and cell phone," Matt said. "You should know that the FBI has a lot of computer talent. We have retrieved your emails. Text messages. Some vague, many questionable. We will put everything together. Agent Sloane Wagner works for me. She was assigned to your unit to investigate both you and Agent Thornton because we knew the leak to the media came from someone in your office. And there have been some cases that have been ignored, dismissed, deprioritized that are suspicious."

Rebecca paled. "Brian—"

"I authorized it, Rebecca."

"I— Oh, God."

"Bryce was obsessed with all the cases that Kara Quinn and Colton Fox worked," Matt said. "He had a stack of them in his office, in addition to every case my unit worked. Sloane took a picture of the files on Monday. We didn't note that one of the files on his desk didn't fit with the others, until we realized that it was gone."

Rebecca didn't speak, so Matt continued. Sloane deserved a commendation for finding the needle in the haystack with this one.

Brian spoke softly. "You know what file he's talking about."

Silence.

Matt said, "Bryce was looking at a case you buried related to Sunflower Group Homes. It's one of the twelve nonprofits run by Zarian and others, but there had been multiple complaints and the group was sent to the FBI for investigation. You squelched it. Bryce pulled the file—I suspect because there was a very loose connection between Chen and Sunflower. Because of Bryce's obsession with Kara, he looked at everything that may have touched her. He unknowingly uncovered your own crimes."

She was shaking her head, but she didn't say a word.

"Bryce was obsessed with Kara," Matt continued, "but he also was a seasoned investigator. He saw something, maybe just that you had cleaned up after Zarian. Or that you lied about the case. You couldn't have Bryce looking at you or your friends, digging for crimes that you'd spent years covering up. You had motive to want him gone, and better, you had Kara's gun. We know you tracked her through her FBI phone. She was at the dog park, so that's where you sent Thornton. It was just lucky for you that she broke her phone there, suspecting someone had tracked her to Colton Fox's house. You sent Bryce there, and you killed him."

Rebecca didn't say anything, sat frozen, not looking at either of them. Brian moved to sit next to her. "Do you want your family to go through this? The investigation? The trial? The rumors?"

"What?" she said. "No. My family has nothing to do with this. Leave my family alone!"

"We're going to try this in the press," Matt said bluntly. "Everything we know, what we can prove and disprove, will be leaked to the press. In a case like this—with so much money lost through graft and corruption—the way to win is to turn the public tide against the people involved. The press conference was brilliant and stupid at the same time. Because *we have the files*. We have everything. We know your son is on all the paperwork. That he coordinated every single grant, funneling it to friends and family. He will go to prison."

"No," she gasped. "No. He didn't know. He didn't know!"

Jonathan Avila stepped into the living room with a young blonde woman that it took Matt a moment to recognize.

His wife. Dorothy Duncan's daughter, Annabelle.

Annabelle was very pregnant. She had been crying, but stood tall holding her husband's hand tightly.

"I need a lawyer to draft up an ironclad agreement because I will not talk if I go to jail." He looked at his mother, but his words were for Matt. "I knew. I chose to look the other way. I can give you everyone—Lydia, Dorothy, Theodore, Krista. They can all rot in hell for all I care. But, Mom." His face softened as he directed his words to Rebecca. "Mom. This is murder. I never signed on for murder. I didn't think you had, either."

Rebecca began to sob. "I killed Bryce. Please, please forgive me."

44

I woke up Friday with a job to do and the excitement to do it. It wasn't until the end of the day that I realized it was my mother's birthday. She would have been fifty-five today.

I left FBI headquarters with the promise to return Monday and help put together the final reports. They wanted me to give another statement, and then return to show the cybercrimes division how I figured out what the hacker had done to the system. They said they would pay me a stipend for my time. I agreed, even though I would do it for free. I realized that no matter how nervous and worried I was about other people, when I talked to my fellow nerds I felt a lot more comfortable.

Maybe I was making progress. Maybe I was growing up.

I didn't have a job anymore, but the mayor gave me six months' severance. I could have kept my job, could have fought for it, but I didn't want to. The money would help while I found something else. I wasn't worried. As Michael Harris told me, I was smart and resourceful. I believed it, maybe for the first time in my life.

I had my mother's remains cremated, but then I paid for a small space at a cemetery in Burbank. They had a wall of sealed urns and hers was second from the top, four from the right. I sat on a bench and didn't know what to say. To her. Or to myself.

My phone rang, and I almost didn't answer—it seemed wrong to answer a phone in a cemetery. But I did because it was Will, and we hadn't really talked since yesterday morning.

"Hi," I said quietly.

"Where are you?"

"Visiting my mother."

"Can we meet?"

"Now?"

"Can you?" He sounded hopeful.

"Okay, sure. Where?"

I met Will at a pub near my house. I came here sometimes because it was comfortable and the bartender was nice and I didn't feel awkward sitting alone. Will was there already. He was drinking a beer; I ordered one, too.

"Amy and Ian are going to interview me on their podcast on Monday," Will said.

"That's good. You'll do great." He would. Will was very smart and articulate. He would be able to explain what happened so that the average person could understand. Better, he was an advocate for changing the system. How the government dealt with the homeless crisis wasn't working. Will knew how it could work.

"I appreciate your confidence," Will said with a grin. "I spent all afternoon with the mayor. Literally, three hours with the man who never has meetings longer than five minutes."

"He must like you."

Will laughed. "I don't think so but he doesn't hate me, which is a start. He wasn't involved in all this, and if he was, he's hiding it very well. He might lose his election, but I don't care. I'm getting it in writing."

"Getting what in writing?" I asked.

"I pitched my nine-point plan to get people off the streets. I told him one of the problems was a California state law that required all government-funded drug rehab facilities use a harm reduction program, and we needed city facilities that required sobriety and helped people achieve it. He told me he would do it my way, and if the state challenged it, he would sue them. That's a huge plus."

"Wait—he's going to implement your plan citywide?"

"No, he's not *that* brave. But he's giving me a small region and a substantial grant and my own team at homeless services. I'll have twelve dedicated social workers at my disposal. I can use existing staff or hire new staff. Train them. The grant goes to First Contact for housing, rehab, cleanups and staff. I made sure my contract requires me to provide monthly reports of our progress, so everything is transparent. I will prove that accountability works. And I need a good computer person, someone who sees the homeless as people, as human beings, not as profit makers. Who knows the system and how it works. I need you."

"You want me to work for you?"

"Yes. I can pay you now. I'll pay what you made for the city. Together, Violet, *we* can make a difference. If I run this pilot project successfully and prove that I can get people off the streets and turn them self-sufficient in three years? Maybe they'll expand it citywide. Statewide."

"You're an optimist."

"Yes, I am. And you're a pessimist. And together, we make a good team."

He took my hand and didn't let go. "At least," he said quietly, "*I* think we make a great team."

I looked down at our joined hands. I didn't know where this was going, but for the first time in forever, I felt a hint of hope… of optimism for the future.

For my future.

I smiled. "We do make a great team."

45

Kara had been sitting on her condo's roof for an hour before Matt found her there. She was lying on a blanket she'd pulled out of her closet and staring at the night sky, listening to the ocean waves and trying to figure out why she was so miserable.

He sat next to her. She didn't say anything, but she liked having him there with her.

What could she say? She didn't know what she was going to do with her life. She wished she'd brought up a six-pack, but she hadn't thought to, and then she didn't want to leave the comfort of her roof.

Finally, she said, "Lex told me I could come back. Detective, promotion, any precinct I wanted. No undercover work, but I can pick my squad. Narcotics, Homicide, Property, whatever."

Matt didn't say anything.

"I quit."

When he still didn't say anything, Kara said, "I blew it."

"You didn't do anything, Kara. None of what happened this week had anything to do with you."

"Not that. Fuck—I'm always ready to take the blame when things go sideways, but this is the one time that none of it was my fault. But—I quit. I'm not a cop anymore. I'm not an FBI agent."

"You will always have a job with me."

"I don't know if I have it in me, Matt. I don't deal well with FBI bureaucracy, I don't want to go through the FBI academy— and I don't even know if they'd accept me, even with you helping to smooth the way. I recognize that I got in through a back door this last year—but I've been really lucky. I don't handle office politics well, and I don't really like a lot of people. A lot fewer now than last week."

She wasn't angry. Oh, she had been angry. She had never been so mad in her life. Now she was…heartbroken. Just…so deeply hurt she didn't know how she was going to crawl out of this pit.

"I have been worried for months that I wouldn't be able to come back to my old job. That because of Chen and everything else that had been going on at the beginning of the year I wouldn't have a job anymore. It terrified me to lose it, thinking I was nothing without it. This—this is ten times worse. I trusted them. Elena. Lex. And especially Colton. I trusted all of them."

Her voice cracked and tears fell. She hated that. She didn't want to give any of them tears. They didn't deserve it.

But maybe she did. The loss she felt was so big, so vast, she didn't know if she'd ever get over this betrayal.

Matt wrapped his arms around her shoulders and pulled her against his side. She turned her face into his chest and closed her eyes, trying not to sob, silent tears streaming, soaking into his shirt.

Kara didn't want to need Matt, she didn't want to need anyone, but right now she was so grateful that he was here with her. What had she thought before? That Matt was the man who was behind her, in front of her, at her side. She wanted him… but she didn't want to want him. Everything had changed—

she had changed—and she didn't know what the future held for her, for Matt, for them.

But in this moment, she needed him.

She had never needed anyone before in her life, not like this.

Matt pulled her face to his and kissed her. His lips, his tongue, his touch. He held her to him as his mouth clung to hers. They sat there on the roof, under the stars, the waves crashing in the distance, two different songs coming at them from two different directions, and he held her.

When she could breathe again, she looked at him. The intensity and love on his face almost undid her. What could she offer this man? She had done everything in her power to keep him at a distance, but he kept coming back to her. Making her a whole person.

She didn't know what to think about that revelation, didn't want to think too hard on it. But she didn't want to let him go.

She feared she would have no other choice.

Matt reached into his pocket and without a word handed her a familiar object.

Her LAPD badge.

"Matt—I—"

He kissed her. "I talked to Lieutenant Gomez this afternoon. Then we went to the chief of police."

"I don't want—can't—work here."

"No. You can't. You deserve better. But, you're right, there are hurdles you would have to jump through to be an FBI agent. Hurdles that are there for a reason, and I believe in them, but I also know that sometimes those same hurdles keep good people out. If you want to stay on my team, your slot is there. I already talked to Tony, and he's completely on board. Same agreement. You work for LAPD, on permanent loan to the FBI. They pay you—in fact, they're giving you a raise—and you keep your badge *and* your promotion."

Kara stared at her badge. Closed her eyes. "Matt—"

"Don't say no. Please."

"I wasn't going to." She smiled. "I didn't think this was an option. I thought—I don't know. I didn't know what I was going to do. But this feels right. This feels like where I need to be."

"You earned it, Kara. You are a good cop, and my team is better because you're on it. I also talked to Sloane tonight. Brian Granderson offered her a job with his team, but she declined. She asked to be assigned to Montana, where her family is. I offered her a job on our team. She's going to think about it. I don't think she was expecting the offer, but I hope she takes it. I even sweetened the pot with a promise she can commute from Montana."

"Commute? How would that work?"

"She'd be on our team, but deploy out of the Montana office. I think she'll take it."

"Good."

"You like her?"

"Yeah, I do. She's different than all of us, sees things from a different perspective, and she's calm, like Ryder. It's all good."

"I agree."

They sat holding hands and it felt so right.

"Kara, I'm a better cop and a better man with you as a partner—working and off duty. I love you. I know you don't like to hear it, but I do."

She looked over and thought she saw a gleam of moisture in his eyes, then it was gone.

She kissed him. "I'm going to sell my condo. I don't know that I can come back...and I want to find a place on the East Coast."

"You'll always have a place with me."

"I know. And maybe...someday...but I need my own space right now. It doesn't mean I don't love you."

He stiffened, tightened his grip on her. "What?"

She didn't realize what she'd said until the words came out.

"I don't know what love is, Matt. I've never had anything like this before. But earlier, as I sat here and thought I would be saying goodbye to you? It hurt. I've never felt that loss, that emptiness. And when you gave me my position back, the emptiness filled with joy. More than joy. Not just because I have the job—that's part of it—but mostly, because I don't have to leave you."

He kissed her, all over her face, her neck, held her tight against him. "Dear God, Kara, I love you. Get your own place, I don't care, I know you need your space. I'll take what you can give, and hopefully, over time, you'll give me all."

"I'll give you a key," she said with a half smile. "And maybe a drawer."

She got up, a bit awkwardly, and held out her hand. "We need to go to bed. I may not say I love you a lot, but I know how to show you."

"You've never said you love me."

She looked at him and realized he was nervous. That was so not Matt, those kind of nerves. "Well, I guess I do love you." Her voice cracked and she laughed. Matt wasn't the only one who was nervous.

"Does anyone come up here?"

She shrugged. "Not often."

He pulled her back down to the blanket they'd been sitting on. "I'm willing to risk it."

She grinned, kissed him. "I love it when you break the rules, Mathias Costa."

★ ★ ★ ★ ★

ACKNOWLEDGMENTS

Research is an important part of all my books—I learned the hard way after making a few embarrassing mistakes in my early novels. Now what I can't learn in books, I ask experts—people with hands-on experience. As always, I may take a few liberties with the facts for the story, and sometimes, I still get things wrong. Any mistakes are mine and mine alone.

For this book, I wanted to be as authentic as possible about what the homeless experience on a daily basis and what my character Violet would face trying to get her mother out of the cycle of addiction. I read dozens of articles about homelessness, harm reduction, rehab, addiction, government funding for homeless programs, and more. In the process, I put together a list of people I wanted to interview. Kevin Dahlgren was the first to answer back.

Kevin is a national homelessness expert with more than two decades' experience working daily with the homeless. He answered every question I had, provided me with statistics and articles to follow up, and made himself available by phone while

I was editing. He explained how the grant process works and what he, as a social worker, is allowed to do and not do. He even read the first chapter and prevented me from embarrassing myself when I made a major mistake. I wish I could put everything I learned from Kevin into this book, but that would be a book in itself.

Sometimes, research changes a writer. The last time what I learned changed me deep down was when I was researching human trafficking for my 2009 book *Fatal Secrets*. Until now. What I learned about the homeless industrial complex and the plight of people on the streets—and those profiting off them—has forever altered the way I view this crisis. Thank God for people like Kevin who are walking the walk, and I'm glad I can call him a friend.

Others also helped with some of the details. Katy Grimes, a Sacramento-based reporter, wrote an article exposing a non-profit as being a pass-through account for homeless grant money, enriching the CEO and treasurer at the expense of the people they are supposed to help. Katy greatly helped me understand how the money flows.

Jonathan Choe, a Seattle-based reporter, helped me understand how harm reduction works on a daily basis.

Every time I write acknowledgments, I have to shout out to Crime Scene Writers, an amazing group of experts who answer simple and complex questions for writers. For my questions about the military and homeless veterans, thanks to Will "Skate" Parks and Justin Landry for reaching out to me. And when I needed help with the legal process and grand juries, Michael Giannecchini answered the call. I hope I didn't mess up too badly.

Jeff Greene is a longtime friend—more than three decades. He's worked in county government for years and was *hugely* helpful in explaining how graft and corruption might work, county approval processes, and the layers of bureaucracy at the local level.

As my longtime readers know, I have many friends in law enforcement to tap for information. Now I have family! My daughter Katie Miiller, now a four-year veteran of the force, is my go-to person for details. We have spent hours talking about what cops face on the streets because of drug addiction and the rapid increase in fentanyl use. Be careful out there.

As always, the team at MIRA is fabulous: my editors, April Osborn and Dina Davis, who help make my book as strong as possible. My publicists, Justine Sha and Sophie James, who do a terrific job. The art department—the covers for the Quinn & Costa series are just amazing. And of course, everyone else from the publisher to the marketing team to the copy editors to the sales force. A lot of people are needed to bring a book from me to you: thank you to all of them.

My agent Dan Conaway is, as always, my partner and guide in this business. He helps keep me sane and focused. Dan's assistant Chaim Lipskar keeps *Dan* sane and focused. Ha. Seriously, I have an amazing team at Writers House and I am grateful for everyone there.

Last but never least, my family. Every day I feel blessed that my mom is with me. She was the first person who told me to write if I wanted to write, and she reads all my books. My husband, who has finally—after thirty years—accepted (realized?) that I will never be as neat and tidy as he is. Thank you for still making me laugh.